Dear Reader,

I'm so glad you've picked up *A Duke, the Lady, and a Baby*. It's emotional and funny. Through the twists and turns, I will deliver a happy ever after. So enjoy the ride.

Welcome to the Regency, where rules of society reign, diversity and upper ward mobility exist, and everyone—rich or poor, whole or broken—searches for soul mates, those persons who understand and cherish them despite circumstances.

I hope you love Patience, Jemina, Lady Shrewsbury, and the Widow's Grace. In the cutthroat world of intrigue and scandal, strong sisterhoods are needed to provide strength in the storm—and maybe offer a gentle piece of advice to keep a girl from wrecking her life.

Rogues and Remarkable Women is a three-book series. *A Duke, the Lady, and a Baby* is the first novel, followed by *An Earl, the Girl, and a Toddler*. The last book, *A Duke, the Spy, an Artist, and a Lie*, wraps up the collection while reuniting you with your faves.

Keep in touch. Go to VanessaRiley.com and join my newsletter to be abreast of book secrets, history tidbits, events, and more.

Be blessed,

Vanessa

Praise for *A Duke, the Lady, and a Baby*

"Riley gifts readers a sparkling love story with deep wells of faith and feeling. . . . It's refreshing to read historical romance that reflects the true diversity of the era. . . . At its heart, *A Duke, the Lady, and a Baby* is about overcoming trauma, a testament to love forged in adversity—a love that both leaves space for and hastens healing."
—*Entertainment Weekly*

"Riley is at her best when she lets her Gothic impulses out to play. . . . Readers on the lookout for Black or disabled characters in historical romance will not want to miss this."
—*The New York Times*

"Riley loads her expertly crafted romance with intrigue, droll banter, and steadily building passion. Readers will be hard-pressed to find a flaw in this bighearted Regency romance." —*Publishers Weekly,* starred review

"Mystery and simmering passion unite to keep you turning pages until the duke, lady, and baby find their happy ever after." —*NPR*

"Riley delivers a fine first outing in what looks to be a promising new series, welcoming a determined West Indian heroine to the Regency subgenre." —*Library Journal*

"With brilliant pacing, memorable characters, and witty dialogue, the premise elevated beyond our expectations. *A Duke, the Lady, and a Baby* portrays black people in a beautiful way that makes us relatable and takes us out of the stereotypical maid and slave roles. We definitely give this novel a strong five out of five stars." —*AAMBC*

"In addition to the deeply emotional story of the protagonists, gothic touches and a mystery keep the plot moving smartly through this book. *A Duke, the Lady, and a Baby* is a book to savor." —*Frolic Book of the Week*

By Vanessa Riley

Rogues and Remarkable Women

A Duke, the Lady, and a Baby

An Earl, the Girl, and a Toddler

A Duke, the Spy, an Artist, and a Lie

The Lady Worthing Mysteries

Murder in Westminster

A DUKE, THE LADY, and A BABY

Vanessa
Riley

ZEBRA BOOKS
KENSINGTON PUBLISHING CORP.
www.kensingtonbooks.com

ZEBRA BOOKS are published by

Kensington Publishing Corp.
119 West 40th Street
New York, NY 10018

Copyright © 2020 by Vanessa Riley

All Kensington titles, imprints, and distributed lines are available at special quantity discounts for bulk purchases for sales promotion, premiums, fund-raising, and educational or institutional use.

Special book excerpts or customized printings can also be created to fit specific needs. For details, write or phone the office of the Kensington Sales Manager: Kensington Publishing Corp., 119 West 40th Street, New York, NY 10018. Attn. Sales Department. Phone: 1-800-221-2647.

ZEBRA BOOKS and the Z logo Reg. U.S. Pat. & TM Off.

First Zebra Books trade paperback printing: July 2020
First Zebra Books mass market paperback printing: February 2023

ISBN-13: 978-1-4201-5523-5
ISBN-13: 978-1-4201-5224-1 (eBook)

10 9 8 7 6 5 4 3 2 1

Printed in the United States of America

To all who've loved and lost and are brave enough to start again—you are blessed and beautiful. I wish you happiness.

To all the wounded warriors—thank you for your service, your bravery, and your hearts filled of love. I wish you joy.

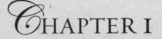CHAPTER I

February 1, 1814
London, England

It was a universal truth that no matter her background, face, or charms, a widow in possession of a fortune would be targeted for theft. In my circumstance, I'd been cheated of everything, even my greatest gift. Now was the time to defy authority, to strike and win.

I'd almost been caught.

My breath came in waves as I leaned against the closed nursery door. I squeezed my stomach tight, as tight as my shut lashes, and waited for someone to push inside.

So close, only to be captured . . .

My heart ticked, numbering the follies of my life. So full of memories—sliding down a sloping banister, the chatter of silly sisters, a stranger's whisper at sunset, a blur of signatures on a marriage contract, then a well-written note of love . . . of suicide—my soul was about to explode.

Laughter filtered beneath the door, then the haunting footsteps moved away. Maybe a maid entered a bedroom down the hall. I swallowed the lump building in my throat. The knot of bitterness went down slow. It burned.

This was my house. Those servants once worked for me. Now, I was reduced to sneaking inside Hamlin Hall.

With a shake of my head, I stopped thinking of my failures and focused on my mission, my sole purpose, my Lionel. Feet slipping in my borrowed boots, I tiptoed to his crib and peeked at my baby.

His wide hazel eyes seized me.

Tiny hands lifted, but he made no sound, no cooing or crying. I pacified myself thinking my smart boy didn't want more trouble dropped on my head, not that he'd learned to soothe himself from neglect.

Pity my heart knew the truth, that Lionel was a prisoner.

And these circumstances were my fault.

I stole a breath and pinned a smile to my lips. I was grateful to see my boy's face.

"My little man. Hungry?"

I unbuttoned the placard of my borrowed nankeen shirt, then unwound the bandage I'd wrapped about my bosom. This made my charms appear flat, manlike.

Scooping up Lionel, I put him to my breast. "Hamlin Hall is different tonight, Master Jordan. Is that your doing?"

My little man's suckle was so strong. Those distant concerns about how often he'd been fed crept forward.

My insides broke into more pieces. "I'm sorry."

I wasn't smart, and now my Lionel suffered.

He made an extra slurping noise as if he'd spooned runny porridge. The funny notion calmed my frets . . . for now. "Tonight, you eat big."

Our change was in the offing. I felt it. I knew it would be so.

"Your mama's a spy again. But tonight, I was almost discovered trying to retrieve my trust documents. I had to scurry back to the catacombs, running at top speed through the secret door at the stairs. The old butler was too drunk—"

Something heavy dragged outside in the hall.

The new carpet? It would be ruined.

Hushed whispers bubbled.

Did I hear something about ruin or ripping?

That carpet was imported from the East Indies.

My hands flushed. My cheeks followed.

The fine tapestries of woven rust and gold silks I'd installed to give this two-hundred-year-old house new life would be torn up, discarded . . . like me.

A loud curse soared, then a clear complaint about a guest—a Rep? Reynolds? Remington?—his arrival, the servant said, was imminent.

Was this a constable from London?

A magistrate from Bow Street?

Or an administrator from the lunatic asylum?

Any of these men could be coming for me.

I shook from the sole of my boots to the collar of my coarse shirt.

They dragged me, the mistress of Hamlin Hall, from this place, from Lionel. My jet bombazine mourning gown, once so proper and refined, was wrinkled and stained as they hauled me away.

The servants and Markham, my late husband's uncle, said I looked crazed, a yellow-eyed loon. I remember sobbing like a lunatic, but the hope in my heart said, *Cooperate, all would be well.*

All lies. All tricks. All meant to crush me.

I wasn't going this time, not without a fight.

I was at war—one made for mothers, especially foreign-born women. I had Papa's knife in my waistband. Forged in gold and white topaz, the pretty thing would be drawn to wave at them. I'd hurl threats and put on a menacing, crazy face.

But could I actually harm or kill anyone?

My father, the Sugar King, should've forged a golden gun. Something I could use with slight effort and at an unfeeling distance, not up close, not inches away where I'd see a man's eyes.

Eyes, like my Lionel's, were my undoing. They took my

battered heart on adventures, somewhere good, where folks were decent, where I was loved for being me.

Blam.

Something fell and broke. It sounded steps away.

A vase?

An ugly sculpture that came with this house of secrets?

"Get the last of her stuff below without breaking anything else. He'll be comin' any day. Repington will . . ."

The knocking and man-talk sounded closer.

"Finish up, Lionel. Feed faster." I whispered this to his thin curls. I bolstered my spine with lass-talk. "My boy, I'll leave out like I've done all week. Another day closer to getting my trust documents to finance our boat trip. Safety, my son. We'll have it soon."

A shadow slid across the sill at the door's bottom.

My lass-talk abandoned ship. My panic rose like the evening tide. There was no other way out of this room. I'd be discovered.

"Law and order, Repington. He'll take care of the *problem*."

That voice, a roguish Scottish tongue—the drunk butler, one of the many servants who worked at Hamlin these past four years. Was he toying with me? Had he recognized me yesterday and sprung a trap?

The insolent man needed to be flogged with a good island switch, a thick palm frond.

I looked down at the boy suckling at my bosom. "We will win. We'll be together."

My babe released a yawn.

"I'm glad you're excited about this."

Lionel's mouth stretched, and he burped. His eyes closed.

"Done with me, aye? Just like your father."

If he had lived and returned with his mouth full of sorries—could we have started anew?

I lowered Lionel into the crib, then started buttoning up my disguise. I had to look like a man to leave Hamlin. "I'm going to regain custody, and that nice countess, the leader of the Widow's Grace, she's helping me."

Thumb in mouth, my boy looked so peaceful.

Maybe he believed me, but since his birth, he hadn't known much freedom. This was how it had been for me these past four years in England.

Colin's unsocial wife.

Colin's foreign wife.

Colin's distant flower couldn't withstand the scrutiny of the *ton*.

My baby cried out. The short outburst blasted like a loud off-key trumpet.

I looked at the ledge outside the window. If I climbed out, I could avoid detection, but this was crazy, even for a girl good at climbing. If I fell, the *Morning Post* would read, *Crazed widow dressed like a man jumped from a third-floor window*.

"Please, sir. I need to check on the babe. Might need to clean him up a bit."

A feminine voice with clear, proper syllables.

The door cracked open.

A tall girl like me couldn't fit into the wardrobe. I turned back, opened the window wider, balanced on the old rocking chair, and climbed out onto the ledge.

"Mrs. Kelly, the little mongrel will keep. But you need a strong man to protect you from the ghost of Hamlin Hall. Come put me to bed."

This deeper speech, smug and amused—Markham's. His gloating voice repeated through my nightmares. He chuckled again. The blood in my veins chilled, the pain worse than an island girl's first snow.

Hiding from his wrath had to be done. Boots dangling, I steadied myself and scooted to the right. The jagged edges of the hewed stones tugged on my breeches, but I'd made it. I stretched and shoved the leaded glass, closing it to within an inch.

The nursery door creaked, the hinge whining as if it had opened wide. Markham might have joined the nanny.

Stiff and silent against the wall, I waited and hoped not to see his face. Thought to pray to Agassou, the Demeraran god of protection, but I didn't know if he had dominion on English soil . . . or stone ledges.

A woman's hand draped in frills clasped the window latch. "One moment, Mr. Markham. The night air's not good for the baby."

My pulse fluttered. If Mrs. Kelly stuck her head out, I'd be discovered.

But the woman stood there, not moving, her elegant fingers resting against the frame.

"Mrs. Kelly," Markham said. "What are you staring at? Not more snow."

My heart thumped hard like a street singer's drummer, one whooping on his instrument to excite the crowd or rouse a rebellion.

"No. Nothing, sir. I see nothing."

The window slammed shut.

The door whined.

Except for my panicked heart, all was silent.

I loosened my death grip on the ledge and clasped my thumping chest.

Not caught.

Not mocked by Markham again.

Not falling or tipping over . . . yet.

Breathing in and out, I swung my feet as if I sat on the docks watching ships come into Demerara. For one moment, the air smelled fresh like the sea. To go home with Lionel, that was my dream now. And we would be happy and safe, no longer sneaking and hiding, no longer living under rules that made no sense.

Elated, relieved, I laughed. I'd accomplished tonight's mission. Lionel was fed, and there was still time to head back to Lady Shrewsbury's before she discovered her wayward widow missing. I reached over to the window, but the pane wouldn't budge.

It was locked.

No! No! No.

No?

Three stories up. What to do?

Break the glass and be caught? Bedlam.

Stay here and be caught in the morning's light? Bedlam.

Jump and be caught dead? The notion *deserved* Bedlam.

Wait for the ghost of my dream or one of Hamlin Hall's to come and float me down? Yes, Bedlam again.

Staying here was impossible. I'd have to get help or turn myself over to Markham.

My stomach clenched at the thought of being at his mercy again. If my mother were alive, she'd put a root on Markham so that bad luck would be his and only his.

But West Indian magic nonsense was as bad as English ghost lore, and none of it could explain why Markham kept winning—he had my house, my son, my dignity.

I slapped the ledge. My fingers stung, and my resolve wavered. Better to live and fight another day. "Lionel, your mother's not crazed. I tried."

I readied my knife to break the glass, but a flash caught my gaze.

I squinted toward the woods outside Hamlin's stone gates and saw the light again. I put down my knife and used both hands to cup my eyes.

The pattern repeated, bright to dark, bright to dark.

A signal?

It was steady, like the ones on the big ships slipping through the fogged bay. Could that be Jemina St. Maur sending a warning? My friend insisted on coming and keeping watch tonight. Brave woman.

My risk-taking had endangered my friend.

I couldn't surrender and save Jemina, too. Markham wouldn't let me help her.

Sweating through my shirt, I opened my livery. My flailing elbow brushed leaves, the thick English ivy, the long vines I'd admired from the first day Colin brought me to Hamlin. I reached over and pushed at one. It was solid and gnarled like a tree. Like a coconut tree.

Would it hold a reformed tomboy? It was now or never. I wedged a boot into the mortar joint between the limestone bricks.

On the count of three, I'd grab the fat tree trunk.

One.

Two.

Two and a half.

Two and a third.

Three. I started and clung to the vine like it was Papa's waist. The ivy swayed but bounced back like a spring.

Heaving, I climbed down, foothold after foothold.

The herbaceous fragrance of the leaves mingled with my perspiration. The scent reminded me of summer—of sneaking from my bedchamber window to escape chores, to hide from endless dress fittings, to avoid the suitors coming to sway the Sugar King's daughters.

It meant a couple of hours of not hearing Mama's critiques, her coughs, or the awful moment when she'd cough no more.

Hand over hand, toehold after toehold, I lowered myself until one boot hit the ground and then the other. I drew my arms about me and made sure my heart was still inside my ribs.

But it wasn't.

It was in a dingy crib, three stories up.

The hawthorn hedgerows at my hips left tiny white petals on my breeches. The flowers reflected the moonlight, making my menswear look like lace. Mama must be looking down laughing.

I scrubbed off the flowers and headed across the wide field toward the gate, toward Jemina.

A screech sounded, followed by a wave of thunder.

I halted in place.

Then a drum, drum, drumming caught in my ear. It chiseled inside, hammering down my spine. I reached for my knife, but it wasn't in my waistband.

I'd left it on the ledge.

Headstrong, impatient girl. Mama's rebuke rang in my brainbox.

The ground shook beneath my boots.

A fast rider led one, two, three carriages. They barreled through Hamlin's stone gates.

Men galloped toward me with guns drawn, flintlocks, the ones with the long barrels, the ones meant for war.

Kicked-up rocks stung my shins as the first horse passed, but the lead carriage shot toward me. Its large side lanterns blinded, stunning me like an insect mesmerized by light.

Couldn't move, couldn't stop staring. I'd survived Bedlam and the high ledge, only to be trampled.

No surrendering, not me, not this time.

I straightened and faced the raiders head-on.

CHAPTER 2

A MOTHER'S RESOLVE

The tart stench of horses' lather and the odor of burning pitch wrinkled my nose. The carriage moved closer, coming for me, but I wouldn't back down. I'd hidden too much.

My father's blood pumping inside kept me from a faint. His endless talk of insurrection from the American rabble, Samuel Adams, stuck in my heart. I understood and absorbed his troubles, his defiant quest for life and liberty.

Each time I picked up my son, felt his skin next to mine, I became a revolutionary. For him, his life, his liberty, I charged forward.

The driver cursed at me but steered to the right.

I was saved, but I knew from the number of guns I'd seen, the battle hadn't been won. Clenching my gloved hands, I remembered my disguise and waved the carriages toward the steps. I acted like a footman and did what those servants did whenever my husband arrived from Town. I kept signaling with arms wiggling and pointing.

Soldiers ran around me, charging the entry. A few ran toward the secret entrance to the catacombs. These invaders had knowledge of Hamlin, deep knowledge. It took more than two years for me to learn its secrets.

Sweat drenched my forehead. My powdered wig had to stay pinned in place. The dabbed-on theater cosmetic had to stick to my face, or I'd never be able to walk free through Hamlin's gates.

"You! Man the door." A groom pointed to the big carriage, the one that almost ran me down.

I nodded and stiffened my walk to seem more brutish. I prepared my countenance, thinking *burp* and rough things like burlap. Escape was impossible until I passed this test. Bracing, I threw open the carriage door.

A man bounced out, tall and thin, looking cross. "I guess we've arrived. Winning already, Duke?"

The other fellow inside struggled toward the opening, like he couldn't get a good push on the tufted seat. He shrugged and fumbled with a shiny gold watch. "Eleven on the dot. An excellent time to storm the castle." He chuckled. "And yes, we are winning. You. Don't just stand there gawking. Help me out."

My name wasn't *You* or at least it wasn't the last time I'd written it. I pointed to my bosom. "Me?"

The big man flopped a little closer to the door and exposed a heavily bandaged leg. "Yes, you."

"Yes, sir."

The urge to check my white wig for escaping dark hair or adjust my livery to see if I'd wet through pressed. My milk was heavy again, and my nerves rattled like the silver toy Lionel should have in his crib, the one Markham sold off.

"You're a might scrawny, but tall enough for the task."

"For what?"

"To help me balance. You'll do as a crutch. Let's get on with this."

First a *you* and now a *crutch*? I grimaced and tried hard not to gawk at his slow, scooting movements, tried not to think of my baby sister flopping about learning to crawl. Tried and failed to not let missing my family mist my eyes.

The thinner man returned. "I'll have a proper crutch brought to you in a moment. Slow down. Napoleon's not inside, just Markham and a baby."

"And all his corrupt minions, Gantry. We know he's been hiring reinforcements."

The other man shook his head and turned to me. "Minion, don't drop the duke on his head. It won't help."

Me a *minion*? Never to Markham. "I won't, sir."

I stuck my hand inside the carriage, like a girl, like a scared little girl who thought a furry spider might crawl onto her hand. Dukes didn't bite and make sticky webs, did they?

He grabbed my flailing arm and towed himself to the opening. "This one has a sense of humor, Gantry, complete with flopping limbs."

The duke's laugh was full and lusty. He didn't look so mean, not chuckling like a schoolboy. Then his expression sobered. "My soldiers surrounded Hamlin. Markham can't escape. Not this time, not with my ward."

"Yes, Repington." Gantry shrugged and moved toward the second carriage.

Repington? Colin's dead grandfather? How did this man have this name? He looked too solid to be a ghost.

Was this the person the servants said would come to fix things?

I didn't know what new conspiracy had begun, but this peer had my arm, and he'd come for Markham.

But who was his ward? Lionel?

"I'm not one who waits," the duke said. "No more antics. Do you think you can help me balance? From your stares, you can see I'm injured. I need to get inside at once."

Hope built in my veins, pumping me up, floating my heart like a heated paper lantern. I ducked my shoulder under his arm. "Non-corrupt minion here, Your Grace. I can help until a true crutch is brought forward."

The duke's laughter sounded richer, like a full-bodied dessert port. Then his full weight came down on me.

Ugh.

All the wind, all the heated air gushed out of me, but I didn't buckle. I couldn't. The duke was here to stop Markham.

We took a step together, and he stumbled.

"I typically despise assistance, but I hate waiting more."

I sympathized.

Waiting wasn't my strength, either. Charging forward with little hesitation was my special talent. As I strained under his weight, I feared that this time my flaw might be fatal.

The duke and I wobbled, each of us trying to lead the other to Hamlin's grand entry.

"You've a lot of heart, minion, but get in step with me. It will be easier."

Nothing was *easier* when I complied. Submission was a softer shade of hard.

But I acquiesced like I'd done with Colin and leaned in closer. The duke's brawny arm smashed my face into his chest. The white cosmetic smeared onto his ebony greatcoat.

Then I heard him counting. The rhythm sounded strong like a conga rattle. I swayed with him. It became our music. No longer struggling to show him the shortest path, I fell in step, my full stride matched his two half jumps.

My reward was his scent. Enmeshed in his cloak was something heady and familiar. It wasn't like my sweet milled soaps, but something honeyed and peppered with hints of cloves.

"I'm heavy, young man, and you're scrawny. Your employer, well, former employer, must not be giving you a decent wage to fill your belly."

"I suppose you eat enough, Your Grace. You're weighty."

"I suppose I do." The duke chuckled, but this noise sounded forced, as if to cover his winces when we stumbled over rocks hidden in the melting snow.

I felt the tension in the man like I'd felt his laugh. He was more hurt than he wanted anyone to know.

I steadied my arm about him. He'd made me into a crutch, and I'd be a decent crutch. He was coming for Markham. That had to be good.

Yet, this close to the duke, I felt the hardened muscles of his stomach and knew the leanness of his thigh. The man was injured but not indolent or lazy.

His scent hit me again, deeper, more acute. I knew what it was, a blend of fine cigar tobacco and rum.

I inhaled once more. Definitely rum, and it was the expensive stuff. It would be wrong to cling to him, sniffing his coat to see if it was Demeraran rum, but this aroma was the closest I'd felt to home in four years.

"Maybe you're not so scrawny, son. You seem to be keeping me upright."

Both of us heaving a little, we stopped in front of the fourteen perfectly hewed steps that led into Hamlin Hall. Moonlight and lit torches highlighted the strong, curved stones of the portico covering the doors. Hamlin was majestic and isolated, a lovely loner in the countryside.

"Someone lit the grand chandelier. Good," the duke said.

It was the biggest, brightest wrought iron fixture I'd ever seen. As a new bride in August of 1810, I stood under that chandelier and watched my husband leave for London the night he'd abandoned me here.

He said it was for my protection, my comfort, for his, for a hundred other excuses, but I was made to stay at Hamlin and accept his comings and goings.

"What a house." The duke's breathing was heavy, and his voice sounded wistful, but I could barely fill my lungs.

Colin and I had a marriage of misunderstandings, a morass of letters inked with halfhearted apologies, a mattress made for two that, almost always, held one.

Then Markham told me Colin was dead.

All before my twenty-fourth birthday.

"We've caught our breath, son. We move forward, now."

The duke pulled me, but I couldn't move. "How, sir? How do we go forward? The obstacles . . . these steps are too steep."

"Son, it's just one foot in front of the other. That's how I do it, even if I need a crutch."

Where was my crutch?

I had none, nothing to take away my guilt. Colin's suicide was my fault. My last note pushed him into the Thames as surely as his depressed thoughts.

"Young man, you're fatigued. See, my weight is too much. Gird your loins."

"What?" I wasn't sure I had those. My eyes crossed as I stared at him. "What, Duke?"

"Strengthen your hold. I'm not looking to fall, not on a night where I've caught that rascal. Markham will be evicted on the hour. He'll be away from my ward."

That was the crutch I needed, the duke taking Lionel from the scoundrel.

Maybe I should say who I was, a widow dressed as a man and . . . and get tossed out of Hamlin, too.

I grunted, then forced myself to take a step, then another.

The duke, this stocky man of six foot four or more hopped onto the first step. Was he pausing for me? Was I slowing him down?

I made my voice deeper. "Let's continue. I don't think I'll dump you, sir. Yet."

"You have a good sense of humor for a crutch." The duke pulled out his pocket watch. "Only five minutes have passed. Still on schedule."

Gantry stepped in front of us with a wooden staff and presented it as if he held a sword. "Here, Repington. It's better than a minion for keeping your balance."

The duke allowed him to slip it under the arm I held up. Standing on his own, he released me and powered up the next step. "Is the perimeter manned?"

"Yes. Your men are securing the surrounding park now."

Surrounding park? Jemina? The sweat beading at my

brow would soon wash off the remaining cosmetic. I'd be exposed, and Jemina would be dragged through the gate.

"Repington," Gantry said, "would you like me to see what's going on inside?"

The duke nodded. "Good idea. Go on. I'll be in the drawing room at eleven past eleven." He opened his gold watch again. "That's six, no five minutes from now."

Gantry hissed something under his breath, then went up the steps.

All the windows were lit up bright. Hamlin Hall was under full inspection or attack. But what of my Lionel?

The duke turned toward me. His clear blue eyes twinkled, reflecting the fire of torches, and he glanced at me as if he could assess every scandal in my soul. "What's your name, soldier?"

I coughed. "Me?" When in doubt, Lady Shrewsbury said stay as close to the truth as possible. Mama's name would do. "LaCroy, sir."

The duke sniffed and wiggled his nose. "I smell milk or soap. You've been with a cow, LaCroy? Milking?"

His question sounded like a cross between a command and a joke.

But how to respond and not give away my sex?

Between my nerves and the fear that a soldier would drag my friend through the gates . . . I leaked worse than a grain bag with holes.

Then I saw my white cosmetic had smeared on the duke's armpit.

Keeping my hands tight at my sides, I shifted. "Well, you see . . . what had . . . Yes, sir." When in doubt, agree to everything except seeing a ghost. That was the countess's second rule of masquerade but with my amendment to stay out of Bedlam.

"LaCroy, that was more of a joke than a request for an answer. But put the word out, I'll require new staffing including a wet nurse. Based on the reports, Old Markham hasn't employed one, and I hear it's best to suckle a babe to grow strapping men."

He thought to hire a wet nurse for Lionel. A sigh blasted through my lips. My boy would be safe at least this night.

The duke mounted another step and released a huff. "Thank you, LaCroy, but you're terminated. All of Markham's staff will be terminated."

"I failed as a groom so soon?"

"You're able, but you worked for Markham. Won't have any problems or potential loyalty issues in my troop if I start fresh."

He took another labored step. "But I can make an exception for you if you'd swear loyalty to me now."

"I don't swear. My mother taught me better." Mama's only lesson that stuck, that and don't move about when receiving a switch of spiky palm fronds across the legs. "I'd rather be terminated and reapply tomorrow."

The duke moved again. This time a sharp word grunted out of him as he reached the next level. "Well, if you return in the morn, you'll be employed. Do spread the word. Only disciplined people, loyal people will work at Hamlin Hall. LaCroy, I'll remember that name. And your humor. You've my permission to leave. You'll not be harassed by my men."

Badly weaving, the duke hobbled forward, step by step up the portico.

A small part of me wanted to stay and make sure the man didn't tumble headlong onto the limestone steps. And a smidge of me wanted to see Markham cower for all the suffering he'd caused.

But I'd lived to see another moment. That was enough.

With all the changes in the hires, this could be an opportunity. Maybe the countess would allow me to be employed to care for Lionel until I could claim my son as my own.

It wasn't right to be a maid, but it had to be better than sneaking in at night. I turned to catch a view of the third floor and the nursery and smacked into a soldier.

"Halt." The man brandished a weapon at my forehead, and the smell of gunpowder wafted. It made me nauseous. It made me remember. These fellows weren't common folk. They were warriors under Repington's command.

Another came and waved me forward. "The duke is signaling. This footman has been given permission to leave."

Half pivoting, I saw the duke still on the steps. He motioned some sort of salute with his arm. He'd made my passage safe. Perhaps this Englishman had some honor. Maybe his word could be trusted. I hoped he'd protect my son tonight.

"Go on," the soldier said. He joined the others unpacking the carriages. More weapons. All being stashed in Hamlin with my baby.

Fists balled, head down, I started again toward the gates, toward Jemina, hoping she remained hidden. I needed her help when I returned tomorrow to fight for my son.

CHAPTER 3

WINNING OFF THE FIELD

Busick Strathmore, the Duke of Repington, marched up the first landing of the grand stone stairs of Hamlin Hall. Well, "marched" was an exaggeration. His valiant ascent consisted of a series of hops with a foul wooden staff.

But still valiant, not tumbling or requiring assistance.

He started again, step by step, to the top without a fall, definitely not looking weak. Or so he thought, until he spied his friend and confidant, the cautious Lord Gantry.

The viscount's face held a tight grimace as he stood near the doors, three steps higher. "You sure you don't need help? Everyone needs assistance, even a great commander."

"Just taking my time. Don't you approve of my caution?"

"If a raid with fifteen soldiers rampaging a country estate full of drunks and wayward rabble is thoughtful plotting, I'd hate to see reckless."

Tired and annoyed that someone would question one of Wellington's trusted strategists, Busick banged his crutch as he took the next step. "I'm effective."

His friend shrugged. "You are, but I don't see how you lose on this one."

Busick wasn't losing anything ever again. He held his breath and pulled up to the last blasted stair. "Gantry," he said with a grunt, "is my ward secure? I don't trust Markham. He'll steal the boy."

"We have the fiend surrounded. Surrender is eminent." He regarded the duke closely. "Your balance is good?"

"Yes, I won't stumble. No lumps or bumps to be added to my thick skull."

"Very thick." Gantry sort of smiled, clasped the door handle, then stopped. "You're not winded?"

Of course Busick was winded, but he loathed admitting weakness. "Stop, mother hen. Save the smothering for the young soldier inside." The duke waved his hand forward but controlled the motion as to not sway and prove the viscount right. "See, I knew you'd be perfect for this mission. I'll meet you in the drawing room at twenty past. A slight adjustment since my caution is slowing me."

"More schedules? And all this over a baby. Just a baby." Gantry shook his head and entered the house.

It wasn't "just" a baby.

It was all that was left of Busick's cousin, Colin Jordan, the man who'd been like a brother to him before wealth and women and war came between them. Was it Busick's fault his line was to inherit the dukedom? Or that he and Colin fell in love with the same beautiful women?

Well, that part probably was Busick's fault. Before war sobered him, there wasn't a pretty face he'd refuse. His position and inheritance garnered many offers.

His cousin gave him no credit for falling out of false love quickly. The last heiress disagreement birthed a ten-year silence. Then, when trouble befell Colin, there was no one for him to turn to but Markham.

If Busick hadn't been nursing his injuries, he would've come to his cousin's aid, apologized again, and stopped the man from giving in to despair. Too many of his fellow veterans wrestled with the same fatal decision.

Thoughts souring, Busick shifted and turned to view the

estate. Torches highlighted the enormity of Hamlin as his men took positions along the walls of the perimeter.

The young footman stood at the gate leading to the surrounding park. Busick swiped under his chin, a final signal sent to his guards to allow LaCroy safe passage.

The swinging motion of his arm whipped up that familiar scent. A milky, slightly soapy, slightly sweet fragrance permeated his greatcoat sleeve.

It was unforgettable.

The perfume of a mother and babe. His top officer, a studious young lieutenant, brought his wife and newborn to the Iberian war front.

A mistake, a costly one.

But LaCroy probably had a wife, a woman nursing her child. "Good for you."

Sullen, more than a conquering warrior should be, Busick entered Hamlin, then rested under the massive wrought iron chandelier. The limbs of the light carved in the ornate style with ribbons and filigree towered above like an octopus caught in a crystalline net.

Lifted high by ropes and pulleys, the chandelier was brilliant, brighter than the sun, illuminating the ice-blue walls of the hall.

Blue?

Not stark white? Hmmmm.

He brushed the irritation from his mind. "The man who lowered the chandelier and lit it, an extra guinea is yours."

None of his men answered, and the reward didn't stop the grumbles uttering from servants his soldiers had roused from their beds. These men—stocking caps, unshorn beards, and slouching postures—all lined up, being given severance, then let go.

No loyalty problems. None.

Busick passed them, his pace slowing as he reached the nook of statues by the stairs. It had been ten years since he'd last seen the three enormous marble warriors, classic Roman soldiers bearing armor and sharp spears.

A curse jumbled with his titled name made Busick look to the line of terminated servants. "Did someone call?"

A portly fellow jerked away from the soldiers. Unlike most of the others, he was dressed in a silver livery and wore a powdered wig like LaCroy.

"Yes, Your Grace. It was I."

Busick signaled to his men to allow the grump forward. "You are?"

"Charmers, Your Grace. I worked for your grandfather. I'm the butler now."

This man Charmers was not charming but frumpy in his wrinkled clothes. "I don't remember you."

"I was the undergardener for your grandfather."

"Well, with the unkempt lawn, I suspect you've been busy in the house?"

"It's been snowing a lot, but Colin Jordan appointed me to be inside. I'm glad you're here. There's too much waywardness happening. I hope you've come to put things in order."

To know Busick's grandfather, the late Duke of Repington, the man knew Strathmore scandals. So, what type of order did he seek?

The pacification of an invalid father?

The firm hand offered by Grandfather?

The wild antics surrounding Mother?

"Your Grace?" The gardener-turned-butler stepped closer and swatted at Busick's coat, brushing off white powder. "I heard you'd been mighty hurt in Badajoz or San Sebastián."

No more hurt or broken than Busick's surviving men. His soldiers looked resplendent in their cranberry regimentals. Unless one stared, one couldn't see the missing arm or fingers that his valet's padding hid.

"Badajoz. You're dismissed."

"But . . . But . . . Your Grace."

"You're dismissed. Get back in line or forgo your severance. Markham will be tossed out shortly. You can follow him. His household might need you."

Busick powered across the hall and stormed into the drawing room. He rested a moment perched at the door, his eyes soaking in more changes. A pianoforte with an exotic olive patina sat in the corner where a suit of armor once resided. A new sofa and a sideboard completed the design.

New furnishings as well as a yellow paper treatment on the walls?

If he didn't know how his mother, Lady Bodonel, loathed Hamlin, he would've thought she was here, readying Hamlin for one of her legendary parties. The notion burned his gut, stirring up feelings he'd rather forget.

Moving deeper into the room, Busick's opinion changed. This was far too elegant and sedate for his mother. The light corn-silk yellow pattern of faint fleur-de-lis, the sea-blue chairs and matching sofa were warm, not ostentatious.

The drawing room would make an excellent base for his headquarters. Here he'd plot war tactics, instruct his ward, and maybe even plan a triumphant return to the field.

The Peninsular War still raged.

Napoleon hadn't surrendered.

Strategists were needed as much as foot soldiers.

Winded, his arm going a little numb from strain, Busick made it to Grandfather's desk and dropped like a rock onto the chair. He rubbed his palm along the rich claret-colored cushion of the newly sprung seat, then whipped out his pocket watch. Twenty-three after eleven. He was late, missing his adjusted schedule by three minutes.

Annoyed at himself, he laid his head back in the chair. He was still learning how not to fatigue so easily. Tiring tacticians were of no use to anyone.

The door slammed shut.

The viscount marched into the room, fists pumping.

Like a magician's cloak, Gantry shed his dark chocolate cape, whirling it in the air before sending it flying to the sofa. It looked like one of his mother's watercolors, the brown earth lying upon the blue sea, missing only nakedness—scantily clad sailors or mermaids.

"I can't believe this, Duke."

Busick should stand for his friend, his fellow officer, but his back wasn't going to allow him to move fast, not if he wanted to be of use, not laid up and ailing in bed. "What has happened? Has Markham escaped? My ward?"

His friend undid the belting of his hilt, and his sword dropped to the floor with a clang. "No, the blackguard hasn't escaped, and the baby seems well, a might scrawny for three months of age."

"Scrawny? I knew Markham couldn't be trusted. But if the boy is alive, why do you look like you've seen a ghost?"

The sneer on Gantry's face could freeze the air and any of the rumored apparitions that walked Hamlin's two-hundred-year-old grounds.

"I've a guard on the nursery. No harm will come to Lionel Jordan, but your uncle Markham . . . Well, I found him attempting to seduce the governess. The woman locked herself in the closet with some fit of hysteria. He's getting dressed. They'll both be down shortly."

Markham couldn't be trusted with anyone, let alone female servants. A man of honor couldn't bed women in his employ. Servants needed to be safe, their wages based on the proficiency of duties, not whims or sexual favors.

Busick slammed the desk. "Lecherous Markham is always up to no good. Is the woman unharmed?"

"Yes. Something other than Markham naked gave her a fright. The widow was upset, mumbling about her lost husband's ghost, not the fiend's tampering."

"So you didn't interrupt them?"

Gantry shook his head.

His friend had a special talent of interrupting couples engaged in the fleshly congress. And the fellow had suffered greatly from his second wife's flirtations and her rumored infidelity.

The viscount went to the sideboard and poured a glass of brandy. "Your uncle is innocent of ravishing the governess, this time."

Busick tapped his thumb along the deepest scar on the writing surface of the desk. "Markham's not my uncle. He was Colin Jordan's uncle from his father's side."

"Yes, your poor father and your cousin's mother were siblings."

"Correct. I'm no part of Markham. The 'uncle business' was to curry favor, since Jordan and I lost our fathers early, but the man is no good and has always been no good. Association with him leads to schemes for money or leisure."

"Money and leisure are no vices. Your pockets are flush, and before the war, you had quite a number of leisurely pursuits."

Busick sat back in the chair, smiling to himself at his history of *leisurely pursuits*. "Ah, the things peacetime affords a man." A man steady on both legs. "Yes, leisure has its place. We'll see how full my dance card becomes once Hamlin is back in order and I've fully recovered."

"Your recovery has been for more than a year, hasn't it?"

Almost two. "Yes."

"I'm devoted to you, Duke. You said you were wounded in the Battle of Badajoz. I expected weakness from a poorly set leg, not that you can barely walk. How bad was the break?"

It was more than a broken bone. Much more. "I'm not a complainer, and words don't change anything. I'll get steadier now that we are out of the carriages. We're not as young as we think we are."

"Duke, you should be off that leg before you walk with a permanent limp."

"More reasons to be away from Town. Now that we've located the child, Hamlin is the perfect place to finish healing. No expectations of social engagements out here." No visits by his mother and her newest special friend, either.

"You'll continue to live as a hermit?"

"Yes, particularly since my friends make married life so appealing."

Gantry tugged at the wilted knot of his cravat. Then he shook free the scarlet ribbon at his back, loosing chestnut locks in dire need of shears. "It has its moments, if there's trust."

Gantry sighed, and Busick imagined fire launching from the viscount's dragon nostrils.

"You and your ward will live here in the country?"

"Of course, and your family seat is not too far away."

"But my father's there. I'd rather stay here or return to my sister's in Bath to collect my girls. I needed to be away. This is a welcome distraction."

Gantry clasped the wrought iron poker. "Fatherhood, when your personal affairs are in shambles, is difficult. Repington, you sound mighty prepared to be an instant father."

"Yes," Busick said. "I've planned for the task, strategized every aspect. I've conferred with all the women who formerly filled my dance card, the women I've allowed others to marry."

If his friend's frown drooped any lower, it would burn in the hearth flames. "You did what, Duke?"

"Many of my former conquests are now friends, more or less. Among them are countesses, duchesses, or respectable ladies of fashion in their own right, all with dozens of children between them. You couldn't buy such wisdom."

Pressing at his skull, Gantry closed his eyes. "So, each of these doves—they sent advice? Duke, you're a lucky man. A lesser one would've been tarred and feathered."

"I've received mostly warm salutations." Busick lifted his index finger. "And just one death threat. Jove has favored me."

"You are most fortunate."

"I've prepared for this child-rearing engagement as I've done all my assignments, gathering as much intelligence as possible. My lady friends have been helpful. Even the death threat provided a regimen for exercise if jumping out of a window was a survivable thing."

"As I said, you're most fortunate." Gantry turned and

leaned against the mantel. "Your cousin, was he also fortunate with his choices?"

"I don't know. After our fathers' early deaths, I had my grandfather's influence. He had his uncle Markham. If Jordan and I had put aside our differences, and he'd followed me into service, I would've protected him. I would've—"

His throat dried.

The memory of shutting the eyes of his fallen lieutenant shook him. Busick forced a deep strangled swallow. "I would've tried to protect my cousin. What's done is done."

"That's another thing upon which we will agree. The past cannot be changed." His friend's voice had become a mash of things that sounded sad, not tightly controlled or spun up like a top. That wasn't practical Gantry.

"When the guards lead Markham and his companion down, we'll press him for the whereabouts of Mrs. Jordan, my cousin's widow."

"Six weeks Markham had you chasing all over England for her and the child when he had the baby all along."

"I wonder what he did to the woman?"

"What are you saying, Duke?"

"No mother, unless she's daft, would leave her child—and never to someone like Markham."

Gantry rubbed his chin. It held two days' worth of shadow, but the latest intelligence meant no stopping—riding through the night with minimal changes of horse—if they wanted to arrive and catch Markham.

Busick could only imagine how disheveled his own appearance must be. He would meet inspection tomorrow—shaved, crisp cravat, pressed shirt.

"Duke, you believe Markham has harmed her?"

Busick shrugged. "I wouldn't put it past him to get rid of anyone in his way, but women do leave, too. That's a possibility."

Jabbing at the coals like he beat an unseen villain, Gantry kept his back to the duke.

The floating ash of savory hickory cleansed the air like nosegay. It refreshed. Busick needed a refreshing. The past was too raw, unforgettable like the scent of mother's milk.

"Duke, you went about this invasion of Hamlin like a battle. You wouldn't have stormed this place with armed guards unless you suspected foul play."

It felt like war, from the first false clues of the babe and mother's whereabouts in Scotland, then Bath. It was a battle to outwit Markham.

But Busick wasn't on the field.

He was in England still recovering, now ready to raise his cousin's son. "It's good that Markham kept the boy alive. I'm grateful we've taken control.

"Well, you've done it. And I must admit this place, Hamlin Hall, is a comfortable house, fashionable on the inside."

And redecorated.

Busick stretched, sinking deeper into the chair's new cushion. "Yes. One might even call it a home."

"Duke, I know you like to win, but we could've used the courts and not a garrison of your former infantry."

"They needed a mission, and the courts take too long. We wait on them to enforce Jordan's will, and Markham could be careless with this child. To keep me from gaining control, he'd harm the boy, maybe even sell him off. I know Markham. He only cares about himself."

"And you, Your Grace, you like winning. You need other hobbies."

"Well, now I have a ward to care for."

"What is it you win with the baby? Best bachelor father ever?" Gantry stripped off his cravat and tossed it atop his discarded coat. "There's nothing to win in raising children, everything to lose."

Busick tried to shift positions in the chair, but it hurt his back too much and would turn the viscount from his moral diatribe to his mother-hen diatribe. "I won't lose on this. I'm doing what's right."

Gantry again leaned against the mantel. "You're a good man."

"And you've done an excellent job. Go, hurry Markham. The sooner he's gone, the sooner you can claim a bed, and I can begin my new campaign rearing Lionel Jordan."

Gantry nodded. "As you wish."

The viscount left the room, still very much the second-best field lieutenant who'd ever served Busick.

The door remained half-open, and he ignored the grumbles coming from the hall and ran his fingers along the carved leg of the mahogany desk. The initials he and Colin etched hadn't been removed. A curly script of CAJ; the straight lettering of BGS. The December strange death notification in the London *Morning Post* followed by a maddening hunt by his solicitors led to this crazy chase.

For Lionel, Busick wouldn't take any threat for granted. Every time he'd been wrong in battle someone paid a price. When he was wrong about a woman, he received an invitation to her wedding.

For Colin's child, he would be cautious, good-tempered, even boring. If the war efforts couldn't use his skills, he'd use them to keep Lionel safe. By Jove, he'd get things right this time, starting with extracting Markham from Hamlin.

CHAPTER 4

THE WIDOW'S GRACE

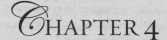

I clung to a tree trunk watching Hamlin Hall. Perspiration fevered my brow, making a sticky paste of the patches of cosmetic remaining on my countenance. I needed this paint gone. I needed to be plain old me, fresh-faced me.

But there was too much activity at Hamlin.

Guards coming in and out, even crawling through the secret entry via the catacombs.

Yet no carriages had left, none of the duke's, not Markham's, either.

"Come down, Patience. We have to go. I kept signaling until the carriages entered the gates. I saw them off in the distance with the countess's scope."

"Jemina, they may move Lionel." I slapped at my thigh pointing back toward the trail, like I was herding goats. "You go to Lady Shrewsbury's. We both can't be caught."

"Oh, no. I'm not going by myself." The lithe little woman tugged Patience's boot. "If you're caught trespassing, you'll never see your son again. Come down. Widows need to be smarter. That's what the countess always says."

Parroting sentiments was what the amnesia-suffering

woman did. If only Jemina could parrot emotions. Then she'd understand the depths of my rage, the girth of my fears. They were wide, wider than the sea.

"I've made sure you were unhurt, but I have to stay for Lionel."

"You can't stop them if they move him. Listen to me, Patience. I know my thoughts aren't always clear, but I've come to realize it takes all of us to win. Come down, and let's go to Lady Shrewsbury. She'll know what to do."

I didn't want to hear this. I didn't want logic. I wanted to be invincible for a moment, to walk into Hamlin, demand my baby, then leave.

That was fantasy.

I clenched the overhanging branch almost throttling it. "But my son . . ."

"We found him. We'll find him again!"

The mousy woman I'd been chained to at Bedlam, the one who only talked in whispers now shouted. I hated and loved that about Jemina, that she'd say her truth and do so no matter what.

Resigned, I swung down. "Let's go see if Shrewsbury's done with me. You think she'll toss me into the asylum again?"

Jemina pulled me into a tight hug. "I'll go, too. It's not as if my memories have returned."

This woman was the reason I had been freed so quickly. When the countess's barrister came for Jemina St. Maur, this lady wouldn't leave, not unless I was freed, too.

"I owe you everything, Jemina. I'd still be there watching the spectators throw pennies at my head. You survived in Bedlam two years. I don't know how you did that. I was in tears every moment, and my imprisonment was a mere ten days."

"Lucky, I guess."

Rays of light emanating from Jemina's lantern showed the truth in my friend's blank, dour eyes. Bedlam and amnesia had stolen her life, one that had a child or children and a husband who probably loved this sweet girl to distraction.

The part of my heart that remembered the love of my sisters thawed. A deep confidence with people who truly cared for me was something I had lacked these lonely years in merry old . . . horrible England.

I nodded, my neck bobbing fast. "I'll be smarter, Jemina, for you."

Wiping her face free of the scarlet hair falling from her chignon, Jemina tugged at the heavy gray scarf wrapping her shoulders. "Then let's go to the countess."

That smile of Jemina's, so innocent and trusting. She'd found peace. Maybe the absence of memories, of no longer remembering loss was best.

But I knew exactly how much had been taken from me.

Hoping for a sign that all was well, I kept looking over my shoulder toward Hamlin. Nothing but darkness met my eyes the entire two-mile walk to Lady Shrewsbury's leased estate. The sound of crickets and an owl's hoot could be heard above the noise of my boots crunching snow, crushing twigs blown free in last week's storm.

Pretty poor signs.

My eternal optimism waned, but I decided that it was just too dark to see a rainbow or some work of a goddess of hope.

The door to the kitchen hung open about an inch, just like we'd left it. We snuck inside. The house was quiet and still. Before I could shut the door, a match struck.

Then another.

Then another.

Soon a wave of bright candles formed a ring about the pale green kitchen. It was as if Hamlin's grand chandelier had been lowered and Jemina and I were caught in its middle.

We were the accused standing in the silent glow of the flames, the frowning faces of the Widow's Grace.

This wasn't the sign I wanted.

The secret society of avengers, women of all sizes, all shapes, glared at us. These widows said nothing.

No words of surprise, no condemnation or *caught you*.

The mix of pink, ruddy, brown, and tanned countenances—all kept their lips pinched.

Then the door slammed.

The finality stopped my heart. The scent of prim-and-proper rosewater fell upon me, resurrecting new shame.

Lady Shrewsbury, the wizened leader of the group, stood at the threshold. She'd shut the door. With ash-blond hair set with curl papers, the countess folded her arms. "Patience Jordan. Jemina St. Maur. We've been expecting you."

I opened my mouth, then closed it. Nothing could be said. We'd broken the group's rules by leaving without permission.

"I'm disappointed." The countess shook her head. The sleeves of her mango-colored robe fluttered from the effort. The luminous pearls at her throat reflected the cheery hue like lavish Poinciana flowers.

The short, buxom woman could be an awakening goddess. But was she one of the good ones, or one who could destroy mankind with a stare?

Eyes down, I stepped in front of Jemina. "I'm to blame, Lady Shrewsbury. Mrs. St. Maur is innocent. I led her astray."

The countess sighed, a tired, heavy one. "What shall I do with you?"

The tone, shrill and crisp, was an exact copy of my mother's. It mirrored her many disappointments in her middle daughter—a torn dress hem, a broken vase, spilling tea on one of Papa's lecherous business associates. Well, that *accident* made Mama's grimace turn into a brief smile. A very brief and seldom-displayed one when it came to me.

"Mrs. St. Maur," the countess said, "you and the rest may go to bed. I must speak with Mrs. Jordan alone."

Jemina frowned but dragged from the room behind the others.

"Sorry, ma'am." I said the words fast but braced for a dressing down.

None came.

When I lifted my gaze to the countess, I felt fifteen years old, gaping at the paled countenance of another disapproving lady, one too tired from sickness to say all the ways her tomboy daughter had brought shame to her door. Mama's ebony eyes possessed the same sadness as Lady Shrewsbury's sherry ones.

The countess came closer. "I want to help you, but you continue to break the rules. Are your circumstances worse than any other widow here? Has your father's wealth made you think you're too good for our rules?"

I never was "too good" or special. I was different and discouraged and alone except for Jemina. Tears welled, but I couldn't swallow more grief. I was about to burst. "I am awful and terrible, but *I'm* a mother. That doesn't make me better than anyone here, just more desperate."

The countess dropped her arms by her side, her gold rings showing beneath her lacy sleeves, one for each of her three husbands. "Are your circumstances more desperate than the widow whose family dumped her onto the streets with no widow's portion or the means for a roof over her head? Or the mother whose husband's aunt has taken her sons, eight and ten, who won't answer her letters? Or the lady whose daughters have been sent out of the country? I have sensible rules for your protection, Mrs. Jordan. You jeopardize the safety of the group when you break them."

"Rules. I'm dying from rules." I lowered my wet face into my gloves. The thin wool couldn't mop up my sorrow. "Since stepping upon these shores, I followed rules, did as everyone said. I was a good wife. My mama would've been proud of the home I kept."

I wiped and wiped. Ashy powder caked on my gloves, my sleeves. "And you, a peer of this land, don't you like how well I've conformed? I've even practiced and practiced until most of my Demeraran accent has fled. But see my reward, ma'am? My son still gets taken away. Rules don't help."

I smeared the cosmetic from my stinging eyes. I wished I couldn't see, but I could. The countess's countenance had that blank look, Mama's look.

The grief of it, the memories of her weighed too much. *Swoosh.* My knees buckled. My livery ballooned out like a ship's sail as I dropped to the countess's feet. Grabbing at Lady Shrewsbury's legs, I held tight, like they were Mama's skirts.

I couldn't let go.

I needed forgiveness.

I needed it now.

My repeated sorries garbled, and I wept upon the hem of the woman's garment. "I don't know how many times my Lionel's been fed. His bottom is so red and pimpled from not being attended. I left him tonight to lay on soiled sheets. Soiled sheets! I don't want to disappoint you, Countess. But how can I be away and let him suffer?"

Lady Shrewsbury bent to me, and I tensed for a slap, but the woman put her arms about me and drew me into the tightest embrace.

Forgiveness.

Not earned. Not negotiated. Not even spoken, but felt through and through, that's what Lady Shrewsbury's arms offered. I clung to her, baptized in her rosewater and kindness.

"It will be well, Patience. You're headstrong but good. Remember that."

How long I lingered in this woman's bosom I didn't know, but the embrace felt like love, like hope. Tonight, that was enough to pull some of my broken pieces together.

The countess tossed away my wig and mussed my frizzy curls. She took a lacy cloth and wiped my face free of the remaining cosmetic. "You are special, Patience. Each of my widows is. But to right wrongs, we have to be smarter. You take too many risks. Tonight, you could've ruined any chance to regain custody."

I straightened and swiped at my cheeks. "I'm sorry, but I don't have to wonder if Lionel ate tonight. For that, I'll never be sorry."

The countess looped her arm through mine and tugged me forward to the kitchen table. The huge walnut furnishing with sturdy benches along its sides centered the Widow's Grace. It was the hallowed place where the women congregated to encourage one another and plot.

"Lionel doesn't like pap milk, Patience. My widow, Mrs. Kelly, tells me she struggles to get him to drink."

I had to touch my jaw to see if it remained attached. The countess had a spy in Hamlin. "You—"

"Sit, Patience. Now is the time for you to know all."

Lady Shrewsbury moved to the stylish klismos chair at the end, one with the harp back like the ones in Hamlin's drawing room.

I shuddered, my head forming an image of Colin brooding in that room, doing his business, wanting no disturbances, needing distance. His comings and goings throughout our marriage stayed with me as did my many regrets.

Lady Shrewsbury's snow-white Angora, the kitty she kept at her side, wagged her head at me. Athena's one green eye, one blue eye saw everything, I was sure of it. She knew I cringed, fearing what her mistress would disclose.

"Mrs. Kelly has been thwarting Mr. Markham's advances, even the rudeness of the current staff, to care for your baby. But all is in place for us to act."

Stunned, barely able to suppress the rapid beating of my chest, I collapsed onto the bench. I didn't know what to think except that all-knowing Shrewsbury was an English version of Erzulie-Ge-Rouge, the red-eyed goddess of revenge. With the cat minion, her klismos throne, and imperial robes, she could be her, if gods wore curl papers.

My brow scrunched, and I clutched the worn wood of the table. "Spy? Markham? What's in place, ma'am?"

"Tea is one of those civilized English things. I think we should make some and then discuss my plans to secure your future with Lionel."

"I don't want tea. I want facts. Do you know that a duke has overtaken Hamlin Hall?"

"I do. I sent for him."

My ears must have stopped working. I twiddled the lobe, more ashy cosmetic coming off on my thumbs. "What?"

"I've been waiting for Repington. This is part of my plan. I pray you haven't ruined it."

This wasn't right.

Lady Shrewsbury lifted Athena and went toward the scullery. Her face held a broad smile, her lips pursed with an I-know-something-you-don't arch.

Fire and nerves exploded in my middle. I trusted the countess, and she solicited armed soldiers to surround my baby. Clasping the table, I tried to make sense of it all, but the one thing I was sure of, my ability to detect good people from bad ones was surely broken.

CHAPTER 5

A TRUE GUARDIAN RISES

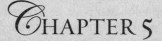

Busick drummed his thumb along the desk. More than forty minutes had passed since the last scout entered the drawing room and reported. All sweeps of the property were fruitless. No widow was located, just trunks in the catacombs and a pile of coconuts.

Odd, but nothing dastardly.

Rubbing the muscles along his neck, he leaned back in the chair. If he could, he'd put a boot atop the desk to gain more comfort, but there was none to be had, not with his thoughts heavy on Colin.

"You were happiest here. Your son shall be, too. To your boy, I'll be a father, the one we both never had. I promise this."

The door flung open with a resounding thud.

Markham, the devil, marched inside. "What's the meaning of this?"

With hands steadied atop the desk and not upon his sidearm flintlock, Busick smiled. "'Tis my duty to inform you, your services are no longer needed. Go on, have a drink, then head out of Hamlin Hall forever."

The man looked as if he could chew through the desk, but he turned and headed straight to the sideboard. With its walnut wood polished to shine, the thing must be a beacon for drunkards.

Markham gripped the furnishing as if he wanted to pick it up and throw it. The lanky man cursed aloud, then seized a crystal decanter. Pour after pour, he downed one brandy and then another. On his third, he walked to the desk.

Wild ash-colored hair scattered here and there, Markham muttered to himself and slurped. "You invade my home. You—"

"This is not your home. It belongs to Lionel Jordan, Colin Jordan's son."

The man gulped all the contents of his goblet, then slammed it down on the desk. The glass spun—*swoop, swoop*—sounding as if it would shatter. "He's a mere babe. He's not fit to handle the business of running Hamlin."

Busick reached out and stopped the glass mid-spin. "But neither are you. Leave now before I have you flung down the steps."

"I'm his guardian. I'm to take care of his interests."

"No, you are not. You know this. That was my cousin's instructions in his will. Yet you've sent me on multiple wild-goose chases across the whole of England to avoid turning over the child. Stop feigning indignation. You fool no one."

A tremble set in Markham's hand.

Good. The firm tone in Busick's voice still held sway.

The blackguard's gray eyes drifted, then he smiled. "Well, you must admit it's been a good chase. I didn't think you'd come this way for another month. That's what I get for not listening to idle chatter."

"Leave now, Markham."

The fiend looked around as if he'd misplaced something. "Give your uncle a little credit. The little mongrel's healthy, and I've kept that awful woman away from him."

"You're not my uncle . . . Awful woman? The boy's mother? Where is she?"

Markham's smile widened, then he turned and walked past the grand pianoforte before stopping. He seemed distracted by the silvered mirror hanging about the fireplace. "Gone, I suppose. Jordan set her up as if she were worthy to be mistress here. The wench even went about redecorating Hamlin as if it were hers."

So Mrs. Jordan was responsible for the new look. "How could she afford it? My cousin was always in need of money."

"Yes, he was. But Mrs. Jordan's father set her up quite well with trusts, plenty of funds to draw upon. I heard she even hid some coins around here. She was suspicious of English banks. Odd foreigner."

Foreigner?

"Lady Bodonel didn't think much of her."

Mother had met her. All he'd seen was a name on paper, Mrs. Jordan, no other accounting of anything, as if she didn't exist or was an afterthought in the legal papers.

He tapped the desk. "Maybe Mrs. Jordan had a distrust in you. That you or my cousin might seize her money. You two have always been awful in handling finances."

Markham undid his wilted cravat and started again. "Her money was his, or it should've been. I told him to press her for our business concerns, but he refused."

Some decency remained in Colin, but he always hated asking for help. Busick hated asking as well. He shifted in his chair. "A man needs to fix his own brokenness before he can entangle others."

"But your cousin wouldn't have had to die if he'd taken her money."

"He didn't have to die at all. That was his choice. Where's his widow?"

"Mrs. Jordan? Not sure. She was very low in her spirits after the birth. She was a danger to the baby, so depressed, feeling so badly about not helping Colin. Perhaps four years alone in Hamlin with its rumored ghosts twisted her mind."

The man turned toward Busick. "I often wonder how

you've kept your head, given all the deaths you've seen. Been in a lot of battles, haven't you?"

Well, well, that was his game, still playing with people's minds. A woman surviving childbirth and the death of her husband could surely be made a victim to Markham's schemes. Busick hammered the desk, the goblet wobbled again.

"Where is she? Where . . . is . . . Mrs. . . . Jordan?"

"The woman ran off, Your Grace. If she hadn't run, I'd have rid the place of her for the child's sake."

Abandon a newborn? No, that didn't feel right. Busick wanted to stand and punch the lies from Markham's lips, but that would show his injured leg. Instead, he pulled his gun and set it on the desk.

"What have you done with her? Tell me now or suffer the consequences."

The smile on the fiend's lanky face waned. "Perhaps if I stayed at Hamlin, I could remember something."

"Your presence is no longer required."

"Are you so set in your decision? Your Grace, I'm sure I could prove useful."

"Out, Markham. I'll locate her."

"You don't want her. She's a danger to the little gold piece upstairs. We could work together. I could help you manage Hamlin. Maybe help replenish your coffers, the ones depleted maintaining your mother's household."

"My purse is fine, but I saw your unkempt lawn, the un-plowed paths. I'll shovel without your *help*. I could offer you a coin or two if you told me where to contact Lionel's mother."

Markham's eyes widened. "Could always use one of your coins, but I'll not bring that woman back here. She dangled the boy over the upstairs railing. She'll hurt the mongrel before the estate is settled."

Dangled? And everything was settled, wasn't it?

Or was Markham still trying to wrangle a way to control Hamlin?

Busick clasped his finger on the flintlock handle. "I'll take up settling the estate with Mrs. Jordan when I find her."

"She's dangerous, Duke."

"Aren't all women a little dangerous?"

Markham shoved his hands in his pockets. "This one nearly killed the baby. That child is all that's left of Colin."

His cousin's uncle was a lot of things, mostly evil, but he'd do anything for Colin. The woman might truly be a danger. He'd sort things out eventually.

"Busick Strathmore, the Duke of Repington, you're still in your prime. You should be courting the socialites of London, not out here in the country with a baby. You and Colin both were popular with the ladies. A child will get in the way."

"Courting is not currently on my schedule."

Yes, that was an appropriate salve to Busick's ego, as opposed to the coddling or repulsion he'd face with his present injuries. He'd never saddle a woman with a sick husband. He'd never turn a wife into a nurse. "Finish your cravat. Leave Hamlin with some dignity. And shame on you trying to deflower a servant."

"She's a comely nanny, but her mood changed unexpectedly. But trust me, the flower has been off the bloom of that woman for years."

Markham folded his arms, making his bottle-green waistcoat appear more wrinkled. "See, nephew. We can get along like old times. We—"

"I'm not your nephew. And I'm done playing games. I found you. I'll find Mrs. Jordan."

"But, Duke, your cousin's creditors are also mine. They've expectations. I spent all my money hiring a staff to care for Lionel. Surely some generosity is warranted."

"I'm sure you'll explain everything to your debtors when they catch you. Perhaps they'll be moved, but not me. Go. Follow your staff—"

"Auug. Help! Help!"

The high-pitched scream came from the hall.

Busick grabbed his crutch. A lady was in trouble. Could his men have found Mrs. Jordan?

He pushed past Markham and went into the hall.

Standing under the grand chandelier, he peered up to the second landing and saw a woman swinging a poker, screaming.

Gantry started up the stairs. "You there, be careful."

"A ghost! It's a ghost. I saw him this time." The young woman tossed the iron but kept moving backward.

Busick charged the stairs, his gaze switching like a pocket scope from how close her foot was to the first tread, then back to the drawing room door. Markham hadn't followed.

The girl teetered, then lost her balance, flipping and flopping all the way down the burgundy carpeted steps. She rolled and stopped at Busick's crutch.

The viscount ran down and picked up her arm.

Markham appeared. He moved quickly and crouched beside her. "Mrs. Kelly, revive, woman. This is the nanny."

Gantry released the nanny's wrist. "She's alive. I feel the blood coursing."

The breath Busick held in his chest began to flow. Powering backward to give the fallen girl air, he pointed his fingers to his troops, summoning two of his men. "Go investigate. More conspirators may be afoot."

Two soldiers marched up the stairs.

Busick glanced down at the woman as Gantry helped her sit. Her eyes had a glow. Some of the girls of the Season used belladonna to add highlights to their eyes. In large doses, it could make a person subjective. Was Markham up to his old tricks?

Mrs. Kelly's wits returned, and the petite blonde bolted up.

"What happened?" Markham asked. "Are you much hurt?"

She clutched the man's waistcoat. "I saw it this time. Not just noises or strangeness. I saw it with my own eyes. It looked like a shrouded man. In the shadows. My own eyes. I saw my late husband's ghost. He's sorry for all I've lost."

Markham put an arm about her, but she swatted away.

"Mrs. Kelly, you're in shock from all the soldiers in the house. This uproar is caused by you, Repington. Apologize, Duke. She's obviously frightened by one of your gun-wielding men."

Gantry shook his head and walked back to the line of servants he was dismissing, continuing to hand each a guinea as they left. "These are delaying antics, Your Grace."

Light hair tumbling from a hastily done chignon, she turned to Busick. "No. It was the ghost. Tell him, Markham, about the ghost. About the things missing. The noises."

The man looked as if he'd sobered up. He shrugged. "Mrs. Kelly is the child's nanny, Duke. You're terminating everyone else, but she should stay. She can care for the child."

With the alleged caregiver babbling about ghosts, Busick shook his head. Young women were trouble. Young, confused women more so. Nothing but old matronly women would be employed, that's what Hamlin needed. "Your position is terminated. I need no one spewing nonsense near my ward. Guards. My friend Lady Shrewsbury has rented a house about two miles away. Take Mrs. Kelly there. Tell her the Duke of Repington sent you. She'll take you in and make sure you are cared for."

The woman went with his soldiers and pulled away from Markham when he tried to claim her arm.

When the doors had shut behind them, Busick pivoted and watched his men opening and closing doors of the bedrooms on the second floor.

"Repington, you should let me at least stay until morning."

"No. Be gone. Guards."

Another of his men advanced upon Markham. The soldier's flintlock was pointed at the fool's head.

"This isn't over." Markham pointed his bony finger in the air. "If you get too ill or tire of baby duty, send for me."

"See him to the edge of the property. Don't come back until he's out of firing range."

The door didn't slam fast enough behind the fiend, but Busick knew this wasn't the last of him. The man was bad at many things, except revenge.

A strong baby's cry filled the hall.

"Your baby, Your Grace," Gantry said.

They both moved toward the stairs, but it seemed a hundred treads lay between them and the nursery on the third floor. The urge to recall Mrs. Kelly pressed, but the viscount had started up the steps.

"I'll take care of this, this time."

Feeling a smidgeon useless, Busick watched his friend go forward. "Tomorrow, we'll get new hires, Gantry, you'll see. This is best for the safety of the child."

"If you say so." Head shaking, the viscount reached the third floor and disappeared down the hall.

When Busick turned to his soldiers, one saluted. Another looked tired. They hadn't done intensive duties in months.

"Take turns keeping watch, men. I promise we'll have Hamlin normal and running well by week's end. And we will return to military precision as well."

That wasn't a command but a promise. One to his men and to himself. After a fast salute to his major, Busick made his way back into the drawing room. He scanned the area, looking to see if Markham had smuggled out a Hamlin treasure.

Everything was in place, even the crystal decanter of brandy.

Moving slow, he walked farther inside and tweaked the mirror, which had become crooked.

Odd. Did Markham try to take this huge silver frame with him?

With a shake of his head, Busick pushed his friend's coat and sank onto the sofa cushions, elevating his good leg over the edge. Deeply sighing, he relaxed and let the strain of the chase fall away.

When he opened his eyes again, Gantry stood near, dangling a baby. "Your Lionel, Duke."

Busick sat up and took the boy in his arms. He was small with a big head and a toothless smile. A panic went through him feeling the boy's little heartbeat against his waistcoat. "What am I to do? I mean thank you, Gantry."

His friend smirked. "I'm sure there is some wisdom on your list from your lady friends on how to soothe a wide-awake child."

"Yes, of course. Hello, Lionel. I'm . . . Repington?"

Gantry went to the door, his head shaking as if it would wobble off. "Good night, Duke. Master Jordan."

Unwilling to give the viscount the satisfaction of knowing that being alone with the baby was a tiny bit unnerving, Busick proceeded to hold Lionel as if he cradled a snug blunderbuss flintlock, one that had been freshly oiled and cleaned. But this one smelled a little stale. He must need more oil.

"We'll hire help, Gantry. As soon as morning arrives, we'll send out inquiries."

The viscount leaned against the door, yawning as if all the air in his lungs had left him in that moment. "I'll relieve you in a few hours. Don't crush or drop the boy. And here." He walked back and handed him a cloth. "You might need this."

Busick took it and pulled it about the wide-eyed child like a blanket.

Gantry mumbled under his breath something that sounded like *amateur*. "That's not for that end. That's a napkin to dry him when he wets himself or worse. Night, Your Grace."

Wet or worse? "A waste basin. Gantry, get it from the desk."

His smug friend did so, putting it close to the sofa, then went to the threshold. "Good night."

The door shut, and Busick was alone with the boy he'd chased these past six weeks. He lifted him high in both hands. "And so this begins. I'm your guardian, Lionel."

The boy didn't cry. He seemed to stare back with wide hazel eyes and long lashes. His light olive face had pink poked-out lips. It was sort of cute, if Busick were to note such things.

He settled the boy in his arms. And right before he could navigate to a more comfortable position on the sofa, the child sprung a leak.

"So it begins, little one. So it does." Busick took off the napkin tied on Lionel's bottom and held him over the waste basin.

"First thing in the morning, I'm hiring a woman for your personal care. Your first valet, a baby valet."

Waiting for the watering to end, he determined that addressing this particular need of the child wasn't something he'd be good at. "Lionel Jordan, we'll win this war together. We'll get you a proper nanny and put you on a schedule. My friends say a schedule is important for proper child-rearing."

The boy blinked his big eyes, innocent and wondrous.

"We'll get along nicely, young man."

With an old nanny serving as the boy's valet, one who adhered to schedules and rules, there could be no way to fail. Busick patted and dried his ward and purposed to hire one right away.

CHAPTER 6

WHEN WOMEN PLOT

I stewed over an empty cup at the countess's kitchen table waiting for her to return. The lady's nephew, the barrister who freed me and Jemina from Bedlam, had barged in. Mr. Thackery seemed different than I remembered. I didn't remember that the medium-build man was about my height. I thought him taller. I suppose everyone looked taller when I was chained to a wall.

He and the countess went for a private conversation.

My hope was that Lady Shrewsbury hadn't changed her mind and was not currently giving the barrister instructions to recommit me to Bedlam.

The door swung open. Chuckling, she came back into the room. "Thackery is such a dear. He sends his regards and his wishes for you to be diligent and show more care. He worked hard to obtain your freedom."

Doubt filled me. My stomach fell, and I waited for the words, *You're going back*.

I counted to ten, held my breath, but no condemnation came.

In my softest voice, I said. "I just want my son. Tell me

how to put my world back together. Tell me how to get my baby from the army you sent."

Lady Shrewsbury leaned over and clutched my fingers. "I requested His Grace, but Repington, the military man, brought his troops. I told him that Lionel Jordan, his ward, was at Hamlin Hall. He's your son's true guardian per the will my nephew uncovered when we researched your identity. Mrs. St. Maur is not the most reliable witness, but she was correct about you."

"Jemina is a dear. I owe her everything."

"She is, but let's focus on you, Patience. Mr. Markham planted false clues and had Repington chasing *you* and the babe all over England."

"Repington was Colin's grandfather, and he's dead. The man I met tonight is very much alive."

"Yes, Colin's grandfather, the fifth Duke of Repington, is buried in the family crypt. The sixth Duke of Repington is alive and well, but you must know this, as you met him tonight."

Yes, he was alive and big and limping. I pulled at my livery, clawing to loosen the binding beneath my shirt. "I did meet him, but as a footman named LaCroy whom he discharged."

The grand woman shrugged, and Athena gave a mimicking shake. "On a first meeting, you couldn't stay employed?"

"He terminated everyone citing a need for loyalty, but he did not see through my disguise."

"Then the rake is slipping. He can usually detect the female presence blindfolded."

"A r-rake?" I rolled my *r*, something I did when surprised. "You mean a womanizer? What will he teach my baby? Will Hamlin be filled with scantily clad women?"

"Scantily clad women? That might be the duke's penchant in private, but rakes like him go after difficult prey, Mrs. Jordan, not ones who can be bought." The countess patted her hand. "You'll need to live up to your name and be patient. Your recklessness is a mixed bag of trouble. That's what I get for helping your kind."

My lungs deflated.

The camaraderie and hope I had in my chest for the countess leached. I was again the label of *other*.

Not once since Lady Shrewsbury rescued me had I been made to feel *other*. From Markham or the butler, I wore a shield to protect my soft heart. For the countess, a woman I admired, I was bare.

What was left of my pride dropped to the pit of my stomach. "My kind?"

"Yes. Foreigners. People birthed in England have far more caution."

I ripped off my gloves and looked down at my brown hands. "So, you don't mean Blackamoor or mulatto?"

With Athena purring in her arms, the countess stood over the table. "Injustice looks the same on all women, the same. You're a cheated widow made destitute by your husband's dastardly family. My goal is to restore you and every widow whose been denied her rightful place, like I was."

Her mouth lifted into a smile, and my heart again saw acceptance, understanding, even love.

"Let's have tea. Even Demerarans fancy tea. I've left you stirring over an empty cup long enough."

Spicy rum or tangy sorrel punch made from the petals of sweet hibiscus flowers was a favorite drink of my homeland, but warm tea was lovely.

"Mrs. Kelly is here."

"What? They found your spy? Who will care for Lionel?"

"Calm yourself, Patience."

After motioning to Athena to sit on her throne, Lady Shrewsbury went to the hearth. She retrieved a pot of steaming water. From a high shelf, she tugged down the lacquered, polished box used as a caddy for tea leaves, fresh ones, not used ones.

The countess brought everything to the table. "The duke

sent her to me. He trusts that I will care for her. She was disoriented and fell down the stairs."

The grand stairs? They were steep but so beautiful when the mahogany balusters and newel posts were polished to shine.

Waving the countess's hands from the pot, I steeped our tea, then strained the golden liquid into the snow-white cups.

"My nephew confirmed that the Duke of Repington has not only seized Hamlin but also has made arrangements to stay at Hamlin long-term. I hope the duke trims the lawn in the spring. I hate leasing next to shabbily kept grounds."

I almost dropped my cup. "Lawns?" I bounced up. "If this man is decent, I should go to him and tell him who I am."

"It's not that simple." Lady Shrewsbury waved her hands, motioning for me to retake my seat. "The duke is not easy. He's taken Hamlin Hall with an armed battalion and has dismissed the entire staff. He's not sorting out good servants from bad ones. He's made one quick judgment. We can't have him doing that with you."

"But, Countess, if I go now—"

"He's a bull, a lusty bull. Bulls are not reasoned with. Their suspicions must be slaughtered, killed with kindness and loyalty." The countess stroked Athena's thick fur.

The kitty rolled onto her back as if to demand, *Tickle me here*. Athena had more control of her life and little body than I had of mine.

"Isn't honesty the best path, ma'am?"

"Telling him that you infiltrated Hamlin as a manservant will not bode well."

"But the truth—"

"The truth is not always enough." The countess sat back, her countenance blanking, her lips becoming nonexistent. "Patience Jordan, why did you abandon your son?"

"I did not abandon Lionel!"

"You've never left his side, my dear?"

"Ma'am, you know very well I had no—"

"Answer the question. Have you left his side?"

I looked at the brown liquid in my cup. No help was in there. "Yes, I have."

The countess leaned forward. "Where did you go when you abandoned your son?"

"I didn't . . ." I knew what she'd pushed me to admit. I hated it but had to own it. Shoulders drooping, I coughed low. "Bedlam. Almost five weeks to the day I was told my husband committed suicide, I was tossed into Bedlam."

"If I were my nephew, I'd have my hands behind my back and parade like a prized peacock presenting a winning argument in front of the jury box. I'd press you for the reason you were tossed into Bedlam. Was it a holiday from grief, Patience? An accident? A conspiracy?"

"It was a conspiracy. I was confused."

"That's not what the admission papers say. My nephew had to craft a bit of paperwork to overcome the eyewitness accounts stating you were a danger to yourself and your child. There's sworn testimony about you being so guilt-laden over your husband's death that you claimed to have seen his ghost and that you took the baby and nearly jumped over the stair railing. Hamlin's stairs are steep. You or the baby could have been killed from a fall."

Wanting to hide at the thought I might've hurt Lionel, I brought my palms to my face. "He had us locked in the nursery for weeks. I did what I had to do to keep up my strength and my milk for Lionel. I'd never hurt my baby. Never. I'd give my life to defend him."

"I know, dear. You are good, Patience. A very good mother, but the duke will look at the account like a field report. Until he knows you, he'll believe it. The man will never let you near the child. You have to trust me. We have to be smarter to outdo Markham's treachery."

My cup trembled within my palms; the tea inside sloshed

but didn't spill. The china was sort of like me, so full of heat, but yet I hadn't cracked, hadn't exploded. "Why is Markham doing this? I was good to his nephew. I followed the rules. Hamlin was immaculate. I burned the expensive beeswax candles, not cheap tallow ones, in the grand chandelier to welcome Colin home like a conquering hero, like all was well. I pretended not to notice his absences, his gambling. I even took him to my bed whenever he returned, even when I suspected he'd laid in others' sheets. Why does Markham hate me? Is it my skin?"

"It's never that simple. Yes, you were a good wife, but widows are cheated because of money and power. We find which one enticed Markham, and we'll have the answer."

The countess poured more tea. "Drink, Mrs. Jordan. It's just chamomile."

Staring at my full cup, I hadn't thought it could be tampered with, but my heart believed the best too quickly.

This was my heel of Achilles.

I felt too much.

I saw the deepest love where there was tolerance.

The handsome hero but not the shadow of his demons.

I took a sip of my tea, almost wishing it had something in it to deaden my pain. "I don't want anything more with Markham. I have means, independent of Colin. If I can get into Hamlin and retrieve my trust documents, Lionel and I can live safely."

"Yes, if the duke would allow. But Lionel controls Hamlin and more money. Do you understand the terms of your marriage contract or your late husband's will?"

"Paperwork? Not exactly." I crossed my arms. "My father handled those things."

"No wonder women are cheated. You have to know details. Your late father had doubts about your husband's commitment. He put some rather odd terms in the marriage contract."

The countess fluffed the lacy cuff of her robe. "Your husband was to collect four thousand pounds upon a son from your womb reaching four months of age and another ten thousand upon his reaching three years old."

"Just a son? What if I bore a girl?"

"A mere five thousand pounds at age five, nothing else. I think your father wanted to assure that you and Mr. Jordan kept trying for success, so to speak."

Did Colin know this?

With the money I'd overheard that he owed, he should have believed this baby was a boy. The payment would have been his, not something from me helping him, as he put it. It would have settled his debts. "Would this money come from the trusts Papa set up for my control?"

"No, the payment was separate. There are more inheritances that come from the Strathmore side of the family, investments that can't be touched for some years. Upon Jordan's death, the baby's money goes to his guardian, as does control of Lionel's fortune until he is of age."

Markham would get it.

I bristled on the seat, my heart pounding louder and louder—malicious, malevolent, muckraker. My husband's dying in December kept rewarding his horrible uncle from the grave.

Suddenly, so thirsty, I tried to extinguish my tongue with the tea, but a sea couldn't quench my soul. It was on fire, burning me.

"The Duke of Repington is your son's true guardian. I believe Markham delayed giving the child up to get the payment that is due next month. It's good the duke has assumed custody."

"How do I regain my son?"

"We need proof of Markham's scheme." With her sherry eyes softening, the countess clasped my hand. "To put it bluntly, no one is going to believe you were his victim, not without proof. The prejudices against you being foreign, a mulatto, a Blackamoor, a woman, a widow are insurmountable. If it's found out that you're gallivanting in men's clothes and breaking into homes, you'll be sent back to Bedlam."

"There has to be hope. I survived thus far. I've not lost my wits. That has to mean something."

The countess whispered something to Athena and set the snowball onto the table. The kitty came to me, meowed, then licked my fingers. The touch was soft and calming like Lionel's coos the first night I snuck into Hamlin and he remembered me, remembered how to suckle.

"Please don't tell me to give up, Countess. I cannot."

"Never, Patience. We don't quit. We must gain the duke's trust. He's a good man. Once the duke was informed of your husband's death and the existence of a child, he's been in dogged pursuit of Lionel. The man is logical but skeptical. He'll believe the worst, no matter what his charming face says. Since he needs servants, you and Mrs. St. Maur will masquerade as such in Hamlin. You'll gain his trust while searching for evidence against Markham."

"Evidence? But hasn't Mrs. Kelly been able to find something?"

"No. Between the little time she was allowed to care for Lionel and avoiding Markham's flirtations, she's found nothing. It was a difficult time, and next month is the anniversary of her husband's death."

Lusty, awful Markham would say or do all manner of things to try to have an advantage over a woman. "I must thank Mrs. Kelly, but do you think someone shrewd like Markham left evidence?"

The countess sat back, sliding her pearls in her palm. "He hasn't left Hamlin, even though he knew the duke was searching for him. There has to be something in Hamlin he's hiding."

Did my future with Lionel depend upon finding a secret in a house filled with secret things? Slumping forward, I laid my head on the table on a darkened spot that may have been marred by a hot soup pot. "You think it will still be there when Markham is kicked out of Hamlin?"

"Trust me. There's something there. And knowing the duke, Markham will be lucky to leave with his cloak. He'll shake him upside down to make sure no silver fork leaves."

Hope stirred in my heart. I wanted vindication more than vengeance.

The Angora wiggling around my head, her tailless bottom wagging, brought a small lift to my lips that had seemed cemented into a frown. I shooed her toward the countess. "I'll do as you say. Being close to Lionel is my priority."

Lady Shrewsbury made a *tsk* sound with her teeth, and the fluffy kitten trotted, then jumped into the countess's lap. "Return to Hamlin as a servant, care for your son, and find the evidence we need to prove Markham's guilt."

"If there weren't guards, I'd run back to Hamlin now and grab Lionel and escape."

"Listen to me very carefully, Patience. The duke hunted down Markham. He'll chase you and reclaim his cousin's son. Then he'll have you committed or imprisoned. He has the power to do this. All male guardians do."

The countess shook her head, curl papers bobbing as she stood with Athena. "I know you want to flee. I've felt your desperation in my own head. If we do things the right way, you'll be restored custody. You're one of mine, Patience Jordan. I won't let you run."

Lady Shrewsbury stashed Athena in the crook of her arm. "Your son needs you in Hamlin. I'll take you in the morning and use my influence with the duke to get you hired as a wet nurse and nanny. While you care for your son, you'll gain the man's confidence, and I know you will find the tools to expose Markham. The evidence may even give you peace on Jordan's suicide. I've heard your nightmares. You have no peace."

Could there be another reason than me, my worsening Colin's depression? I scooped up the teapot and readied to dry the leaves. "I'll clean up here and put away the cups."

"This masquerade will work. Get some sleep. Things always look better in the morning."

Kissing her kitty, Lady Shrewsbury moved to the door. "I expect to see you in the morning, Mrs. Jordan. I hope you'll be here."

"I'll go by Mrs. LaCroy for our masquerade."

Lady Shrewsbury nodded; her mouth even offered a smile. Soon her footsteps disappeared.

All was quiet.

I laid out the used tea leaves on a napkin and stacked the cups in the scullery, then rinsed out the pot, the rules for finishing a tea service. Sinking onto the bench, I dropped my face onto the spot the tea had warmed, right next to that communal soup-pot mark. I was grateful for the Widow's Grace, but I wanted my life restored, all my pieces put back together.

I'd serve this Duke of Repington to serve Lionel, but only to get my son strong enough to sail. Once I retrieved my trust documents, we'd escape England. It was time to live by my heart's rules. That had to be the smartest thing a widow could do.

CHAPTER 7

A MAN'S BEDCHAMBER

Groggy from a night of little sleep, I stood at the steps of Hamlin Hall. My head conjured up fears of how my son spent the night in a house teeming with guns.

But my heart, that easily misled thing, told me that the man I met last night would protect my baby.

I should tell him the truth and beg for mercy.

Jemina came to my side, blowing into her bare hands. "Such a pretty house in the morning. Everything is so much lighter than at night." Laughing, she put her palm out, thumbs touching, as if she could measure the changes. "I suppose that is the way."

Offering the girl a side-eyed glance, I nodded. It was all I could muster with my stomach knotting. I stared at the double doors, the shiny brass handles of Hamlin's entry. Doubt swirled about me like the cream-colored fringe adorning my shawl. The tendrils of the spun wool slipped through my perspiring fingers.

"I helped the Duke of Repington reach these steps last night. He said he wants a loyal staff. We're not exactly that. We're performing another deception."

Jemina shrugged. "What a man says, Patience, and what he means are often different. That I remember."

Yes, like vows in front of a minister. I squinted at Jemina. My friend was scary sometimes.

It was as if she could read minds. Maybe that was the good part of the life she'd forgotten shining through her amnesia. I heard the bad parts in the girl's whispers at Bedlam. Jemina had suffered greatly.

I took a half step forward, just a little ahead of my friend, to be alone with my former house.

On a cold November morn, Colin brought me here, even helped me up the snow-covered steps. I was a nervous new bride, and he was handsome and tall with deep raven hair. I'd loved him, love on first jest. He'd made me laugh so hard under a Demeraran sunset. A girl mourning her mother needed humor.

But once inside, I saw the man, his struggles, his sad thoughts. He did his best to assert me as mistress, but only here. He never took me beyond the grounds. I was a prisoner to his moods and fears as much as he.

Now I visited Hamlin, hoping to serve.

A nanny couldn't tell a footman to lower the grand chandelier. Couldn't ask him to find the fine beeswax candles and light them to pretend she entertained fine guests. I'd have to take orders and continue denying myself, but who was I on these English shores?

A mere widow?

A desperate mother?

More so, a woman guilty over things she should have challenged, should've changed.

"I'm ready to go home."

"You're not talking about Hamlin Hall are you, Patience?"

Jemina was at my side again, but I couldn't say aloud that this place was no home, not for me. The rooms I decorated still held bitterness.

The dining room with my menus—never English enough.

The bathing room with milk baths for my complexion—never light enough.

The halls with their echoes catching the purring of my syllables—never sounding proper enough.

Never. Never. Never. Enough.

"Jemina, I'm here, and I'm going to win this time."

Lady Shrewsbury joined us. "Ladies," she said as she adjusted her large straw bonnet bearing a blush pink ribbon, "it's time to put our next act into motion."

She gathered our palms together. The woman was elegant in bishop-blue gloves and a deep violet carriage gown appointed with military-style brass buttons.

The countess dressed as a lady. Jemina and I wore the costumes of servants.

I stopped fretting, stopped lading my shoulders with coconuts and boulders and doubts and listened to Lady Shrewsbury's prayer.

"The holy habitation is the protector of widows, providing relief and favor. This is the Widow's Grace." She clasped our hands and led our aproned and mobcap brigade up the stairs. "Now, we win."

The doors opened before she knocked. A guard, a fellow in a regimental-red military uniform answered holding a gun in his hand. He lowered it. "How did you get past the guards at the gates?"

"Never mind that, young man. We've come to see the Duke of Repington. I'm an old friend, and he's in dire need of our services."

The guard lowered his flintlock. "The commander has not mentioned visitors. Return later."

"Tell him Lady Shrewsbury is here. He'll see me."

"Let me ask." The man closed the door with a thud.

I folded my arms under my shawl, hiding my fists. "He didn't even think of leading us to the drawing room. Colin had his visitors meet there, not that he'd want me in there."

A flash of my husband's last visit, late summer. A few

weeks before I last saw him, he and Markham argued with a man in there. I'd never heard Colin raise his voice. Such words, so rude.

"This soldier was r-rude."

My purring mouth, I swiped at it. "The first guard had better manners."

"That fellow I knew," the countess said. "I helped the man's sister with a little paperwork. The impact of the Widow's Grace is wide."

Jemina clasped my elbow. "Patience, you're shaking."

I was, and no amount of knitted threads could hide it. "We're so close to Lionel. Now this scrutiny and having to be so careful."

Lady Shrewsbury brushed my shoulder. "You need to calm yourself. We must impress the duke."

Another man set to judge me. I nodded and found a smile, a begrudged tug of my tight lips.

The door opened again. "The duke will meet with you at ten o'clock. Return then."

"That's two hours from now," Lady Shrewsbury said. "That's unaccept—"

A baby's loud cry.

Lionel's cry.

He wailed for a moment, then stopped like something muzzled his mouth.

I edged forward, but the countess gripped the sleeve of my gown. Her hold was the only thing keeping me from dashing inside.

"Young man," the countess said, "how long has the baby been crying? I have a nanny here who can help."

"Ma'am," the soldier said. "It's off and on. He's just picked that racket up again thirty minutes ago."

"Racket?" I gasped, shook free of the countess's hold, then ducked under the guard's arm. Sliding across the marble tiles, beneath the shadow of the grand chandelier, I was in the middle of a camp. The hall was a sea of tents—flat white, bell-shaped tan, and flags backed all the way up to the stone gods, the three warrior statues near the stairs. The duke's army had made camp on my floor.

Lionel shrieked again.

"Wait, Mrs. LaCroy," the countess said. "Have some patience, please."

I couldn't.

Not with my baby crying.

I hiked my skirt and sped up the stairs to the second story. Lionel sounded as if he were on this level, not the third floor with the nursery.

"Come down, woman. Stop!"

Soldiers were coming for me. Jemina blocked one, fluttering in front of him with her dark gray skirts.

I spun to the left and then to the right. Which way to my child?

Lionel started again, though softer now, he was indeed on the second floor, in one of the bedrooms. The master's bedchamber?

People were running after me, pounding up the stairs.

They'd drag me out.

Not again. I turned the corner and pushed into the room where my boy's sobs seemed the loudest.

I closed the door, then froze.

Lionel, my baby was here . . . in the arms of a man rocking him . . . in my bed. Through the sheer silver curtains of the canopy, I saw a masculine figure hovering over Lionel. His thick arm half-covered in a billowing burgundy robe swallowed all but my baby's big head.

"You're not wet again, are you, lad? I'm running out of shirts. Come on now, little soldier, milk will be here soon."

My panicked spirit eased. This man was trying to appease Lionel, not punish him.

I took another step into the room, staring at the man, my baby, and the bland white walls surrounding them all. It was one of the only rooms I hadn't redecorated to make it seem warmer, loved. Paint couldn't cover lies.

"Come on, my boy. We were getting along."

That voice. Deep and rich.

The shadows and outline of this fellow half-hidden in the bedclothes were large and overpowering.

And familiar.

It had to be the duke from last night.

I squinted through the curtains to be sure.

Yes, it was him and the memory of him—his heavy arm draped across my shoulders; the hammered muscles of his chest splayed into my cheek—left my mouth dry.

The baby calmed, grabbed at the velvety robe falling from the duke's bared shoulder, one with scars. The man was rugged and masculine with brown hair streaked with blond, making me wonder if, like velvet, it changed colors when my fingers swept through it.

"Easy with my cuff in your mouth. Well, until your milk arrives, I suppose that will do. But my valet's not going to be happy. Let's see. One of my dear lady friends said poetry is soothing to babies."

The duke scrubbed his chin. " 'There was an old woman from . . .' No, that rhyme might not be appropriate."

I wanted to laugh, but my heart felt too cheated. It should be Colin in my bed, holding our son, giving me wrong thoughts—of curling up onto a bared shoulder and listening to his sweet deep voice sort of singing.

Very wrong thoughts, but it was such a dear picture.

One to covet in my heart.

I shook my head and coughed. "Sir. I mean, Your Grace. I think the baby needs to be fed now."

The man seemed to startle, pulling at his blanket to cover his leg as if that was indecent, not his naked chest with the curls of hair peeking over the lapel of his robe. "Who's there?"

I came around to the side of the bed where the curtains parted. "Your Grace, I'm here to help."

"A washerwoman? Barging in." His gaze seemed to travel the length of me, but there was nothing wrong with my maid's outfit. The blue checked cotton was pressed, unassuming, and clean beneath my white apron.

The duke huffed. "I'm not sure how Markham had his staff trained to awaken him, but there have been a number of changes to Hamlin this past night."

Nose wrinkling at the fiend's name, I stood up straight. "I'm no washerwoman."

He glanced my direction again before lowering his face toward Lionel. "Well, whoever you are, you need to leave. You're no longer employed."

"Is the boy wet, sir? I see he's bundled in a . . . shirt?"

"One of my best, and I don't think so. He's hungry. I've sent a footman to find the cows. He'll have milk soon. His first feeding will be"—the duke reached for a watch on the nightstand—"in another twenty minutes. Now please go."

I reached my arms out. "I'm sure he's hungry, Your Grace. I can help."

Lionel started crying and seemed to lift his hands as he'd done for me last night. He surely heard my voice and re-membered.

"See, miss, you've gotten him out of order again." The duke took his big thumb and waved it over Lionel.

The baby grabbed it and suckled the digit.

"The boy and I are friends. If you were a washerwoman, I'd hope you were good at stains. That's the second shirt the boy's used, and his side of my mattress might need to be at-tended, too."

"The babe slept in here with you?"

The duke glanced up with a smile of pride. "Like I said, we've gotten to know each other. Now if you don't mind. Well, look at that. His eyes have changed like my cousin's. They're a darker hazel now."

My father's eyes were also hazel. Who should take credit for this? "Sir—"

With a boom, the doors of the bedchamber flung open. The countess, Jemina, and two soldiers stood there.

The duke shuffled the sheets about his one leg stuck in the blanket. His other foot dangled as if poised to toss on the boots lined perfectly by the bed.

"Men, return to your posts. I can handle women in my bedchamber."

The soldiers laughed and left. The doors shut with a thud.

"Lady Shrewsbury? Does this woman belong to you?"

"Duke, she's one of the servants I have brought to recommend to you. No, don't rise, you seem to have your hands full."

"I hadn't intended, ma'am, since this is my bedchamber and you are intruding."

He glanced in my direction as he played with Lionel's little palm. "Normally, so many lovely ladies in my private chambers is a goal, but not in front of my ward. These days, I have to have more moral goals."

The man preened like a proud papa tweaking my Lionel's nose.

"Lady Shrewsbury, can you please lead this beautiful harem away from my bedchamber? Hmmm, words I never thought I'd utter."

The countess cast pained eyes at me as she passed and stopped at the bed table. "Mrs. Kelly, the young woman you sent to me, says you've fired your staff. You'll need help, particularly with that bundle in your arms."

My babe cried harder.

The duke rocked Lionel a little faster. "Please, son, we were just getting along. Must be all these intruders."

"Son?" Lady Shrewsbury held out her arms and took Lionel. "Duke, you sly thing. Your old habits of loving and leaving have caught up with you and now you've gained this morsel."

He chuckled, a rich full-bodied laugh, and I felt more cheated, even jealous.

"Countess, I'm not one to kiss and tell, but this young lad is the son of my late cousin. I'm just a mere guardian. No lovers lost, not this year, not yet."

All this inane conversation and Lionel was hungry. I looked to my friend to see if she could help, but Jemina might as well have been a lamppost.

She stood at the foot of the grand bed, stiff and stilled by a wheeled chair. The girl looked mesmerized by it.

I rubbed my brow. "Your Grace, sir. Lady Shrewsbury. Let me take the baby. The boy is hungry. I know he is."

Lionel cried again.

The duke reached for him, but Lady Shrewsbury seemed not to notice. She turned and bounced Lionel in her arms.

"Ladies, I'm getting him on a schedule, and you're interrupting." He picked up his gold watch again. "Milk will be here shortly. So please leave."

I undid my shawl and a few buttons of my gown to expose the wetness of my tunic. "Milk is here for the babe."

The duke's gaze fell upon me. "Oh."

That was all he said, but he took his time staring with a cheeky smile that took years from his face. "Ah, yes, ma'am, you do. Of course." He tugged on Lionel's foot. "Be at it. Feed him."

Permission given at last, I sighed and moved fast to get my son.

Then I tripped over those boots.

Hands flailing, I landed headfirst onto the bed. My cheek smacked hard against the chest I'd admired.

CHAPTER 8

THE WRONG MOVES

Naked chest. Naked chest. I'd landed on the duke.

There was no place to put my hands that wasn't scars or muscles, lean shoulders, or taut abdomen.

"Sorry. Sorry. Your Grace."

There was no rule, no protocol for this.

His arms came around my back and held me still. "Woman, don't move."

There was no rule for how I felt in this tight embrace. My cheeks burned.

"Don't thrash, woman. My leg is injured. You'll make this worse."

Worse?

What could that be?

I was sprawled atop him. His breath wasn't sweet like last night's rum, but tart. I stopped twitching. With each twist he increased the pressure of his palms.

My legs sank more into the softness of the mattress and pillows that had surrounded the duke.

I looked up and caught his gaze. His eyes, clear blue with

streaks of mischief gray, held a smile. "There you go. You listened."

"Yes, listen to the duke, girl," Lady Shrewsbury said. "He's supposedly an expert in bed."

The man chuckled, his hands shifting from my waist to my hips, then back. He laughed more.

It wasn't funny to be so clumsy, so awkward. I'm refined. Mostly coordinated. I'd never do this on purpose. I started moving again to get off him and to show I wasn't the compliant bed wench he thought I was.

"Whoa now. I thought we agreed upon you not moving?"

I fidgeted more and caught a whiff of Lionel's handiwork and more duke, a woodsy, earthy smell. "I'm sorry, Your Grace, but I want off."

"In a moment, once you settle, I'll lift you from the bed."

His head lowered to mine. We were almost nose to nose.

"Have we met, miss? That is the correct question to ask being in bed together."

"She's Mrs. LaCroy, Duke. She's excellent with babies." The countess cooed to Lionel as she'd done with Athena last night. "Mrs. LaCroy is so passionate about children, she forgets herself."

"LaCroy? Of course." He nodded. "This is a bit of a compromising situation. Remember, Lady Shrewsbury, when I told you what that one lady tried—"

I put my hands to his chest to push away, but my fingers tangled in his robe. Now I've added naked shoulder to naked chest. "I need to be free, Your Grace. The baby's still hungry and I'm . . . I'm leaking."

"That won't do." His hands slipped down my sides again.

My breath caught as he clasped my hips. He lifted me as if I were a feather and set me on my feet.

"I'm so sorry, sir." I straightened my apron but found more of my buttons were undone. When I glanced at the duke, his smile was wider.

"All that twitching. I suppose we are both disadvantaged, LaCroy."

Cheeks burning like a raging fire, I took the baby from the countess. "I'll take him to the nursery."

"You can feed my ward here. No need for false modesty with you falling all over me." He folded his arms. "Women have done that before, but it usually takes a little more effort on my part. I do like to earn my seductions."

He pointed, his voice hardening with a sense of command. "Miss, use the chair in the corner. My ward doesn't leave my sight."

It wasn't as if I had a choice. I wasn't even sure if I'd be employed. Flopping into the chair in the corner, I slipped Lionel under my shawl and put him to suckle. His cries stopped, and I tried to forget this new humiliation.

"Duke," the countess said, "Mrs. LaCroy will be an asset to your staff. She's not always so clumsy."

He rubbed his face, slow along his jaw. "I think I met your *husband* last night, LaCroy."

"I beg your pardon, sir. My husband is gone. Do you see ghosts?"

His expression softened. "Now it's my turn to apologize. Sorry, I met and, er, um, fired your brother . . . brother-in-law last night. Let him . . . Let him know . . ."

His head shifted.

I felt his gaze wandering over me. I was caught, and I knew it from the way his smile thinned to nothing.

Lady Shrewsbury moved near Jemina, swatting her hands from twisting the bed curtains. "Her brother-in-law returned to his residence after seeing to our Patience LaCroy. He won't be visiting anymore."

The countess smoothed her gloves. "He has his own to protect, and I assured him you'd hire Mrs. LaCroy. Don't make me a liar or leave a woman unprotected, not when you can help."

The duke fumbled with the belt of his robe. "Left, hmmm? My ward and I are still at a disadvantage. With one woman falling all over me, and another giving me sweet or-

ders in my bedchamber, I . . . more words I'd never thought
I'd say."

Lady Shrewsbury pulled back the curtains on the bed.
"That must be hard for a military man to cede ground to his
known weaknesses."

"Well, it's good LaCroy doesn't work for Napoleon.
Bony elbows are definitely a torture."

Bony? There wasn't a bony thing about me. Pregnancy
assured that.

When I looked up to sneer at him, I noticed the duke,
truly noticed him, beyond his looks. The man was in the
same position, half reclining, folded arms, brooding. Something was wrong.

I shifted my greedy boy. "The countess has letters of recommendation. If you can forgive my clumsiness, Your
Grace, I . . . We will serve you well. We will be loyal."

"Loyal? I do value loyalty and honesty."

His stare was strong, almost a summons to come back to
him.

The only man I owed such scrutiny was dead. I refused to
lower my eyes or demure to him. I returned his glances with
boldness.

The duke dragged himself higher, working his shoulders
and pulling closer to the carved headboard, but he sank into
the mattress. "You're forgiven, LaCroy. Lionel has forgiven
you. He sounds content slurping."

My boy was. And I was. I rested in this moment for I
knew it would not last.

His Grace played with the belt of his robe, tugging and
twirling the fine burgundy brocade fabric, but still he hadn't
moved.

"Ladies, go downstairs. When I've had a shave and am
fully dressed, we can discuss employment."

Lady Shrewsbury started pulling down the sheer curtains,
then motioned to Jemina to do the same. "These will need to
be scrubbed, too. And that boy needs mother's milk daily.

Look how scrawny he is. No pap solution of cow's milk will do. That's what I wrote to you."

Wrote to him advice about caring for my Lionel? The countess hadn't mentioned that part last night. I bristled but stayed silent.

The duke wiped at his chin. "Two young women in a house of soldiers is not wise. But I've never been wise about women. Fine, you're both hired. Now leave. Wait. Who am I hiring besides LaCroy?"

Shrewsbury lifted Jemina's chin. "This is Mrs. St. Maur. She'll be a maid. And she'll get to your sheets straightaway."

Jemina curtsied. "I'm good in the kitchen, but Mrs. LaCroy is skilled in bread, sir."

"I'm sure she's good at many things. Many hidden talents."

I patted Lionel, and he offered me a man-size burp.

Proud of him, I fastened up my tunic. "Thank you again, Your Grace."

"Fine. Ladies, I assume Lady Shrewsbury can show you how to begin your duties here at Hamlin. You visited with my grandfather quite a lot and attended my mother's parties."

"Lady Bodonel did throw some nice parties, and the late duke was quite a man. The widower would've made a nice husband for me. Your father was a good man, too."

Anger smoldered in his eyes as if the countess had dressed him down. I didn't understand that, but I felt the fire of his mood across the room.

The countess tugged Jemina toward the door. "As I remember correctly, the nursery is above us on the third floor. Mrs. LaCroy, you'll serve as a wet nurse and nanny."

"Mrs. LaCroy, Lionel Jordan will need care day and night . . . But what of your child if you live here?"

"My child?" I didn't want to lie. Lionel was in my arms. How could I deny him?

I lifted my eyes to the countess. *Help*.

"Duke," Lady Shrewsbury said, "it's painful for Mrs. LaCroy to talk of this, but the child is no longer hers to love. Gone."

The duke's grimace became deeper. "Sorry, ma'am."

His pity-filled voice burned my ears. I liked his flirty commands better. Snuggling Lionel, I held him close to my cheek. "I'll work hard. And it will be my honor to serve Lionel Jordan . . . and you. This boy will have a bath of lavender and a fresh napkin. I fear he's in the process of soiling this shirt, too."

Repington folded his arms. "Ladies, I have quite a few soldiers in residence—"

"My women will be fine and not seek out companionship, but do keep your men in line. LaCroy, St. Maur, let's go get you both acquainted with Hamlin Hall. Duke, I will return with their letters of recommendation."

Jemina nodded and walked out the door.

The countess followed behind.

The door closed before I could slip past the odd wheeled chair.

"Mrs. LaCroy. Wait."

I turned, holding my baby against my bosom like a shield. "Yes, Your Grace?"

"Mrs. LaCroy, is there anything you wish to tell me?"

No confession would come from me. I shook my head.

"Fine. Is there anything you want to ask me, ma'am?"

I shook my head again. "Not a thing."

He nodded, but his expression remained unreadable. "Then, you'll be in charge of Mrs. St. Maur. I like a woman who doesn't ask too many questions."

"Then this is perfect, Your Grace. I don't like asking."

"I'm not sure how to take that, Mrs. LaCroy."

"I should go join the others."

"Why rush, when you are already familiar with Hamlin? Right, LaCroy?"

If he believed I would expose myself, he was mistaken. I

hugged my son tighter. "With a baby about, this place feels very familiar. This boy needs a bath, sir. And this shirt a good scrubbing, more so with each minute we are wasting."

"I don't like wasting time, but a mysterious woman, a pretty one in a house of men, is concerning. I'd hoped to hire a much older, more matronly type. You and your friend are not matronly."

Repington's mood was hard to ascertain, a little flirty, a little mad, but I wasn't going to play fetch, so I shrugged. "Is that all, Your Grace?"

He leaned forward. "You're sure there's nothing you want to tell me?"

"No, I am ready to work."

His face, formerly plains and prisms of masculine pride and authority, softened. "Well, when I'm dressed, I'll find you to go over the rules and expectations. Rules are necessary in my employ."

"Yes, that's what they say about rules. Good day, Your Grace."

I edged closer to the door. Only a few more feet, and I'd be out of his scrutiny.

"La—Croy, I have a feeling you don't follow rules."

The way he said my name, hanging it on his tongue. He definitely suspected that I and the footman were one in the same. I should say something to dissuade the notion, but only a laugh escaped. Another one bubbled up inside, pressing on my chest until it exploded. It was a full giggle out loud.

"What's funny? What has you humored, ma'am?"

I covered my mouth. "Sorry, Your Grace, but I was thinking that maybe you think you like rules, but unlike women, men get the option to break them."

"Interesting perspective, sir. I mean, ma'am."

I curtsied. "If there's nothing else you need, I'll be giving your ward a bath."

"We will continue this discussion later. I'll have my schedule of the boy's activities ready for you this afternoon."

I stopped, took my hand from the door latch. "Excuse me?"

"Yes, I have a schedule. Plans for my ward."

"He's a baby."

"I've made men of less well-behaved people. Lionel Jordan will live up to my expectations. I'll visit you in the nursery at fifteen past one."

"Fifteen past what? Why so exact?"

"Precision is my strength. I'll meet you then, and we can discuss my other requirements for Master Jordan. You'll have to adhere to them *if* you stay."

If?

Oh, that didn't sound good.

But how dare a stranger try to tell me how to take care of my Lionel? I felt my smile freezing, falling off, and shattering on the floor. "Yes, sir."

"Have the child and the nursery ready for inspection."

Servants had to defer to guardians. I kissed my son again. "Yes, Your Grace."

The duke looked like he attempted to rise but sank into his pillows.

Something was definitely wrong.

I couldn't help my gaze pinning to the wheels on the invalid chair. "Fifteen past one."

"Yes, LaCroy."

I fled the bedchamber.

Jemina shut the door behind me. She and the countess had waited.

Lady Shrewsbury offered a *tsk* with her teeth. "Well, that didn't go as planned, but you've been hired. Jemina will work downstairs among the campers. And you, Patience—"

"I'm going to get this one a bath."

"Good." The woman rubbed Lionel's arm. "But take care, the duke has agreed because he was disadvantaged. A commander will lose the battle but not the war. Be sharp around him. Do excellent jobs, or he'll terminate you."

Jemina nodded, her brow furrowing. "Patience is with

her baby, but what's the plan, particularly with all the men and tents, and is that a cannon?"

The crazy, hurt duke had turned Hamlin into a war zone.

"Lady Shrewsbury, where do we begin?" I asked.

"Gather the evidence that Markham has hidden in Hamlin that will prove why he needed to imprison you in Bedlam. The guard at the gate, who let us through, said Markham lingered for quite a long time. He was remiss to leave. The villain has something hidden in Hamlin. Find it."

The countess and Jemina headed down the steep stairs.

I didn't know what to make of distrusting dukes, cannons on the marble floor, or evidence. Everything for me was Lionel and getting him healthy. "Let's go to the nursery."

Up the steep stairs, we danced onto the third floor. Once inside the nursery, I shut the door and looked at the smallish room I'd have to get in order. The tart odor of neglect was all about. The sconces needed dusting. "Lionel, this room will be the palace I dreamed for you."

Holding my baby, I spun round and round. In the light of the day, the teal walls blended with the hazel blue of my son's eyes. He was all smiles, empty gums and all.

Breathing a little fast, I caressed him. "I'm here with you now, Lionel, in the day. And I'm going to do what I can to stay with you till I get my trust documents. Then I'll finance passage for a boat to Demerara. We're going to be safe."

I pulled off the dirty linens and set my shawl in the crib for Lionel to lay upon.

"Time for your bath, Lionel, and to make an ointment for that bottom."

Opening the window, I let a little fresh, cold air inside. The glimmer of Papa's knife shined on the ledge. I stretched and put it in my pocket. It was good that it was here and not on my person when the duke inspected me. I wouldn't have been allowed to keep it, and he'd think I was nefarious to have a weapon about a baby. Yet, until Lionel and I were at the docks in Demerara, we weren't safe. This was a long war. The next battle would be fifteen past one.

CHAPTER 9

A VALET AND A VISCOUNT KNOW

Thunder growled outside his bedchamber window. Busick muttered to himself and rubbed his hip. The sense of imminent rain ached his bones.

Schedule change. No outdoor exercise today. A storm would come. Well, a second one. Shrewsbury and her young women were the first.

He stretched on the edge of his disheveled bed. The new maid he hired, Mrs. St. Maur, had stripped it of its sheets before he could blink. That servant was a good, industrious hire, even if he'd made it under duress.

The other one, LaCroy, was a different matter. Beautiful, deceptive, beautiful, bony elbows, nicely shaped . . . deceptive.

Well, some things didn't change, like him finding the niceties about a woman, even if she was a spy. One of Markham's no doubt.

Busick swiped at his freshly shaved jaw as he waited for

the sharp pain in his back to settle. Sliding on his shirt even while seated still hurt sometimes. His valet left a half pour of rum atop his set of drawers. Rum eased the pain and left him with more sense of control than laudanum or the other medicines his physicians prescribed. He needed to keep his wits with spies and soldiers about.

Gulping a full breath, he pushed up on his staff. Standing, he smoothed the shirttails into his breeches. Done. He'd re-learned to do most of his dressing seated instead of standing in front of a mirror. Anyone coming through his door would probably notice no difference.

Yanking his waistcoat off the chest of drawers, he looped it over his shoulder and swayed. He must look like a Morris dancer, a bad one. He'd been pretty good at preening with the latest feather at balls and private dinners. He was good at many things before Badajoz.

Struggling to button his bone buttons and keep from keeling over, Busick grabbed the knurled edge of the dresser. The glass of rum shook. The desire to down it pressed. It was the only thing calling him to sanity when he couldn't do things that felt normal, but today, he needed a clear head to deal with a spy.

Being made a fool by a woman, a nanny in his household, was not normal. Far from it.

A knock on his door left little time to straighten the bandaging to his leg. The straps and ribbons fastened at his thigh needed a little adjustment, but a quick glance showed he looked decent. "Come in."

Gantry pounded inside. "Duke, a young woman just shook me from my bed. Then I remembered the baby. I should've come and relieved you by . . . now."

The viscount was in need of a shave. His eyes were half-open as his neck swiveled from side to side. "Where's the baby? Duke, what have you done?"

Ahh. The joy of knowing something Gantry didn't. Busick stretched his stiffening shoulder and pulled his cravat from the high back of the infernal invalid chair. "The babe is well. You should return to your room and get a few more hours of sleep. You look lost."

Gantry wiped at his eyes. "If I remember correctly, I left you with a baby, Duke. What did you do with him?" The viscount clasped the drawer pull on the chest of drawers. "You didn't put him away like a cravat, did you?"

"Of course not." Busick put his hand on the ornately carved drawer, keeping it closed. "I didn't fold him like a shirt, either. What do you take me for?"

Seizing the glass of rum, Gantry emptied it. "Sorry, I'm not fully awake. But you're up and shaven. Where's Master Jordan?"

Now was the time to look steady as a swan and pretend he did not stop his friend from opening the drawer. Probably needed more rum in that glass to dull the viscount's wits.

"The babe is fine. He's with the nanny upstairs, one I hired a few hours ago but must terminate now. Could you help me with my jacket? My valet left it over there, hooked to the bedpost."

Gantry's face became a mash of questions, but he moved, collected the jacket, and held it out.

Sliding one arm in the tailcoat of dark indigo and doing a little hop to tug the other sleeve in place, Busick then took a large breath. "Hopefully the rain will stop, and we'll lead the troops through outdoor exercises tomorrow. Maybe my ward will watch, too."

Gantry pushed a hand through his hair and swept aside his too long locks. "One, it's not raining yet. Two, your ward cannot walk. Three. Why terminate the nanny you just hired? It's not that Mrs. Kelly."

"No, not her. A new one." The way Busick's thigh ached, it would rain today. But he couldn't say that without sparking questions of his injury. "My valet is excellent at barbering. He could fix all that hair and put you back into military precision."

"I served my time. My wife, she likes it . . . long." Gantry shuffled his feet and looked down. "The length is fine."

Busick noticed this was the first time he'd brought the wife up after weeks of not mentioning her. "We both know how to avoid talking of things, but you can tell me anything."

"And you'll do the same? Starting with why you can't spend a week or two resting, getting to know your ward, before doing drills. You're stunting your recovery. It's been almost two years since Badajoz, and you're still on a crutch. You must keep reinjuring yourself by not giving the bone the proper time to heal."

Responding in anger would make things worse, especially when he needed Gantry's help. "I'll rest when things are settled. But this morning, I hired a maid and a spy. Patience LaCroy has infiltrated my household. You must find a replacement nanny."

"LaCroy? She's related to Markham's footman from last night?"

"The footman last night was a footwoman."

"Truly a spy?" As if Gantry couldn't decide what to do, he folded his arms and sank against the dresser. "He was a she? Are you sure?"

Oh, Busick was sure Mrs. LaCroy was all woman. Curly auburn hair that looped behind dainty ears. Brown eyes of the deepest topaz and a figure full of curves . . . Well, none of that gave her away as the footman, but the unmistakable cleft in her chin on her heart-shaped face was the concluding evidence. That and his valet asking how he had theater make-up on his coat.

"Yes, Gantry, my nanny was the footman."

"Duke, are you sure? Are we that out of practice socializing?"

The past years left little time for women.

Avoiding his wayward mother's attention took up the

rest. A hint of an injury would bring forth Lady Bodonel's "caring" role. She'd find a way to enable a compromise with some socialite's daughter for those grandchildren she claimed to want. But what she actually longed for was access to better parties, ones his union to a lady with the right connections would solicit.

"Yes to both. We are hermits, and she's a spy. Is she working for Markham or someone else? Maybe Colin's debtors?"

The viscount rubbed his jaw. "Not that it makes any sense, but why would a spy want the baby? And why did you give the boy to him—her?"

Why *had* Busick?

Was his vanity that great?

Or was the sorrow in her eyes when she lay upon him, like her world would burst if he refused her? "I suspect she's harmless but here to feed some information to someone."

"And you are now dressed, shaved, and in one of your best coats to do what? Interrogate the lady spy?"

Busick fiddled with the buttons of his waistcoat again, pushing the disks through holes. "I'm not sure, but I'll need you to find a new wet nurse if I don't get the answers I want."

Gantry tapped the empty glass and smirked. "Well, if you are going to go interrogating, you'll need sleeve buttons." He yanked open the drawer and steeped his hands into cravats . . . and that mechanical thing, that awful thing.

Busick wasn't quick enough to stop the viscount. He should've remembered that Gantry was similar to himself, not letting anything go until he'd found answers.

The silence deafened.

Then Busick heard his heart beat loud, loud, louder than the thunder outside. He counted the seconds for his friend to ask his questions.

Why didn't Busick say he needed an amputee's stump?

Does it hurt? Does he need to be coddled?

But Gantry didn't lift his head. He poked at the leather

strings attached to the lifeless piece of wood carved to take the place of a limb.

The fasteners itched and pinched when Busick strapped it to the stump that remained of his leg.

"I think my valet put the buttons in the second drawer."

Gantry closed up the top one. "You're right. No sleeve buttons here. You're good without . . . them. I'll keep looking."

Busick kept his gaze steady. No signs of weakness or hesitation would show. He wasn't defined by a leg. He was competent and in command, but others decided with their dour eyes and sappy pity that he was no longer of use. "Yes, do so. Check the second drawer. I'm good, but sleeve buttons will make me perfect."

Gantry frowned, but still refrained from asking the things he must want to know.

So Busick decided he'd answer. "Badajoz. It took a year for the nerves to stop throbbing like fire and many more months to balance and then walk. Almost two years to mostly recover. And it *will* rain." He slapped his thigh. "What's left of this leg says so. Anything else you haven't asked but want to know?"

A knock at the door ended this one-sided staring match.

"Your Grace, may I come in? It's Mrs. St. Maur."

"A moment, ma'am."

The viscount located a pair of pearl sleeve buttons. "Is that the spy?"

"Not that one. Well, Mrs. St. Maur could be an accomplice. Their letters are on that chair."

The invalid chair, where he'd spent a year, more when he had setbacks.

"Take those letters of recommendation and investigate. See if I need to terminate both women."

The knocks became more urgent. Mrs. St. Maur beat upon the door. "I have fresh linens. They're heavy."

"Impossible, Gantry. The woman just took up the bed-sheets barely an hour ago. They are in this together." He started tying his cravat. "Come in."

The door opened, and Mrs. St. Maur entered with a bundle of linens. "It won't take me long to dress your bed, sir. And don't mind the piles in the hall. I have a great deal of rooms to clean. We'll have rooms for all your men. No need for tents."

"Where did you find—"

"Your Grace, Mrs. LaCroy sent soldiers into the catacombs to retrieve trunks."

Lips thinning as if he now put stock into what Busick said, the viscount fastened the sleeve buttons, one in each of Busick's white cuffs. "How would she know where to look? Or even to look there? Duke, I guess she really is a sp—"

"Special, Gantry. The word is *special*. It seems Nanny LaCroy might be a little too clever."

"She is clever, sir," said Mrs. St. Maur. The maid beat at wrinkles in the bedsheets. "She's very smart and very kind."

"See that, Gantry, I've hired a clever and kind nanny."

"Those are good requirements." The viscount caught Busick's arm as he tried to pass. "Do you know what you are doing?"

"Yes. It's ten after one. I have five minutes to make it to the third floor to see my nanny. Wish her luck."

Frowning, Gantry adjusted Busick's collar, smoothing it. "For what?"

"That LaCroy passes inspection. I think it will be difficult to find another nanny so quickly. It would be a shame to terminate her on her first day."

In the mirror, he saw his comment had the effect he wanted.

Mrs. St. Maur clasped her hands in prayer, but Jove wouldn't save them. The women needed to know he was onto their games. He'd not be made a fool by anyone.

His friend stepped in front of him again. "You think you should be going up those steep stairs? I could bring her down to the drawing room."

He punch-patted Gantry's forearm. "No, mother hen. And you should head back to bed and sleep for a few more hours. Hopefully, Mrs. St. Maur—when she finishes up in here—will make some of the delightful bread she talked of earlier. Everyone needs a good dinner before the day ends."

"Yes, sir." The woman's frown became bigger, and she slapped at the sheet like it was a person; hopefully not Busick. "But it's Mrs. LaCroy who's the bread maker."

He powered through the threshold. "Off to my appointment."

Gantry followed him out and again put a hand to his shoulder. "Sorry, Your Grace. I'm truly sorry."

Busick's jaw tightened, and he clutched his crutch tighter. "Just another challenge. You know I like challenges."

His friend nodded. "You're good at blustering through things."

Gantry's words stung, along with his glance. It wasn't a soldier's deference to his commanding officer, or soldier to soldier, or peer to peer. It was the fretful look of the doctor saying the leg had to come off.

He'd rather a look of annoyance than pity. "I'm fine, Gantry. Go get some sleep. You've earned it."

As LaCroy earned a firing for being a spy. Sad eyes and a fine figure wouldn't save her.

CHAPTER 10

THE NURSERY

Stairs were awful, evil things.

That was Busick's new opinion of them. The steep treads to the third floor were nearly impossible. He hastened his steps, but midway up, he tired and slowed his rhythm—breath held, crutch pointed, strain, breath released. Again. He repeated this until he'd reached the third level.

He started to pull out his watch to see how slow his timing had been but decided against it. Since Busick set the schedules, he'd break them today.

At the nursery door, as softly as possible, he pushed it open.

His pique diminished at the sweet scent of lavender.

Freshness. He pushed inside.

Piles of sheets lay on the floor, balled and rolled up as if there had been a struggle. Doors to a wardrobe lay open. Drawers pulled out and emptied. It was chaos as if she'd been looking for something.

Then he spied the crib.

It had been polished and scented with orange oil. His sol-

dier lay fast asleep on fresh sheets. The little fellow's snore
was sweet, like a tune cranked from his mother's music box.

The nanny spy had her back to him, and she looked out
the window. Her chin was raised, and whatever she saw
through those wide eyes held her captive.

Easing a little more into the room, he couldn't help but
admire her profile. Long auburn tresses, curly and thick, had
escaped her mobcap and rested upon a slim neck. Her posture was straight, as if she'd been taught to do so. A printed
fabric of blue checks draped gentle curves that screamed
woman.

How could he ever have thought LaCroy was a man?
Busick's senses must be slipping.

Stepping closer, he noted her lengthy lashes. They could
curl about Lionel's pinkie, maybe Busick's, too.

How long he studied her, he didn't know. But her appeal
had nothing to do with her hiring status. "The room doesn't
pass inspection, Mrs. LaCroy."

She didn't look at him. Her face remained steady toward
the glass. "I have to start with the basics, Your Grace.
Everything must be cleaned and dusted. Nothing in here was
up to my standards, so I know it fails yours."

Oh, she was a good spy. For how would she know what
he liked? He stepped over one of the piles. "I despise disorder. This reeks of disorder."

"It r-reeked of a great deal more. Once I'm done, it will
r-reek no more."

The rolling of the *r* sound was faint and soothing like a
stream lapping upon the shore. This woman had spent some
time abroad, but where? Spain? One of England's colonies?

"I trust that you'll have this done in a timely fashion."

"I will, sir."

He cleared his throat, but she still did not turn. Her attention remained committed to what was outside the glass.
"I've come to talk . . . about schedules."

"Yes, Your Grace."

Her voice sounded tired, and her gaze remained distant.

A panic stirred inside near his well-developed sense of vanity. Maybe she couldn't look at him. Perhaps she, like Gantry, couldn't engender respect because of his injuries.

Anger stirred in Busick's gut. A missing limb didn't limit his abilities. It did not change his stature. He navigated closer. "I'm your employer. I demand your full attention. I'm due that."

When she turned, there were tears in her eyes. Those polished stones leaked, and his heart shook.

It seemed as if he intruded, but on what? Was it grief for her lost child? Something else?

"What has captured your attention so completely? I was able to come fully inside the nursery without you stirring."

Her lips twitched then moved up as if she'd just remembered to smile. "Memories, Your Grace. Some hold on a little too tightly. I'm sorry I'm not attentive."

Her voice was winsome, and Busick remembered the countess said she'd lost her own baby and husband. That had to be true, for sadness like this, those quivering leaky eyes couldn't be feigned. Her season of stolen joy must be terribly sad and recent.

A knot formed in Busick's gut, forcing him to think of his fallen lieutenant's wife. No one could stop her from seeing her husband cut down by cannon fire. And no one, not even Busick, could prevent her when she took up her husband's sword and charged the enemy.

He blinked, sniffed the orange polish, and forced away the remembrance of war. "My sympathy goes out to you, Mrs. LaCroy, but we must speak of our situation."

Wide, delicious eyes, orbs of topaz with hints of honey gold and henna stared at him. It felt as if an assassin had marked him. A small part of him didn't mind being in the line of fire, her fire.

"Yes, Duke. We're not ready for your inspection." She moved to the crib. Her steps were graceful—chin held high, shoulders level—so very tall for a woman.

"And Master Lionel, he didn't seem to want to keep your schedule. He went to sleep after his sudsy bath."

He looked again at the baby swaddled in fresh linens. The whisks of jet-black hair had been brushed to the center of his head and tied with a green bow, like Gantry's. "The boy seems at ease, but was the ribbon necessary?"

"He's too young for a top hat, and he's c-catching his hair in his nails and scratching. The bow will work for now. He's far too young for his first b-barbering."

Her voice sounded stronger, but a few of her words meshed with stuttered breaths.

Busick started to rethink her termination. He didn't want to be her next disappointment, the thing that made tears leave her sweet eyes. "At what age do you suggest cutting his hair?"

"Six. He'll have a wonderful head of hair for the first trimming."

"Nooo. He doesn't have to wait until he's breeched."

She pivoted. Lines riddled her forehead. "He's already born. How can he go back to be a breeched baby? What do you know about infants?"

How did the conversation change to be about Busick? He swayed a little as he lifted his hand to his temple. "You're not from England, are you, LaCroy? For a boy to be breeched is a term of elevation. At age six, he transitions from pinafores to pantaloons. Where are you from?"

"A little colony of no consequence."

"You've never been a nanny before. Have you, LaCroy?"

"Never needed to be one. *Sir*."

The way she tossed in *sir* was as if she remembered herself and who was employer and employee. Well, employer for the moment.

"I suspect my Lionel will have his first set of man's clothes and a haircut, early. Maybe in a few years. With my training, he'll excel."

He put his palm on the boy's head. It was warm, not with

fever but from rest. The lad was at peace. "So much to look forward to with this little one."

When he glanced at her, there were more tears in her eyes. She blinked heavily. "Do we pass enough of your inspection, Your Grace?"

"You seem to be getting the nursery in order." He ran a finger along the edge of the crib's carved rail. "No dust."

"I'll take that as a yes, for now. There's more cleaning to be done."

Bad news was best served cold, direct, no emotion. But he had an emotion about her, about terminating a teary-eyed woman who'd polished bed rails and put bows in his ward's hair. Wrong. It felt wrong.

Good thing he never listened to feelings. "How long did you intend to go along with this act, footman?"

Mrs. LaCroy brushed at her face, that cleft in her chin. "As long as it was convenient."

He kept his jaw from dropping. "I didn't think you'd admit to things so easily. At least humor me and ask how I figured it out?"

She clasped her bony elbows as if needing to do something with her hands. "If you must, tell me of your brilliance. You never forget a face, especially one brought in such close proximity."

"No, your falling all over me wasn't . . . Well, your knees and bony elbows were uncomfortable. And you're correct. I don't forget a face, even one disguised in white paint. Not with that delightful cleft in your chin. But knowing where to send my men to retrieve trunks from the catacombs was your downfall. You've spent time there before. You've worked here."

He moved and sank into the rocking chair close to the crib and eased his crutch to the floor, next to the broken shell of a coconut.

Coconut?

Poking at the smashed-up white flesh, the dark, thick outer husk, he shook his head, then looked up at LaCroy. "A newly hired woman wouldn't know this. What will you do with coconuts?"

"Lots of things. It's a dependable drupe. You would call it a stone fruit or nut."

"No, ma'am, I'd never call a nut dependable."

She glared at him, those hands now flexing at her sides. "Linens, clean linens are needed. Mrs. St. Maur has buckets of scrubbing, including your shirts. And this baby seems to have been on dirty sheets far too long. Oil from the coconut is for his bottom. You did notice how red it was?"

"I just cleaned and wrapped. That wasn't right?"

"You did good." She smiled a little. "Your shirts are the cleanest thing he may have worn in weeks." She sniffled, and a big fat tear rolled to the tip of her arched nose.

Some women didn't cry and look beautiful, but LaCroy did. And her face looked tanned and healthy without the paint she'd worn last night. Her complexion was smooth, a little darker than Lionel's. Was she mulatto or Blackamoor or both?

It didn't matter, when she looked like a choice rose sprinkled in morning dew. He dug into his pocket and handed her a handkerchief. "Please stop crying. It's so much easier to dismiss a soldier. This almost feels like the end of a courtship."

That made her frown and step away. "What?"

He raked a hand through his hair hoping to tighten his skull and keep more stray thoughts from uttering. "You admit to working here. You purposely tried to deceive—"

"I *told* you I'd reapply in the morning. That's what I did."

Well, that was what she said last night.

Busick raised his hand to complain but instead clasped the chair arm and rocked. "Why dress as a man?"

Her mouth opened, then closed, then opened again. "You were right. I was here. I worked hard, but I could not stand, Mark . . . Mr. Markham. He put the things needed for efficient running of the house down in the catacombs. I knew exactly where he'd tossed the linens and things for the baby.

Unfortunately, the elements and dampness have gotten to some. There're more trunks down there, but I don't think they have linens. I'll need to go to Town to get more for the baby unless you've come to Hamlin with an endless supply of shirts."

The energy in her voice extinguished all his thoughts of LaCroy spying for Markham. She was dedicated to the care of the boy. Passionate about it. Isn't that what he wanted in a nanny?

He felt foolish and looked at his content, snoring ward. "That answers some of my questions. But why dress as a man?"

A smile spread across her lips and even stretched to her eyes, adding a sparkle like freshly glossed boots. "What's easier to spot, a woman coming and going through the catacombs or a man?"

"You chose a disguise to find bedding and baby things because you hate Markham. I don't think so, LaCroy. I think—"

The baby started crying.

Busick wanted to pick him up and comfort him as he'd done last night, but the chair moved when he tried to get out.

Mrs. LaCroy cut in front of him. Without asking, she scooped Lionel up and held him to her bosom. She rocked him until his cries stopped. "We're talking too loudly."

"Letting go of employees is nasty business. It will be well, little soldier. The secretive lady will be leaving. I'll get you a new one, one who can be honest."

She half turned and Busick panicked. He was stuck in the chair, and she was about to feed the babe. As much as he was an admirer of the female form, some things needed to be private.

"'*Il était un petit navire. Il était un petit navire.*'" She sang the words, her voice low and pretty.

Lionel stretched and hooked a pinkie upon LaCroy's full lips.

Then she stopped singing and looked at Busick as if he'd

caught her doing something wrong. "I'll do this in English. English is better for you." Again, she sang, "'There was once a little boat. There was once a little boat.'"

"But it was lovely in French, LaCroy. '*Ohé! Ohé! Matelot.*'"

Her eyes brightened, and he sang her tune a little louder. Bits of gold shone like shooting stars in the darkness of her irises.

He liked surprising her.

Then he switched to English. "'Ahoy! Ahoy! Sailor, sailor sailing on the high sea.'" He paused and pursed his lips. "Should we sing Lionel a lullaby about a shipwreck? One where the men . . . the sailors eventually eat each other? I hardly think it appropriate."

"My friend, Mrs. St. Maur, she hums it often. I suppose if you examined it closely, one wonders how something so sad could become a child's lullaby."

"True, but maybe it was made for boys. We require adventure." He gave up trying to get out of the chair and relaxed as she sang more.

Then Lionel snored, and the world was perfect again, except here was a woman, a kind woman, a woman who'd be sweet to his ward even when Busick wasn't looking, and he had to terminate her employment. "So, what am I to do, LaCroy?"

He swept his gaze over her, neat in her finely button-up gown of blue checks, her spotless white apron. "I do think I like you better as a girl."

"If I hadn't been so clumsy or if I hadn't bothered to assist you to the stairs, you wouldn't recognize me, and I wouldn't be facing unemployment."

"I would have figured it out. I'm very observant. And being up close in my face twice, without a wig and with your figure free . . . Did I say I liked you better as a girl?"

"Yes. Well, thank you, I think." Her lips curled up, but was that for Lionel or him?

It didn't matter. He reached for his crutch. He should

stand for this last part. "This is unfortunate, for we are back to where we were last night. Me having to terminate you."

"What, no option for a loyalty oath?"

"Your mother taught you not to swear, remember."

"If I learned more from her, maybe I'd have better fortunes. I can be loyal. And look at your ward, he's clean and happy."

"It's a bad precedent. I make an exception for you, then what lapses will I allow next? It's obvious you've worked here before, and I terminated all who did."

"Then rehire me." She set the baby back into the crib and picked up the crutch he'd been struggling to grasp with the chair moving.

He caught her palm. "Why were you sneaking in and out of Hamlin? Why risk your employment here?"

Her eyes, her luminous eyes, looked away. "I can't sleep sometimes. This property is very convenient to where the countess put me when she took me in."

"And dressing as a footman does what? Keep men from bothering you?"

She slid her hand from his. "I don't like to be bothered, and I'm not one to beg, not to a man who's made up his mind. At least keep me on until you find another wet nurse."

"Do something to assure me that you can be trusted. Convince me. Can't you see that I want a reason to go against my rules?"

"I hate rules. I despise them. I'm suffocated by them."

"This is not helping your cause, Mrs. LaCroy."

Her neck, lovely and long, tilted to the side. Was she studying him? Were his buttons misaligned?

She knelt before him.

His pulse ticked up. She was close, and his mind stuck at the no begging. "Please—"

Everything stopped when she put a hand on his knee. He didn't feel her warm fingers. She'd chosen the leg that was missing a knee, a shin, a foot.

She straightened the stuffed form his valet had made to

look like a heavily bandaged foot. It had twisted with his fumbling to get out of the chair. His deception had worked until this moment.

He waited for the questions that always came.

But none did.

No gasp, no awkward pause. "The knot seems to have slipped; I almost have it, Your Grace."

Did he stop breathing when her nimble fingers searched his thigh? That he did feel, as much as the twinges of what was missing, the aches and itches where flesh had been sutured. The doctors said the searing jabs were normal and would lessen, and they had, except on days like today when it looked like rain.

Her ring finger, the one with a simple silver band, found the knot of his straps and tugged it higher, adjusting the ribbon under his breeches.

"I can be trusted, Your Grace. And I won't let you go about your duties poorly served. Or have a house bared of linens when I know the solution would put my position in jeopardy."

The unmasking was not just his to do. She'd figured out his secret *and* was clever enough to know sending his men to the catacombs would bring her trouble.

When she rose, the gentle slow movement was like a queen's, as if she'd stooped to expose him. Was she above every conspiracy running through his head?

"Your Grace, it's time to feed your ward. I must ask you to leave. I'll stay until you find a proper replacement. I'll even go to Town and help stock up supplies for Master Lionel's care. There are things he should have."

"Make a list. I'll see to the items." He pushed up onto his crutch and moved to the door.

She slipped past him and held it open. "Do we have an understanding?"

Why did it feel as if she'd turned the tables? And why did he become a little more lost in wide eyes that held no scorn, or shock, or disgust. He edged through the threshold. "Yes.

You shall stay a day or two, but I will find a suitable replacement. Keep waging the war to make the nursery pass inspection. Tomorrow at one o'clock, when you set the babe down for his nap, come to the study. We can go over Lionel's schedule."

She nodded and closed the door on him, leaving him leering at the paneled wood like a witless fool.

But his questions remained.

Why would she be sneaking about Hamlin? What other secrets had she unearthed? And how would he pay for allowing her to stay a couple more days?

Gantry would find a replacement nanny, even if it meant allowing LaCroy to stay a week or two. Given more time, the widow might make a full confession. Keeping her around shouldn't cost him too much.

CHAPTER II

SIXTH DAY ON THE JOB

I hummed as I looked at Lionel asleep in his crib. He'd suckled a bigger breakfast than he had the past two days, even bigger than the first day in my old . . . in the duke's bedchamber.

Misty-eyed, I folded the rest of Lionel's clean linens listening to his snores.

Last one done and stowed in his wardrobe, I stretched, looking about this room that was once our prison. It never made sense why Markham locked me and Lionel in here. Maybe he thought the isolation and my grief would break me.

Nothing would break me when it came to protecting Lionel. I'd defy all who tried.

Shaking my head, I focused on the beautiful sea-blue walls and the large shells I again displayed on the wardrobe. The conch with its colors of pink and gold were one of the treasures I'd brought from home. The room looked like how I had wanted for Lionel, clean with his crib fashioned as a ship's berth. He was the captain, the master of his fate.

I wasn't the master or mistress of mine, however. Lionel would have to do better than me.

Somewhere in the house one of the grandfather clocks chimed. Time to meet with the duke and stare at him as he requested updates on the linens and baby care.

Staring at him wasn't a terrible task. It was quite easy, particularly when he wore his uniform—scarlet regimentals and white sashes wrapping about him like a present. I didn't remember liking soldiers, but the ones visiting Demerara weren't as kind or as thoughtful as the duke. He made sure Jemina and I ate, and he kept his men courteous to us, addressing us as ma'am, none of the slurs I'd heard Markham or Hamlin's old servants utter.

I leaned in close to my baby, watching his chest rise. "Being a servant in our old home is easier than I thought. Must be because you are so easy to love. You think your mother can make it through the week here?"

Lionel arched his hand and swooped the tiny digit like an eagle to nest in his puckered lips.

That had to be a sign of confidence.

I stroked his forehead. "Brilliant boy."

Yes, thumb-sucking was something all babies did, but Lionel did it with such elegance. I took it as a symbol of good luck.

I tiptoed from the nursery and shut the door, refusing to dwell on whether today would be my dismissal.

Fine. I dwelled.

Guilt, self-incrimination, and Jemina were my closest friends. I lifted my chin and focused on the good. I was grateful to be near Lionel. My boy was fed, clean, and happily thumb-sucking.

The beautiful burgundy tapestry looked resplendent beneath my slipper. It only needed a beating to remove the dirt left by Markham's servants. I listened to my heels bopping against the thick rug. I hit my hands with the rhythm and tapped to the beat of conga drums.

I reached the stairs, my fingers slipping on the fresh polish of the rail. It was slick and ready for sliding.

I paused.

No one was coming.

The duke had all his men outside with his drills.

Feeling freer than I had in a long time, I held my thumbs
up, just so, to figure out where I'd land if I hiked up my
skirt, climbed upon the sleek wood, and swooshed down
like at Papa's big house. Nothing like flying with the sultry
sea air cooling my face.

For four years in Hamlin, I'd thought of doing this, but
the house was never this quiet. If someone caught me, how
would I seem dignified to the servants? I'd heard their whispers—Jordan's Demeraran wife, so unusual, so exotic, so
sullen, so tragic.

That wasn't me.

I once was funny, a little headstrong, and I had a lot of
heart. I wanted to be me again. As a servant who could be
terminated for much bigger things, what was one slide down
the stairs?

My palm anchoring to the rail, I wondered if my fingers
retained the memory of how to hold on and keep my balance
to fly. What did the rebel in me have to lose?

A knee bent; a leg went up.

I heard a noise, a creak from above, and slammed my
foot on the tread. What was it? The attic? I held my breath.

No more sounds overhead. No more movement.

Everything became quiet, like before.

But now, I was wary and weighed down in caution.

"You should do it, you know," Jemina said. She stood at
the lower second level, leaning on the acorn-carved post, the
baluster of the rail. Her arms were stacked with linens that
she tossed as she leaned on the newel post. "No one who'd
tattle is in the house, no one but us."

Did that mean she hadn't heard the noises in the attic?

Jemina's impish smile grew as she brushed a curl from

her eyes. Her voice is loud, louder than before. "I'm not going to say anything. I won't even remember, on purpose."

No one was in the house. No one would tell.

Picking up my light gray skirt, I backed up to the rail again. I was tempted by the thrill—the rushing air as I slid, the pounding of my heart telling me I was alive.

The creaking sounded again.

Reminded of my place, I released my skirt. The jaconet muslin flounced to my ankles. The way the air fled the twilled fabric—it judged me, too, saying, *Not now, no*.

"The stairs to the third level are far too steep. It would be unwise," I said in a proper tone with crisp English syllables, then descended the treads.

Standing next to Jemina, I leaned over the rail and looked down at the empty hall. The encampment had gone. The slightly warmer weather let them do more outside. The soldiers seemed to enjoy actual beds to tents. The cannon, however, remained.

"The marble gods should be happy that the soldiers have left the hall."

"What?" Jemina kicked at a pile of dirty sheets. "What gods?"

I pointed to the statues below. Colin said they were three Roman soldiers with spears and bucklers, but I knew their true identities. "There are Agassou and his helpers."

Jemina looked over the rail, then back at me. With her freckles and red hair, the girl could have had Irish or Spanish roots, so she may not know what I meant.

She shrugged. "The tallest one, his spear with the sharp point, looks particularly painful. It's best you changed your mind."

If sculpted of ebony granite, not the whitest marble, the three would definitely be Agassou, made to protect Hamlin. But since nothing had gone right here, maybe it was just marble. "We are high up."

My vision swirled and looped, and I clasped the baluster

to keep my balance. The night they dragged me away, my skin had gone cold, then boiling hot, tingling like ants biting my arms. Then I saw something coming at me and Lionel. I scooped up my son and ran as fast as I could.

Had I tried to slide down the rail? With Lionel?

No. Even addled, I couldn't imagine endangering him.

Jemina put a hand on my shoulder. "What is it? You've paled as if in fright."

"Do you believe in ghosts? That those you've disappointed might haunt you?"

She put her warm, lavender-smelling palms to my cheeks. "No. My nightmares aren't coming for me, so yours can't be coming for you."

I hugged my friend. "Yes. Nothing's coming that we can't handle."

"Tell your soul you're safe, Patience. Repeating that helps me." Jemina offered a bigger smile.

She might believe that. It might even be true for her, but I wasn't safe. If the duke knew the truth of Colin's death, he'd take Lionel from me forever.

Pulse slowing, I pulled free, bent, and helped pick up the laundry she'd dropped.

When we'd folded the fresh sheets, Jemina set them down with her other bundles. "Patience, you should've taken the risk, but I suppose you are too refined."

"That, and I'm not the lithe girl who came to England."

"You're beautiful, my dear. And you should be bold and unafraid. Things are like vapors, before you know it, everything is lost. In the next moment, all is good again."

I put my fingertips to Jemina's cheeks and looked deeply into her brown eyes. "When you learn everything of your past, choose to be *this* you, this lovely girl who is good inside and out."

She hooked her arm with mine. "This is our third day cleaning at this level. One doesn't realize how massive of a house this is." She closed an open bedchamber door. "West wing, east wing. We'll get it done."

"At least all of Hamlin is being used. For years, I was in this house with servants and little company, a few business associates of my husband came to visit, but they never stayed. It's good to see Hamlin teeming with life."

"Ummm." Jemina's head was down, and she counted her fingers while pointing. "Six. There should be six piles of sheets."

"Well, you left one by the stairs."

"I counted that one. There should be five here. One, two, three, four. Only four. That makes a total of five, not six."

In the time I'd known Jemina, I'd seen her become flustered, her cheeks turning fiery like her hair when she thought she'd lost another memory.

Distraction. That's what Lady Shrewsbury did.

I took my friend by the hand and turned her around and around, then stopped at the stairs. "These steps leading down to the first level are not as steep. These would be the ones to slide down if we were bold and daring."

Jemina put her hands to her forehead and breathed in and out. "Yes, it seems that way."

She nodded. "Yes. I must be mistaken." Jemina tapped a few of the baluster supports, the strong mahogany posts holding up the rail. "Five bundles, not six. No one steals dirty sheets."

True, but my cherubim friend made a point of noting things. It was as if she'd decided never to forget anything else. So, I believed that something was missing—that one of the duke's men might have taken it for mischief or target practice.

I scooped up a pile. "Let's get these to the pump room."

Jemina looked left and then right, then leaned close to my ear. "We'll have cleaned all the bedchambers today. So far, I've found nothing suspicious. What about you?"

"Nothing. Nothing was in the nursery. Not a thing on the third level to show Markham's guilt. We need to check the drawing room and parlors below, but I think the man was too smart to leave anything pointing to his guilt. What if Markham locked me away just because he hated me or he thought me reckless with Lionel? Couldn't both be true?"

"Now, don't you start blaming yourself. Markham had a reason other than his distrust of you. We'll find what it is. We'll get the proof, and we'll prove it's Markham who's a danger to the baby, not you."

When I found a way to hire a boat to take me and Lionel back to Demerara, would Jemina want to go? I couldn't bear the thought of leaving her unprotected. I caught her hand. "I know everything will work out, and I'll take care of you always as you've cared for me."

"Female bonding always seems like a conspiracy."

The complaint came from a weighty baritone voice.

Glancing down, I saw the duke standing in the nook next to the marble gods. His bright scarlet regimentals contrasted the white marble like the striated petals of a lily.

Now the thought of the duke and beautiful flowers would stick in my head. I rubbed my temples. "Did you come from the catacombs?"

He pushed closed the secret door in the niche. It had been made to look like the wall with the same color paint and molding. "Yes. I need to see what else my nanny has spied down there."

I bristled. The man knew how to goad me, yet his sunny smile, full and wide, dimmed my pique. "How long have you been standing there spying, sir?"

He leaned on his crutch. "Enough to know plotting."

Jemina's eyes went wide.

"He's joking, Mrs. St. Maur. He doesn't realize how much we need our employment and how unsettling his teasing is."

I'd made my voice lofty and airy, and it seemed to do the two things I most wanted. My friend's stance relaxed, and the duke's countenance changed. It held a repentant dimpled frown.

"Sorry," he said in a softer tone. "So, what have you two done while my troops drilled? Gossip?"

"Bedsheets, Your Grace," I said. "We still have more to do. But you, you appear from nowhere. Perhaps you're the conspirator trying to steal bedsheets or wanting to scare us like a ghost."

"No thefts from me. That's stealing from Lionel Jordan. It shan't be done." He thumbed his chin. "So you've heard the rumors of apparitions walking the property. You're quite safe. I'll protect you."

Straightening from his hunched position, he chuckled, his laughter rich.

My pulse raced as I studied the man, the soldier.

His jacket hugged his body and tucked neatly into light gray breeches. Nice and snug about his muscular figure. Today, he wore a burgundy sash about his hips, contrasting the white satin one that I'd become used to seeing.

So coordinated, so orderly. Perfection, even if it was probably rule-based.

"Do I pass inspection, Mrs. LaCroy?"

My face fevered, but I offered a stiff nod. How long had I been staring?

"More cleaning," Jemina said, and darted into a near bed-chamber.

"Inspections are difficult things to pass, Mrs. LaCroy."

"I'm . . ." I rubbed at my hot cheeks. But then I glanced back at the man I couldn't deny admiring. "You pass, but why did you enter by the catacomb? I could've studied you much better if you'd entered by the front doors. What a sight for the Duke of Repington to arrive under the grand chande-lier."

I glanced at the wrought iron and crystals and noticed his men had raised it without the glass housing and candles. "Of course, I'd have to have a great deal of notice for the chan-delier to be lit in your honor."

His laughter was infectious. It pulled chuckles from me.

"Such an honest answer."

He pushed to the first stair tread as if he waited for me to descend. "I hadn't expected you to admit it. You keep surprising me."

"Some days feel more liberating than others, sir. Perhaps widowhood coupled with your indecision on the length of my employment have given me a more care-for-none attitude."

"More unexpected candor on top of an offer for a hero's welcome, I don't know what to do with myself."

Balancing on his crutch, he slapped his lower thigh, the one I knew was missing. He wore boots, both boots.

"Mrs. LaCroy, you know from your skulking of the underbelly of Hamlin, the catacombs have a gentle slope. That's a much less taxing way to enter Hamlin when I have this on." He hit that leg again, and it made a *click, clack* sound. "I tire more with this Potts's artificial limb. One of the reasons I choose not to wear it."

Blinking at this admission, I set down my sheets and came down the stairs as if all was normal, like I hadn't examined my employer from head to toe and that he hadn't volunteered a private truth.

There was a rhythm in my head, sweet and danceable, matching the uptick in my pulse. "Did you have a good morning, Your Grace, drilling for imagined raids of the castle?"

"Imagined?" His brow cocked. "Napoleon has not surrendered. If he wants Russia, his eyes very well could be set on England. Hamlin will be prepared. My staff and my ward shall be protected."

I stood near him and wished I had one of my fancy silks, one with Mechlin lace on the sleeves, something that made me look dainty and as fragile as I felt. Then a man like the duke would understand how I cherished words like *protection* and *security*.

"If you say so, Your Grace. I do feel safer."

He turned and walked under the chandelier. The tiny sound of clicking surrounded him.

I followed. The scent of snow, maybe a few bush clippings, fresh and herbaceous, hung on him. It felt honest and true.

"Safe with me, LaCroy? It's good to know you trust me." As he spun to face me, his jaw had tensed. "You do trust me, don't you?"

We stood together, two people in each other's confidence beneath an unlit chandelier. It didn't seem odd or humorous. The moment held a touch of normalcy, something I could grow used to, if he wasn't my temporary employer and I wasn't masquerading as a nanny.

"Well, madam?"

"With my position hanging in the balance, *trust* is not a word that fits us, but I do take comfort in your preparedness. And I appreciate that you've made your men camp in bedrooms, but they need to leave the cannons and muddy boots outdoors."

"These are serious drills, ma'am. Tomorrow at two, meet me again in the drawing room, we'll discuss more changes to my ward's schedule."

That would make a whole week without being terminated. "Yes, sir."

He adjusted his hat, a half-moon shako. "I'm going to review the troops from the rear balcony. You and Mrs. St. Maur could come watch me . . . my troops."

The invitation was fraught with that strange tension that made it harder to breathe. "We have work to do that can be accomplished more efficiently in a quiet house."

"Then, perhaps, we'll have to add some time in your schedule for a review. Keep avoiding conspiracies, Mrs. LaCroy. The drawing room at two tomorrow."

He smiled a knee-weakening smile, then headed down the rear hall whistling my lullaby. The tiny clicking of his stump disappeared.

His voice was strong, not quiet like Colin's. Maybe that's why I liked hearing it.

I turned toward the stairs to help Jemina. Should I let her know we were promised another day's employment and protection against Napoleon?

What more could a girl want?

I didn't hear the duke's voice anymore, and I wondered if he dismissed nannies while singing.

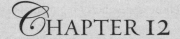

CHAPTER 12

THE DRAWING ROOM

I sauntered into the drawing room at ten minutes to two. The duke and his men had finished in here earlier.

My nerves for this meeting should have lessened after seeing the way Repington and his soldiers gobbled up my bread for dinner and my rolls for breakfast. They loved coconut bread, the gooey sweet texture beneath a hearty crust.

But this drawing room was Colin's. He was always so distant after spending any time in here. I hadn't been allowed inside when he resided at Hamlin, only when he left.

The last time I saw him go into the drawing room, he argued with a man and Markham. He scolded me for entering, even though it was to bring him and his guests tea.

"Ma'am."

I jumped, my heart pounding like I'd been caught rifling through the desk. With a hand to my racing heart, I curtsied to the duke's friend.

"Lord Gantry."

His jacket was well tailored on his thin frame, but civilian and simpler—no braiding, no sash. He whipped off his hat, a normal top hat, not the duke's shako.

"Mrs. LaCroy, you and Mrs. St. Maur are doing an excellent job of whipping Hamlin into shape."

Gripping my white apron, I curtsied again. "Thank you, Lord Gantry."

The tall man stripped off his gloves, then called to a soldier.

An older fellow in cranberry regimentals stepped inside. "Yes, sir."

Lord Gantry put his hat to his side. "I can't stand women carrying things, particularly heavy bundles. I helped Mrs. St. Maur carry at least ten large platters to the scullery yesterday. Captain, if any of the ladies have need of anything, I expect you to continue to aid them. Pass the word around."

The soldier nodded. "I'll help where I can with my one good hand. The captain at the front door has both his. Well, most of them, just missing a thumb. But I'll make sure everyone knows to help."

A quick glance at his padded jacket arm confirmed the truth.

The duke hadn't hired mercenary soldiers merely to storm Hamlin or prepare for a fake invasion. He'd employed wounded men, probably ones sent home from the fight. From the smile on this soldier's face—his lifted jaw, the proud dimples, Repington had given them hope.

That was priceless.

That was honorable.

I choked up a little, thinking how decent of a fellow the duke was. It was most inconvenient to gain more respect for the man I was forced to deceive.

Smoothing my apron, searching for pockets in my jet gown, I cleared my throat. "Thank you, sirs. Mrs. St. Maur and I try to be industrious. And, Captain, thank the men who went down into the catacombs for supplies."

"Just make some more of that sweet bread, and we'll be at your service."

His easy posture returned to attention, and he saluted the viscount, then moved to the door.

I pulled a cloth from my pocket and began wiping smudges from the sideboard. When I turned, Lord Gantry was still there.

"Is there something you wanted, sir?"

"Nothing," he said. He fingered the ribbon anchoring his shoulder-length hair, brownish chestnut and wild if not for the ebony tie. "You remind me of someone. Coconut bread, that was a particular favorite of hers."

The distant look in his blue-gray eyes—he wasn't thinking of my masquerading as a footman. He'd lost someone dear.

"I'm sorry, my lord," I said, before I could stop myself. "It's always difficult missing someone."

The viscount nodded. "You just don't know how much you miss a person or what you'll miss until they are gone."

He blinked and startled as he'd realized he'd been wistful aloud. "My apologies."

Lord Gantry withdrew at a fast clip, disappearing into the hall.

I moved to the pianoforte, swiping at the dust. The trust documents my father gave me were hidden in the big desk in the false back, a compartment I'd found within my first ten months at Hamlin, while Colin visited Town.

There had to be enough money in the trust that I could draw quickly to secure passage for three to Demerara.

With the duke heading here any moment, I couldn't get them now and risk being caught and looking like a thief. Timing was everything. When it was right, I'd have them.

Away from here, I could stop dreaming and asking those questions about Colin, about Colin and me, about what went wrong. And I certainly needed to be gone from Hamlin before I started asking questions about upstanding dukes and the nannies who fancied them.

My cloth had become dark with dust. The olive patina of the pianoforte's lid shined when given proper care. I swiveled to the mirror to do the same.

"You look very fine, Mrs. LaCroy, you don't have to peek in the looking glass for confirmation."

The duke had crossed into the room. "But do wipe Markham's fingerprints from the mirror. I think he tried to take it with him."

"When did he do that?"

"The night I seized Hamlin. I left him cowering in here when there was an uproar in the hall. But you know the chaos of Markham's household." He sailed his hat to the sofa, a perfect pitch with it landing on the center cushion. "You never told me why you worked for Markham."

I took my cloth to the beautiful edge of the gilded mirror and swiped at the delicate filigree, making certain the grubby prints were banished. "Chaos, you say. The man knows how to soil things."

The duke came farther into the room. His movements were quiet. The strain in his jaw showed the great effort it cost to make his footfalls silent. "Selective hearing? You don't have to tell me, but it remains another secret you're keeping from me."

I didn't reply and instead put more effort into shining the mirror, testing how it rocked. I'd never noticed that before. Something was behind it.

Repington moved to the sofa and started to lower himself but stopped. "This thing is very comfortable and too soft. It's almost as difficult to get out of as the rocker in the nursery."

Hmmm. Was that how I'd take Lionel? Leave the duke stranded on the sofa? No. That wouldn't do.

Arriving at the big desk, he rested against it. "Should we talk schedules or your resignation?"

"Schedules, Your Grace, unless you've changed your mind again. I hear that is something men in your position do."

His brow scrunched. "What do you mean?"

"Nothing in particular, but aren't men of your ilk flexible, given to whims?"

"My ilk?"

"R-rakes, sir. Lady Shrewsbury explained . . . your popularity."

His face lit up like the grand chandelier shining with strength and joy. "I suppose popularity can make one flexible. Sit, LaCroy."

I stuffed my rag in my pocket and came to the chair he pointed to, a nice mahogany klismos seat. One I'd ordered.

He rubbed his hip. "Don't know about flexibility anymore, changeable perhaps. Is this an appealing trait?"

"Not at the moment, Your Grace. Your flexibility is quite frustrating. You offer employment at night and rescind it in the day. It's quite taxing."

He chuckled and swiped at his hair. It was thick and definitely more brown today than blond. But the eyes he cast upon me, they were ever clever and clear. Clear like ice or glass prisms made to sparkle.

He leaned forward. "I wonder what other offers you've had extended, then rescinded. Never mind. It's just one more question I have about you that shall torture me." He pulled his hands together. "I'm still revising a schedule for Lionel. Until a replacement is found, if I decide to find one, you'll need to comply with my requirements."

"May I ask, Your Grace, that you make up your mind about this termination business or please stop repeating it. Do you want me to dread seeing you?"

"No. I'd rather you not. I'm looking for a reason to decide firmly in your favor. Other than being dishonest when we met, you seem to be a very kind woman and very loving toward my ward. You and Mrs. St. Maur work hard. Instead of remaining idle in the nursery where no one would bother you, you've come down and helped with the washing and cooking. The men are raving about your food."

Was he truly torn, or merely toying with me? I looked down and kicked my slippers against the leg of the big old desk.

"Help me, Mrs. LaCroy. I don't want you to dread seeing me." His voice was soft and sweet like honey. "I'd rather you'd enjoy spending time with me . . . in the mutual care and concern of Lionel."

The way he looked at me, it was as if he meant something else. Maybe this notion was only in my head. I was never a good judge of intentions or feelings. Or men.

"I have a question, ma'am."

His countenance remained a cross between a repentant fellow and a scalawag. Now I had to know his thoughts. "What type of question?"

"A personal one."

"Yes, sir?"

"Your husband, how did he die—sickness, the war, old age?"

"Sickness." That was a way to put it that sounded nice and noble, not wrenching to my gut or difficult and guilt-ridden.

The duke clasped my fingers. "Mrs. LaCroy, I didn't mean to make you cry."

Was I? I touched my wet cheeks. "My husband's death was unexpected."

"How would you have told your child about him?"

This was so personal. I leaped up. "Enough. I beg you, please stop these questions. They're intrusive."

The duke clasped his palms together as if in prayer, a supplicant's prayer to some English god of nosiness. The African and island ones knew better than to pick at scabs.

"I meant no offense."

"Truly?" I folded my arms, glaring at the man who could banish me, but the right words, the appeasing ones defied my tongue. "You did cause offense. Meaning and doing are two different things."

"I apologize, Mrs. LaCroy. I just know someday that little boy upstairs will ask about his father. As a mulatto child, his path will be more difficult. I don't want to say something to make things worse or to not be the encourager he'll need."

In Demerara, with my father's wealth, the boy would be a prince. "Perhaps you should send him to a place where he'll be respected."

"Send him away or trot the boy out for parties to show him off, pretending to be a saintly mother."

"Mother?"

He hooked his palm about the base of his neck like he'd developed a headache. "Please sit, Mrs. LaCroy. I'm going to have to tell him *something*. I know nothing of his mother other than she was a plantation owner's daughter. I grew up with a sickly father, a strong grandfather, but my cousin, poor Lionel's father . . . He committed suicide."

I sat stunned at the anguish in his voice. "I'm sorry, Your Grace. There was talk that Jordan's finances were careless, that Markham forced him into unwise financial schemes."

A deep, dry sigh escaped the duke. "Careless finances are not heroic and not worth the sacrifice of a life. It's not the same as dying for God, king, and country."

The edge in his words mirrored my hurt and how often I had to balance my sadness with selfishness—it was selfish of Colin to leave us, selfish of me to want him to stay when he was so unhappy.

I sank against the chair, letting the angel's harp be my spine. "I wish Colin Jordan had been more heroic, like you or the men you employ."

The duke rubbed his jaw. "I'm not a hero. I was lucky. I had a duty to perform. That kept me going, but I understand the disappointments that can make a man think his life is worthless. The struggle is hard. Some don't make the right choice. I wish I had been available to help my cousin."

"You'll find the words." Not that I intended to let Lionel stay in England that long. I twisted my apron, but all I could see was my white stationery and that last letter I'd written to my husband—telling him my hurts, all of them. I shouldn't have written it. He couldn't withstand the truth.

My cheeks burned, then a leak from my eyes put out the flames. I hadn't thought of how to tell Lionel about Colin. I didn't want my boy to think ill of his papa. Or that my letter had killed him.

"I'm sorry, Mrs. LaCroy. I didn't mean—"

Swatting at my tears, I waved at the duke before he could offer platitudes. Evidence of Markham's conspiracy would prove that his scheme caused Colin's death, not me. He was the last to be with Colin. Markham had to be the final stone that forced my husband into the depths of the Thames.

"Mrs. LaCroy?"

"Tell Lionel his father was sick, and the sickness led him to be misguided. That he sunk to a place no love could reach him. And that if he lived, he would've loved Lionel. Tell the precious boy that."

A handkerchief dangled in front of my face. I took it and wiped my tears.

When I looked up, I saw my reflection in the duke's clear blue eyes. His gaze held me in place.

I felt caressed, embraced, understood.

But the man hadn't moved.

His arms were mercifully at his sides. "LaCroy, I'm changing my mind again. We'll take your employment month by month. Gantry will need to get back to his daughters in a few weeks. When he's in Town, he can solicit agencies for a proper replacement."

"Wonderful, I have a whole month."

"We'll see how we—you and I—work together. I need to ask another question."

"Haven't you had your fill?" I waved at him to proceed as I snorted into his handkerchief.

"Was Lionel's mother here when you were hired?"

Tell him. Tell the duke and end this farce.

"Your Grace . . ."

"Yes, Mrs. LaCroy?"

He glanced at me, and again I was captive, this time with fear.

The duke would turn me out for playing another masquerade.

Or he'd not believe me, thinking I was a crazed widow

who tried to claim another child as her own. I bit my lip a moment and told the truth he'd accept. "Markham hated her. He rid the place of her. I think that's how he put it."

"Or the woman ran off. Depressed over my cousin, she might have run away." His head lowered for a moment. "I have one more thing to ask."

"Another ting . . . thing? Go ahead, by all means. Read me like a book of sport."

"A Shakespeare reference, *Troilus and Cressida*. Such a learned nanny. What other surprises do you have?"

Lord Gantry knocked along the threshold. "Repington, sorry to interrupt, but your box is here."

"Oh, good. Mrs. LaCroy, we'll need to continue this conversation later." He popped up and dropped in the chair behind the desk. "This will be such an improvement to the outside."

My stomach flip-flopped. I'd been dismissed for a box. I swiped at my eyes. "What needs improvement? You've cleared snow, even trimmed the brush that awakened in the warmer weather."

His impish smile returned. "You'll have to wait. You're not the only one with secrets. Good day, Mrs. LaCroy."

I'd been set aside. Lord Gantry and the duke ogling a wooden box meant sending me away like Colin had when I interrupted that last loud meeting.

My rise from the chair was slow. I watched as an outsider to the glee the men shared, spreading out the mysterious papers coming from the box.

I looked away, my eyes catching the sparkle of the silvered glass.

The mirror.

The one that held Markham's fingerprints.

There was a secret behind it. This one could set me free.

Finding time to get to it was all that mattered. I would not be distracted by the duke's questions or the feeling he actually cared about my tears.

CHAPTER 13

STORMY NIGHTS

A storm raged throughout the night, but that wasn't what kept Busick awake.

He took a swig of his rum. His leg had ached all afternoon from the vigorous marching regimen. Now this turn in the weather set him in agony — rain, more snow. The change brought pain.

His back felt stiff, achy.

Maybe he was doing too much outdoors.

But inside the house had its own dangers.

Nanny LaCroy was dangerous. Always surprising him with her candor and that calm sense of rebellion.

A faint cry sounded over his head.

The nursery was above. Had the storm frightened Lionel?

For Busick, being in Hamlin had always made it hard to sleep. Maybe it was that way for Lionel.

He pulled on his dressing gown, taking care with his sore back. The last thing he needed was for it to begin aching so much he couldn't keep his balance.

He stared at the invalid chair.

The three-wheeled monster propelled easier on hardwoods than carpet, but it was stable and dependable.

His hand tightened about his crutch.

The contraption with its nicely sprung seating and wicker chair was a symbol of dependence, of his always needing help. It made him want to run and punch fate.

He fought despair, finished his rum, and headed for the third floor.

All was quiet when he made it to the nursery.

The room was spotless.

But Lionel wasn't alone. Curled up in the rocking chair was the nanny.

Bare brown feet.

Bright white nightgown with lace and ribbons—something elegant and denoting a refined lady.

Who was LaCroy?

What was her background?

And why did he like the shape of her small feet?

With a shake of his head, he returned to his mission.

"Hey, little soldier. The storm has you awake, too."

The babe lifted his arms.

If Busick felt steadier he'd pick him up. Instead, he lowered his hand, letting the boy have the cuff of his robe.

Lionel caught it and batted it about.

But Busick's gaze lifted to LaCroy.

She sighed and curled deeper into the chair. That blanket had fallen away, exposing a hip and more of her long legs.

"Such strength, little one. Man-to-man, do you want to keep your nanny?"

The boy dribbled on the trim piping on Busick's sleeve.

He wasn't sure if that was a yes or no.

Lightning zipped out the window. Thunder crackled.

The nanny sprang out of the chair with a gold knife raised.

Her eyes were wild.

"Nanny LaCroy?"

She trembled. Hair spilling from her mobcap.

"Is that a weapon in the nursery?"

Blinking, she lowered the knife and started pulling a blanket up around her. "You startled me, Duke."

Why did her tone sound as if he'd done something wrong checking on his ward? He knotted his robe belt into a ball for Lionel and handed it to the boy to chew.

"Is this a new way to raise children? With knives?"

"Yes, sir, it's something Greek. Or maybe tribal from the African shores. It certainly can't be English to feel the need to be protected."

Words were a dangerous thing. There was no way to retract a barb. It cut as much flesh going in as it did going out.

The wide-eyed woman was hurting. A joke wouldn't do. He put his hand on hers, taking the knife from her, dropping the expensive jeweled thing to the floor.

Thunder crackled, and she shivered.

The woman was frightened by something that wasn't him and nothing made more sense than to draw her into his arms.

But he wouldn't.

That would be a dangerous line to cross, to take her in a tight embrace, to press her delightful curves to him. Could he chase away her fears? Would he add new ones?

Busick wasn't a heavy-handed lord. He was a soldier and a lover and a protector of all things beautiful. LaCroy was beautiful, with a cleft in her chin that should hold kisses, topaz eyes that needed to turn black with passion.

Crossing this battlefield was fraught with too many risks.

Explosions of feelings, cannon fires of desire, made a wonderful way to pass the time until morning.

Nonetheless, Lionel needed a good nanny more than Busick needed to explore the attraction that existed between them.

So he stood there with his hand upon hers, listening to the storm, wishing their circumstances were very different.

* * *

The duke held my hand, and I looked up into eyes that saw me.

Did he know my fears, or was he preparing to terminate Lionel's jittery nanny?

He didn't say anything, didn't talk about the audacity of pulling a weapon on him.

Well, it wasn't as if I could tell him I'd been imprisoned in here for about a month, so soon after the birth of my boy. That I didn't know if I would eat or see anything beyond these walls.

I couldn't even tell him that I was sorry for having to be a party to the deception enacted by the Widow's Grace.

Yet, I'd deceived myself for years, pretending to be a passive dove. Why should the duke of Repington be any different?

"LaCroy." His thin lips held my fake name like a kiss. "Tell me what you saw when you awoke. It wasn't me, at least I hope not, with a knife in your hand. If it was me, we may need to reconsider this employment situation."

His rough palm clung to mine, not letting go, not that I wanted him to. Was it wrong to want to be held by him, when thunder and lightning danced outside the window? Was it horrible to hope to put my head on his shoulder, to nestle away my fears, hiding in him?

My eyes closed for a moment. I needed a savior, not a duke, not a man I had to lie to to be near my child.

"LaCroy, I asked what has frightened you. You can tell me. You're the keeper of my secret. You can trust me with one of yours."

Those words, trusting someone who wasn't Lady Shrewsbury or Jemina, stiffened my floundering spine. I took my hand from his and pulled my blankets around me.

"I'm fine, Your Grace. Just startled. I didn't expect you up here."

"I do like surprising people. But you have proper quarters. Though I admire your dedication, you don't have to stay with my ward every moment. Why are you sleeping in here?"

There wasn't an answer that sounded plausible or sane. I stopped returning his gaze and went to the crib.

Lionel had fallen asleep gumming the robe-belt ball.

I took it from him and wiped it on my blanket. "Is it wrong to be dedicated to my charge? He's so small and innocent."

The duke was behind me.

I felt him close. I smelled Demeraran rum on his breath, felt the softness of his robe. If I took a half step backward, I'd be in his arms, whether he wanted me there or not.

It was only a few seconds, dreaming while I was awake about that savior, about being comforted in strong, unyielding arms. Thoughts of the texture of brocade fabric slipping along my cheek, the heat of a man's chest holding me close, made me stand still, made me wait.

But I wasn't brave enough to turn, to ask or take what I wanted.

His palm fluttered over my shoulder, then landed softly on the crib rail. "Lionel is sleeping well. You should rest. In a proper bed, lying in pillows and sheets, a blanket on your bare feet . . ."

He rubbed his forehead. "The late hour makes me babble. Sorry, LaCroy."

A savior was needed, that thing bigger than the duke or me, that would make everything good. That would melt away distance and distrust between us. "I'm sorry, too."

Thankfully, regrettably, he moved. I heard him sit in the chair. "Hand me my ward, Mrs. LaCroy."

When I turned, his face was stone. None of the softness I'd seen earlier. This was an order.

I scooped up my son, my precious boy and put him in Repington's arms.

"You go sleep until this soldier's next feeding. I'll stay with him."

"That's too much, Your Grace."

"No. I think an extra measure of protection is good and perfectly suited for me, as I don't sleep well most nights."

He told me another secret, and I still hadn't told him my name.

"Go sleep, LaCroy, in a decent bed. I have the little fellow. No one is going to take him from me. I'll even keep your little knife for protection."

Whether he made fun, or was trying to tease me, didn't matter. Lionel was secure in his arms, bundled within his robe.

The man looked incredibly good and natural playing . . . no, being a father to my son.

I bent and picked up my knife. "I know he's well protected, but I still have to make it back to my room. Never know what's in the shadows."

"Don't tell me you believe all those foolish tales of Hamlin's ghosts. I'm going to have to speak to Lady Shrewsbury to stop spreading tales. Now go, before Lionel decides he'd rather milk than my robe."

I moved to the threshold. With a final glance, I eyed the precious picture of the two. Then, I left.

On the other side of the door, I lay my head against the panels. I was dizzy, my heart stuttering with the pounding of the rainstorm.

When I left for Demerara, how much will Lionel remember of Repington? How much will he miss him?

How much would *I* miss him?

This draw to the duke would drive me crazy.

Well, crazier.

My eyes adjusted to the dark, and I saw nothing. I needed to keep seeing nothing as I moved six or seven paces to the servants' quarters.

My gaze strayed to the end of the hall.

Nothing. No ghost. No guilty manifestations.

I snuck back into the bedchamber Jemina and I shared. She was asleep, and I settled onto my bed, wishing for Lionel to cry so I could take him into my arms.

Tomorrow, I'd have to contact Lady Shrewsbury. The Widow's Grace needed the next phase of the plan started before it became impossible to get Lionel or myself away from Repington.

CHAPTER 14

PLANS FOR MY LIONEL

A week of rain and snow flurries made Hamlin unbearable for me. The house abounded with restless men. Scarlet regimentals to the left and to the right, coming and going to the catacombs, slamming doors, loud talking. It was chaos except when the duke enforced nap time, Lionel's nap time. Someone even tried to set up another tent in the grand hall, but the polite implied threat of no more coconut bread made it disappear.

I stood under the grand chandelier as another delivery arrived. Soldiers in muddy boots hoisted lumber, lots of hearty oak, through Hamlin's entry.

Lord Gantry trotted down the stairs. His shirtsleeves were rolled up, and he still had a few buttons to finish on his green striped waistcoat. "Sorry, Mrs. LaCroy. I know you like a tidy house. This should be the last of the big deliveries."

I nodded and hoped it to be true, but my heart shook when one fellow's boards almost whacked the marble gods. Did they know the wrath that could come from awakening them?

I didn't, either, but it had to be big.

"Sorry again, ma'am." Lord Gantry shrugged. He smiled and escaped through the not-so-secret door to work on whatever project the duke had him doing.

I had to get into the drawing room. I was convinced that evidence against Markham was in there. Jemina and I had checked everywhere but that room.

Yet, if none was there, if nothing hung behind that mirror, then I'd go back to my strategy of getting my trust documents from the desk and booking passage to Demerara. Lady Shrewsbury would have to come up with a new plan, one showing me how to tell the duke who I was and that I'd be leaving with my son.

Deceiving the duke was now unbearable.

His bonding with Lionel, holding my baby every night, sharing with him dreams and plans, pierced so deeply into my soul. I was going to break.

Jemina came from the rear hall and joined me with her wash bucket. "These marks are going to take a bit of work. Men and their dragging boot heels."

I dipped my rag in the sudsy water and started scrubbing.

She knelt beside me on the cold hard floor, each of us engulfed by the shadow of the grand chandelier. In a way, each of us were still imprisoned to our plights, her amnesia, mine deception.

"Nearly two weeks, Patience. We're no closer to finding proof. Is this the big plan, to be maids?"

This was honest work for a couple of dishonest women. I shook my head. "This rain stops Repington's army. Of course it would affect our progress."

One of my lacy coiffed mobcaps covered my friend's fiery curls, and she'd hemmed another of my mourning gowns to offer her a change of clothes. With me in a muted blue India print, we were the fanciest maids in the countryside.

"There's something in the drawing room, Jemina. We have to get to it."

"Can't you use your influence and just ask the duke to leave the room?"

"Influence?"

"You two look mighty cozy whenever Lionel is about. The duke's eyes follow you at dinner, don't you know?"

"His eyes followed the basket of bread. I merely happened to carry it."

"If you say so. It's a nice big basket, a beautiful one."

It was. My mother had made it. Entwined with plaited reeds braided into a handle, it had a deep brown bowl that was big enough to put two Lionels.

"The duke is truly loving your bread and basket."

To prove I wasn't falling for the duke, I decided to go to the drawing room. I stood up, smoothed my skirts of wrinkles and went to the door.

When I lifted my hand to knock, I heard the duke's baritone mention Wellington's name. Then something about war.

Then something about Lionel.

Eavesdropping wasn't something I did. Well, a few times I overheard Colin and Markham arguing about nonsense. Then there was that volatile last meeting in the drawing room.

Yet, I was locked in place wanting to know what the duke meant. Wellington was the commander of England's forces in the ongoing war.

Was that why the duke drilled so hard, to return to battle?

My heart stopped as fear enmeshed it, crushing it tight.

"Patience."

Jemina's loud whisper made me jump and knock into the door.

I turned to her and made eyes at her, but the woman waved me forward, bolstering me.

The door opened and a man with officer's braiding on his uniform came out. "The commander will see you now."

I didn't think I was expected, but, having knocked, it wasn't like I had a choice. The pit of my stomach looped and knotted, making a bow.

Stepping inside, my first time in days, I saw the duke sitting at the big desk. He wasn't in military dress but relaxed in a bronze embroidered waistcoat and buff breeches. My gaze fell to his bandaged foot, and I wondered how he could think of returning to war with what it had done to him.

His hands laced upon a pile of papers. "Mrs. LaCroy, you must be prescient. I've made improvements to my ward's schedule. Or has Lionel told you of our talk last night?"

His smile, warm and inviting, mirrored the one his face held when we danced at Lionel's crib. Dance was the only way to describe what we did each night—the close but not touching approach to the baby, him slipping to the left, me to right. His breath teased my neck as he passed. Then we parted with the exchange of scents—his rum and sandalwood, mine lavender.

"Lionel didn't mention any changes, and I didn't think I was on your schedule."

"True. We do our best work at night . . . with Lionel."

I should laugh at his joke, but I didn't know if he was joking or if he saw my confusion, my belabored heart. We *were* good in the quiet night. We took care of Lionel well. My boy was getting stronger, and he reached for the duke as much as me. If the man had milk, I might be replaced.

"I've been thinking about us and Lionel. Please come forward. You don't need to be at such a formal distance. This is a welcomed meeting, nothing more."

I wanted to clutch my pianoforte. I was safe at this distance, but when the duke called, his nanny was expected to come.

Head tossed back, I walked the long distance to the desk and took my seat.

His expression turned pensive. "Mrs. LaCroy, have you ever traveled?"

Travel? Maybe he found milk and I was being sent away, a nanny retirement? "Yes, Your Grace. I have. I'm from Demerara."

"My favorite rum."

"It's more than rum, sir."

"I know. I haven't had the pleasure of visiting, but some of my friends have. My cousin, I believe . . . went."

I stared at him and didn't blink. If he'd finally put it all together, I would not lie. I was tired of this secret stuck between us.

His strong jaw held steady; his countenance was blank with those beautiful eyes boring down at me. He'd be good at playing whist.

"The war is continuing. I've written to Wellington about his need for a strategist. I was very good at strategy."

I leaped up. "You are done playing guardian? You're going to leave us?"

"Sit, LaCroy." He pointed me back to the seat. "If I go anywhere, Lionel will come. I'm the only dependable family he has."

That didn't comfort me, and it was far from true.

"Mrs. LaCroy, I was wondering if you'd come with us. Officers can take family. Lionel needs supervision."

"Was that the secret project—to figure out how to put yourself and Lionel in danger?"

"The war needs to end. Men are dying every day. If you can step up and help, you have to do it."

"Why you? Haven't you given enough? And why put the baby in danger?"

His face turned beet red. "No one has asked me to do so. I have yet to prove that I'm handy on a horse again."

"Small blessings."

"Were you this opinionated when you worked for Markham, or was there a reason he gave you special privileges?"

"What are you talking about?"

"You float about here as if you own the place. Were you Markham's mistress?"

A little vomit rose in my throat. "Certainly not. I'm not that kind of woman. Why would you think this?"

"You're very pretty, Mrs. LaCroy, and well-endowed, and—"

"The countess told me you've had your share of pretty women. Shouldn't you know the type, someone like me who's difficult versus someone more eager to please?"

"You are far from eager. My conquests were not Markham's. My friends were independent women who knew exactly what they were getting, a man who loved war more than domestic life. But Markham, he has a habit of going after servants and women under duress. I sense you to be strong, Patience LaCroy, but everyone has a breaking point. Markham thrives on breaking things."

The grip I had on my collar eased. "I've been through the worst, but never would I debase myself with the likes of Markham. Have you preyed upon servants?"

"I haven't. I'm very careful with those I employ."

There was something in his expression before he raised his countenance to the coffered ceiling. Something that said if they were equals, meeting as strangers, there might be different possibilities.

But this was a distraction.

Colin would do the same when he wanted me to hush. I wouldn't be silent. If I'd spoken up sooner, I might have prevented my husband's death.

"You're a confident man, Your Grace. You know substance defines a man. Not a limb, but yet you go through this pretense with everyone wearing that padded bandage. I know nothing of war, but I saw the soldiers come to Demerara—close quarters, men crowded about. It will be difficult to hide your amputation. And why hide it at all? You were injured in service to your country."

"You are correct, ma'am, and I don't doubt myself. I doubt others. I spent my youth on the battlefield. Any hesitation in a leader's ability can lead to problems on the field. That's a disaster in the offing."

"No one here doubts you."

"You do."

"Never you, but your judgment, yes. How can you even

think of becoming so involved in Lionel's life and then put yourself and him at risk?"

"I suppose taking a wily nanny along wasn't insurance of Lionel or me returning unscathed."

"No. It's not. Even if I wanted to save you, how could I? I'm just a nanny, a foreigner."

"Well, we'd all be foreigners in Spain."

"This is not funny. You'll have to wait for a land invasion to reach Hamlin to show off your fancy strategies. Or you could return the boy to his mother. She could make sure that the baby is unharmed."

"Now you're talking crazy, LaCroy. I can't trust Lionel with a woman who ran off. Mothers leave, and it's never for a noble reason."

I couldn't stand hearing his low opinion of me or bear to think of him going to war. I wanted to confess, box his ears, and hold on to him to keep him from harm.

Instead, I slapped my forehead.

This was me feeling too much, too soon. I couldn't let my heart do this to me again. As fast as I could, I moved toward the door.

"LaCroy, stop! Where are you going?"

"To go check supplies for the land invasion. If you're called back to duty, you can be assured Hamlin is running well without you. Be assured, nannies don't leave, not without their charge."

"Stay, Mrs. LaCroy."

"Why? Because you haven't asked me to withdraw?"

"I haven't, but I want you to stay. I want to reassure you that I'm not reckless and that I take Lionel's concerns and that of his outspoken nanny very seriously. Come back. Sit. Let's pretend I said nothing of this. Let's review Lionel's schedule for next week."

His smile was tentative. Those dimples seemed sincere, not a tool to twist my emotions even more.

My feet were slow, but I came back, slipped into my chair, took the paper he offered.

Repington's lips lifted. Dimples definitely showed. A dimple was dangerous on a handsome man.

I looked at the schedule and gasped. Ten o'clock, eleven, one, and more. "An hourly schedule? Sir, you're serious? A baby sleeps and eats and then relieves himself, and then he does this all again, but with loving hugs and reading to him and brushing his hair and smoothing his little face with lavender. None of these things are on this page. They matter."

"That's what you are to do in between these more formal tasks."

"Raising a baby doesn't need to be this formal, R-Repington, it needs to be a work of the heart with all the passion a mother can muster."

His eyes went wide, and he bit at his lip.

I bit mine.

I didn't mean to call him by his titled name as if we were equals. Or had I? We should be equals when it came to Lionel.

"True, Mrs. LaCroy, but *my* baby needs all those things and a schedule."

His? Lionel wasn't his. He wasn't. The duke didn't birth him, didn't spend months with him in his belly talking to him about seashells and coconuts and dreams, good dreams.

"You have a problem with a direct order, madam?" He handed me the list again. "You can add those mothering things, too, but I thought if I set a time for hugs it would seem a little heavy-handed."

"No, we wouldn't want you to seem that way."

"This is what I want for my Lionel."

His again? Lionel wasn't his. I glanced up, ready to tell him what to do with his schedule but stilled.

His face.

The pride in the duke's face, pride for my Lionel, stopped me, gluing my hands to the seat.

That was the sentiment he'd expressed in the nursery the first day, and it made my eyes sting.

Swallowing lumps and my own pride, I put the list upon my knees. "I'm at a loss for words. You've gone above my expectations."

"I do like amazing people." The duke's look was thoughtful, but his smile slimmed to nothing. He glanced at me as if my river of emotions had reached him and swept him away.

He clasped the edge of the desk and leaned in a little. "Comply, LaCroy. I know best."

No. No, he couldn't. He was trying to prepare my boy to go to war. To advance him to be less of a concern on the battlefield.

I didn't want my boy pushed and prodded and made to fit into the duke's world. I held my breath, counted to ten, then slid the page back to him. "These r-rules are r-ridiculous. It's not appropriate. Not for a baby."

The duke sat up from his slouched position. His mouth twinging as if it hurt to do so. He offered the paper again. "I think it is, and it shall be done. My little soldier needs training. You will follow my schedule, all my rules."

"But—"

"That's an order."

I bristled. There was no room in his crisp command for debate or even an extra syllable.

"Mrs. LaCroy, do we understand each other? I heard your thoughts on war, but this is what I want here at Hamlin."

"It's still not appropriate."

"We agreed on a month-to-month engagement. By Jove, you are a difficult one."

"Now, don't go calling down your gods on me."

"What, LaCroy? Jove is an expression for my one God." He held up one finger, then folded his arms. "Are you telling me that our month-to-month engagement is too long and that I need to find a nanny who understands her place?"

A second was too long when it came to my child. My foolish heart had begun to lead me astray. Thinking of the duke as a substitute father was foolish when he was just a drill master. I'd say anything to stay until I could steal Lionel away. "I understand."

I took the paper and shoved it into my pocket. "May I go?"

"You may, but this schedule starts tomorrow, Mrs. LaCroy."

Think happy thoughts, Patience. Demerara, Demerara. Demerara. I offered a salute and headed out the door.

The first opportunity to gain access to my trust documents, I would. All I needed was a chartered boat and a head start. My son and I would be away before the duke succeeded in turning my Lionel into his perfect little soldier.

And before I had to watch the fool man return to war.

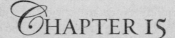CHAPTER 15

BACK IN THE SADDLE

Busick tossed his jet shako upon his head and cupped his eyes as he stepped out of the catacombs. Days of rain ended yesterday, but it didn't snow. The effort to clear the fields wasn't wasted.

Hamlin's grounds weren't perfect for outdoor exercise, but these were the best conditions he could hope for before more showers fell. The darkening clouds, the musk of rain in the air, meant it wouldn't be long.

He stretched, shifting his weight between his stump and his crutch, then looked to the balcony for the storm called Patience LaCroy.

She churned these past days, blowing into his mind like a cyclone, overturning tables and breaking up dusty cogs, challenging his commands with her passive resistance.

Pretend passivity.

The woman never complained. She was too smart for that. No, she complied with one-word answers, a yes or a no.

The absence of complete sentences irritated Busick. The occasional *sir* or begrudged *Your Grace* made her seem tragic and long-suffering.

That wasn't her.

Patience LaCroy was passionate and stubborn, and he'd witnessed glimpses of her compassion before he put his foot down. The woman didn't want him returning to war, but the notion of her coming along, of her being a woman to fight for him and Lionel had been shredded.

She'd not follow him across the hall, let alone the continent. It was folly to think she would. But he and folly were old friends.

One of his field officers approached. "Your Grace, your men will be in position in fifteen minutes."

"Good. We must begin on time, Colonel."

The man saluted with his good hand and then marched out to the troops.

Busick squared his shoulders and took a few steps toward the huge platform he'd designed. Gantry had his misgivings, saying the structure was something one would see outside of Newgate Prison to hang offenders.

This construction was needed.

Today's exhibition with his troops in front of his guests and his nanny would show how far he'd come in his recovery. If LaCroy saw him looking strong, handling his horse, she'd see he was right. All would know he was capable on the field.

Maybe their rapport could improve, and she'd forget about their argument in the drawing room. That was his hope, but women were different than soldiers. They didn't take commands well, not when they thought they knew better.

He'd forgotten that.

With the last two years focused on recovery, he'd forgotten a great deal, like how he enjoyed challenging eyes and passionate lips not pressed in a frown.

Moving toward the platform, Busick steadied himself and straightened his posture. Today would decide everything, showing his mettle was strong and that he could lead on horseback. He'd return to being one of Wellington's trusted men.

The viscount leaned against the platform, as a groom, one of Busick's second lieutenants, held on to a wonderful mount with a dapple-gray coat.

"Repington, your great secret has been completed." Gantry knocked his elbow into the structure. "Finished late yesterday, built to your specifications. Board by board, inch by inch. Nail count to within two, plus or minus."

"A two-nail discrepancy, Gantry? Hopefully, it's overdesigned and won't collapse. I've been told I'm weighty."

His friend laughed, and Busick circled the twelve-by-twelve platform, touching the shoulder-height boards that served as the flooring he'd walk on once he climbed its steps. "When I'm up on the decking, I can literally stroll into the saddle from the rear."

"You mean to mount using your horse's backside? You had me build a rump deck, Duke?"

Busick craned his head, felt his face frowning. "I wouldn't put it like that. I can also approach from the side. Straddling my mount from the outset will prevent any balance issues."

With a shrug, Gantry handed him the reins. "If you say so. And without further delay, your fine piece of horseflesh. Also, per your instructions, backside included."

Trying to remember this was his friend, Busick tugged off a glove with his teeth. He held it there a moment before the leather slipped to the ground. Lowering to retrieve it was tricky. He'd have to balance between his reliable crutch and the mechanical appendage strapped to his thigh.

No falling today, not in front of Gantry or his balcony guests who still hadn't arrived. Where were LaCroy and Lionel? He didn't want to begin until they were well ensconced in the chairs he'd set.

Taking his time, Busick sized up the horse and sank his palm into its pewter-colored mane. The coarse hair—thick, tangle-free—was wonderful. It'd been two years since he'd ridden. To have the opportunity to do it again almost brought him to his knees.

"Magnificent. You're magnificent. Look at the slope of your shoulder. By Jove, the lines of your legs would make any Englishman jealous. No offset cannons or upright fetlocks. You're the ride I've been waiting for."

"Do you need privacy with the Shire horse?"

The viscount chuckled again, but the man seemed troubled. The bags under his eyes were thick. He patted the horse's neck as if it were a fellow soldier. "Zeus is a strong one. You will enjoy him."

"Zeus." Busick nuzzled the horse's nose. "Here, I told LaCroy I had one god and you bring me another."

"What?"

"Roman mythology. Zeus, king of Olympus . . . Never mind. The horse is fantastic."

"And coupled with an easy temperament, he's perfect for today."

"Easy?" Busick glared at his friend. "You think I like easy or that I need easy?"

Gantry frowned and picked up the glove. "Neither of us is easy, but it would be better if we took the less hardened path upon occasion."

Thunder clapped in the distance as Busick circled the horse, stepping back to look at Zeus's hocks and the height of his withers. Shire horses were strong specimens, workhorses, and occasionally horses for war. "Is it winning if it's easy?"

"We can still win and not make things so difficult. That's a lesson for me, too."

"Easy. Difficult. It's of no consequence. As long as the weather holds and that coming storm delays, I'm winning today."

Busick looked over Gantry's shoulder and caught a glimpse of LaCroy coming on to the stone balcony. Did nannies choose the easier path?

Zeus deserved his attention, not the brooding nanny that he needed to impress. Checking the saddle, he tugged on the girth. It was tight. "Time to give this a test."

Tossing him his glove, Gantry followed him to the steps of the platform. "Repington, you sure you're ready for this? We could review the troops like we always do, then head in for whatever the ladies have prepared for breakfast."

With a deep sigh, Busick shook his head and clasped the rail of the stairs. "No. We . . . I'm committed to this path."

He looked at his haggard friend—pale countenance, disheveled dove-gray tailcoat—and decided to offer more charity. "You haven't been sleeping. The bags under your eyes could transport supplies."

"They're not so big. And I'm hungry."

"Heartache won't be solved by eating, Gantry."

One tired eye shot up as his man shoved his fists into his pockets. "A lot of things can be solved by breaking bread. Or offering compliments and apologies."

Would complimenting the nanny make things better between Busick and LaCroy? An apology for wanting his old life back—never. But for the tone he used to express his differing opinion—maybe?

Gantry climbed the steps behind him and leaned over the built-in horse pen. "How is this hangman's platform going to work?"

"Simple." Busick tugged on his riding glove. "Second Lieutenant, lead the horse to the front of the stall as if you were stabling it and then back him in," he said to the soldier. "Use a gentle pressure on his reins. Show him his respect."

The viscount glanced down to the soldier. "Let's not keep the duke waiting."

The man hastened his pace, circled Zeus, then aligned him into the structure.

With the flooring surrounding the horse like a dock, it was easy to imagine the Shire being moored into place, like a sailboat. For Busick, it was time for a maiden voyage. "Gantry, you followed my instructions perfectly. I can walk

around on three sides, even check the reins again. I don't
have to depend on anyone to ride, I could even back Zeus in
myself, tie him off, climb, and mount. Excellent. Most excellent."

His friend reached the overarching beam. "A hangman's
noose could sit here." He gave it a pound. "But, no descend-
ing rope for you. You're going to hold on to this traversing
board, the guillotine part of your structure, and lower yourself onto the horse?"

Noose? Guillotine? His friend's doubts weren't subtle,
but they wouldn't shake Busick's confidence . . . much. He
handed his crutch down to the groom and took a few un-
aided steps. The strapping at his thigh was tight and rubbed
as he moved, but it felt steady. The muscles in his back felt
strong and in control.

Good. "It's not a guillotine for there's no blade. And yes,
I can use my arm strength to hold on to the board and ease
onto the saddle. No additional help required. It's fantastic."

"I and a groom could just hoist you onto the saddle. It
wouldn't be any trouble, and it's far less risky."

True, but that would make Busick a burden to others.
That would never do. "Why waste a good guillotine?"

"Tell that to the peers of France."

"*Non*." Busick clasped the traversing board. With a grunt,
he pulled his torso up to it and then lowered onto the saddle.
"See," he said between gasps. Clutching the pommel, he
stayed upright in his saddle. "Zeus, I know this is a unique
experience, even for an *easy* horse like you. We'll get used
to it."

"What goes up must come down, Duke. And at least it
was not unceremoniously done. Good."

Busick took up the slack in his reins and chuckled to himself. The viscount hated to be wrong. "Everyone, move."

Gantry leaped down the steps and motioned to the soldier
to let go.

Busick steered the gelding forward. "I have Zeus now."

"You're good up there, Duke? You sure?"

"How is that even a question? I've kept my troops and my civilian audience waiting long enough."

His friend grasped the horse's bridle. "You could still practice in private with just me, maybe a few of your most loyal men."

"Do you think I'm going to fail? I'm not."

"I'm concerned." Gantry saluted. "But if you fail, you'll do it better than any man I know. Keep your head up."

The horse jerked a little, and Busick felt his abdomen tighten, but he kept his seat. Situating his stirrups, he made his mount circle back. "There's another reason we have an audience. I invited Lady Shrewsbury. She knows everyone in society. She must know your wife. The woman, whom we won't talk of, can be found by the countess. I know you miss her. I know you want to make things right."

"How would Lady Shrewsbury know where to find an enigma?"

"It was the countess's connections that led me to Markham. Unless Lady Gantry has gone back to Demerara, Lady Shrewsbury can find her. She knows how to locate women from the West Indies."

Gantry folded his arms. "I haven't mentioned her much."

"It's in the not asking, the not saying, the not sleeping. If you were done with the woman, you'd tell me how awful she is. You'd try to use my connections or your father's to see what can be done to sever things. We have two beautiful widows in our midst, and you haven't even looked at them."

"You mean in the manner you gaze at Mrs. LaCroy? How you keep glancing at her even now?"

The way he said it made it sound as if the flirtation was one-sided. It wasn't. Busick was sure of it. And her not asking—her one-word responses—had to mean something other than stubborn.

They were much better at night.

They didn't need words.

Just two souls with a common mission. He needed them back to that place, where he felt her support and care. Their situation had to be fixable. One or both of them should be flexible.

He made his horse do another circle, this one tighter and more controlled than the last. "She's a beautiful woman. She noticed me. And I haven't been admired in a while."

"She's not admiring you. She's tolerating you. Trust me. I know the difference." Gantry kicked at a patch of snow. "And if Lady Shrewsbury can find anyone, why can't she find your cousin's wife?"

That was a good question.

But the answer was obvious. No good mother would be away from her child. She'd died or she'd gone on with her life. If the answer was the latter, Lionel didn't need her.

Busick pushed his shako higher on his head. "Perhaps Mrs. Jordan has met a foul end. Markham, or Markham's and Colin's creditors have destroyed her. I've hired runners, but they've found nothing. I'm going to focus everything I have on Lionel. He must be orphaned. I'll make sure he never falls prey to the Markhams of this world."

"Especially its prejudices." Gantry's head slightly bowed as he spun his wedding band about his finger. "Or the subtle slights your viscountess endured for your sake that you glossed over."

"Lady Shrewsbury can be useful." Busick turned his good heel toward his mount and applied a gentle pressure. With taut fingers on the reins, he nudged the horse forward, straight to the balcony. The stone structure looked like a trapezoid with angled stairs on both sides. Balancing to favor his weak leg, he slowed the Percheron and doffed his hat. "Ladies."

The countess waved a dazzling ostrich print fan. Her serious face changed to lightness.

He'd interrupted another conspiracy.

"Looking very spry this morning," the countess said.

"Feeling spry, good lady. Morning to you, Mrs. LaCroy."

Lionel was in the nanny's lap nestled in a blue blanket against the folds of her rust gown. It was good to see LaCroy in a color, something other than blue or gray. He rode closer, close enough to claim her gaze, every bit of those wide topaz eyes. "How are you and my ward this morning?"

Her cheeks fevered. "Fine."

The countess chuckled. "Your leg is better, but don't be reckless and rush your recovery."

Not her, too. Gantry was enough of a mother hen. He adjusted his hold on the reins. "Reckless is in the eye of the beholder, Lady Shrewsbury. Lionel, you'll ride someday. I can't wait to select a pony for you."

"He's a baby." Mrs. LaCroy's hand tensed on the arm of her chair. "I mean. Good."

Two sets of three words. Progress. "It won't be tomorrow. He has to master crawling and walking first."

The countess laughed. "An old bull like the duke was practically born on horseback. He'll be a great teacher."

He winced at the comment, the unavoidable reference to his scandalous mother, but the nanny didn't smile or offer a pacifying head nod. "I suppose, I'll just have to show you how well I can handle a horse. You'll learn to trust me."

He tipped his shako again and turned his horse toward his men.

Once the parade was done, he'd repair the good working atmosphere he'd begun with the nanny. A last glance at the tense LaCroy, and he knew the battle would be difficult, but he'd win. He was Wellington's best when it came to war strategies.

CHAPTER 16

A PARADE WITH LEMONADE

Hoping the duke knew what he was doing, I cradled my son and waited for the pressure in my stomach to ease. The thing knotted again and again as the duke's horse leaped ahead of his marching men. The grounds of Hamlin were sloshy and wet. Sliding would be too easy.

"Dear," the countess sank deeper into her chair, a finely carved seat of zebra wood. She tapped the lion head sculpted into the leg. "We're outside on the balcony. It hasn't started to rain. A lovely military theater is before us. Why do you look as if you might be sick?"

Because I was.

"I should be happy this wasn't one of the duke's crazed baby drills. Three-month-olds do not crawl. They tip over. They don't repeat words. They burp. Lionel's passage of man-size gas was not a sentence."

Well, I was sort of proud of that. It meant his little belly was full.

The duke stopped in front of his eight-man battalion. One person shouted. The soldiers, sharply dressed in scarlet regimentals, tossed flintlock rifles over their shoulders and marched in lines of four.

As if he knew I was fretting for his safety, the duke decided to canter his horse around and around the procession.

One misstep and both man and horse could fall.

The duke's balance had to be perfect or he'd hurt himself. Or worse.

Something could happen to expose his war injury. The private man loathed to acknowledge it. I understood this. I felt his pain in having to risk others' scorn.

I splayed a pinkie over Lionel's lips. "If the clouds don't hold, rain will come. It will get very slippery, and men could fall."

Thunder crackled in the offing. Strong and loud, heading for us.

"Dear, he'll be a wet duke on a horse. He's fine. And Lionel looks quite comfortable. What has you so anxious?"

Nothing I could say aloud, but every muscle felt ready to rip apart. Disaster loomed. I hadn't been this way since Markham locked me in the nursery, complaining I was too loud and that I talked too much when I'd said nothing to him. "This all makes me uneasy."

I tried to hug Lionel for comfort, but his wiggling and coos didn't work their magic, not this morning.

From her reticule, the countess pulled her gold-framed theater lens and stared at me. "You're one of his marks, but you don't look tampered with."

I almost jumped to my feet. "What? What, ma'am, are you insinuating?"

"Has the duke pulled you aside into one of Hamlin's secret corners to give you a private lecture, one that involved kisses and promises that go nowhere? We call that tampering in England."

"The man has lectured on schedules but nothing in a corner. And definitely no kisses."

But my cheeks flushed when he complimented my bread

and when he insisted Lionel and I oversee his troops this morning. I leaned closer to the countess. "I'm not looking for promises from anyone but you. I need to be employed long enough for the Widow's Grace to figure out how to regain custody of my son. He wants to take my boy with him to war."

Lady Shrewsbury set down her lenses. "You must've misunderstood. You . . . Oh my!"

With Lionel hugged to my bosom, I jumped up and scanned the field. "What?"

"Just making a point." The countess groaned. "You're besotted by a man in uniform. Didn't they have those in Demerara?"

"Yes, we had soldiers. Plenty of your soldiers. One of your regent's brothers, too. Prince William Henry was known to strut about our shores, dance and become a drunkard in the island hotels."

I returned to my seat, easy like I was light with no cares. "I'm not besotted. I'm concerned."

Jemina came onto the balcony bearing a silver tray with a pitcher and glasses. "She's not besotted. She just won't admit to liking the duke, that's all." Jemina set the tray onto the table with a heavy plunk. "Lemonade?"

The countess poured herself a glass of the tart yellowish liquid and sniffed the contents as if it were medicine. "Very lemony."

Pushing up her dark gray sleeves, Jemina sat in the vacant chair among the three. "Extra lemony." Her voice sounded happy and loud, no longer mouselike. She'd grown stronger working at Hamlin. That was good, for she was good.

Lady Shrewsbury set the glass aside. "Have you two found anything? You've been installed here a little over three weeks. Your father's payment will be sent soon. Once that's dispensed, the main reason we suspect Markham of trying to harm you would be no more."

Jemina's lips puckered with each sip of her concoction. "We've found nothing, but we haven't been able to search the drawing room. If anything is here, it has to be in that room."

I tried to keep listening, but my head kept turning to the field. The duke raced back and forth again. I held my breath until he slowed.

The countess coughed.

Those cheeks of mine felt on fire. "Yes. We've found nothing so far. I'm confident that there's something in the drawing room. But the duke or Lord Gantry is always in there, or the house is too full of soldiers."

"You have to search that room. Markham's still in the village. If he had what he needed, he'd be gone. There's something in this house that has his attention. We must find it."

The skunk stayed close.

Jemina lifted her fingers, she seemed to be counting. "There's no one in the house now and on the field, there are less men. Have they disappeared, too?"

"Too?" I caught Jemina's hand. "What do you mean *too*?"

"One of the loaves of bread we made is gone. There are only eight in the kitchen. We pulled and twisted nine. Each baked perfectly, golden brown in the hearth, I might add."

And Jemina's laundry bundle went missing.

Had it been stolen? Those odd noises I heard coming from the attic. I still believed I heard something in the attic the other day.

Was there a thief in the house?

Or was Markham somehow getting into Hamlin? That jittery feeling in my stomach lodged and turned cold and black with fear.

The countess clasped both of our hands. Her gold rings clinking against Jemina's and my wedding bands. "Do be at ease, dears. The duke has let some of his men go this morning. They've returned to their families. He doesn't need as many men now that he's secured Hamlin. A soldier surely took a loaf as a meal for the journey home."

Lady Shrewsbury moved to the knee wall. "His Grace is keeping a smaller contingent. Those fellows marching can keep Markham and his ilk away. A smaller number of men mean—"

"Less things to clean? Less things missing?" Jemina lifted her glass as if it were a goblet for a toast. "This is wonderful. The soldiers left a ladder under the grand chandelier. They didn't finish setting it. Some of the glass globes aren't even on it."

What? Half cleaning the chandelier? I looked down at Lionel and tried not to fume. I wanted things back in order, how I had it when Hamlin was under my control. "The chandelier should have all its globes."

The countess looked to the field for a moment. "I guarantee you two will have more liberty to search the drawing room. Perhaps tonight, when everyone is asleep."

Lip biting, gaze narrowing, Lady Shrewsbury placed a palm about the beaded trim of her redingotes lapel. "I hate to say this, Patience, but our friends in London have uncovered staggering debts for Colin Jordan. The tally at a few gaming hells are over two thousand pounds. Hamlin may even be encumbered. My nephew is checking."

I closed my eyes. I sought to be numb to Colin's recklessness. We'd be so unprotected if not for my father's provisions. "My husband was clearly bankrupt when he committed suicide. I thought the fact that his grandfather willed Hamlin to his mother and then to him meant this place was special."

"Desperation changes things. My nephew is looking for a financial transaction. The encumbrance is speculation. The gambling vowels are most pressing. The holders of those IOU debts are not the type to take excuses. Markham will lead them here for payment."

Perhaps the duke's battle plan would protect us against creditors.

Jemina sat up straight, her eyes scattered like she'd seen a ghost. "Is that why Markham is lurking in the village? Is he going to try to take Lionel for ransom?"

The countess bent and covered Lionel's escaped feet. "Markham can't best Repington's men."

Jemina stirred her concoction, then clanged the glass pitcher with a wooden spoon. "But if anything happens to the duke, Markham is next in line to be guardian. Then he'd again control Lionel's fortune."

I looked at Jemina, the way she held the spoon and her cups, pinkie extended, she either had a societal background or was a teacher of etiquette like a true governess. My friend and her scary insight fit well with Hamlin and its secrets.

My heart pounded when Repington slipped a little on a turn. I wasn't numb when it came to him. I was a slow rolling boil, a lobster pot trying hard to not foam over.

The duke took another jump. I pretended to drink the lemonade and glanced at him between lower lashes. How does one dissuade a man from folly? Nagging, letters . . . subtle requests. Begging. Submission.

None of that worked with Colin.

Nothing broke the grips of his depression or his belief that Markham was always right, that he needed to be loyal to the cretin.

My stomach couldn't hold more knots, any more than I could hold my tongue. "This has to end. I should tell the duke the truth and all that Markham has been about. The duke needs to take more care."

"Be at ease. Repington likes risk, but he's no fool." The countess reclaimed her chair. "He's relaxed his forces, but he hasn't reduced them to nothing. The man likes to show off, but he's settling into life here at Hamlin. The truth now would be inconvenient. We need proof of Markham wanting you gone. Men are guardians. Mothers, particularly ones who've fostered deception, have little say."

"This mother needs to say more. We need to be done with this masquerade."

"I think you're right," Jemina said between sips of her lemonade, wetness circling her upper lip like a mustache. "And he won't dismiss you. Who would he stare at if you weren't here?"

"Maybe he'd pay more attention to that horse if I were gone."

I snuggled my son as if he'd slip away. No more duke's or countess's rules but mine. I needed my trust documents. Lionel was healthy enough for a boat trip.

"Lady Shrewsbury, we need more cloth and linens. Can you convince the duke to allow us to go to Town? Perhaps there's something Jemina and I could discover while we're there. My husband stayed in London often."

I blew kisses to my son and made a face that made him squeal. "Wouldn't you like to go to Town?"

"I'll see what can be done," Lady Shrewsbury said, "but I doubt he'll let you take Lionel. You sadly underestimate the power of an instant father, especially a man determined to prove something."

"What is there to prove? He has the power. He's Lionel's legal guardian."

"Busick Strathmore's father, Lord Bodonel, was sickly. Then he broke his neck in a horsing accident."

"What?"

"Yes. He was an invalid for years. Everyone's fighting something." Lady Shrewsbury grasped my hand. "There's nothing to fret about. The duke is healthy. He can handle a horse. Can't you see how he's enjoying this? With Markham still poised to strike, he'll not risk Lionel being out of his sight."

"I don't know."

The countess released a little huff as if she knew she were imploring a stubborn daughter. "Patience, see this through. You'll have custody. You must learn to trust."

"I trust you, Jemina, and my own strength. Is that enough to win?"

The countess picked up her glass of lemonade. She drank

it, her mouth drawing up to a pucker. "A woman has to stake her claim and fight for what she's due. You're a fighter, Patience. You will win, my dear. Your prayers to be safe with your son will manifest. We must continue to be diligent. The Widow's Grace will prevail."

I put Lionel's cheek, soft and sweet, next to mine. I may have even nodded in agreement, but my heart was in the drawing room getting my documents.

"My nephew is approaching peers at the Court of Chancery for advice. All have said that things may go easier with evidence of Markham's duplicity. It could outweigh you being committed."

May and *could* were not the same as *will*.

Lord Gantry came up the stairs, his footfalls rushing. "Lady Shrewsbury, Mrs. St. Maur, Mrs. LaCroy." With a quick dip, he bowed his head, then stopped in front of the countess. He rolled his beaver-domed hat in his hands as if his nerves had gotten to him. "May I speak with you, ma'am? The duke says you're good at finding people, and I've decided this is what I must do."

"Me, finding people?" She fanned and offered him demure eyes, demure red-goddess-controlling eyes. "I have a few connections. Who are you looking for, sir?"

"May I speak to you alone, Lady Shrewsbury?"

"Yes, let's take a walk. Mrs. LaCroy and Mrs. St. Maur can occupy themselves as we take a turn." She took his arm, her long crimson pelisse trimmed in Vandyke lace flounced above her sleek short boots. "The scarlet and yellow pimpernel flowers have burst through the snow. It looks hopeful, battling against the grips of winter. A perfect place to exchange confidences."

Her hint to Jemina and me was not subtle, but we watched as the dear woman claimed Lord Gantry's arm and headed him down the stone steps.

Jemina rose. "Let's search the drawing room, Patience. We don't have much time."

I rose and cooed at Lionel. "You want to help Mama look for the secret? Of course—"

The duke rode close to the balcony. "Mrs. LaCroy, I've dismissed the troops. See? Nothing to worry about. Stay put. I'll be right back."

So much for searching now.

The duke wasn't done showing off, and I wasn't done fearing for his safety.

CHAPTER 17

IN THE CORNER WITH YOU

From the stone balcony, I watched the duke spirit his horse to the odd wood structure he'd erected. It was an eyesore to the newly manicured grounds, but he seemed gleeful riding at top speed toward it.

A groom handed him his crutch, and he charged back to me.

I turned to my friend. "Later, I suppose. When everyone's asleep, we'll search."

Jemina stood and smoothed her charcoal gown. "The duke's trying to impress you. Let him know you are. Then he'll take more care."

She slid the beverage tray closer to me. "Give the man some lemonade. It's refreshing after a hard ride. I'll go set out breakfast before the soldiers return to the house."

My humored friend went back inside, but her words made me think. If admitting that I was impressed and fearful made the duke slow down, that would be best.

"Mrs. LaCroy, here." The duke rode up close to the balcony knee wall and lifted his crutch to me. "Grab hold of this."

Cradling Lionel in one arm, I gripped his staff with the other.

He waved at a groom but looked dead at me. "Did you enjoy the review? Was my ward attentive?"

The baby stuck his hand onto my lips. Lionel's eyes were light and searching. Maybe he did see.

"Yes, I guess."

"Three words? Was that a torture?"

"No."

A soldier came to the gray horse and grasped the reins.

The duke lifted his one leg over the pommel until both boots were in front of him. Then the foolhardy man jumped. He hit the ground with a little wince, then straightened.

I wasn't going to let him fall. Lionel and I went to him, dragging the crutch behind me. "You're not toppling over, not if I can help."

"Woman, I'm not—"

"Hush." I put the crutch under his armpit. "There."

He held on to my hand before I could withdraw. "That was more words you've said to me than all of yesterday, but don't fret. There's one child at Hamlin, and he's on your hip. That's not me, though his position is enviable."

The duke tugged off his gloves and put his big thumb on Lionel's nose. "You hold on tight, little soldier. Hold on to her. She's a difficult one to befriend."

Friendship? My face fevered. "Sorry."

"I won't fall, LaCroy. I'm in command, but I'm reasonable. I know the value of a fretting woman."

Thunder crackled.

A hint of rain perfumed the air.

And the heat of his eyes sizzled like lightning.

"At least you were able to see my regiment before the weather set in. By Jove, we beat the storms."

So glad he was safe, I thanked his god, too.

My pulse ticked up, tick, tock, rattling like the grand-father clock in the dining room. I was too near the duke with

Lionel caught between us. This was very much like our dance at the crib, except he wasn't moving, and neither was I.

This terrified me, this family moment.

My heart grew used to things too quickly. I moved from the duke, me and Lionel fleeing up the stone steps. "There's lemonade on the balcony, Your Grace. Let me get you some. You look very heated."

"More words to me." The duke smirked with dimples and a touch of a hero's swagger as he joined me on the balcony. He seemed very steady in his boots, only leaning a little on the crutch.

I poured him Jemina's beverage, then settled in a chair with Lionel bouncing on my lap.

The duke took the glass I'd offered and gulped it down, his lips puckering like Lionel's. "Tangy. You don't like shows of force?"

"I do. I just want you to take care, to take your time. Who else will set Lionel's onerous schedules? In fact, he's been fed and is ready to nap. I should go put him down and keep your latest dictates."

"We can relax his schedule today." Whipping off his hat, he stashed his gloves inside and set it on the table, then sank into a chair. "It's nice that you care, Mrs. LaCroy. I don't think I told you that the other day. I should have. I know I was rude."

He reached out and smoothed my forehead, his rough thumb slipping across my skin. "I want no creases on that brow on my account."

My heart went into my throat and stuck there somewhere between being beguiled and stupid. I remembered this breathless feeling. This dizzy rush meant I'd fallen for Colin, now it meant I was stupid, again. I had feelings for the duke.

"Is that a command?"

"Yes."

"See. Simple answers are best."

Wincing a little as he shifted his weight, he took Lionel from my arms. The duke looked very good holding my son.

My boy reached up and swatted at the duke's brooch with the star, the graceful medallion he wore on his ivory sash. That was new. He'd made himself extra fancy for us.

Assured that no one would fall, I lowered my clenched palms to my rust-colored skirts, one of the demure gowns of my old dresses. It was not a full-mourning gown, far from it. I didn't want to be at the duke's parade grieving.

With a quick glance to the door, the vacant hall behind us, I thought of my trust documents. Maybe this would be like the nursery and I could leave my son safe with the duke and head to the drawing room.

"Lionel, you have to believe in your abilities in spite of others' fear or doubts, right, LaCroy?"

I looked at the duke, truly looked into those strong, wintry eyes. "I may be guilty of fretting more for you, because I know of your injury. I'll admit that. But I'll always be concerned for your safety. You're Lionel's guardian. You should be safe."

"Lionel, you like medals. Believe in yourself, and you'll win them. Believe when no one else does, then you always win."

Winning. Winning. I was sick of the talk, especially when my side kept losing.

The countess and Lord Gantry returned.

"Looking very good on parade, Duke," she said, taking Lionel from him.

The boy cooed. His smile held dimples, dimples like Repington's?

Lady Shrewsbury snuggled my baby like he was her kitty. "Lord Gantry, you have two daughters. Are any this small?"

The man's chest puffed up, his smile broadening as he helped the countess sit. "Once, but now they are three and four. I'll collect them from my sister next month."

His lordship looked more at ease. Whatever he'd confessed to the countess seemed to liberate him. Lady Shrewsbury had a calming way about her.

"My dear," she said as she tapped my hand, "why don't you go get paper, so we can make a list of the things you need?"

"Yes, ma'am."

The duke held out his hand and blocked my path. "I can provide for her."

"I'm sure you can." Shrewsbury poured Lord Gantry a glass of the lemonade. "But she needs some personal things."

Lifting from his seat, the duke moved to the doorway leading into the house. "There's nothing I cannot get for her."

"It's just paper, sir. You know? The thing you use to make schedules. I can go get it while you sit and have more lovely lemonade."

He frowned, puckering his lips. "No, thank you. Stay, ma'am."

"Mrs. LaCroy, go get it," the countess said. "Duke, sit. She needs things that I know you are familiar with, but I am sure she'd rather you stayed out of her stays."

"Oh," the duke said as he mouthed, "stays and corsets."

The two were giving me orders like I was a compliant rag doll but witnessing the duke murmur about my undergarments was too much. I moved quickly and slipped under his arm. I didn't touch him, didn't brush against or wrinkle his pressed jacket or the sweet sashes.

"Quick thing. I'll follow, Mrs. LaCroy. I have something to ask you."

The duke caught up, a boot length behind me. There would be no gathering my papers today, not with him giving chase.

Done with being on edge, I stopped, and he bumped into me.

His arm went about my middle as if to steady me. "Sorry."

I wasn't. His chest was solid, the hold was nice. His medallion pressed into my spine. The prick of the star's points might be the only thing keeping me from turning my cheek to his.

"Are you steady now, lass?"

"Are you sorry to hold me, sir?"

The duke released me. "No. Yes. We must talk."

Why talk now when I was all ruddy and bothered and sure to make a fool of myself? I scooted behind the marble gods for protection. "You go get the countess some foolscap. It only takes one of us. One."

When it seemed as if he'd heed, I blew out a breath and sank against the hidden door.

Jemina was right about me liking the duke and about the chandelier. Someone had raised it without all of its glass globes. The job was half-done. The velvet sleeve covering the pulleys was pulled down, exposing the mechanisms. Very sloppy.

The duke barged into the nook. "Mrs. LaCroy, we need to talk now."

It was inconvenient for him to tower over me with his wonderful height covering me in shadows. Fine job of Agassou! No protection at all from the duke's pretty eyes. "What do you want, Your Grace?"

"Admit that I'm not reckless."

"No."

His head reared back, almost knocking into the sandaled heel of the lesser god. "Will you admit that I held my seat well? I was good on my mount. Shires are a gentle, sturdy breed, smooth in their stride, like me."

"You didn't fall. Great."

"I saw you observing, LaCroy. You could have more enthusiasm."

Were observing and fretting the same thing? I nodded. "Perhaps."

"Well, you're not one for flattery. Or do you simply loathe being wrong?"

"Both."

He raked a palm through his hair, the shift stopping on blonder locks. His distance remained respectable and aggravating, not the caress of before. He stood close enough to have his ears boxed but far enough for me to admire how well he looked in his uniform, the shine of his brooch.

I covered my eyes. "Your Grace, is this chat done?"

He sighed, his breath citrusy like an island breeze. "At least that wasn't a one-word answer."

"Yes."

The duke sighed again. His fingers clenched, then slacked to his sides. "Why do you have to be so difficult?"

"You want me to flatter you? Why, Duke, you look r-really suited for the saddle."

He glared at me, his eyes frowning, his noble chin elevated, seeming formal and above it all. "Is that the best you can do? You were more convincing of actually caring posing as a footman."

Maybe it was the challenge in his voice. Maybe it was days of being forced to agree to his rules for my son. Or maybe I wanted him to notice I wasn't a rag doll. I shouldn't be ordered about. I wasn't going to be put on a shelf like Colin had done. He assumed I was too delicate to be seen in Town, anywhere away from Hamlin. Lies.

I grabbed Repington by the sash, the one that crossed his wide chest, and shoved him a little against the gods. I hoped they minded their business as I put my palms to his lapel, massaging the rough wool between my fingers.

In a low voice, sultry like a singer, I said, "I've never seen anyone so skillful with his mount. Your Grace, I'm overcome in admiration."

His brow lifted. Did he see me now? Was he shocked?

"That's your best, ma'am?"

Could I do better? I stepped closer. Our shadows entwined. I skimmed my pinkie down the brass buttons of his jacket—*plink, plink, plink.* "I'm not sure what my best is. I don't know what I'm capable of anymore."

His smirk went away, and his eyes had darkened to mirrored glass, but in those reflective pools, I saw a wild woman, a wanton one. And it looked wonderful to be free.

"Has your widowhood liberated you, or has working for me stirred rebellion under that mobcap?"

"Both."

"One-word answers!"

I stilled my fingers on the brooch Lionel had touched. "Is this what you want, another sycophant to be in awe of you, your power?"

"No."

"Oh, now it's your turn for one-word answers." I leaned into him and put my cheek so close to his I could feel his breath. I knew he felt my panting. I knew I was slipping from pretend to that dark place of need I long denied.

But this wasn't Colin who'd turn me away.

I think the duke wouldn't flinch if my lips met his.

Footsteps sounded overhead.

Pushing back on my heels, I retreated. "The house is filling, Your Grace. Please have your soldiers finish their household duties. They didn't replenish all the glass globes on the chandelier and left the ladder in the hall."

His jaw tensed, and he put his hand over mine. "So you're done with me? A few questions, a request for truth, and then you send me away. Errands, madam, over an admission that you were wrong. I thought you were more honest than this."

"Errands are tasks to be added to a schedule. Your orderly heart should love it."

"Anytime you're ready for me to school you about orders and schedules, I'll willingly indulge. Do pull me away when there's a lot less distractions. I don't like to be interrupted."

"Well, that's impossible with soldiers milling about and Lionel needing me. Do you have a one-word answer for false promises?"

He lifted my palm and kissed my knuckles. His hands were rough, but his lips were gentle, such contrasts against my skin.

"I'm thinking of another one-word answer for you. Tease."

"Tease?" I shook free. "A tease is what men do, tease of

love and happy forever when they only mean for a moment."

A crackle sounded above, sharp and quick like a branch breaking. The house settling or was that thunder? "I should go get Lionel before the weather turns."

The duke's mouth opened, more sweet breath released along with a deeper groan. "I'd never tease you. Never."

"But you have others, Lady Shrewsbury says so. How many have you led to believe in the sweeping power of a moment? How many have you made follow rules that you later broke?"

I smoothed his wrinkling sash. "Duke, I want to be you. The one with the power. The one controlling so many destinies. The first to withdraw when I tired of playing games."

I'd silenced a rake with my stays in place. I curtsied. "If you will excuse me, I must go retrieve the paper per Lady Shrewsbury's request."

"No. I'll withdraw first. It's my paper. It's the least I can do to set up a task to gather your stays. It's a tangible thing, since you think only lies and games are my forte."

He took a step. Then turned back, planting his crutch, the thud matching the storm's moaning outside. "Have you considered it's possible to have a changed heart? Can a rake choose to reform?"

"A man can choose anything today. Tomorrow? Well, tomorrow is tomorrow. Thunderstorms come and go."

"No. Hearts can change. A man can be saved from himself. I was saved. I saw a woman, a beautiful Spanish peasant—"

"Duke, I really don't want to hear of your exploits."

"Listen. Everyone, including myself, discounted her as my lieutenant's indulgence, but this woman . . ."

I saw a hard lump go down as he cleared his throat. "This brave lass . . . she picked up her slain husband's sword and mortally charged the enemy for him, for the memory of him. I wasn't fast enough to stop her. She died for him. She sacrificed everything for their love."

His voice grew lower. This was no jest, but something he carried with him in his chest.

"Their baby, I had to deliver to her parents. He will grow up with neither of them and will never know the depth of her sacrifice."

A gasp left my lips, my feet chilling as I stood in my own hypocrisy. I'd expected a clever retort, not something so raw and anguished that I'd be left blinking, breathless, even a little more broken in my spirit.

"That type of devotion is never earned by a man who's not honest in his dealings, never given to one who's faithless. I want to be the kind of man who can engender that kind of noble passion in a woman."

I was caught, caught by the sadness in his voice. I'd tried to discount him as a pretty rake, a schedule-happy dictator— anything to justify or diminish the draw I felt for him. I had to admit that he was all of this and none of it. I hated that I'd made him feel less than what he was . . . honorable, and he'd chosen to be honorable to me.

The duke turned to the hall. "Go on onto the balcony. I'll bring both ink and paper. I've a correspondence to send before the storm comes. It will rain soon. I feel it in my bones."

He walked away, heading toward the abandoned ladder.

I stood alone in the nook, shamed, listening to the distant rumble of the coming weather.

Snap.

A loud pop sounded as if something stretched and broke.

I searched overhead and found nothing, then glanced at the duke. He closed the ladder and leaned it on its side.

Could someone truly turn from his past?

Could I turn from mine? I didn't trust anyone but Jemina and the countess. A good man should be added to that list.

I had to apologize. "Your Grace, wait."

He pivoted on the slick marble tiles. "Yes."

And that's when I saw it.

The tremors of the lights above. The glass prisms strung on the chandelier shifted, casting shooting stars about the hall. The heavy wrought iron fixture jerked and descended a few inches.

It would fall.

The chandelier would drop and crush the duke.

There was no time, no one-word warning to shout.

I ran as fast as I could and hit the man at top speed. The blow sent him reeling forward, and I fastened my arms about him to keep him moving away from the danger.

Snap. Snap. Rip. That had to be the pulley ropes.

I couldn't tell. My face burrowed deeper against the duke's shoulder. I kept pushing us forward.

We crashed to the floor, my head hitting the marble. The world behind me exploded. Glass bits shot at us, stinging my fingers, lacing into his hair, cutting his smart uniform. The world blurred as our momentum turned us over and over.

My arms stayed locked about him.

Dust covered us.

The thunder of his heart, my heart, became distant.

I stopped breathing.

CHAPTER 18

THE LAST LETTER

I beat my hands and tried to awaken, but I was trapped. He passed beside me. His haunted hazel eyes were so close to my face.

A chill covered my skin as I followed Colin.

He locked himself in a room. I heard shouts, threats, murderous threats.

When I opened the door, he turned to me, his face twisted, ghastly twisted in grief. Then, I heard Colin. His voice was faint but growing louder. "Your fault. Your fault, you killed me."

Shaking, sobbing, I opened my eyes.

A candle burned, but everything was a blur. I blinked until I could focus.

Breathing made everything hurt.

Nothing seemed right. I was a ship too far from the shore. Tangling in a bedsheet, I swam upstream, swinging my arms until I sat upright.

I wasn't dead or caught somewhere in between, was I?

Not with aches like this. I had to be among the living.

But where was I?

A window dressing in fine muslin and sheers sat open, blowing cold air into the room.

This wasn't the bare servants' quarters in the attic.

Rubbing my jaw, I studied the walls, the jonquil yellow paint.

Not Bedlam.

One of the bedchambers of the second floor? This wasn't right at all.

The sun wasn't outside the window. I saw stars in my vision and in the dark sky.

It was the dead of night.

The fallen chandelier.

The duke and I escaping its collapse. Did we both escape?

The bandage on my hand, the lump on the back of my skull said I wasn't unscathed.

The duke? How was he?

And where was Lionel?

I gripped my neck. The high collar of my rust gown was gone. White muslin wrapped my limbs, not Bedlam's chains.

My heart pounded as if it had become a drum. The musicians in me beat it hard and crazy. I had to get up and make sense of things.

I stood on my second attempt.

A momentary win.

The noise in both my ears made me fall back. I crashed onto the mattress, headfirst.

"Dearest? You're awake." Jemina helped me sit, then hugged me. "You do remember me?"

"Yes. I remember."

Jemina kissed my forehead. "I was so afraid you wouldn't. Your nightmares were so vivid, I didn't think you'd be free. Not everyone can keep their memories."

I put her hand to my heart. "We widows have lost enough. No more. It wasn't smart to do what I did to save the duke, but I had to."

"It was better than smart. It was brave. The poor duke was shaken. He's very concerned about you. It's why we are in the room connected to his."

The connecting bedchamber.

The room that would have been mine if Colin hadn't insisted I have the best bedroom. It didn't mean he'd stay, but that was the love he could give.

My foggy thoughts were too fluid, drifting in too many directions. I clutched the bedpost to keep from swaying. "Where's Lionel?"

"He went to sleep an hour ago. Your baby's fine. Lady Shrewsbury stayed with him as her physician made sure you were well. The duke took over his care and has had your son ever since."

The duke was well enough to care for Lionel. My crazed action had helped.

The notion brought me some comfort, but my head raged. My stomach felt wobbly and readied for a revolt. I forced air in, in and out, in and out. "I need to see . . . see Lionel. Lionel needs me."

"He's well." Jemina bounced up and grasped my arm and kept me upright. "The duke is like a father returned from war, not letting his babe out of his sight. The countess had to defer to him."

Repington could have been badly maimed by the heavy chandelier. He could've died, and I'd have let another man suffer. Not again. "I acted. I didn't think of much else. I knew I had to help."

"Patience, he might've not been hurt, and you could have escaped with Lionel in the confusion. Lady Shrewsbury would've let you go. Instead, you risked your life." Jemina put her face close to mine. "Why? Why take such risks?"

My shoulders rose before I could stop them.

I looked down at the bandages on my hand. The cut underneath stung, but not as bad as the daggerlike feeling to my chest when I saw the chandelier fall. "The duke's a good man. He didn't deserve to be hurt. I could've helped my husband, but I waited for him to ask. I can't sit around anymore waiting for words. Does that make sense?"

Jemina nodded. "Perfect sense. You always act with your heart." She helped me stand and take a step. "Is your heart telling you to act for the duke?"

I couldn't admit it. I wanted to run, but the room spun. Jemina was my anchor. "The man is irritating. He's full of rules and schedules, but he has been nothing but kind to Lionel. It's only been a few weeks, and he's shown more love to my son than any man. I'm grateful. I had to help."

"It's fine to admire the duke. He's handsome and polite."

Polite?

That wasn't the way I'd describe him. He was terribly handsome, awfully rule-conscious, painstakingly diligent. My heart melted to a dripping puddle when he sang to Lionel or made plans for him. "I need to get my son back before this goes any further."

Following close behind, Jemina hovered as if she thought I'd fall. With my stomach lurching, I just might.

We reached the adjoining door, but I couldn't go through that one. I couldn't have Repington looking at me like some sort of bridegroom in the bed that used to be mine.

I pushed away and wobbled to the hall. "We'll go in through the main door. It will be more private if they are both asleep."

The dim light of the hall made my vision worse. The ache in my skull intensified with each step, but I pressed forward. I had to see Lionel.

Easing the door open, I saw my boy's crib. It gleamed next to the wide bed, but he wasn't inside.

My heart would seize, but it was too tired from all the upset and the drummer beating on my head.

The duke, the back of him—thick, touchable hair, more brown in the candlelight—sat in his wheeled chair. In the crook of his arm, Lionel's patch of curls peeked out.

My son wasn't crying but making that sucking sound with his gums.

"Come on, young man. Just a few more sips. That's an order."

The duke's deep voice was a whisper.

"Not quite what you're used to, son? This cold pap dish with warmed milk isn't a woman. It's not flesh. Not the plump bosom of a vibrant soul. Oh, there I go prattling away. But the stories we'll share when you are older, I can offer advice about choosing ripe melons."

He chuckled.

I wanted to box his ears.

Then I wanted to hug them both.

"Lionel, maybe you could share a thing or two since you've tasted such goodness. What a surprising woman your nanny is? The beautiful minx. One minute, exasperating. The next, not so. I'd like . . . I'm going to have to save this talk, too."

Lionel's hiss sounded louder. Maybe he disapproved of someone talking about his mother like that, like a woman to be desired. One of flesh and blood and yearnings.

Yes. The duke needed to save that talk.

I pushed Jemina out of the room. I had to be gone before my face burned with fever.

"Sorry, I guess Lionel doesn't need me."

"Of course he does, but he's fine. Now go back to bed and rest."

"How can I? The duke is growing more attached to Lionel. He'll not let us leave."

"Is that a bad thing? I see how you blush, how you stare at the duke. I lost a lot, but some things are unforgettable. My thinking is addled sometimes, but I see that there's something between you and him."

My friend had such an innocent expression, but my head wasn't innocent. It was covetous, thinking of Repington, admitting I wanted his kiss. And hoping he wanted mine.

But I told myself no. There was nothing but heartache that came with Englishmen. Colin left us with his depression. The duke would abandon us for war.

"I'm done with this masquerade. Let's get my trust documents. I'll admit to who I am and leave this place ready to buy passage on a ship for you and my son."

"A boat? Journey across the sea?" Jemina's face became dour, her easy smile fading. A memory must've returned to her. It couldn't be good.

"We'll sort everything later. Now we must go to the drawing room."

I turned and wobbled to the stairs. My vision spiraling, my nausea whirling, but I made it down to the grand hall.

It was quiet.

Wall sconces were lit, but the shadow of the chandelier was absent.

My heart sunk.

I'd lost a dear friend. The grand chandelier—the sparkle of crystals, the smoky silvered globes, the ebony iron limbs—it was the first thing to greet me coming to Hamlin. The last thing I saw when Markham carted me away.

Jemina put a hand to my shoulder. "You're not well. You're not thinking clearly. Remembering what is lost is never helpful."

"But I do remember. I remember my life. This was my house for four years. That man upstairs will know tonight."

"And then what? We haven't proven that Markham tricked you and sent you to Bedlam. We've found nothing to show a conspiracy."

"I don't care anymore." I took a candle from a sconce and stole into the drawing room. I lit up this darkened place. No more shadows. No more lies. No more thinking that all of this was a nightmare.

I looked at my reflection in the mirror.

I was pale.

My hair was down and wild.

And in my eyes, I saw a coward's stare. I kept blaming myself, blaming Colin, kept circling the poison of our union in my heart, my soul.

It was easier to stay stuck, to keep reliving the past.

Neither the duke nor Colin was responsible for me being moored in one place. I was my crutch. I needed to be free.

"Jemina, you don't have to stay. You can go back to bed."

"I'm with you, Patience." The girl moved to the polished gilded frame. "This is crooked. It must've jostled when the chandelier fell."

She put her hands to the frame, but it wouldn't straighten.

That was the mirror Markham had touched before being tossed out of Hamlin.

I turned away from the desk. "Let's take it down. The nails might be coming undone. Or it might be hiding what we've hunted."

On the count of three, we lifted it from the wall. A small compartment door was now exposed.

I'd never seen it before, but Hamlin was a house built with secrets. "This must be what Markham's after."

Jemina started prying the slotted door opening. "One way to find out."

We tugged together. Soon, the heavy door made a loud noise like its hinges opened a crypt.

"Oh no," Jemina said. "That's loud enough to wake everyone."

Someone would come.

I knew how voices and noises carried in Hamlin. "Then we must hurry."

Hoping not to be bitten by one of those furry spiders, I slid my hand inside the dark vault.

I found letters, not insects.

The ones I'd sent to my sisters, my father. All were here. Colin never sent them.

I flipped through them. They'd been opened, read, then carelessly creased and closed.

I'd lost contact with my sisters and my father these past four years. My husband had kept my letters. He didn't think my words were worthy to be sent. *How could you, Colin?*

"Patience, what is it? And what is that? It's a book."

My face must seem so troubled. I hid within myself, something I'd learned to do on these shores. "Jemina, I'll get it."

I pushed past the dozens of letters, even fought the stinging of my eyes and drew out a book. The leather thing was brown with a torn spine. Stuck in its gold leaf pages was my final letter to Colin.

I set the book into Jemina's hands, but the letter I kept. My heart pounded as I unfolded it.

The paper was stained with tears, old ones from the day I penned it. And new ones leaking now from my eyes.

My clever handwriting, the curly script of my *d*'s—*dearest, disappointment, don't.*

All my words, all my heart—my wanting to leave him, my needing to go home, my hurts—all stared at me.

I felt the same, except I wished he'd been strong enough to hear me. I wished this hadn't pushed him into the Thames.

I killed Colin. Here was the proof.

He was ill. Why else would he try to keep me away from everything?

Jemina was on the floor flipping through the pages of the book. "This makes no sense." She counted her fingers. "No one would do this."

"What didn't Colin do?"

"These are IOUs in your husband's name and Markham's."

"Yes. They owed money. We knew this."

"But these have been canceled." She lifted the vowels to me.

These debt markers had indeed been marked paid. "The papers indicated a man named Sullivan canceled them. How much debt? Is Hamlin encumbered to this Sullivan?"

"Still adding."

Jemina's fingers of both hands were involved. She'd have a sum in a moment or two.

"Patience, it's at least 2,804 pounds, all paid by an A. Sullivan." She stood next to me and pointed to entries in the book. "The debts are tied to Grapes, Brooks, Watiers, and Piccadilly. What are those? And look at the list of men's names, varying amounts, and then this Sullivan's mark."

Why was Colin keeping a diary on this man? And why did that name Sullivan—A. Sullivan—sound familiar?

My dream. The voices. The ones condemning, threatening Colin—was one of the accusers this A. Sullivan?

Nauseous, dizzy, I tried to reason why Colin would have such records, but then I looked in the compartment at my letters, my unsent letters to my family. Maybe there was no reason. Maybe Colin was simply unwell.

"Patience, I see you. I see the fear in you. This diary and these canceled IOUs have to be what Markham wants. A. Sullivan would know. The Widow's Grace must find him."

In my heart, I knew this Sullivan person was the key. But my heart was never a good judge of anything.

Jemina took the diary from me. "Let's put the mirror back. We'll study this in our room."

I was swimming again, trying to wake up from this new nightmare. "I don't know the man I married. Why would he have so much debt, and why would this man he tracked pay for it?"

"Extortion. Sounds like this diary was enough to convince this man Sullivan to pay off the debts."

My friend was guessing, but she was good at puzzling things. Colin an extortioner? That made no sense, but Markham . . . that sounded right. "His evil uncle would do it and trick Colin into helping."

"If we locate this A. Sullivan, we could ask him. He would admit to how much your husband was involved."

That didn't sound like a good plan. I didn't want to hear of Colin's duplicity. He was my son's father. There *had* to be some good in him. I rubbed at my temples, my renewed headache. "I know what the man who came here and threatened my husband looks like. I think he was called Sullivan. If we find him, I know he'll admit that Markham was the mastermind."

Jemina caught my hand. "If we can't, the fact that Markham incurred so much debt might be enough to sway the Court of Chancery. He locked you away because you knew he gambled, and he didn't want you to tell and remove him as guardian."

It made sense, except that Repington was the guardian, not Markham. "My baby's father can't be a criminal."

"Perhaps. But this book has to be what Markham wants."

Flipping to the last pages, I scanned the final figures and dates. The last entry was dated a month before his suicide, a few days before I gave him my letter. "Sullivan is the key to everything."

Footsteps.

Jemina tugged my wrist. "Someone's coming. Help me put the mirror back, Patience."

I tossed my awful letter into my pocket, then we forced the squealing door closed.

When we lifted the mirror back into place, we couldn't get it straight. It tottered on the nails.

Jemina collected the IOUs, stuck them into the diary. "We must—"

The door swung open.

The duke and one of his soldiers stood there.

I wasn't sure if he was going to toss me and Jemina out.

But I didn't care.

I'd been through too much to be scared.

I looked in those seeking eyes of Repington's and wasn't afraid. Too much was at stake.

CHAPTER 19

BE A LITTLE WEAK

Busick waved his soldier out of the room. "I can handle this disturbance. Get some sleep, man."

He tried to appear calm, and even waited for the fellow to leave before he reprimanded his remaining troops, his female troops.

The door behind him closed.

He leaned on his crutch and folded his arms against his brocade robe. His sleeve had pap-milk stains from his noncompliant troop upstairs.

"Mrs. St. Maur, I thought I asked you to alert me when Mrs. LaCroy awakened."

"I . . . I . . ."

LaCroy swept in front of the other widow.

Exactly what he would expect the superior officer to do. "I'm responsible. I wanted to come down and write."

"We were talking about paper before . . . You need to write now?"

"Yes."

Her pale pallor made him fearful for her health. He stepped closer. "Woman, do you feel well?"

She put her hands to her temples. "Yes, Your Grace. A headache."

She didn't make much sense, and if he could, he'd sweep her up into his arms and carry her to bed. "LaCroy, does the physician need to return?"

"No. Yes. I need Lady Shrewsbury. Send St. Maur for her. Please, Jemina, go to her."

He couldn't deny the request. LaCroy's healthy olive skin looked very gray, even green. The good woman had risked her life for him. He owed her everything. "You want Lady Shrewsbury, you shall have her. St. Maur, dress and have someone send for a carriage."

Mrs. St. Maur stooped in a low bow with her hands behind her. The demure miss came from LaCroy's shadow and backed to the door. "Yes, sir. I'll run now."

Arms folded under her thick shawl, she fled the room.

Busick returned his gaze to LaCroy.

The look on her face was unreadable. Her hair was loosed, full of tight curls. Not the orderly lady, so neat and tidy. Not the woman he was used to seeing.

More mesmerizing than ever.

Pallor aside, she seemed calm and in control. Yet, a smidgeon of him wanted her to break, to come to him with need, asking for advice, seeking him to make things better. "You've too many secrets in your eyes."

"Perhaps, you shouldn't look." She slipped to the sofa and leaned against it. "If you're finished with your questions, I should go lie down and wait for the countess."

"Sit here and wait for her. I won't risk you growing dizzy and toppling over the stairs. I won't be so lucky a second time that you'd be mostly unharmed."

Her lips tugged to a brief smile then drooped again.

"Why is it you seem one step ahead of everyone? Ducking in and out of Hamlin. Detecting my injury. Noticing the chandelier."

"Lucky, I guess."

He moved closer, her scent of lavender and liniment

hinted at her enticing femininity and her bravery. "That kind of luck will get you killed. I wanted to see you when you awakened. I needed to thank you."

Her eyes squinted as she peered up at him. Then, she touched the bruise on her forehead. "We did peek at you, but you were busy, Your Grace. You were instructing your ward on melons."

"Oh"—he rubbed at his neck—"that would be awkward for you to interrupt. Melon selecting . . ." Maybe Busick did hit his head.

"You're very good with him, but that's not new. We spend too much time together in the nursery for you not to know how much I think of you and Lionel."

"Thanks." Her compliment almost brought a smile, but this moment of vanity was a trap. He waggled his index finger. "No changing the subject, young lady. You like risk. You don't care about tempting fate."

He moved closer. "It's not wise for someone with a head injury to be up so soon. You thought differently, so you had Mrs. St. Maur ignore a direct order."

"Yes. Yes, I did."

She swayed, and he braced against the sofa to hold her up.

Hands about her waist, he drew her near. His gallant reward—the feel of her rapid heart beating against his chest.

"This isn't saving you from a falling chandelier, but it's something."

He strengthened his hold. She was easy in his arms, and he liked thinking he comforted her. "I don't want you falling."

"Your Grace, let me sit. Then lecture me."

"You're trying to soften me. You're in the wrong. I won't soften—"

"Must you talk?" Her fingers curled onto the lapel of his robe; her cheek laid upon his shoulder. "Sssshhhhh."

He groaned, part frustration, part this intangible thing that made him so aware of her breathing, the tickle of tresses along his neck, the curl of fingers against his skin.

Holding this woman was dangerous.

Yet, his arms stayed in place. His heart beat with hers. "You like the strong, silent type?"

"Well, you're strong, but not silent, so I may never know."

"Grandfather was a man of few words. He'd sit at that desk over there, dictating commands to me and my cousin on everything from posture to penmanship."

"Do you have a beautiful hand?"

Busick flexed his palm, the shrapnel scar near his thumb. "No. Colin did. Exceptional. Better than any. Markham tried to claim credit . . . I'm rambling."

"A little."

"Except for his rules, I suppose you'd like Grandfather's reticence. Was Mr. LaCroy quiet? Did he do as you asked?"

She pushed away. "I'm feeling better."

Busick should've followed her request and remained quiet. Then he'd still be holding her, glancing into her dark eyes, hoping to know their secrets. When would her unexpected honesty manifest into a confession that she desired him, too?

His horse should come inside and kick him. Strathmore men didn't chase after women in their employ.

"I'm fine, Your Grace. I'll be better when the countess arrives."

"You don't have to be so strong. You can be weak. I'll not think less of you."

"Weak?" She slipped farther away. "No."

He hated how much room existed between them. "You're the only one who's made me rethink my convictions. That's my weakness."

"But I can't be weak, Your Grace. It's not allowed. I'm sure there's a rule against it. I was taught to be strong—the perfect helpmate, hostess, and a hundred other things. I wish I had the luxury to be weak."

He pressed forward, the distance between them evaporated. "There's strength in a shared weakness. Confide in me."

Shaking her head, she moved toward the unlit fireplace and stared at the mirror. "Confide in you? Fine. My thoughts are desperate enough. My marriage was not a happy one. I tried very hard to please my husband, to warn him of bad influences. He wouldn't listen. He said he'd protect me from the slurs against our union and my heritage. I was to be away from every slight he imagined."

"Some can be horrid."

She lifted a shaky finger and pointed to her reflection. "His different wife; his difficult wife. His dark wife."

"So, Mr. LaCroy was of the gentlemen class. There are expectations of whom he's to marry, a society darling with proper looks, money, and connections. You're beautiful, but not what the *ton* expects."

"They want my money absent my face."

"That's a shame. It's a very nice face. I take it your late husband squandered your means and you now find yourself a governess?"

"Something like that." She folded her arms about her. "It's a little hard to be weak when my husband . . . his family has cut me off from everyone. It's hard to trust."

Busick sat on the sofa arm. "I'm sorry."

She stared straight ahead at the mirror. "I was strong. I could take the slights if we faced things together."

"Even a misguided man wants to protect his lady. There's nothing wrong with that."

LaCroy brushed curls and tears from her face. "It's wrong when he can't take the weight of it, when his shoulders were already laden with his depression."

The pain in her voice dragged through him, stinging like hot metal fragments shredding flesh. "You take too much upon yourself."

"Not being able to help my lost husband hurts. Learning more of his darkness and what he's done, crushing."

"Be weak. Let a friend . . . let me support you, then rebel again in the morning."

She picked at the bandage on her hand. "Is that a command, Your Grace? Does it require scheduling? You said to rebel in the morning. Before elocution practice for Lionel or after?"

Straining, his back aching more, he stood beside her.

They were a sight to see in the mirror. She was the right height for him to put his arm about her without bending. One little stretch and he'd have a proper hold on her waist, an inch of hip, an ounce or two of bosom. A perfect clench. But that wouldn't be proper.

"I asked if that was an order."

"Yes. For ten minutes, be uncontrolled. Cry, punch, make me a proxy for all the things that have made you sad. I owe you that."

She turned to him, staring with that blank look she often offered, the one where he couldn't read her thoughts, couldn't see into her heart.

"Punch at you? Is that what you'll teach your ward, violence and conflict?"

He kept his hands at his sides, not testing that perfect clench. "LaCroy, we need to get better at negotiating things. Let me be of aid to you."

She smiled a little.

Then swayed a little more.

He caught her and held her. When he couldn't stand not kissing, not crossing that line, he stroked her chin. "Duck your arm about my shoulder and let me help you sit."

Miracle of miracles, she followed his request. LaCroy slid her hand behind his neck, then leaned into him.

They walked together as they had that first night, but her robe didn't hide her curves like the footman's livery. The press of her thigh and thin nightgown felt different from her breeches.

"I do like you much better as a woman. I say that respectfully."

At the desk, he sat, set down his crutch, and then lifted her beside him. Hip to hip, he kept her hand.

"Duke, you smell like rum and floury pap milk."

He chuckled and smoothed the stain to his robe sleeve. "The former was needed to ease the pain. My back twinges upon occasion. You slammed into me pretty hard. I wasn't expecting such a hit."

"If you had, I'm not sure I would have been able to move you."

Did she shudder against him? Or was the tremble the swoosh of his blood coursing hot in his veins?

He stretched, almost put his arm behind her, but drew his palms to his lap. His resolve was in danger of slipping, and the desk was sturdy. Without the fears of balancing, he could court discovery, the flimsy nature of her nightgown.

But he wouldn't.

LaCroy wasn't the type of woman you dallied with and then let go. She was one to keep, to argue with and deal with forever.

"The second stain is Lionel's fault. Why settle for less when you've had the best?" He blinked. "Ohhh, that wasn't the thing to say."

"It was honest. Thank you."

"I want to say thank you again. Patience LaCroy, you risked your life. I am grateful. But, soldier, that was crazed. You could've been killed. I don't want you taking such risks."

"Would you tell Lord Gantry to not do what he felt in his heart? You'd keep him contained?"

Heart? Busick was in her heart?

Not touching her, not tracing her satin skin was proving more difficult. Yet, when he looked again into her eyes, he saw shadows—caution and something else.

It was time to be a better man.

A man Lionel would be proud of. He anchored his hands to the desk. "I know what's going on here."

"You do? You finally figured it out."

"Yes. We'd just had words. I said something I should've kept to myself, and then you risked your life for mine. That's when I realized what was between us."

The relief in her eyes disappeared. "Between us?"

"Yes. I hurt you with my commands, my crossness, my orders. You're in love with me. Who wants to be ordered around when they've fallen in love?"

"*What?*"

"I figured it out. It's not like I hadn't seen the signs before. Your injuries are my fault. This risk-taking is my fault. My attraction to you makes things worse."

A sour look, sort of like Lionel's face when he sipped the pap milk, crossed LaCroy's. "I think I should return upstairs."

"Please. We have a level of honesty and acceptance between us. Let's talk this through. Women becoming attached is a common thing, and usually I'm much better at ignoring the draw. I'm trying to do better to not lead anyone astray, but you're different. I find myself drawn to you. I'm enthralled."

She put her hands to his skull, her fingers sinking into his hair. "Did you hit your head, too?"

His pulse quickened as if his troop had taken on cannon fire.

"There has to be a lump or a hole up here for Your Grace to say something so stupid."

His face dipped closer to hers. "Is this hysteria? I'm trying to be easy with your feelings and mine."

The woman laughed. "And, of course, now I'm terminated."

"Well. I . . . I hadn't thought that far out. I don't want you terminated."

LaCroy chuckled harder. She tried to smother them with her bandaged hand, but they escaped. "Please go on."

Was she laughing at him or their situation? He played with his cuff. "We'd have to see if we can still work together. It shouldn't be too painful for either of us. I don't want misunderstandings. I value your friendship."

"Let me help you, my dear Duke of Repington. I'm not in

love with you, and I quit my employment. I end this farce now."

"No. Don't." He reached for her hand, but she'd jumped from the desk. "I want you to stay. We can forget this, just like we forgot how we met and go on, like normal."

She tottered a little and turned back to him. "Sorry. I must be swooning again. This love. It's too much. Yes, I must quit it."

"No quitting me. The boy needs you . . . I don't want you to go. I like you here. I like being able to talk with you."

"Why are you so willing to say such things? Are you sure my ploy to win you by saving your life didn't work? Have you not accidentally fallen for your hero?"

Maybe he had.

Why else was the thought of her leaving abominable? He clasped her hands in his. "This speech made a great deal more sense when I was telling Lionel."

"Did he give you advice on your direct address?"

"It actually put him to sleep. So I've made a fool of myself."

"Yes, you have. It's endearing, though."

"Could this be another of the things we don't talk about?"

"Once a thing is said, it's pretty hard to ignore."

"This is why I have a rule of no young women in the house." He crossed his arms and hung his head. "This is the first time I've disgraced myself. LaCroy, you've been gracious and kind. You've kept my secrets. I've done nothing but put you at risk."

She put her hands to his shoulders, then slid them behind his neck. "I can see how you could leap to such a conclusion. You must be used to women being charmed by you, but it's time for me to quit."

The woman was being kind, but she was no quitter.

He clasped his palm about her elbow, stroking her arm through the thin fabric. "I feel . . . I feel quite foolish, and now I've ruined things for Lionel. I know how you care for him. You'll do what you must but consider him. I need you here to care for Lionel and to make bread that the men rave about. I want you, need you . . . to stay."

"I must quit, for there is something else I must do."

She leaned in close, all those inches to his lips and drew him into a kiss.

CHAPTER 20

A KISS CAN SET YOU FREE

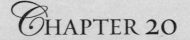

Arrogant, endearing man. Still laughing, I put my mouth to his.

What I'd intended as quick and chaste, deepened.

His arms tangled with mine and drew me off-balance. I willingly went.

Then I was lost, as his skillful palms slid to my hips, his practiced hands searching my shape.

I let him.

I wanted to be discovered. The real me had been hidden too long.

Oh, the pressure of his lips changed, demanded more.

I teetered as he swooped me up onto his lap. The silent command to cling to him had me drawing closer.

This moved too fast, felt too good, changed too many of my notions of dukes and dreams and decorum and desks. With a sleight of hand, the duke had me flat on his desk, caught between his theater maps and his schedules.

"I always wanted a nanny." He chuckled, then blessed my lips again.

Hadn't I just made fun of the notion of falling for him?

Surely, I was on the losing side of this battle. Repington won with the way he touched me, the way he looked at me like found treasure. From hills to valleys and back, his fingers made a fiery path on my skin, a campaign straight to my heart.

I can't surrender like this, on the drawing room's desk, in the place I last saw my husband before he left Hamlin forever.

I pushed on Repington's shoulder, but my pinkie betrayed me, finding warm skin bared by his open collar, his unbuttoned nightshirt. "More talking, Duke. We need more talking."

He nudged my hand to his chest. "*Non, ma chère.*"

His thumb stroked my ball-of-fire cheeks, and he kissed me so gently, so sweetly, that I forgot my fake name, my real name, and would answer to anything.

"A moment, Duke?"

His laugh is rich and knowing.

With my palms to his jaw, I searched his eyes for something other than a reflection of me wanting him. Yet, that was all I saw or maybe all I allowed my soul to see. I can't be swept away. I won't lose everything. I pressed against his chest again; my fingers splayed along his scars. "Repington, this won't do for us. I must get my documents."

He let me slip away. "What? Wait. What?"

I rounded the desk and opened the top drawer. Tossing books and foolscap away, I cleared everything from the secret panel. A couple of taps slid the door open.

"Come back here. You said we needed to talk."

"Seems as if we'd finished *talking*. I'm getting my documents."

"Your employment papers are upstairs in my bedchamber. Neither of us will go there, not with Lionel's sleeping."

"My trust documents, Duke. The one's left to me by my father."

"Mrs. LaCroy, when did you . . . These are from before, when you worked at Hamlin?"

"I never worked here, not before you. Well, that's not quite right. I worked at Hamlin—decorating it, keeping it immaculate for four years. But I wasn't employed."

"How could you be here and not be employed?"

I yanked free my paperwork. The crisp, folded parchment of legal terms and amounts. "They *are* still here. Markham never found them."

"Why would he want . . . What does he want? I don't understand. And I don't want you quitting. We can forget about this. We should try."

I waved my trust documents. "Can you truly forget? We've been in this quandary of you waffling on terminating me for weeks. I'm happy to quit to have control over me again. It's liberating."

"I didn't know if I could trust you about Lionel. I've seen other young women who cared more about the latest parties and mischief than their charges. Then you proved worthy. Annoying and resistant to orders, and beautiful, but very worthy. But what are these papers and how were you at Hamlin and not working here?"

"Repington, you do babble when you are trying to figure things out. Perhaps you need Lionel's counsel."

He held out his hand. "Give me these documents, and if I'm quiet will you kiss me again? Now that you no longer work for me, things can be different between us. I'm attracted to you. I've hidden it, struggled with it for an eternity."

He started to pick up his crutch, but I put my hand on his.

"I need you to be at eye level when I say this next piece."

The duke gripped my hand. "You could kiss me again, but please don't cry. I really hate—"

"The mistress of Hamlin Hall is not a salaried position."

His arms wrapped about my waist. His lips savaged my neck with fire. "I suppose she's compensated in other ways, but I haven't offered that position, not yet. I love how you don't mince words. You are direct."

"You are not listening, Cousin."

His fingers fell away. "Cousin?"

"Yes. I am Patience Amelia Jordan, daughter of Patsy LaCroy Thomas and Wilhelm Thomas. I am Colin's widow. These are my trust papers that prove my identity."

"But she . . . You?"

He took my trust documents and flipped through the pages as if he wanted to tear them. "These . . ."

"Think, Duke. Markham took my son and shipped me away. I fought to return. I snuck into Hamlin through the catacombs, ones I discovered living here for four years, to feed my son. I dressed as a footman to care for my Lionel. That's how we met. I was the cow. I'd just fed my son."

He looked down at the papers again. Crafted in Papa's exquisite hand and certified by his London solicitor, the proof had to be indisputable. But this was the doubting Duke of Repington.

"Not that I believe you, Patience LaCroy, but why hasn't Mr. Thomas come to see after you? Why did you wait to tell me?"

"It's Patience Jordan. I haven't heard from my father in a long time. Markham tore me away from my son after he'd kept us captive for weeks. I didn't know if you'd be any different."

"I'm not Markham."

"Well, that is good, 'cause I swore to cut my tongue out if I ever kissed him."

"Don't. That would be a waste of a treasure."

My cheeks felt hot again. "And hopefully you've come to know I'd never hurt my child. That I'm not crazy."

"Why would I think you crazy? Because I met you dressed like a man?"

I closed my eyes, held my breath, then decided to blurt out the horrible truth. "Because Markham locked me away in Bedlam so that I'd never have custody of Lionel. Do you know what it's like to be put away from society like you have no purpose and ripped away from the only thing that matters?"

He flinched, but not from pain. Something else.

If it was pity, I wanted none of it. I only wanted Lionel.

"R-Repington," I said in a tone that didn't demur, *r*'s rolling. I needed him to know I was his equal. "Do you understand why I had to deceive you? I'd risk everything to be back in Hamlin caring for my son."

"Why tell me now? You're good at your deceptions. You could have kept at it."

I brushed at my loosed hair and stared into his eyes. They were cloudy like blue bottle glass. "Because I'm tired of deceiving you. Because I think if I haven't proven to you that I can be trusted I never will. Because you love Lionel as I do."

His face hardened, muscles tensing.

I was dizzy and tired of standing, but sitting next to him didn't seem right.

"You are here for custody? Do you mind if I have these documents authenticated? I fought too hard to assure the boy's safety to be easy with it now. Did Lady Shrewsbury know of this ruse? Who is St. Maur? The countess's sister?"

The Widow's Grace could not be unmasked. "I take responsibility for my actions. Jemina's no relation to the countess. She's an honorable widow, like me until Markham forced my hand."

"Lionel is not going anywhere, and I need to determine what to believe."

"This will now work to your favor. When Wellington recalls you, you'll know Lionel is safe with his mother."

"No one has made a decision on anything. I have custody of Lionel. That hasn't changed."

I wanted to press him, but how could I, dropping this secret upon him. Though I felt free, he looked confused.

My heart stilled. I clasped my elbows. "I expect nothing less. You shall twist over every aspect until you've come to the right decision, the only one. You know what I'm saying is true."

He set the trust documents down and rubbed his chin, the light stubble that had tickled my cheek.

"If this is the truth, you've deceived me twice. How long were you going to keep up this charade?"

"As long as I could stand you ordering me around and telling me how to care for my own flesh and blood. I needed to prove I'm no danger."

"Well, you're dangerous, but not to Lionel."

I didn't understand why he had a distinction, but I wouldn't argue with him.

"And Lionel's part my flesh and blood, too, via Colin. And I haven't done so badly."

Emboldened, I dared to touch him again and smoothed his lapel. "You have done wonderfully. If Colin were here and thinking clearly, I think he'd be proud of how good you've been to his son. I am."

"He wouldn't be proud of you kissing me or me returning the favor." He stared into my eyes. "Are you sure you're not in love with me, even a little?"

"No more than you love me, R-Repington. Everyone knows that's not possible. You don't believe in such sentiment."

The duke's smile returned, one that made his countenance seem more at ease, more kissable. Then it disappeared. "What's not possible? For me to love or for me to love you?"

"Does it matter? We have a common problem. Lionel's custody."

"Lionel's no problem. We'll figure this out. Colin made me that little boy's guardian. I'll not be remiss of my duty."

"That duty has to be his safety. Colin and Markham owed a lot of money. I suspect Markham is still lurking, hoping to gain custody. My father structured a payment via my marital contract, one that will pass to my son's guardian. Markham could be trying to harm you."

"What are you talking about?"

"How do things go missing? How does a two-hundred-year-old chandelier suddenly fall? I suspect he's getting in the house, causing mischief."

"The chandelier was old. Things break."

"Perhaps, but Markham's still in the village. My father's payment is four thousand pounds. It's to be paid next month when Lionel turns four months. Quite the incentive."

"Well, that will buy a new chandelier."

"Repington, you're at risk. If you are incapacitated, Markham becomes my son's guardian. He gets the money and who knows what will happen to Lionel or myself."

He leaned closer, tugging me to his chest. "Whether I believe you or not, you should know I'd never let anything happen to you or that baby."

"But the chandelier still fell. You should put Lionel and me on a boat to Demerara. Then everyone's safe."

"No. No one's leaving Hamlin. You'll not run from battle, soldier."

I smiled inside. In spite of all my deceptions, the duke believed me. "Then I must find proof of Markham's duplicity to prove that you and Lionel are in danger."

"No, LaCroy—Jordan—woman. That man is dangerous. He's already hurt you."

Those eyes of Repington penetrated my chest and spotted my softening spine. I was weak for the duke, but wasn't he like Colin, who wanted me to obey orders, to live and do as he said? How long before he tired of my spirit . . . or my bed?

I wouldn't be compliant.

I hadn't risked all to surrender to fleeting feelings. Love didn't last.

Backing away, I decided to be a picture of a woman who cared for nothing. I trailed my pinkie on his nose. "I'm not going to follow that order, Commander. As long as you take care and protect Lionel, I can do what needs to be done. Markham thinks I'm locked away in Bedlam, so I'm safe. I can work discreetly on determining his guilt."

"His guilt? What are you thinking he's done?"

I wasn't ready to say that Markham was more responsible

for Colin's death than my letter. "I'm not sure, but I will find out."

"Patience, you will defy a direct order?"

Glancing at this man, with honor glimmering in his eyes, I nodded. "My son and you are in danger. Markham is our enemy. Colin didn't turn to me, not when he needed help. And I could've saved him. He didn't think I'd pick up his sword and fight for him. I'll defend his memory to Lionel by proving Markham's guilt."

The duke frowned, sort of like my baby before a burp. "It's too risky, and none of this brings Colin back."

"It will change what I tell Lionel. I can do this, unless you intend to toss me out."

"If I did, you'd sneak back in dressed as a man. I told you I liked you better this way, even better in soft muslin." He pressed his lips together for a second, then cleared his throat. "I still have to verify things, but I don't toss out women. They usually leave me."

I turned, but he reached out and clasped my hand, spinning me to him.

"Repington, I'm ready to withdraw."

He was silent, staring, but lightly holding me in place. I could slip his grasp if I wanted.

I didn't want to.

"You've explained a great deal except why you kissed me. Why, Patience LaCroy—or Patience Jordan, or whoever you are?"

With my fingertips, I combed a lock of his hair that had dropped onto his furrowed brow. The motion made him blonder, more godlike. Definitely one of those archangel types in regal burgundy.

"Why a kiss, Patience? Do you have feelings for me? Why risk anything for me?"

His tone riveted through me, trying to awaken a heart that had been put to sleep with my unhappy marriage. Playfully, I tugged at Repington's lapels again. "You were blathering, and I didn't think you'd let me kiss you after I confessed to another masquerade under your nose."

"You could've just covered my mouth like Lionel does. You do love me, don't you?"

"*Non*."

"But you do like me?" His sigh, his rum-anointed breath smelled good, as his whisper fell upon my nose, my mouth. "Don't you?"

If he felt my pulse racing, he'd know how I felt. If I hadn't had my heart broken by the same kind of man, one who could only love me if I complied, I'd be fool enough to fall for Repington.

"Outside this room, Your Grace, we should keep up the pretense. Me being the nanny, you the crazed field commander."

"Crazed? Who's been to Bedlam? And it's not crazy to demand order. I'm not sure if I like this arrangement. I don't like falsehoods or pretending."

"Would you rather it be known that the commander was deceived?" Very lightly, I put my hand on his thigh. I was careful with my touch, light and honoring what I knew of him. "I think you care what people think."

The duke picked up my hand and clutched it to his chest. "Thoughts are meaningless. How one is treated is all that matters. I like you, Patience. You don't treat me like an invalid. Don't start now. And you're mistaken if you think you have the upper hand."

"Well, you have that hand now."

He released me and fumbled with the belt of his robe. "I don't have to go along with anything. Is my old friend the countess in on this, too?"

"I'm a widow. Lady Shrewsbury has a heart for widows. She'll help any woman in trouble, no questions asked. My circumstances are dire. I'm at your mercy as much as I was under Markham. Male guardians have all the power on these shores."

"There's much to consider. But as I said, I'll not toss you out. And I certainly won't if these trust documents prove authentic. Besides, Lionel hates pap milk. He's a taste for the good stuff. I don't blame him."

His joke—was it a failed attempt to cover the longing in his voice?

I took a long breath savoring the scent of him, rum, sandalwood, masculinity. "You know that Markham is the threat, not me?"

"Perhaps. But your pretty lips have lied to me twice."

"I did what I had to do for Lionel."

"And kissing me, was that for the boy, too?"

"Repington, some burdens are easier to bear than others."

"Seems to me you haven't been burdened enough. By Jove, your lips haven't been kissed, not often enough. How can you be Colin's widow? He was an amorous fellow."

The light banter betwixt us died as shame and hurt and all things unrequited welled in my windpipe. I moved from him. "Your god knows Colin wasn't himself, not in the end. You can stay in the master bedchamber, my old bedchamber, but I'm taking my Lionel next door to the adjoining bedroom."

He reached for his crutch like he planned to give chase. "I am sorry—"

"No. Stay. Read my trust documents, pray to your Jove, and come to the only conclusion. I am Patience Jordan."

"I'm not sure what I'd pray for in this moment other than there to be nothing but the naked truth between us. Nothing."

I didn't want to guess at his meaning, so I fled into the hall.

Looking up at the darkness of where the chandelier had been, I swam in my guilt, guilt for making eyes at my husband's cousin.

Colin couldn't be replaced so easily in my heart, my bed, my son's life. Could he?

"If you're here haunting, Colin, know I'm sorry. I won't let you down this time."

Carriage lanterns flashed outside.

Repington came from the drawing room and walked toward me. My documents stuck out of his robe pocket.

The doors of Hamlin opened. Lady Shrewsbury and her snowball Angora, Jemina, and the barrister came inside. They swept me up and ushered me to the stairs.

The duke was left standing in the hall, gaping at the invasion. I was glad he was down there and I was out of his reach.

CHAPTER 21

THE PROBLEM WITH CRAWLING

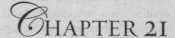

Busick's men marched back and forth over the fresh snow. No leading them on horseback today. The riding platform was slick, too slippery to risk climbing, especially with his back aching. He'd need to be careful or he'd end up flat in bed for weeks.

A groan stirred deep inside as he leaned against the platform. Busick wasn't the cautious sort, but what if the nanny was right? What if someone sabotaged the chandelier?

He pulled out his watch.

Five minutes to eleven.

Crawling practice with Lionel would begin on the hour. That is if what's-her-name complied.

Mutiny stirred in those lovely dark eyes, but would she lie about concerns for his safety?

He crossed the field and took his spot beside Gantry.

Puffing his chest, Busick readied to dismiss the men. "Take care on patrol. We are a smaller contingent force, so we must be more vigilant."

The snapping of palms of his men matched his salute and sounded crisp.

After the force dismissed, Gantry turned to him. "It's good that you are keeping things light today."

Suppressing a yawn, he checked his watch again. Ten to one. "Everyone was pushed very hard yesterday."

Gantry nodded. His eyes showed his now trademark weariness. "Lady Shrewsbury had to return with another doctor last night for Mrs. LaCroy. I hope all is well."

Busick didn't know. He didn't answer and paced to the balcony. He waited for Lady Shrewsbury and Mrs. St. Maur to tell him if Patience What's-her-name was well, but they'd taken her to the third floor. The nice-looking gentleman— the too-nice-looking man flashy in an emerald-green waistcoat—in consult with the women didn't bring him any comfort.

Jealousy was something he didn't think he was susceptible to. If someone were to be his, they would be. Still, Patience was vulnerable.

Gantry met him at the balcony. "You look pretty sour for a man who escaped death again."

"Sore. Not sour."

"Would this mood have anything to do with nanny problems?"

Busick stopped and planted his crutch with a thud. "Why would you say that?"

"No bread this morning. I hear a woman bakes when she is happy."

"Or when ordered to do so."

"But you'd never do that. And you haven't had to order her to do anything these weeks. When I passed her in the hall this morning, she didn't look happy, either."

"You saw her. She was up and about?"

"Yes. Moving quite slowly."

The low clouds didn't obscure his view of the vacant seats, the nannyless table. "I should cancel crawling practice today. She may be more hurt than she let on."

The viscount's face twisted. "Ummm. Crawling for a babe not yet four months old?" His friend steered in front of him and stopped at the base of the stairs. "Never mind about that. Tell me, what has occurred between you and the nanny?"

"There's nothing."

"Look at me, Repington. We've been friends for years. Your leg is amputated, and you never say a word. Don't you trust me?"

"I trust you, Gantry, with my life. But you know how I am. I don't want a fuss to be made."

Tugging on his ribbon-tied hair as if he'd rip out a clump, the viscount moaned. "Then I won't even ask why you're back to the bandaged limb."

"My leg is sore. The mechanical contraption is heavy. The straps chafe. It clacks when I walk. Falling with it wasn't the best for my leg or my back."

"Use your design mind and create a new one. Or get your nanny to whip you up something soothing. I hear she solved your Lionel's red bottom issues with her coconut mash."

Was Lionel still Busick's?

"Duke, tell me."

"The nanny. She says she's my cousin's wife, Lionel's mother. I think that part is true, but I don't know. How do I trust her when she deceived me?"

"Um . . . She nearly killed herself saving you from a falling chandelier. What type of sign are you looking for?" Gantry folded his arms and tapped his nose in a knowing fashion. "You're brooding. And irritable. Yesterday, you were as nervous as a true mother hen over this woman. Is this agitation about her hiding her identity or something else? Did you get rebuffed by the nanny? Did she send you to bed without dessert?"

"First, I always get dessert. That usually eases my troubles, but I may have been a little insensitive to her . . . about the deception."

Brow cocked, Gantry stared at him.

"Well, maybe I was a lot insensitive about a lot of things, but she misled me."

"Women have their reasons. I think we might have to be more open to listening."

"Oh, this marital difficulty is working you. Buck up, man. We have to have principles."

"Yes. Principles. Yours and mine, have done us quite well. I'm wifeless and you're irritable with no bread. We've been quite principled."

Busick wasn't alone. He was still Lionel's guardian, and for a good stretch, he had a woman who cared about him.

The faux nanny, more-than-likely wife to his late cousin, did push him out of the way of the chandelier's fall.

She did kiss him last night.

Kissed him like a suitor.

Then left him like a rake and went upstairs with a stranger.

"Duke, soldiers for hire don't quite make a family. But a woman of substance and a child I know you adore, that has the makings of a fine dessert.

"You sound like my mother. Always trying to arrange things to make up for her scandalous behavior. Lucky for me, her latest friend has kept her from darkening my doorstep."

Another glance at the empty balcony heated his gut. "You're missing the point. The nanny has lied to me twice. Would anyone respect me if I overlooked this?"

Gantry put a hand on Busick's shoulder. "You've earned your respect on the field and off by how you treat your men and your friends. You're your worst critic pushing yourself when you don't have to."

"That's the man I am. That's not changing."

"No one wants you to change, but I for one would like you happy. You're filling your world with the things you're used to—soldiers and drilling. What about things you've never had, like a woman who truly loves you?"

"Don't they all claim love until something doesn't go as

it should? What type of fool will I be if there's another deception she's hiding?"

"I'll do some inquiries for you. See what can be determined about Mrs. Jordan. Wouldn't your mother be able to identify your cousin's widow?"

"Perhaps, but then I'd have to see Lady Bodonel." Busick wanted none of her meddling or treating him as his invalid father. He pulled out his watch. "I'll invite my mother here along with your father. Won't we be an unhappy quartet?"

Gantry looked as if he'd bit into a sour lemon. "Your mother is nothing like my father. She's actually proud of you."

"When she has time or wants to impress a new friend. No, Gantry, you have an unwanted gift, a healthy father invested in your life. I want to be that for Lionel without all the manipulation. I will be a source of stability regardless of his mother."

"Well, your nanny has showed on the balcony. Go make nice. We want bread tomorrow."

Busick turned and spied Patience Maybe-Jordan carrying Lionel, cooing at him, like nothing had happened.

She and Mrs. St. Maur spread a blanket between the chairs, just like normal.

Gantry straightened Busick's jacket. "Well, Commander, go forth and conquer."

Busick picked up his pace, climbed the stone stairs, and gazed at the nanny. A gown of the deepest black swallowed her whole, hiding the figure that had been in his arms last night.

He started to pull out his watch but stopped. La . . . Jordan . . . Patience was on time. He moved to his chair, but the stare between them remained unbroken.

"I'm going to leave. Time to dust," Mrs. St. Maur said, then scurried back into the house.

Patience sank onto the blanket six feet away. She whispered something, then put the baby on the fuzzy wool.

Her mouth opened, but her typical complaint about

Lionel being too young to crawl never came. She looked at Busick coolly. "Go, Lionel. Go to the commander."

The boy lifted his head, big and wobbly, and burped. Wait. Was that a smile for Busick?

He slapped his thigh. "Come to me, son. You can do it. I believe in you. You're capable."

The baby tipped over onto his back, then rolled onto his stomach.

That was new.

Patience offered a bit of a smile, her eyes getting big. Pride in her son? Maybe a little approval for the duke as well. His trials were working.

"Your Grace, Mrs. St. Maur and I will be heading out this evening."

What?

And that didn't sound like a request.

Dragging his chair onto the blanket until he was next to Lionel, he scooped the boy up. "I said you didn't have to leave. Lionel is not going anywhere."

Her lids closed. "I hadn't intended to take him with me. This time."

"When and for how long?"

"It should take no longer than a day."

"You will be coming home as soon as this errand is done?"

Her lips trembled. "I'll return to Hamlin, but home for me is Demerara. If you don't think you can handle taking care of Lionel for such a long time, I'll . . . I'll ask Lady Shrewsbury to send a new widow."

"No more women in this house. The current widows she's sent have upended things. I can handle Lionel."

"I know you're quite capable. I couldn't do this, couldn't be away if I didn't know how you loved my son."

But she was still leaving. "May I ask where you're off to?"

"You may, but nothing requires me to answer. I'm just informing you of my decision."

"I don't like not having a say."

"Duke, you're not my father or my husband or my employer. So, no say."

"I liked you better as LaCroy, at least you listened to me."

"As LaCroy I'd have to sneak out. I don't want to do that. From now on, when I say something to you it has to be the truth."

"Well, that is a good development between us, you not deceiving me."

"No, I'll save that for others."

She smoothed her sleeves. A nervous response?

"I only did what I thought I had to, Repington. Know that keeping my identity hidden was one of the hardest things I've done."

"You have to go, today?"

"The thought of leaving Lionel for a moment breaks me up inside. But you are a capable guardian. He's safe in your hands. You must keep him safe."

"I have guards again on the catacombs, if that will make you feel better." He adjusted Lionel's clean pinafore. "You will be back?"

"Of course."

She smiled at him, definitely *at* Busick. The first since their argument.

He rather liked her smiling at him. "I must insist that you tell me where you are going. What if something goes wrong for you? How will I come for you?"

She stood up with a palm shadowing her face. "There's too much light. The way the sun reflects off the snow hurts my eyes. May I be excused?"

The woman did look uncomfortable.

Busick handed her the wiggling boy. "Let's return to the house."

He stood and held his free arm out to her.

She didn't take it, but neither did she retreat.

They were in the house where less than a day ago everything turned topsy-turvy. "It's safe here. Stay. Don't leave Hamlin."

She adjusted a blanket about Lionel. The boy looked so content in her arms. The flare of his nostrils—was that Patience's nose?

"I wouldn't leave Lionel if this was not important."

"I'll not stop you, but you should tell me what you are doing, Cousin."

"You believe me?"

"Mostly. And mostly, I want you safe. Here under my protective arms."

Another brief smile set on her lips. The lines of her neck tensed less. "You don't have to be concerned. Lady Shrewsbury's nephew, the man from last night, he will be going with me and Mrs. St. Maur. He'll make sure we have safe travels. Your arms will have to find another occupation."

"You trust a man you met last night?"

"He's the barrister who rescued me from Bedlam and led me to Lady Shrewsbury. Yes, I trust him."

"He's sort of your hero. Any chances of you being taken in by that hero business?"

"No more than you. If you will excuse me."

She took Lionel up the stairs and he watched her form glide up, tread by tread, step by step.

The thought of Patience being out of arms' reach and leaving Hamlin wasn't good.

Busick wasn't about to allow Patience to be in danger.

A practiced strategist would cede a battle but not the war. He'd agree to allow her to leave, but she wasn't the only one who could employ secretive tactics.

CHAPTER 22

WATCHING AND WAITING

I sat next to Jemina in Daniel Thackery's carriage, an elegant conveyance of polished ebony exterior with brass side lanterns and four riders atop. I'd ridden in it before, wearing rags, with Jemina glued to my side, like now.

Today, at least, she looked good, a nice clean dress of light gray. She held my gloved hands. "It will be well."

Thackery shook his head, maybe even rolled his eyes.

Lady Shrewsbury's nephew was a nice-looking man bearing the tanned skin of a Corinthian. He'd freed us from Bedlam, and I was grateful for his efforts shepherding us to Town, so I'd forgive his staring at Jemina and me as if we were witless.

I released my friend's hands and clutched my knees. "Out with it, sir."

Thumbing his waistcoat buttons, he slouched on the seat, his coal-black eyes lifting. "I do many things for my aunt. She's the dearest—but traipsing about London with a woman dressed as a man is lunacy. We should turn back."

Jemina waggled her finger at him. "It will work. Mrs.

Jordan has been playing a man for a month. She does it quite well."

He leaned forward, caught her finger, and lowered it. "Spirited little creature, aren't you? Don't take this the wrong way, but didn't I collect you two from Bedlam? All three of us should be headed there now."

I glared at him as if I were the duke, tough and assured. "I can do this. And this is your fault."

"Mine? Hardly, madam . . . sir . . . Hmmm."

"You saunter into Hamlin and tell us that A. Sullivan, the man who canceled over two thousand pounds of my husband's debt, could be the name of an inspector working at a gaming hell. Today, you say it could be a reverend who gambled with Jordan."

"My apologies. I don't saunter. My stride has been said to be confident. I don't spend time gambling, so I have no way of knowing who A. Sullivan is."

"I do. That's why I'm in this getup." I tugged on my jet waistcoat with silver stripes. "If the man I saw arguing with my late husband is the Sullivan the inspector and not the fallen priest—"

"Minister, ma'am. Though gambling during the week and proffering Communion on Sunday isn't quite a paragon of virtue."

"Well, if it's the inspector, then we know this diary holds entries of a conspiracy. We know that Markham wants this back. This is why he wants me gone. I can identify Sullivan. I'm a witness to the conspiracy."

The barrister's expression sharpened. "If this Sullivan is the inspector, the man responsible for collecting and settling credit at Piccadilly's gaming hell, this book denotes a treacherous conspiracy. It still doesn't prove the other two things."

"It's a start to answering questions."

He folded his arms and leaned his head back. "I'm hoping for the gospel of the dice. Then there will be no encumbrances on Hamlin, and your son's legacy will be clear."

That was a good possibility, but not the reason I donned menswear. I was desperate. This Sullivan caused my husband's suicide. Not my note to Collin, not my failure at being an understanding wife or turning the other cheek.

I tugged on my crisp white cravat, then slipped my perspiring hands again to my pantaloons. "If he'd borrowed money or won from this minister, wouldn't that be in the diary, too? Like my dear friend, my husband was precise about numbers."

"His records are detailed, but are they complete? Is anything missing?"

My letter was missing. I'd stashed it in a drawer in my room. I should've burned it. Set it to flames.

That would take away my frustrated words but not my pain.

"Mrs. Jordan, do you truly understand what this means if Sullivan is an inspector?"

Jemina flipped through the diary again. "Extortion. No one would cancel IOUs because of choice words."

"Does that matter, Mr. Thackery?"

"It could mean your husband's death was no suicide."

Jemina looked at me and I at her. I hoped she couldn't read my thoughts. It couldn't be murder. I saw the note he'd left, accusing me of making him so depressed that he wanted to die. Colin was steeped in anguish. His careful script was broken, even sloppy, so not like him. I burned his note. I had to.

"Ladies, well, Lady and LaCroy. You have to ask yourself, why would a man with canceled debts kill himself? One who would be getting a small fortune of a marriage settlement in a couple of months? You had written him again that you'd borne a son?"

"Yes. I kept writing him. Then I wanted him to come see our son, right away. The next I know Markham appears telling me Colin's dead." That suicide note and Markham's hideous smile as I sobbed—I'll never forget either. Never.

Thackery rubbed his hands together. "Delightful. My

apologies, but I haven't tried a capital case in a year. I'll have to convince the Lord Mayor for the assignment."

The smart barrister looked gleeful, and my innards twisted. "My husband was depressed. He suffered moods."

"True. When a person decides he's done, it's hard to stop him, but I'm inclined to think that whatever caused an inspector to cheat his gaming hell might lead him to rid himself of the problem, permanently."

I rubbed at the pain in my neck. My headache returned. "Now you have me rooting for the minister."

Jemina nudged my shoulder, then settled in with her embroidery. "Don't let Mr. Thackery's bluster make you lose heart. You identify Sullivan, and we'll be off to Hamlin and Lionel to determine the next steps."

My babe.

I missed Lionel, but my boy needed the truth, and I hoped the truth was that Markham was at fault. If it was mine, then I'd own it and work every day to make it up to my son.

But I had to know.

I took comfort that my boy was with Repington. I knew he'd be safe. Repington would never let anything happen to Lionel, even if his mother courted danger.

Thackery adjusted his brass spectacles, then set down the diary, stashing it on his seat. "Mrs. St. Maur? You don't seem very quiet, very different from when we first met."

"Chains at Bedlam will steal your tongue."

He tweaked his lenses. "Or perhaps it's been liberated with all the sneaking and danger of the Widow's Grace business. Do you approve of this adventure?"

"I approve of Patience. If this is the lengths we must go to discover the missing parts of her husband's life, then I'm for it. A woman needs to know what she needs to know."

"'Tis true. My compliments to your sewing. You butchered my waistcoat and breeches quite nicely for Jordan here. I know where to come if I'm ever in dire straits and my tailor is busy."

My friend raised her needle, then lowered it as if she

thought better of the action. "Since waiting on your lawyering and the Widow's Grace has proved slow, we are called to act."

Jemina's tone sounded sharp, and I had the feeling that she'd tired of waiting, of hoping for someone to arrive with the information needed to save her.

I clasped her pinkie in solidarity. I would help her even if it meant delaying our trip to Demerara.

Staying wouldn't be so bad, giving Lionel a little more time with the duke. It would be dreadful if my baby couldn't have some part of the honorable man.

The duke might be crazed with his drills, but I felt safe with him. He might not believe that someone could get in the house, but he added patrols to the catacombs. I saw them as we left.

Was this an indication that we could work together for Lionel's benefit?

The lights of the near village dimmed. It would be an hour or more before we reached London. My palms were dripping wet.

"Justice is slow sometimes, Mrs. St. Maur, but I don't see you traipsing about in refined menswear. You don't have the height for it?"

"Silly goose." She started her needlepoint again, long scarlet stitches. "Too many of us could raise suspicions."

The man chuckled. "Yes. I don't want to raise suspicions, going to gaming hells with pretty men at my side."

"Men drinking or under the influence of the games won't be looking for anything but luck. I won't be discovered."

"You obviously haven't been a man long enough."

I didn't know what to do with Mr. Thackery. The only man I had to explain myself to was at Hamlin.

Fixing my powder wig, I closed my eyes and waited for the true games to begin. It wouldn't be long before I knew if Jove or Agassou smiled on me at last.

* * *

In the drawing room, Busick sat at his desk with Lionel on his lap. This dance of getting the teary-eyed child to drink the pap milk was getting old. Patience should be here giving the boy what he wants.

Trying again, he tipped the pap boat to the babe's mouth.

Lionel sucked down a little, then stuck his pink tongue out as if Busick had given him sour milk.

He sniffed the beverage in the pap dish, a long-necked vessel stretched like a gravy boat. It didn't smell bad, but when did floury cow's milk have an inviting scent?

"Come on, young man, you need to eat. Then you'll grow up big and strong."

"Duke." Gantry paced from the pianoforte to the mirror and back. "Didn't you have a woman employed for this?"

He did the trip again, back and forth, with a letter in his clenched fist. "I'm sure you had a woman for this."

"No need for jests. She had an errand."

"Both of them, Duke?"

"Someone had to go with her. Mrs. LaCroy Jordan couldn't leave Hamlin by herself."

"She's a widow, not a single maiden. She can go places respectably by herself."

Busick hadn't thought of that.

The woman wasn't forthcoming, and he didn't want to show how concerned he was. Maybe he should've.

The major he sent to scout the countess's leased house knocked at the open door.

With Lionel still sticking his tongue out, Busick didn't stand and unsettle the boy more. "Come in."

"Mrs. LaCroy remains inside with Lady Shrewsbury. But Mrs. St. Maur, she left with the barrister and an unidentified man about a half an hour ago."

"Mrs. St. Maur? Do you have an idea where?"

The fellow had a bubbly look on his face. "To a gaming hell, Your Grace."

"To gamble? I didn't think that one had it in her. Good work, Major. Do you have someone watching the house?"

"Yes, my replacement showed." The man pumped his fingers as if his arm was bothering him.

"You've done enough for today. You're off duty."

The man saluted, turned on his heel, and left.

Gantry poured a glass of brandy. He lifted the glass bottle high as if to make a show of the amber liquid, but merely sipped at it. "You let Mrs. La . . . Jordan, Mrs. Jordan go on her errand but are having her watched. Hmmm. Hypocrite."

"How is that wrong? If she's right that Markham is a threat, then she'll benefit from my protection."

Feeling quite satisfied with himself and his planning, he hummed and rocked until Lionel went to sleep. Busick was in a much better mood. His nanny didn't go off debauching.

"Don't you think it's a bit wrong, that you and I are here watching your baby and the women who should be caring for this infant are gone, one even to a gaming hell?"

"Gantry," he said in a whisper. "Could you get the basket?"

"Basket? The bread basket on the sofa?"

"Yes. Mrs. Jordan didn't bake any today. Put the blue blanket in there and we'll have sort of a Moses basket."

With a shrug, the viscount brought the basket and set it near the desk. "Just don't test this in a tub of water or a moat. It's not going to end well, Pharaoh."

"I'm not putting this boy at risk, but the handle is something I can grasp and still maneuver with my crutch."

His friend returned to the sideboard and scooped up his glass. "You seem awfully upbeat. Your nanny's not here. The other woman is headed to corruption."

Maybe he meant to empty the brandy this time, even smack it to his lips, but when Gantry was wound up, wound up tighter than a watch spring, it took him forever to finish anything. "Why again are we here watching a baby and not out gallivanting like your subordinates?"

"Well, for one, you are still married."

"Lady Gantry left me, remember? I'm as free as I wish."

"Nonetheless, I need to be here when my nanny comes home. She's obviously in some sort of pique. I think she pretended to be away to prove a point."

He settled the snoring Lionel into the reed basket and covered him with a blanket. "A pique, a point. Women and games. What's a gentleman to do?"

With a roll of his eyes and a hard shake of his head, Gantry began pacing again, back and forth across the room.

Why was he struggling?

His friend wasn't trying to get Lionel to eat or struggling to determine the best course of action with Patience. That m-word, *marriage*, had started to rear its ugly head. It was a proper, convenient arrangement to share custody of Lionel for two people who needed to be in close quarters, in each other's faces, every day to raise this baby.

Busick wanted to punch the desk leg, right on the curlicue scripted *J* for *Jordan*, and then his own *B.S.*

Colin had been dead a few months, not the respectable eighteen months society wanted before anyone should become attached to the man's widow. Well, he didn't know LaCroy to be her when he became attached, but so was his luck with women.

His friend paced faster, the poor wound up clock.

Was he doing this for Busick's sake?

"Spit out what has you so uneasy. My bread basket is full of a sleeping soldier, but my ears are open."

"Six weeks, Repington. A full six weeks since anyone has seen Lady Gantry."

"Yesterday was five weeks and six days of her being missing. Why is this evening different?"

Waving the letter, he started moving again. "My sister says she sent her a birthday present and gifts for the girls."

"Nothing for you? I didn't know you were the sentimental type."

"I don't want a present." He stopped, dropped his head, clasping his neck with a loud slap. "I want her."

"Then, what's keeping you from finding her? If you are staying because of me . . . Don't. I have things well at hand. Aren't we good, Lionel?"

The baby snored, but pap milk was on his green pinafore as well as Busick's cravat. He'd awaken soon, looking for the good stuff. "Bear with me, son, your nanny will be back soon. Or maybe we should go get her."

"Son? You are in the family way, Duke. Has the bachelor father thought of his plans for the mother?"

"No. I still need to . . . verify—"

"You don't need to verify anything. Your mother would know her. She'd make a point to see the woman at least once just to savor the gossip of Jordan's foreign wife."

His voice broke a little.

Then, Gantry returned to the sideboard and finished his half-finished drink. "In your gut, you know Mrs. LaCroy is Lionel's mother. What are you going to do?"

"Nothing. Not until she's back at Hamlin."

"And that's why we are the best of friends, so stupidly similar. I've tried doing nothing these past weeks. I'm out of my mind, wondering where my wife is or if the fool woman is intending to leave."

"I thought she already left you."

"No, you daft, Duke. Leave England. Return to Demerara."

"Well, if you are done with her and she wants to go, let her. You can't keep someone who wants to leave."

"And you can't sit around testing them to see if they will stay. You care for Jordan's widow, but you goad her just to test her character. You should know her by now."

Was that what he was doing? Testing her dedication to Lionel and to himself?

"Duke, this woman has Wellington's great general on nursing duty while she's free to do whatever."

"She didn't go with the barrister and Mrs. St. Maur; she stayed with the countess."

"Well, St. Maur will be back soon from her adventure."

"Why?"

"As soon as she learns gaming hells only allow men, she'll see her mistake."

"Only men can go into a gaming hell?"

"Yes, only men. You know this. We've been to a few."

"No, not for a long time. All men?" Busick rubbed his chin. "Lieutenant, repeat the field report from the major."

"Why?"

"Just repeat it, man."

"Mrs. St. Maur left with the barrister and an unidentified man about a half an hour ago. To go to a gaming hell."

Busick jerked up, his back twinging from the motion. "Gaming hells only admit men or those they *presume* are men."

"Duke, you think the nanny is impersonating a man again?"

Patience had a notion in her head, and the fool woman would see it through. "Send for Shrewsbury. She is the key to everything. She may even know where to find Lady Gantry in Town. She'll definitely know where to find my gambling nanny."

Gantry wiped through his hair. He looked poised to run. "I'll go get the countess myself."

"Tell her that I need her for Lionel. That will hurry her."

His friend left at a glorious speed, and Busick looked down at his ward.

Sometimes, mothers don't come back. The wanderlust in them needed to be released. But some needed to be chased after and given reasons to return. Busick didn't know which camp Patience belonged, but she'd know his opinion on the matter posthaste.

CHAPTER 23

GAMBLING STAKES

The stench from the gaming hell had to be in my clothes, my hair, even my skin at this point. The cigar smoke was thick, as thick as the cursing, the spilled liquor, and my disappointment. I brushed at my emerald-green tailcoat hoping to clear away the last hour.

"Patience." Jemina asked as I climbed into the carriage, "Did you find Sullivan?"

"Yes," I said, only the one word, for I had nothing else to offer. Hearing my husband's character run down as Markham's pigeon stole everything—words, sentences, reason.

"Patience, I don't understand. You look ill."

"Things became a little unsavory." Mr. Thackery dumped his top hat on the seat. "I think we've done enough tonight. If we leave now I can make my standing appointment."

Jemina and I both must have shot him shocked looks.

He held up his hands. "Fable reading to my daughter before bed. Nothing sinister, but I am a widower, a bachelor for what it's worth."

I hated that, to deprive a child of her father, but we were

so close to the truth. "Please. We can't be done." I folded my arms about me. I was shaking, shaking hard. "This man we just met wasn't the Sullivan I saw arguing with Colin, nor did he relieve any debts. He can't be a reverend. He was foul. His cigar, his clothes, his mouth—all foul."

"Sorry, Mrs. Jordan. But we did learn some things. Your husband was known to gamble."

That was a nice way to put it. Hearing this Sullivan laugh at how Markham used Colin—taking his money, soiling his good name—I was disgusted.

Mr. Thackery patted his rumbling stomach. "I suggest I take you both back to my aunt's."

The barrister seemed quite calm and even debonair as he took the drunken Sullivan's foul comments on Thackery being a half-breed. The dear man did not strike out as I wanted.

I seethed for him. "We've not found *my* A. Sullivan."

"Yes, but we haven't been caught, either. My reputation is spotless. I'm not in the mood to tempt fate again. There's only so much hatred one can take in an evening before something unfortunate happens."

I saw fury swirling in Thackery's eyes and understood. This wasn't retreat but self-preservation. I wondered how much abuse he had to ignore to maintain his position. Colin had been right about Town. At least on this, he'd tried to protect me.

Jemina balled her fists. "No, Mr. Thackery. No, Patience. We've come all this way; we have to see this through. We need answers. Let's go to Piccadilly."

The duke would see things through. He didn't wage half battles or come at things unprepared. "Jemina is right. We made it out of here without harming your reputation. Can't we try the next gaming hell?"

Thackery sighed, a desperate throaty noise. "My reputation is important. I don't have the luxury of my colleagues to fail. Ladies, my walk has a delicate balance."

I stared at him but couldn't fathom why a man, even one of mixed raced, would ever have to be so careful. Men had all the advantages.

When he pulled out his pocket watch I thought about Lionel and Repington. Since working at Hamlin, this was the longest I'd been away from my son. I tired of disguises. I'd done enough hiding with Colin.

"Patience, you've heard the barrister. You've heard my opinion. What do you think? Is this masquerade done?"

I put my hand in my pocket and grasped my father's knife. Trailing my thumb over the jewels, I felt my courage rallying. "We must continue. If the inspector at Piccadilly isn't my A. Sullivan, then we need to start over. I'd rather know that now."

Thackery held up his hand. "Will it give you peace to know your husband was an extortioner? Some women would prefer their men to be decent."

I picked up the diary from Jemina's fingers. "If this is indeed a record of extortion, then I know Markham was involved. You heard the drunken minister's sermon. Markham's the controlling one."

"Or this gambit could prove nothing. There's that possibility."

I picked at the buttons of my waistcoat, so pretty the clinking sound of the brass. Pretty wasn't a shield. Truth was. "I need to know that I tried everything. Let's go to the gaming hell in Piccadilly."

Thackery straightened his stylish waistcoat of bright blue, then knocked on the roof of his carriage. "I figured you would say that. At least Piccadilly has decent food. You up to pretending to be a man one more time?"

"Yes, Mr. Thackery. I am."

I'd been able to work the room at this hell, observing everyone without being seen. This was a practiced gift Colin had given me. It saddened me that I'd learned the lesson so well.

* * *

A half hour of my stewing passed as the barrister's carriage rumbled along the street. Through the window, I saw the scattered stars. My thoughts mirrored the jumbled sky.

Colin, Markham's dupe—how much did my husband suffer?

How could I have made things better?

Now the harsh words I'd overheard between them made more sense. Colin was agitated at Markham, but the fiend had such a hold on him.

The carriage stopped. A footman opened the door to an elegant neighborhood, very different from the shadowy one we'd left. "Piccadilly?"

"Yes. We're not far from the famed White's gentlemen's club."

Thackery rolled his top hat in his palms. "It's quite brilliant to place an elite gaming hell so close to where titled pigeons can fly in, perch, and lose their inheritances. My father visited quite often." His laugh sounded scornful. He scooted closer to the door. "Ready, Jordan?"

"It's LaCroy. Always when I pretend, LaCroy."

"It's best," Jemina said. "The last thing we need is for gamblers to decide you need to pay his debts."

Thackery popped on his hat. "Mrs. St. Maur, you continue to amaze me. The way your mind works, adding up numbers and loose ends. You're right."

His full lips drooped into a frown. "This may take a little longer than the last. Will you take care?"

Jemina's brow scrunched as she threaded her needle. "Why longer? Is there a bigger wait to get in? A secret handshake you have to teach Patience?"

"No, I've heard their beefsteak is superb. If you two have me dragging about at this late hour, I will be fed. Shall I bring you something back? A treat perhaps."

"No favors for me." She handed me my hat. "Take care of LaCroy."

She grabbed my hand. "You'll have luck at this one. We'll know the truth."

I hoped she was right and feared that she was, too.

With a nod, I followed the barrister out of his carriage and up the steps of Piccadilly.

We checked our hats, but I kept my dinner gloves and shoved my hands behind my back.

Brutish walk in motion, stone face in place, I followed behind Thackery.

"By Jove."

I'd said that aloud, but at least it was the right god, the English one, to express my wonderment.

Mesmerizing. This was no hell, nothing like the last. It was a clean, orderly place. Exquisite furniture with klismos and Egyptian-styled chairs.

Footmen in silver liveries stood along the walls. Had I been in my servant's disguise I would've stood out as too simple and plain.

My pulse swooshed in my ears. It was louder than the yells of the man waving his cards boasting of his stakes as he stood at a crowded table. A collective shout of yeah came from men at a long green stand as they watched a fellow rolling dice.

"Yes, LaCroy. The same cribbage cards and hazard tosses you saw at the last establishment are played here. It amuses me how vice can look different with better lighting. Shall we?"

"Yes, Mrs. St. Maur notices the same about light."

My heart went to Hamlin, missing its lights—my Lionel and my duke, who were the same, morning, noon, and night.

Part of me, that woman with the easily broken heart, missed being at Repington's side, him barking out commands while sheltering me from his perceived harms.

"Do keep up, LaCroy."

Thackery looked cross, but then he sort of smiled as he rubbed his pocket watch. He seemed uncomfortable, as if we were still in the dingy gaming hell.

He coughed. "All is well, my friend. Circulate."

Circulate? He had to be kidding. I followed close behind the barrister like a puppy, not breaking stride, not slowing until we stood under the grand chandelier.

Shiny clear crystals twinkled above. They grabbed the light of the sconces and scattered it about the room. Pretty and serene, like my old chandelier. I missed it. I missed Hamlin. I was ready to go, ready to make peace with the duke and trust we could work together for Lionel's benefit.

Thackery circled back and knocked my shoulder. "Sir, you need to keep moving if you are going to enjoy all that the club has to offer."

I nodded and moved in the direction he pointed, a long bar. "The waiter is pouring drinks. You could use one."

The man filling goblets wore a dark livery with a starched cravat.

So similar to the duke. I could smell Repington's starch, his rum.

This cosmetic must be burning me up, making me emotional, making me think such odd things.

With a shake of my head, I cleared away these girly feelings and repeated manly things—gambling, excess, boots, polished and glossed black.

Then I heard a voice that cut up my insides.

Markham.

The blackguard was here.

Over my shoulder, I saw that high, pinched nose lifting in the air.

The knife in my pocket called to me. I hated him enough. From what was said at the last gaming hell, I knew he'd taken advantage of Colin as much as he had me.

Hand on the bulge in my pocket, I turned.

At the door, the fiend stood. The above-it-all sneer on his horrible pale face once drove fear into my heart. Not now, not with my baby safe with Repington.

Something caught my arm. The jerking almost flipped the knife from my fingers.

Thackery handed me a glass of wine. "I may have forgotten to mention Mr. Markham frequents this establishment. Take a sip and go to the bar."

"He's responsible for all that has happened. All that has gone wrong."

"Yes, but you are responsible for your future. Turn around. Let the anger pass. Let clear thoughts prevail."

That was the opposite of everything I wanted, but I forced my feet to move. I had to be smart, smarter than I had been before.

Swirling the crystal goblet, I watched the deep burgundy kiss the sides of the glass, then leave tinted legs, little rose breeches before dripping and settling.

As I put the wine to my lips, the hair on my arms and the braids under my wig stood on end.

Markham stood beside me at the bar.

Not spitting or cutting my eyes at him, I kept my head down, sipping slowly from my glass. If he saw my gaze, he'd know my face and the hate in me.

"LaCroy, there's Sullivan." The barrister pointed across the room. "I believe he's who you need to see to get credit. You lost enough at the last club."

Markham slammed down a coin. "Sullivan's a little light tonight."

"I think my friend will take his chances. He's very persuasive. Go, LaCroy."

I put down my nearly empty glass, but something inside said not to leave my drink near the worm, Colin's uncle, so I handed it back to the waiter. Then I made my boots move.

"Wait," Markham said.

My heart thundered.

My breath stuck in my throat. Fingers again curled about my knife, I looked over my shoulder, daring him to acknowledge me. "Yes."

"Let me know if he does lend money. Good to know he's still in the business for others."

My head nodded, and I started away.

It was better that the fool didn't recognize me. That's what I told myself, but I clutched the knife in my pocket, wondering if I was finally ready to strike.

Standing a few feet away from the man I'd hoped was Sullivan, I saw that meeting unfold in my head.

Shouting, long and angry. I came waddling down the stairs, away from the marble gods sweeping under the shadow of the chandelier. I posted outside the drawing room and heard the boasts, the threats.

Fearing for Colin's life, I went inside.

The one called Sullivan had his hands about Colin's neck.

The fiend had a mole on his nose, close-set eyes, veiny hands.

I squinted and blinked. This man in the corner with the mole, with those eyes was him. It was A. Sullivan.

The man stared back at me, and I panicked. I was sure my face was awash with perspiration.

"Sir," he said. "Are you looking for credit? Have you been sent to meet a man for credit?"

"Yes, Sullivan. An old friend, Jordan, said you were good for it."

My words were bold, and I hoped they wouldn't get me choked.

His veiny hands balled. "The welch is dead and with him my IOUs. Get new friends if you expect any money to be lent. Him and that slick Markham are not good references."

I put my damp palms to my sides. "You're angry, almost like they took your personal money. IOUs would be for the club, no?"

He lowered his voice. "Like I said—"

"LaCroy."

"Like I said, LaCroy, get new friends. The convenient death of the blackguard doesn't solve everything. Excuse me."

The man pushed past me and headed straight for Markham.

My voice died in my throat. If he told him I'd mentioned Colin, Markham would confront me. He'd recognize my face and expose me in this club.

Crossing my arms, I felt sticky. My nerves had done it. My milk would soak through the bandaging to my chest.

Tugging on my jacket, I wanted to leave, but my gaze was caught by the man entering the club.

The Duke of Repington had come to Piccadilly with my bread basket in his hands, one covered with a blanket that kicked as if it carried my son.

CHAPTER 24

LESSONS OF A RAKE

Busick glared at Patience.

No disguise could hide her from his anger.

He scooped up the handle of the bread basket with his sleeping ward and marched toward her.

She didn't retreat. She didn't hide.

He liked that she was bold.

Her daring nature was something he hoped Lionel inherited, but that he'd learn good sense from him.

Balancing with a cane in one hand, the basket in the other, he maneuvered in his boots to stand near her.

Powdered wig, face slathered in paint, she lowered her head to Lionel kicking at his blanket. She shook her head. "Repington?"

"Yes, LaCroy. I believe we've met."

"Yes."

He set the basket down and leaned over and adjusted her cravat. "Nice tailor, but your waistcoat is getting damp. Perhaps you should leave and get some fresh air."

"We should go."

"Not me. I'm here to gamble." He picked Lionel's basket up again. "Nice seeing you again, LaCroy."

That look—wide eyes, quivering cleft in her chin—touched his heart, softening the well-deserved ire built up every mile to London. It was a long trip with the countess and a babe who wouldn't drink his pap milk.

But Patience needed a lesson.

He stepped around her and went to the hazard table. The jade-colored baize table was crowded. Dice rolled down the length to jeers and cheers.

"You ready to roll, sir. The man just threw out with deuce aces."

The operator dropped the two white cubes into Busick's palm. He cast them down the table with just enough pressure to make the long distance.

It took two rolls, two adjustments to the force of his throw before the dice stopped on a nick of five. Gambling wasn't something he did, but he admired the strategy of the game and beating the odds.

He hit his streak, winning his shots, casting the dice and nailing his nicks—fives, sixes, and an occasional twelve.

Luck was on his side, and Lionel had fallen back to sleep, the gentle blue blanket shifting only a little.

The shadow of thinner legs fell on the basket and that sweet soapy smell came from behind.

"Your Grace, don't you think you've proven your point?"

He shook the die in his palms. "No points can be proven unless someone admits that flouting authority is wrong. Does one recognize the governance of a superior officer? His wisdom?"

"Duke," the operator said. "It's your roll. You're still winning."

"Yes. Yes, I am. LaCroy, why don't you go try another game? You like games."

Her penitent look turned petulant. "As you wish, Commander. But take care of the bread, Markham is here."

No sooner had she said those words than the devil appeared on his right.

Markham hissed and chuckled. "See? I knew you'd want to go on and enjoy living."

"Back away from my roll," Busick said, "I don't want your luck."

Patience slipped away, retreating to a safe distance beneath the chandelier.

He saw fear on her face. That wasn't the lesson he wanted for her.

Busick shook the dice. "You're still here, Markham. Do they know you're bankrupt?"

The man's pinched faced caved in better than what Busick's fist would do.

"Nothing is over, Duke. You haven't won. In fact, I hear you have one foot in the grave, or was it that you left one there?"

Busick tossed the dice and hit his mark. "I'm still in a better position than you. Take your broke pockets, your bluster, and leave."

The operator tapped the table. "Your Grace, it's your roll. Is this gentleman bothering you?"

"He is."

The operator waved his hand, and two footmen came on either side of Markham. "Eject him."

"I'll go. Wait, what's moving in—"

"Quiet, Markham." Busick smiled. "Take him away."

The men gripped Markham by the arms and dragged him away.

Markham twisted and struggled. "This isn't over, Duke."

"But it feels like it. Take him and toss him out on his ear."

Soon, the fiend was a memory. Busick shuffled the dice in his palms while the operator apologized for the disturbance. He let the cubes roll down the table.

Boots stomped and congratulations sounded as he hit his nick again, lucky number twelve.

But one jeer was missing.

When he glanced at LaCroy, he frowned.

She sat with the barrister.

Busick turned back to the hazard table. He wasn't done winning, and he wouldn't allow jealousy to snatch it from him now.

CHAPTER 25

A RAKE'S SURRENDER

There's a moment in your life when you wonder how you arrived at the point you are at. I glanced at the duke and my baby's bread basket. I sat near Mr. Thackery at a table covered in white linen, trying to figure out how I'd gone so wrong. Agassou couldn't help me. Mama's wiles, Papa's money and brawn brought no answers. Repington and his Jove were winning. They'd even defeated Markham for the moment.

This was punishment, and I was angry, fearful, and sticky.

Smelling the thick onions and gravy on Thackery's beef-steak made my stomach rumble. I wished I could bathe in the gravy. Never again would I fail to eat before cavorting about in menswear with a mocking duke giving chase.

"You doing well over there, LaCroy? You look a little green."

"My headache of yesterday returned, and I'm a little tired of being punished on these shores. If I brought you my trust documents, could you arrange passage for three to Demerara?"

"Three?"

"Myself, Lionel, and Mrs. St. Maur."

He shook his head, even grunted a little. "Would this passage be done with the duke's permission?"

I lowered my eyes to the nearly empty plate. "That wasn't my question."

"It needs to be. I survive by upholding the laws and rulings of the Crown. I'll not knowingly break the provisions of a will. The duke is Lionel Jordan's guardian. He sets the rules. It would have to be extraordinary circumstances for me to break my oath."

Where were these honorable men when I sought to marry? "Then forget what I said. Perhaps your aunt has someone else who could do what I need."

Thackery forked the last bit of his meal, bits of gravy spilling on his chin. "Maybe you need to rethink what you need."

I handed him a napkin. "Are you done? Jemina's still waiting outside. You go on and take her. Knowing the duke, your aunt might be outside, too."

He took the cloth and wiped at his mouth, patting his mouth. "You have transport? Repington seems to be in good spirits."

I looked over at the duke, straddling the bread basket, winning another hazard roll. "I think I have a way back."

At least I hoped I had.

The duke's posture was a little bent, but that was probably from hovering over the table.

He looked very smart in black trousers and an ebony-striped waistcoat. His cravat was still crisp, but he wasn't lugging a cow in his shirt.

Sullivan came to the other side of me. "Mighty young for the duke to bring his page with him. I thought a good page was a Blackamoor child that could walk or at least be able to follow a lady around with a satin pillow. Right, Thackery? You know how it's done. Weren't you one for your father?"

The barrister put his fork down. "It's time to leave."

The awful man chuckled. "Just a little jest, Thackery. The

little thing is quiet and must be bringing His Grace luck. The duke's on quite a streak."

"The Duke of Repington is eccentric and does as he pleases." My voice held steady, but I was ready to hit Sullivan. I didn't slap like a girl. My mother taught me how to deliver a blow.

"Now, LaCroy, your friend Mr. Thackery knows I'm joking. In fact, I should be nice to him. I hear he's set to inherit a title when his uncle finally dies."

The barrister stood. His countenance hadn't changed from blank. "LaCroy, finish your business with Sullivan, I'll go watch the duke and see if his luck doubles."

When Thackery left, Sullivan stepped closer.

"LaCroy, you do have better people to vouch for you than those deadbeats, Markham and Jordan. Let me know when you need credit extended. I'm sure I could work out an offering, even one without management's extra fees. Jordan mentioned this?"

"He did. I'll keep this is mind."

"Yes, come to me alone. I can give you better terms than the house."

I nodded. "I'll contact you once I figure out how much I'd like to gamble."

When Sullivan moved back into the crowd, I sat back down.

After a few minutes, Thackery returned, slipping into a seat. "Well, LaCroy?"

"My husband was involved in a conspiracy to defraud this club with Sullivan. Colin was guilty."

"Did the man mention Markham being involved?"

"Just as a deadbeat. He hinted at Colin knowing about Sullivan's lending money at better terms than the house."

"Well, Jordan's diary must be a record of these deals. That must be the tool Colin used to get his IOUs canceled. His extortion worked."

That was no comfort. How could my husband run a criminal pursuit?

The sight of my sleeping angel beginning to punch at his

blanket was too much. I hungered to be with honest souls. My head had mapped out the quickest route to my babe and the duke. I'd cede to the lessons the clear-eyed commander wanted to teach.

"Mr. Thackery, good evening to you."

"I'll sit here for a moment and ensure you do have transport. You're under my protection. I won't chance leaving you, not here, not disguised as you are."

Again, the fussy man surprised me, but I knew Repington. I could count on him. "I'll be fine."

Slowly walking, like it was my last mile, I went to the hazard table and brushed his coat. "Duke, I think it's time to go. You have appointments and schedules."

"No, relax, LaCroy. Go sit back with the barrister. Lionel will tell me when it's time to go. Unless you know of a reason, a good reason for me to stop."

A few gentlemen looked my way with frowning lips, almost menacing. "Continue, Your Grace. Win at all costs."

He offered me a wicked smile. A cross between *two can play this game* and *wait until I get you home*. Neither would be well for me or my traitorous racing pulse.

I slipped away, plotted murder in my head, and wondered if I stole Lionel's basket from between the duke's legs if I could make it out of the gaming hell before one of the footmen stopped me.

Swatting my way through the crowd, I walked back to the barrister.

"How long will the duke make me suffer?"

Thackery slid me his glass of wine he nursed. The level of it looked untouched. "LaCroy, you look like you need this more than me."

A groom came and pressed a note in my palm.

I took it, my hands visibly shaking.

It was in Lady Shrewsbury's script. She was outside and wanted to know how everything was going. "Mr. Thackery, your aunt's in the duke's carriage. I think you should collect her and Mrs. St. Maur and take them back to Hamlin."

"LaCroy, you don't seem to be doing so well in your present negotiations. Perhaps you should come, too. The duke is only going to stay as long as you do."

"I've had enough games and disguises, sir. I understand my limits."

The barrister settled the bill, tossing a few coins from his purse. "Don't lose heart. You have a duke and a baby chasing after you. You must be some kind of woman. Evening, LaCroy."

Thackery strolled to the door, and I heard claps from the hazard table.

Seems the duke won again.

I sniffed the barrister's wine and took a drink. If I wanted to be drunk and deadened to pain, I'd down the thing. The way my heart hurt right now, as if it had been ripped from my sticky chest, it was clear the duke had won everything.

Busick held the dice in his palm and watched the barrister leave.

"Come on, Repington," the operator said. "Don't let that arm grow cold."

He rolled again and won his nick. "I think it's time to stop."

"Your Grace, you need to give the house a chance to win back its money. Surely, you want another turn?"

"Roll 'em." One man started the chant, then another picked it up, too.

It wasn't the same as his soldiers voicing their meter in a march, but it was stirring. Wellington eschewed gambling, so Busick would, too. He passed the dice to the man on his right, then hefted the bread basket.

Lionel started to stir, wiggling his blanket. Any moment he'd fully awaken and would be ready to dine.

He made his way through the crowd to where Patience sat.

Was it wrong to admire the shapely cut of her legs, or the

way the pantaloons made her backside a viewable work of art?

He stopped staring before he became known as even more eccentric. "LaCroy, would you like me to drop you off somewhere?"

She didn't glance at him, her gaze stayed steady on the blanket. "I'm quite ready to go."

Patience took the basket at such a speed, he thought her capable of fleeing, but Busick knew she'd not run from battle. She'd hear him out first.

"I'll get your hat, Your Grace."

He let her retrieve it, and then they walked side by side onto the street.

She released a sigh. It was deep, shaking him at his core.

Had she suffered as much as he, thinking of the jeopardy her scheme afforded?

His carriage pulled around, and he leaned in, thinking Lady Shrewsbury would mediate, but it was empty. They'd be quite alone.

Patience put Lionel's basket on the seat. Then she bounced back out and went up under his shoulder, helping him balance. Her scent of cigars and soap was an interesting blend, wrinkling his nose as he was hoisted by his petard, his nanny-petard up the step.

"I needed no help."

"You're leaning more on your cane. You haven't straightened in an hour."

The door closed as they settled inside. "So observant. Did you see how cross I am, or are your observations selective?"

She didn't answer but fiddled with Lionel's blanket. "He went back to sleep."

"Ignoring me won't work this time. Nor will one-word answers." He tossed her a handkerchief. "Take that foul cosmetic off. Make yourself look like the infernal woman I know."

She scrubbed at her face. "You didn't need to come."

"Who are you to tell me what I can or cannot do? You don't listen, Patience. Why should I listen to you?"

"Your Grace didn't tell me I couldn't come."

"You didn't tell me you'd dress as a man going to a men's-only gaming hell."

"Well, that's true. Sorry."

"Are you saying that to appease me or because you mean it?"

"Both."

"Not the one-word thing again. I'm not in the wrong."

"You brought my son to a gaming hell. How is that not wrong?"

"It was to teach you a lesson. To teach that lovely stubborn head a lesson."

"You're not my father. I need no lessons from you."

"I'm very glad not to be your father. No more than you are my mother concerned with my posture. Actually, you're like that woman with your risk-taking. You're on your way to becoming a careless rake. What if something had happened?"

"Mr. Thackery was with me and Mrs. St. Maur, too."

"You thought enough to bring a chaperone to this folly? I don't want to talk of you and another man."

Her brow lifted. More of her normal warm coloring showed, not the ghastly ashy paint. "I had to go. I had to track down a man named Sullivan."

"If you needed a man, I'm here. Patience, I'm not going anywhere."

"What?"

"You heard me, madam. If you wanted adventure, I could give that to you. You don't need to go out and search for it. And you don't need any other guides to debauchery. I'm plenty capable."

She tugged at her cravat as if the flailing thing choked her. "You think I left Hamlin because of boredom?"

"I know I seem settled or dull. I know I'm order-driven."

"Order-driven?"

"Yes, I have a lot of rules. I like rules."

"Rule-driven? *Obsessed* would be a better word, Repington."

"I can give you what you need if you tell me what that is."

She freed her hair from the awful wig. In the glimmer of the carriage lantern, he saw her crowning glory—wild and bushy curls of gold and brown and black. Her tresses were braided and falling upon her shoulder.

She rocked trying to fish her way out of her tailcoat.

He stretched to assist but tugged her to him.

She was kneeling on the carriage floor with her arms tangled in the coat.

He settled a palm to her chin. "Adventure, affection. I'm here for it. Use me, Patience. Test me."

"I suppose I do like pushing limits."

Busick lifted her even as she reached for him. He had her up in his arms before he had a chance to talk himself out of kissing her.

And why not? Why shouldn't he prove to her he meant every inch of his challenge?

Unexpectedly compliant, she molded against him. Sweet, hot, and sticky, his fingers found her beneath her waistcoat.

Her lips were soft. Her mouth tasted of berries. And he schooled and scolded her with lips on her neck mapping the way she moved against him when he stroked here, teased there.

He checked again, tasting the soft flesh of throat hidden beneath the collar of her shirt.

A strategist needed to be sure.

Busick tore at her waistcoat buttons. He wanted Patience LaCroy Jordan out of this disguise, freed from all the pretending.

Lionel cried out.

Her fingers on Busick's shoulders were weak, a slow, half-hearted push.

What a time for the little fellow not to share.

This crazed connection between them was more than

Lionel, more than convenience, or adventure or even jealousy.

"I need to feed him. Did he drink any of the pap?"

"A little, but he's had the good stuff." He put a hand again to her waistcoat and finished undoing the final buttons one by one. "I'm a fan of the good stuff, too."

She hooked his finger on the last button. "This is not as wonderful as you think. I need privacy with my son. Then we need to discuss us, everything."

Lionel's cries grew louder. She picked him up and held him against her shirt.

The boy seemed very hungry wiggling against her, his tongue kissing at the wet linen as if he gloated.

Busick reached and stroked Lionel's cheek. "For you two, I'll make a stop. Somewhere I never go." He tapped on the roof.

The carriage stopped, and the compartment door opened.

His driver stood outside. "Yes, Your Grace?"

"Take me to Lady Bodonel's in Mayfair. It's not far from here."

The driver looked stunned but nodded and shut the door.

"Lady Bodonel? Colin's aunt. Your mother?"

"One in the same."

She put her face in her palms. "She's going to see me like this?"

"No one is more scandalous than my mother. Her son stopping by with a woman dressed as a man carrying a baby should be nothing to her."

Patience didn't look convinced.

A tiny, tiny, tiny portion of his brainbox wondered if her fretful look was for a last deception she hadn't shared.

If she wasn't his cousin's widow, he'd know shortly.

The question would be if a final deception would kill what he felt or if the truth would erase his guilt for wanting to seduce his cousin's widow.

CHAPTER 26

A LAST-MINUTE STOP

Confusion twisted about my head like a vise's grip.

Did this happen to male spies or just widowed nannies who hadn't taken care to protect their heart?

I didn't know what I felt or what could come of it, but I knew I was in danger once again. I fell for Colin so fast I couldn't think straight, and now I was falling for the duke. He made me think too much about being happy and whole and not hiding any piece of myself.

Could this last? Could a thing built on deception be true?

The carriage stopped outside a large stately manner. Lots of windows and lights, but the structure was not as big as Hamlin.

Did it have ghosts, too?

From the fretful look on the duke's face—his smile slimming to nothing—it had to.

Repington caught my hand. "My mother and I don't have much of a relationship, good or bad, but if I had to pick, I'd describe it as mostly bad. This will be difficult."

"I'm not delicate. I can withstand her criticisms. I weathered yours."

He held me in place. His eyes, cloudy blue in the lantern light, seemed to plead with my soul. "If I need to know anything before we go inside, tell me now. I'd rather have it said betwixt us, just us."

I had nothing to tell him, and I wasn't ready to share how much I liked his kiss or how I welcomed the heat in his gaze, the strength of his arms.

I shook my head and offered my shoulder to help him from the shiny black carriage. The masterful team of horses looked ready to bolt. I didn't want to be here, either.

The duke waved me from the opening. "Onward, then."

I waited for him to ease from the carriage, straighten, and then secure his balance on his cane.

Lionel's cries started up again.

My poor son's patience had worn away, but I wasn't ready to expose myself and be more vulnerable to the duke.

Nonetheless, hadn't I exposed what I felt when I didn't shy away from his kiss?

I rocked Lionel in the basket. He seemed tired of bouncing. I was pretty tired of my waffling, too.

The duke put his hand on mine along the basket handle. He smiled down at Lionel, who stretched and shoved at his blanket.

Up three steps, we arrived at the door, which opened as if it had been waiting for us.

I'd left my hat in the carriage, not that this would help our cause.

The hall was littered in portmanteaus, big ones, small ones, even bonnet-size boxes.

A woman, a little younger than Lady Shrewsbury, came halfway down a plain set of stairs. Blond, shorter than me, about Jemina's height, Lady Bodonel threw back her head and blotted her cheeks with a handkerchief.

"Busick, you've come to see your mama but with no notice. Well, it's a visit."

He looked up to the plastered ceiling. "Mother, I don't

mean to interrupt your evening. It's obvious you're stealing away in the middle of the night."

"No, silly. In the morning."

She came all the way down the stairs. Her sheer peach-colored robe and matching mobcap were quite fine, each trimmed with satin ribbon along the hems. "You did pick a good day to see me before my scheduled travel."

"So that's where you get the tendency for schedules, Your Grace?"

He glared at me. "Bite your tongue, Patience."

"Son, what's wrong with you? You're on a cane."

He lifted the cane and hocked it in the crook of his folded arm. "A little injury, nothing to stop your travels."

I took Lionel from the basket. I had him settled a little in my arms, but it wouldn't last. "Lady Bodonel, may I have the use of a parlor?"

The woman wrinkled her nose, and then stepped closer. "You brought a little piece and a baby here? Are you coming from a masquerade?"

"You don't recognize her, Mother?"

She went to a drawer on the console and pulled out something that looked like theater glasses. Moving about me, she examined me up and down, head to boots, like a foreign woman in menswear with theater paint smearing her cheeks wasn't an everyday thing.

My chuckles came. Laughter was all I had.

This woman would pretend she'd never met me, that she hadn't sipped tea on my silver at Hamlin.

I didn't care about this slight, but I did care about Repington.

The small smile he had for Lionel on the steps had been taken away. He thought I'd lied to him.

Demerara, Demerara. Demerara. The incantation needed to take me away. One of these portmanteaus needed to turn into a boat and sail me across the sea. I gave up on Agassou. No protection would come for me.

Lionel started crying. His hungry wail was too much.

"Is it allowed to use a parlor for the baby? He needs to be tended to."

She clapped her hands and a man in an indigo livery came forward. "Take her to the close one."

"Mother, why are you pretending not to know Mrs. Jordan, my cousin Colin's widow?"

Lady Bodonel took out her theater glasses and stared at me again.

"Oh, yes. Mrs. Jordan, to what do I owe the pleasure?"

I looked at Repington.

But the duke wasn't looking at me at all, and as many times as I had defied him, I'd never seen his cheeks this red in anger.

Slamming his cane with a thud, he stepped in front of me. "Why haven't you visited Colin's widow? Why didn't you attend her when she was grieving? You're an expert on such."

"Well, son, I was told that she didn't like people. That's what Markham said."

"And you believed him?"

"I was busy." She came closer. "Odd, tall creature, Mrs. Jordan."

Lionel began to cry. I knew this yelp. There would be no placating him. "Ma'am, I need some place for privacy. I need to feed my son."

"This is my house, Mrs. Jordan," the duke said. "Go to any room you choose to take care of my ward, my heir."

A footman bowed and moved his hand for me to follow.

"Oh, Colin's boy. Such a yellowish-brown little thing. Does he look like Colin to you?"

"Mrs. Jordan, hurry. We need to leave as soon as possible."

Opening a door to a parlor, the footman lit sconces and then pointed inside.

Once seated with the door closed, I disrobed and fed my hungry boy.

I tried to distract myself from the conversation in the hall.

The voices were low, but the duke offered many one-word answers, several of them noes.

Lionel's suckle was strong. "Were you a good boy for the duke?"

The answer seemed obvious. His appetite was too big, too hungry.

"You didn't eat a thing for Repington, did you? Naughty Lionel."

Lady Bodonel's pitch became higher. I couldn't understand what she said, but it sounded like one long set of syllables, no spaces, no breaths.

I felt sorry for the duke.

My own mother was difficult, but I'd been able to get a few words in—angry ones, even repentant ones at times.

Not enough repentant ones.

Lionel should hurry up. I'm not sure what we'd come into, but I knew this was no place for us or the duke.

Busick stood up as straight as he could as his mother circled him in the grand hall of the house he leased for her. A nice, expensive Mayfair address was the cost to keep her from his smaller townhome in Town, where he'd convalesced these past two years.

"Son, you've been back from the war front for a while, and this is the first time you stop by to see me, in the middle of the night with a woman?"

"You sound as if you are shocked. Remember when you left me with Grandfather for four years? I did enjoy the letters for my birthday, though I'm surprised you found time between that string of special friends. A duke, an earl, a marquess."

"You weren't unhappy. The late duke enjoyed having you about." She folded her arms and strutted about in her nightgown and robe as if auditioning for her latest paramour, complete with pouts and tearful mopping with her handkerchief. "This widower duke may decide to be a permanent friend."

"Mother, this one is no more likely to commit than the others. They all figure out you bore easily."

"What do you know of commitment, son? Last I heard, you were unwed without the benefit of even a bastard."

He rubbed his skull wondering what he'd done to have such a mother. "Just when I think you can't shock me anymore, you do."

Her brow raised, and she offered him that devil-may-care-but-she-didn't look. "You're popular like me, son. If I were a man, such popularity would not draw censure."

"When Mrs. Jordan is finished, we'll leave you to your packing."

"But that woman, Busick? That unusual creature with a baby. Is that what they wear, men's tailcoats and breeches?"

"Mother, Mrs. Jordan . . . It was a masquerade. I cared for the baby while she was away. I should tell her there are fresh napkins in the basket."

Lady Bodonel held out her hand. "Wait, she made my military son, a commander of English forces, a nursemaid? What has come over you?"

What had indeed?

Busick didn't want to admit to the thoughts he had in his head about Patience. He retreated and leaned more on his cane, balancing becoming more difficult, his back aching. "She's under my protection. Markham is a threat to her."

"Does that mean you are in possession of Hamlin Hall again?"

Oh no. No. He could see the cogs in her head turning, stopping on bad. He put a hand to his neck, the strain of standing and his mother's scheming becoming impossible to bear.

"Lionel Jordan is in possession of Hamlin. I'll see that his interests are best served. That does not include your parties."

"Hamlin was a place for such lovely gatherings. It should be yours. It should never have gone to Colin."

"But it did. I wonder why Grandfather would do such with you constantly trying to sway him?"

Her ageless face pinched up. "The man was spiteful. He taught you to be spiteful."

At this, Busick chuckled. "I've been told that I'm very much like him."

"So what are you going to do, Busick?"

"What?"

"This is the first person you dare bring to see me. You must have taken a fancy to her."

"My ward was hungry. It's a two-hour ride to Hamlin. The woman is not going to undress in front of me to feed him."

"Son, you should think about regaining Hamlin. Colin's widow is a little brown but not bad on the eyes. I'm sure she looks quite well, dressed in a gown, and that hair done up in a proper chignon."

"What?"

"Marry her. Return Hamlin back to the Strathmore line."

Marriage wasn't a bad notion, one that popped into his head more and more when he thought of rearing Lionel with Patience, but he'd never admit that to his mother.

"Think about it, son."

He gripped his cane tighter. "When have you ever cared for the Strathmore line? I thought you were angling to be on another family tree. You never change, always scheming."

"And you're just like me. You lust for adventure, going from bullets on the battlefield or bonbons in your bed. Why else would you take up with this exotic creature, your cousin's Demeraran wife?"

Perspiring, he lost the grip on his cane and slipped. He grasped the console to keep from falling.

"Are you hurt, son?"

"I need to leave."

He navigated through the litany of portmanteaus. "I've

been in your presence for twenty minutes, and you've already tried to marry me off for a house, one you never cared about when you lived there, when my father lived."

"Well, I've changed my mind on a great many things. Maybe I've been waiting for you to come show your old mother some care. I want to start anew."

She came close and put her hand to Busick's arm, but he jerked free and tripped over a trunk.

He hit the floor hard with his back going one direction, legs in another.

The amputee stump stayed on, but the strap dug into his flesh.

Patience ran out of the parlor, Lionel's basket swinging in her hand. "What has happened? Repington!"

She knelt at his side in seconds. "Are you much hurt?"

"No, I just like making faces. Help me up."

"I'll call for a physician. You don't look well, son."

He knew the signs since the chandelier fell. His back was going to go out, but this couldn't be the time. "Patience, help me up. I've enough strength to stand if you help."

"Duke, maybe we should stay for a doctor."

His mother hovered over him. "Let me take care of you, son."

She clapped her hands for servants, but Busick wouldn't be here a moment longer.

He grabbed Patience's cravat and drew her close. "Get me out of here." This second part of his order, he set at a whisper. "I beg of you."

Her eyes grew big.

Did she understand? Or would she defy him, thinking she knew better? Better was not here.

"No, Mrs. Jordan. I'll get a footman and put him in a room. He's too hurt to leave."

He flopped back. He was about to be trapped with his mother.

"Sir, on the count of three." She'd put Lionel's basket down and had Busick's arm. "One, two, three."

She pulled him to a seated position. "Now, up sir. Again, on the count of three. One, two, three."

Clasping his cane, he held his breath. It took all his power to withstand the pain in his body when he rose, but he did it. By Jove, with her help, he stood.

Patience ducked under his arm. "Commander, let's walk together."

With a thud, he set down his cane. "You keep counting, Patience. I'll not pass out. Proceed."

Taking up the basket with her free arm, she started them moving, step by step to the door. They fell into a blessed rhythm.

"Busick, you're being stubborn. I can postpone my trip a few days. Let me take care of you. I took care of your father. I'll have you good as new."

Those words were the scariest he'd ever heard. He wasn't his father, wasn't an invalid. And he'd never let a woman he didn't trust have any control over him. "Night, Mother."

"A mother should take care of her son, not a stranger."

He ignored her and held tighter to the woman he did trust.

His mother went in front of them with her arms wide. "Mrs. Jordan, I order you to stop."

"I'm sorry. I have a different commander. Out of our way."

He wanted to smile, but everything hurt.

It seemed like an eternity before they reached his carriage.

She waved at the grooms, and they hoisted him inside.

Patience climbed in and put Lionel's basket on the floor. She knelt beside Busick's seat.

"Repington, are you sure you don't just want to stay? The carriage will jar you all the way to Hamlin.

He stretched and put his palm to her cheek. "You're the only woman I trust, Patience Jordan. Get me back to Hamlin, nurse me to health."

"I'm serious."

Busick held his breath and drew his arms together, folding them over his chest. "In fact, wear something fetching. I'll recover faster, chasing you in my thoughts."

"A nice dress will help you heal?"

"Yes, that and you agreeing to marry me."

"Now I know you fell and hit your head." She touched his temples as if to check for fever. "You need to stop this crazy talk. We'll get you back to Hamlin, and you'll recover, and everything will be normal again."

Nothing would be normal, not for him, but he didn't have the strength to convince her of the seriousness of his offer. It took too much to bite back the pain from the carriage wheels hitting every divot in the road.

"Fine. I'd rather be an invalid at Hamlin than any other place."

He closed his eyes. He didn't want to see the doubt straining her countenance. For the first time in a long time, he knew exactly what he wanted. Whether he could walk or not, he'd regain his strength and win Patience.

CHAPTER 27

CARING FOR THE DUKE

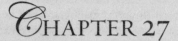

I stood outside Repington's bedchamber, fretting as I had for the past three days. Upon returning to Hamlin, I'd sent for Lady Shrewsbury's physician. This was against the duke's orders, but I had to know how hurt he was. I didn't understand everything the physician said, but he had my duke on laudanum and left instructions to keep him flat and isolated.

The duke hated it and begrudgingly followed the physician's instructions.

Lord Gantry came out of the room and shut the door behind him.

"Is the duke any better?"

Gantry shook his head. "He needs to get back into his routine."

Not knowing what to do with my nervous hands, I fiddled with my apron. "Can he see his men drilling from the window?"

"If he were up to it."

The tone in his voice sounded too settled, too accepting of this fate.

I couldn't.

A man who'd journey from a horrid injury back to riding a horse and had built a contingent force to face Napoleon wouldn't accept it, either.

I glanced at his lordship. "Then maybe you should get his men drilling. We need to act like everything is normal."

The viscount shrugged and went down the hall.

No one could be the duke but the duke. I should be mad at Lord Gantry, but he'd received a letter that left him brooding. I knew how deadly letters were, how they could kill a spirit, so I let him be.

Mustering my courage, I cracked open the door, hoping to see the duke sitting up and picking at the food I'd given to his valet.

Nothing was touched. The full tray was on the bed table.

Repington was flat on the bed. No pillows, no moving.

His eyes were closed. This quiet, this not declaring orders, unnerved me.

Moving to the bed, I arranged the sheers. "One word. Just one will do."

No answer. Nothing for my hopes.

But what could I do?

I went into my room, the adjoining one next to Repington's, to check on Lionel. We didn't move back to the third floor when he'd placed us here after the fallen chandelier. Now I couldn't be far from the duke.

My baby's smile wasn't there. It was probably my imagination, but my boy surely noticed the difference in the house.

Jemina swept into the room. She held Colin's diary. "How's the duke? Is he any better?"

"I'm not sure."

My friend leaned against the door. "The night of the gaming hell changed so much. We found Sullivan. We know of the extortion, but you and the duke are not the same."

"He's injured, of course things aren't the same."

"But *you're* not injured. You're tentative. Tiptoeing everywhere. You're not you."

I wasn't me.

I didn't know who me was.

Jemina took my hand and sat me at my vanity. "You talk in your sleep, you know?"

"I do?"

"Yes. You have nightmares of Colin Jordan, and now you talk of the duke." She spun me toward the mirror. "Where's the bold girl who snuck into Hamlin? Who slipped away every night despite the countess's orders and threats by Markham?"

I stared at my reflection, the frightened island girl staring at me in the mirrored glass.

Jemina leaned in close. "I see the mistress of Hamlin. She needs to run this place, and she needs to see about the duke."

I *was* afraid.

Wasn't I pretending that we hadn't crossed a line in the carriage?

That he hadn't hurt himself chasing after me?

But mostly, that I hadn't turned down his proposal?

What would make me commit to a marriage where I'd have to walk on eggshells? Lionel and I were meant for Demeraran seashells.

"This is all my fault. I've taken away his Jove's favor with all my masquerades. Why else would he be hurt now?"

Jemina put her hands to my face. "You and the duke are so similar, so stubborn. Don't let fear come between you. You deserve to be happy. For a woman, that means being brave. For a widow, it means learning to be brave again, not just smarter."

She was right.

My fears, my guilt pushed me back into that quiet life of just moving about Hamlin wondering how to please Colin.

Repington wasn't Colin.

And I had ideas how to please the duke, at least a little.

"Help me find a beautiful dress. That's what the guardian of Hamlin requested."

My friend nodded and began creaking open my trunks, the rest of them brought up from the catacombs. After plowing through this shift, that gown, Jemina lifted a muslin dress with a silver overskirt. Points of Vandyke lace circled the hem and edged the bodice.

It was beautiful. Perfect for a dinner party I thought Colin and I would attend. The muted colors, the airiness, the nonexistent waist for a girl with hips wouldn't do. "Let's try my other trunk."

She opened it, and I thought I could smell the sea.

Her hands dipped into the linens and silk, the rainbow of colors from the mud cloth for shoulder scarfs. Then she tugged out the last dress my mother made.

Long sleeves, made of smooth shiny silk, this grand robe had a luster that caught candlelight. This beautiful dress of a marigold hue with gathers at the waist was perfect to me, always perfect, worth the fittings and the admonishment for fidgeting. Mama. I loved her so. She was my chandelier, that bright lady who gave light to everything she touched.

I wanted to be like her, bringing light to my son, to my duke.

"Repington can't ignore me in this gown."

My friend nodded and laid the dress on the bed to prepare it for pressing.

This traditional fancy dress of Demerara would do the talking for me if words failed.

Holding my breath, I opened the door between our connecting bedchambers.

The duke stirred. "I don't want to be disturbed. Please leave."

I crossed around to the footboard and peered through the sheers. "No. I've let you stew too long."

His eyes opened, fluttered closed, then opened again. "Do you need to force another physician on me? Is this a warning?"

"That was for your safety. I needed to know how badly you were injured."

"I already knew. It's my body. My shrapnel-laden spine. I knew what he'd say, and that he'd force laudanum down my gullet. I hate laudanum."

"Do you feel better? The rest—"

"I can't get up. I have to wait this out. I'd rather do that with some sense of control."

Swishing my airy skirt and adjusting the bright madras scarf of orange and rust about my shoulders, I prepared for the duke to see me. I knew my appearance was the furthest from full- or even half-mourning as it could be. I was a walking English scandal.

"Repington, I must speak to you."

It seemed like an eternity times three before I heard him stir again.

"Patience, you may speak."

Speak, run to him, fly forward, I rounded the bed and stood in the very position where his boots lined up, the spot I fell upon him on that day long ago. "I needed to see you."

Eyes closed, nightshirt parted, exposing bits of his chest, he lay under bedsheets with hands flat on the mattress.

His face held three days of shadow. So different from his tidy appearance, but I didn't mind rugged.

"You've seen me. Regrettably, I'm in the same position as when we arrived from Town."

He released a long sigh, his blank expression not changing. "You're going to tell me that I'd be up and around if we stayed with Lady Bodonel."

"No."

"You're going to tell me I should've had my crutch if I was going to make a point of carrying Lionel about Town?"

"No."

"You're not going to tell me that all my foolish drills, trying to prepare to return to the fight is now wasted?"

"Never. This is my fault. You're hurt because of me. My risk-taking has done this."

He opened his eyes. "What?"

"You came after me. If I hadn't gone chasing after Colin—"

"Colin is dead. There's nothing to chase, unless you believe in ghosts."

"I don't know what I believe." I shook my head. "Actually, that isn't true. I believe in you."

He raised his hand like he wanted me to come, but I saw a wince on his cheek. His arm dropped. "Well, rest assured. I'm not going anywhere. You've seen me. Stop fretting. I'm not wasting away."

"You haven't eaten."

"Broth? A sick man's food. Shouldn't a prisoner have smuggled bread?" He laughed and then winced.

"I'll get you bread. Anything you want."

"Anything?" Now his eyes were wide open. "A miraculous sentiment coming from you. But, by Jove, you're pretty, Patience."

"Your god would approve?"

"Yes, lass. Now, if my god could answer my one prayer again, I'd show you how much."

"I struggle with trust. Things are so different here than where I was raised. English versus island deities, so much conflict. And those marble gods downstairs are completely useless. You should toss them out."

He chuckled even as his face scrunched. "Don't make me laugh. It hurts to laugh."

I threaded my hands through the bed curtains. "I believe that a man who has such good in his heart, who does good, will be rewarded."

"On this side of glory? Or the other?"

"Hoping for both, Duke."

"I walked before. By Jove, I'll walk again."

"If you know this, why tell me to go? Tell me anything else to do."

"Anything, again? Patience, you weren't good at following my orders under my employ."

"It's hard to listen and to trust."

"That I know, but you've seen me. I'm glad you came, but you can leave. In a week or two . . . I'll determine what's next."

Next? Was he referring to the proposal again?

I knew walking out the door wasn't the right path. I avoided Mama's last days because I couldn't face life without her.

The duke wasn't dying, but his spirit was. I couldn't let him alone like I did Colin hoping things would improve. Not this time, not when I could do better.

As if I were moving toward the adjoining door, I rounded the bed, spread open the curtains, and eased onto the mattress. I didn't want to jar his back, but I needed to be next to him.

He groaned from my scooting. "What are you doing?"

"Sharing your view. I used to lay here and study the canopy, count the stitches, hoping to hear Colin's carriage. He stayed away for weeks. There were always reasons for him to be away."

"Well, you'll know where to find me if you're looking for me."

The uncertainty in his voice hit me hard. I didn't know how to tell him, how to say all the thoughts crowding my skull.

I stopped thinking, stopped listening to excuses.

I gripped his hand, turned into him and kissed his cheek, then his nose.

Crouching on my knees, I leaned into him and tasted that mouth, that delicious, doubting wonder.

"Patience, you do know where I am."

His hand reached my neck, stroking that spot, that gullet exposed by my *coiffe*, the silky mobcap covering my braided chignon. "You're not going to let me waste away. You're going to force me to live, aren't you?"

"Yes, but I do like knowing where you are. And that you won't be leaving me. I like not being afraid to touch you even more."

With my pinkie, I traced his cheek. "Rough, very different, you not in full compliance."

He brushed my knuckles against his lips. "This beard won't last. Don't get used to it."

Clear blue eyes settled on me. The shadows I saw in the carriage and when I stood at the footboard seemed to have lessened.

Yet, a shadow was still a shadow. Regret or mistrust still remained. It was time for a full confession; well, an admission of the truths I knew.

"I went with the barrister to two gaming hells to search for a man named Sullivan. We found him. He runs credit at the Piccadilly gaming hell. I think he's changing the amounts owed and pocketing the money. I believe Colin and Markham were extorting him."

"That's a serious accusation. A man's debt are a matter of honor."

"Colin kept a record of these transactions. We found a diary. The notations in it are confusing. I want to think Colin's moods got to him. The latter pages show the trembling of his hand, must be from his deepening depression."

"My cousin's script was something he prided himself. You're sure it's not some sort of misunderstanding with Sullivan? I didn't think Colin would threaten someone for money."

"Threats sounds like Markham. I think this is why he had to get rid of me. I can identify Sullivan. I must be a witness to the conspiracy."

He clasped my fingers. "You're rocking. Snuggle close, then don't move."

Those were orders I could follow. Lying beside him, I put my cheek to his shoulder. "Rattle off more commands, and come up with a strategy on how to win this war and prove Markham's guilt."

"I'll stew on this and review the diary. But I'm intrigued about your new willingness to follow orders, Patience."

With my chin tucked high on his shoulder, I didn't resist when his other arm found me.

The gown I'd pressed, each gather at the bodice, the lacy puffy sleeves, would wrinkle and deflate within the heat of his hold. I cared not.

The drumming of his heart, the rhythm mirrored what I felt down deep in my battered soul.

His moan was loud when he held me. It wasn't pleasure. He'd forced himself to move, slipping his mouth along my jaw until he'd taken full possession of our kiss.

I wanted him to command me, to tell me what to do to make his pain go away. In this instance, I'd let him mold me into the woman he needed.

A loud groan like a cannon's belch ripped from my duke. He eased back onto his pillow. "Well, that's enough seduction for me. I'm glad you found me. I'm glad, but you can go."

Kneeling over him again, I put my hands to his sides, soft and easy, all those years of walking on shells put to good use. "You know I don't do well with orders."

Then I arched my back and stretched and finished this kiss that needed to be his. Three days of fearing for him, of hating myself for his injuries disappeared in the taste of him.

"With you rallying me to health, I'll walk again."

One palm cinching my waist, expert fingers scorched my melting spine. The duke's silent commands encouraged me to continue.

"I'm not hurting you?"

"Of course you are, but that doesn't mean I want you to stop. With pleasure, sometimes there's pain. I'll let you know when I've had my fill."

Lionel's sweet cry filtered into the room.

"Or he will let us know. Take care of my boy. Tell him to enjoy the good stuff."

Easing from this mattress made for two, I smoothed my gown, but before I went to my son, he stopped. I peeked through the door, and he'd fallen back to sleep, thumb in mouth.

The duke chuckled. "I need to speak to him about sharing. I'm beginning to take these interruptions personally."

My cheeks burned, but I knew I wore a smile. How could I not? This intimacy was the best time I'd spent in this room.

The duke made that face, one that said he was hiding the pain. The bottle of laudanum was on the chest of drawers, but so was a container of his rum. I filled a tiny glass with the perfume of Demerara's best, then poured a second with the laudanum. I presented both to him. "For the pain you're hiding."

"Put them on the table. I need to see how long I can endure before I need either."

No longer questioning how he chose to manage his injuries, I set the glasses onto the bed table. "Tomorrow, you think you might eat something?"

Lionel started up again. "I should go to him."

"Send up bread tomorrow. A thick cut of your coconut bread. I hear happy women bake."

Almost skipping, I sailed through the door into my bedchamber.

Picking up my hungry boy, I found it quite easy to adjust my gown to him. The duke seemed to have helped in advance with buttons and such.

Soon my baby filled his belly.

He burped and sort of giggled before I set him back in his crib. I sung his lullaby, in French and English. For a little while, I heard a baritone echo.

Then two snoring men.

This was good. The duke just needed to heal.

A cacophony of curses sounded below, in Hamlin's front hall.

Commotion and slammed doors echoed.

Rushed footfalls pounded and screeched below.

Righting buttons as quickly as I could, I slipped from my bedroom and ran into the hall.

I heard Markham's voice and froze.

Part of me wanted to get Lionel and hide in the duke's bed, but both of them needed me strong.

He saw me and added an expletive to my name.

In front of the useless marble gods, he stood and blasphemed, and they left him whole and not struck down. It was up to me.

"Markham, you're not welcome. Leave."

I said the words with power as if I wore a stone buckler and shield.

"You!" He pointed a bony finger. "How did you get back in here? You're supposed to be in Bedlam."

Gantry came from the rear hall. "How did you get in here, Markham?"

"Does it matter? Let's say Colin's ghost let me in. Right, Mrs. Jordan? You've seen him. How could you allow that crazed woman here?"

I clasped my shaking hands to the newel post of the stair railing. "You are trespassing. Get out."

My voice was strong, and Repington's men took up their arms and pointed them at Markham's ugly face.

Gantry pulled his sword and waved more soldiers forward. "Leave now, before you test my accuracy."

Markham backed up. He now stood in the space where the chandelier's shadow would have swallowed him. "She doesn't belong here. I'll get Bedlam's administrators after you, maybe all of you. Where's Repington? Are his mother's words true? The duke has fallen and can't get up."

Without a thought, I slid down the banister. My pretty shimmering skirt lifted like butterfly wings. I landed in front of Markham and slapped his face. "Repington will stop you. He won't be manipulated like Colin. You're not welcome in this house. Garbage be gone."

Gantry nodded, and two men gathered Markham by the arms and dragged him.

"The duke's a fool and doesn't know that you'll endanger that gold mine. Have Repington come down to the drawing room. I need to get my things from there anyway."

"Nothing here is yours. You, evil man, you're never to be welcomed here."

Gantry opened the doors. "Guards, take the man and dump him far outside the gates. You trespass again, you'll know my sword."

"This isn't over. I'll get the administrators on Mrs. Jordan and Repington. Tell him I won't let this stand . . . like him."

He sneered, and I wished I could slap him again.

The fiend struggled, but the soldiers overpowered him. "The duke has to be insane to side with Mrs. Jordan over the boy's safety. You know what you did to that boy. You know what you let happen to Colin. May he keep haunting you."

That was a curse from the gods, to have Colin not at rest, still hurting.

The soldiers did their duty, carting Markham away. Soon, I saw nothing more of his dusty boots.

This was a momentary battle.

Hamlin wasn't safe.

With the duke hurt, his men had become lax.

"You were right, Mrs. Jordan. We need to get back to drills and security."

Gantry's words faded. The evil man's threats repeating, repeating in my brainbox.

Markham wasn't just coming for me and Lionel. He was after Repington, too.

CHAPTER 28

OLD DREAMS, NEW DREAMS

I bolted up in my bed.

My heart raced around my chest. It had no place to hide since my lungs had shriveled. Gasping, I saw my Lionel sleeping soundly in the crib next to me.

He was safe, but I still wanted to run, to throw off blankets and flee.

But where could I go that my horrible dream, my guilt wouldn't follow?

Colin.

Two days ago, Markham, that blackguard, called him down to haunt me once more.

Laying back on my pillow, I found it was damp. Did I cry in my sleep again?

One swipe at my sticky eyes said the truth.

Gaze pinning toward the ceiling, I dare not drop my lids again, for he'd be there, screaming at me the words in his last note. *You did this. You did this.*

"I didn't mean it! I didn't."

"Patience. Patience."

That wasn't Jemina's voice.

She'd returned to sleeping on the third floor. This was the companion room to the duke's.

Not knowing what or who called, I fingered my bed table and found my knife. I picked it up and went to the light spreading beneath the connecting door.

"Patience."

My rattled thoughts cleared. That was Repington's voice. Was he in trouble?

I pushed open the door that separated us.

The duke had raised up an inch or two and looked as if he'd tried to stand. He groaned and lowered to his pillow. "Come to me."

I dove headlong up the mattress.

He scooped me up into his arms as if I were Lionel. "I have you. Nothing will hurt you. Talk to me, Patience."

His lips sought my fevered brow, and I held on to him.

"I heard bits of your nightmare."

"Nothing. It was nothing."

"My greatest fear is to be of little use to you or Lionel or my men. Tell me, unless all your encouragement was a deception."

I didn't want to talk. I half clawed my way through his nightshirt to hide.

He put a hand to my cheek. "Either you trust me or you don't. Tell me your secrets."

It wasn't a command. I knew how his voice dispatching an order sounded—harsh notes, crisp syllables with those dimples disappearing. This wasn't it.

My choice was to trust my heart.

"Markham had me committed because he said . . . I was a danger to Lionel."

"Why?"

"I saw Colin. His ghost railed at me. Before he died, I wrote him a letter, telling him how much wrong there was in our marriage. That's why he killed himself. My angry words pushed him into the Thames. That's why he haunts me."

"You're not responsible."

"I am. I must've freed myself from the nursery where Markham held me captive. Colin's ghost came at me. I ran blurry-eyed at top speed. Markham, the servants, all said I tried to slide down the banister to get away from his ghost. I could've killed Lionel if I'd fallen."

The duke released a long breath. I felt the muscles of his arms relax. "You were trapped in the nursery under duress. Markham plays tricks, making people wonder about their strength and sanity. The night I took control of Hamlin, he'd drugged the nanny to take advantage of her. Patience, when you say blurry-eyed—did someone describe your eyes as yellow and bright?"

"Maybe."

"You're definitely not crazed." He lifted my chin. "I know you. You are most trustworthy."

I held on to Repington. I might even have cried. I didn't feel worthy, not until I looked into his truthful eyes.

Sheltering the trembling Patience in his arms, slipping her betwixt bedclothes and pillows, Busick made a list in his head of all the things he needed to do when he recovered from this bed.

First, find that gardener-butler fellow, the servant who'd worked at Hamlin since Grandfather, and confirm Markham's treachery to Patience.

Second, order a few barrels of rum, the good stuff.

Third, he thought, as he curled one of Patience's lithe fingers within his own. Put a ring, a Strathmore wedding band on it. It was time to claim her as his own.

He wiped his thumb along her nose. "I need you to marry me."

"Am I that hysterical that you must make jokes to lighten my mood."

"We're beyond kissing cousins. I asked you to marry me in my carriage. I meant it."

"I suppose lying in bed with you twice in three days is too much."

"The problem is it's not enough." He laced his fingers with hers. "I try to lead a very moral life."

"Now you want to make me laugh."

"Well, since I have a ward and you keep flopping into my bed, perhaps it's best if there was a legal reason to explain this. Marry me."

"If I said no, you'll make me leave this room?"

"Yes, ma'am," he said, claiming a spot on her neck that seemed particularly sensitive to nips.

"Isn't this something to discuss when we both can get up and leave?"

"Wouldn't a matchmaker prefer a groom who couldn't?"

"I'm not a consolation prize. Marriage doesn't solve all ills. I thought wedding Colin would make my mourning for my mother go away. It just brought a different sadness."

"Gantry told me about Markham's coming here. He's conferring with my mother."

"I thought Lady Bodonel was going on holiday."

"The chance to lord over me would make her delay her friendships."

"That's a shame. She looked happy to be going."

"Yes, I wish she had gone, too. Now, the odds of her coming to visit have doubled. I don't like those odds."

She frowned at him, like she'd drank Lionel's pap milk.

That soft heart of this woman even cared for Lady Bodonel, someone who'd snubbed her.

"I wish my mother had what she's looking for, but you're trying to deter from my point. It won't work. Getting me to babble won't take away my offer."

"I'm not what your world, your English world, expects for the wife of a peer—a duke, no less."

"You're not what anyone expects. That's why I fancy you."

She turned away, putting her back to him. "I'm not ready

to hear how I took advantage of the Duke of Repington while he was indisposed. Tricked him on laudanum."

"I do hate the stuff, but no one takes advantage of me. You're a rake in training. I'm seasoned."

"I don't look like what they want for you. The duke's dark duchess, his difficult wife, his different wife. I'd be safer in Demerara, all of us would be. You'd love my father's house. The sea air will be good for your recovery. I can picture you and Lionel rocking in a hammock."

"That sounds sweet, but I must tell you—"

"Hush." She kissed his lips.

The taste of her tears and coconuts, the sweetness of her bread flavored their embrace. This lady was so dear. It tore him up to break her heart.

"Tell me you'll think of it, Repington. We could be safe. I wouldn't have to be fearful another minute. Markham is after you."

Patience cared for him. He knew that. Somewhere beneath her silky mobcap and glorious braided chignon was bravery and dignity and hopes for their future.

It was his duty to set her straight. "You'll be my beautiful wife, Patience Amelia Strathmore, the one educated by the finest tutors, fluent in two languages."

Claiming her eyes, officer to officer, he prepared to tell her the worst. "Beautiful Patience, the daughter of the late Wilhelm Thomas."

"The late . . . ?"

"Yes. His brothers have taken his plantation and sold it off. Your trust and everything he settled for you in England is still intact."

"Still an heiress, I suppose." Her jaw trembled, then she wept. Sobs puddled in that sweet cleft in her chin.

Busick risked his returning strength to secure her in his arms. "I'm so sorry. On route to the gaming hell, Lady Shrewsbury and I had a long conversation about you. Then Gantry did some checking. My solicitors are quite good, as good as Mr. Thackery. He's been searching everything about

Colin, but nothing more about you. I wondered why a father, a powerful one, wouldn't come to his child in her time of mourning."

Her stuttered breaths punched his gut. "How long?"

"A few years."

"Is that why Colin didn't send my letters? Could he have known and sought to shield me?"

Busick didn't know, but he'd afford her the comfort of thinking Colin's misguided notion was an effort to keep her safe as opposed to a twisted need to control her.

"My sisters?"

"Still hunting them. They will be found. That's my promise."

Her sobbing ramped up again.

When it slowed, he blew a sigh onto her temple. "Listen very carefully. I've plotted this out, weighed the pluses and minuses. The equation says it is to our benefit to marry."

"How?"

"Patience, if I die, Markham becomes Lionel's guardian. If someone bribes counsel to say I'm unfit because I'm somewhat incapacitated, Markham gets the boy. Lionel will always be in jeopardy if I'm unable to protect him. And you will be unprotected, too. I won't have that."

"Marrying you will make everything better?"

"I think it will. It's something I can do and not move a muscle, and it will remove me from this state of wanting you and just having a piece of your great big heart. I'm not satisfied with a taste."

Her head shaking vibrated through him down the spine that refused to behave.

"I rather think it's a little lonely sleeping in this big bed knowing you're up next door."

"It's not too far."

"It is when I can't get to you, when I can't hold you and tell you everything will be well. I heard your nightmares. I've heard them before, when you risked your life for mine. Let me risk this for you."

Her dark eyes looked scared. He'd never seen the bold girl frightened by one of his requests.

"I don't know what to say."

"Yes. That would be an appropriate one-word response."

"Do you see me? Are you sure?"

He saw her, her strengths, her flaws, her heart and wanted it all. Looping her fingers, he clasped his thigh, the leg that missed a knee and more. "You saw me first. A marriage will also protect me if I truly become an invalid."

His hands had more strength than yesterday, and he traced the figure that he coveted.

She swatted his fingers.

Busick laughed. "See, I'll have to marry you to gain Lionel's privileges."

Her face glowed in the candlelight. He loved that about her. Just so many things to love about her.

"Then care for me, Patience, in any erratic, chaotic manner you choose. It will be better than anyone else making decisions for me."

She jerked up. "But I'm not even in half mourning. I last saw Colin in July, but he died in December. This is a rush."

"You are considering it if you're questioning silly rules."

"What if I did see his ghost? What if he haunts me? He wasn't happy. How would he take us?"

"Colin is free. I hope he'd be happy for his son. You need to be free of guilt. I know you. I know you tried to make my cousin's life beautiful, but a man has to *want* peace."

"You will regret settling down."

"This is what I want."

"Lady Shrewsbury says you've changed what you wanted a good number of times."

"Not quite true. It was a mutual parting. Our goals didn't match. Your goals and mine match. And if you're going to make me act like a henpecked husband chasing you about London, give me the benefit of being a henpecked husband."

"You make this all sound so logical."

"Logic and strategy are my strength. Do I need Lady Shrewsbury to catch us like this for an old-fashioned compromise?"

"With my father . . . with my father gone, who'd force you? I should go back to my room." Brushing at her cheeks, she scooted free. "See you in the morning, Duke."

"Busick, Patience. My wife should call me by an intimate name."

"I haven't agreed."

"Stay until you do. I'm staying."

"Even if Wellington says he needs you?"

"He'll have to learn to share me like Lionel must learn to share you."

"No jokes. None, please."

He strained and caught the sash of her robe.

Her turn was slow, but he hoped she saw he'd choose her, her and Lionel over Wellington. "Before you leave, I've worked on a new schedule. Here, Nanny Jordan." With a grunt, he reached for his paper that sat atop Colin's diary on the bed table and pressed it into her shaking hands.

"You're moving better, maybe? You'll walk soon. We don't have to discuss marriage."

"Yes, we do. Read the schedule."

Clutching it, she looked down. He saw more tears in her eyes.

"You will see a wedding marked at two this afternoon. Please attend. Have Lionel ready. He and Gantry, they will serve as my best men. Wellington is not invited."

"How could I refuse—"

"Patience, a marriage of convenience solves this little problem we have. You kissing me. Me liking it. That's a bonus, an extra benefit, truly. Our attraction will only grow, but I know you trust me. I trust you. This will give that boy we both love the benefit of us as a team. And if anything were to happen, I will rest well, knowing you're protected. Give me this. As a man, I need this."

"Repington . . . Busick."

"Follow orders, Jordan. I expect you here at two with Lionel. Then this door between us will never be shut. I think we'll both sleep better with nothing separating us."

"That's not a declaration of love. But I had one of those. And in the end, it meant little. It's a practical arrangement."

"With benefits. My title and such."

Waggling his brows, he hoped she'd laugh or at least smile.

"This is crazy, Commander, but since I'm a former inmate of Bedlam, why not? Yes, I'll follow your schedule."

He drew his hands behind his head and watched her wobble like she shifted through dessert jellies returning to the adjacent room.

She left the door separating them wide open, and he hoped that was indicative of how they'd continue. He picked Colin's diary back up, looking for the final clues that would set Patience free.

CHAPTER 29

A CEREMONY OF CONVENIENCE

Never thought I'd marry again.

Or that one of my bridesmaids would be a cat. The countess's kitty had gotten a hold of the bouquet Jemina made of the brave pimpernel flowers from the field. Athena took them and ducked under the duke's bed.

I knelt and tried to coax her out from under the bed. "Come, girl. I need you, dear, to r-return to me."

My nerves showed as I stumbled over my words.

The countess snapped her fingers, but the kitten had too much fun shredding the red and yellow petals.

Well, it added color to the celebration.

The duke laughed. "Let her be. Gantry has the rings. Athena can litter those petals to decorate our makeshift wedding chapel, this lovely bedchamber."

He was in good humor and took my hand. "Begin, sir."

The parish minister began his speech.

Lionel lay beside the duke. He'd rolled over, surely a result of the baby drills.

My free palm smoothed my skirt, a huge white cotton *gaulle* draped with a gold-and-scarlet madras shrouding my waist. The gown spoke of Demerara, of my lost home. I wore a hat, a slim cream-colored bonnet, very English, very much what a free woman would wear on the island. It was a proper memento of my papa, much better than carrying my gold knife.

No wearing gray or black. I was done mourning. I proudly rolled my *r*'s on my duke's title.

The minister, a man wearing a powdered wig with a very pale face, made me laugh, thinking of my masquerades. But this was no act. It was true. I was wedding my duke.

"Do you, Busick Strathmore, take Patience Jordan to be your wife?" the minister asked.

Slightly sitting up, with his cranberry uniform draping his shoulders, he wore the brooch Lionel loved. "I do."

His face wrinkled when he held my son, and he seemed to pay more attention to my baby than the binding words the minister offered.

"Do you, Patience Jordan, take this man to be his lawful wife?"

"Yes."

Jemina nudged me.

"Oh, I mean I do."

This brought a new round of chuckles.

This was a marriage of convenience. Admitting to more would ruin things. The tightness in my chest as I looked at Busick would be my new secret.

Athena ran by, dropping petals at my feet.

The countess made a coaxing *tsk*.

Jemina and Lord Gantry couldn't stop their chuckles.

I decided to ignore them and focused on the new band on my finger.

It held no fancy script or initials, just an ounce or two of smooth yellow gold. It was different from the silver band Lady Shrewsbury had given me to make up for the one Markham had taken.

I was glad for this ring. It symbolized strength and practicality. I'd be a good wife to the duke.

Lord Gantry took a paper from his jacket. "This is the special license for the archbishop."

"Well, it's done, Duchess." Busick picked up his watch from the table. "And in such short order. Who knew a ceremony could be so short?"

His beautiful clear eyes, sweet blue eyes held a smile and me.

I was a Strathmore, Her Grace, the Duchess of Repington.

Lady Shrewsbury kissed my cheek.

Jemina offered a big hug.

Boom. Boom. Boom. Gunshots.

My heart went into my throat. "Markham?"

"No, dearest." The duke wore a full grin, his dimples beaming. "My men. A tribute for us."

Jemina caught Athena and the flowerless bouquet and stood at the window. "What a tribute, Your Graces."

The snowball licked at my dear friend's fingers.

I'd never had a salute with a hail of bullets, or a celebration, for that matter. Colin and I left right away on a boat. If I'd known it would be the last time I saw my father, I would have stayed. I would've held on to him for much longer in the Demeraran sun.

Grief and hope filled my heart. Who would be victorious?

Turning from the window, I watched the duke play with my boy, letting Lionel bat his medals. Then I knew hope was the stronger warrior. It would win.

Lady Shrewsbury took Jemina's arm and mine. "Congratulations, Duke, Duchess. Walk me out, ladies."

The duke nodded and whispered something that made Lionel's gums blow spittle.

In the wide space of the hall, I shuttered as I heard another gunshot. "So does this count as a win for the Widow's Grace? You promised to restore my custody. This marriage does this."

"I've come to know you, Patience, as well as I know Repington. I knew you two were well matched, but this is an unexpected blessing. May this union restore your heart. But take care, Markham's not done. You're secure, but Lionel is still vulnerable. My nephew says Markham's been making a fuss in legal circles."

The joy I'd been trying to hold on to slipped from my grasp. I clutched my elbows, the billowy sleeves of my gown deflating. "Will I always have to be afraid?"

"In a little more than three weeks, the payment from your father's trust will be made to Repington. Markham will have nothing more to fight for. He will tire. His need to have custody of Lionel will diminish. Mrs. St. Maur will stay to help you stay vigilant."

Jemina spoke up. "That diary I think is the thing Markham wants. Without it, he can no longer extort Sullivan."

Jemina was brilliant. That must be why he wanted back in the drawing room. Without the diary or my father's payment, he had no way to get money.

"Stay alert, but don't let uncertainty of anything cheat you of joy. Widows have to be smarter, but we have to have peace, too."

Peace, bravery, intellect—I was weighted down by all these things I was supposed to have.

Guards opened the entry doors.

Kitty in one hand, her shawl in the other, the countess descended Hamlin's steps to her carriage. Her gooseberry-gold–colored skirts and matching cape flapped in the sweet breeze. "Stay alert."

Jemina and I waved at her.

The air smelled of powdered snow and gunpowder.

I looked at the steps. I no longer saw Colin there but the duke, the night we'd met, me helping him arrive at the entry.

The doors closed.

Jemina and I passed milling soldiers. They were in good spirits, drinking the sorrel punch I'd made.

"My Demerara is gone."

She kissed my cheek. "You have a new home, here."

My friend kept moving up to the third floor.

Walking deep inside the master's bedchamber, I saw the duke asleep with Lionel on his chest.

My boy snored his crickets.

I scooped him up and resettled the blanket on my husband, my Busick. Then, I pushed open the door between the connected rooms.

Singing to my baby, I sank onto my bed and fed my hungry boy, but my eyes drifted to Busick's bedroom.

When night fell, I didn't like the quiet of my room and how far away I was from Repington.

I'd kept the big bread basket and settled Lionel inside.

I put on my nightgown and carried my boy into the large bedchamber.

I set the basket near the duke's boots, where he could watch over him, then scurried to the other side and climbed aboard.

When I rested my head, Busick clasped my fingers.

"Duchess, is our boy asleep?" His voice was lazy and filled with gruff boulders and gravel.

"Yes, he has a full belly."

"Good."

I held my breath and scooted deeper under the covers, closer to him.

His face held an amused smile.

"I'm still a bit immobile, you know? This spine will loosen any day. What will you do with me then? You won't be able to take up all the room on this mattress."

I glanced up and saw something in his face I hadn't seen before. It wasn't quite vulnerability or his normal bravado. It was something in between.

He sank his fingers into my braids, tossing away the *coiffe* head wrap. His thumb tumbled along my ear. "I snore sometimes, you know, in those moments when you're not trying to seduce me."

Busick took my palm and kissed the lifeline of the palm.

"You don't have to stay. My mother never shared a bedroom with my father when he took ill. You don't have—"

Crouching on my knees, I brushed my nose against his, then kissed him silent, stopping the foolish drivel coming from his delicious mouth.

Surely, he knew I wasn't his mother.

And he wasn't his father or mine.

His hands found me slipping the edges of my nightgown, the lace covering my bosom. I curled into that position under his shoulder, that spot that had become mine, rib cage to rib cage.

The groan leaving Busick matched the one I held inside. That shimmer of a spark had to be extinguished, put away for later.

"Not exactly the beginning of the wedding night I imagined, Patience."

"I suppose you're used to more excitement." A forced yawn pushed out, and I snuggled closer to his pillow. "Well, I will wait with bated breath."

He released a growl. "Waiting is supposed to be good."

I was at peace knowing Busick would be there in the morning, but that murmur wasn't pain. It was restlessness.

My warrior was frustrated. He forewent his portion of rum and drank laudanum, then clenched his eyes.

"Busick?"

With a patronizing pat to my hand, he turned his head away.

What words would the commander heed that would assure Busick I was content as things were? I needed him here, next to me, more than I wanted passion.

With his eye closed, his face pinched, I wasn't sure he felt the same.

CHAPTER 30

A MARRIAGE OF INCONVENIENCE

Busick sat by the window watching Gantry lead his troops. They looked crisp, marching on the fresh snow. It ached deep in his gut that he couldn't be out there. It had taken another week since the wedding, but he could now sit without agony vibrating every muscle. Yet none of this was enough for a man who'd lived to push for excellence.

The soldiers made a ninety-degree turn that seemed more like a hundred. Their first miss, and Gantry didn't correct them. He was too far ahead on his horse to see.

Busick should be out there. The lineup of men was wrong. He banged his fist on the side of the wheeled chair.

He struck the side again.

Pumping his hand, he looked up and saw Patience at the door, her arms full of bundles.

Schooling his face to appear impassioned, even calm, he glanced at her. "My wife does not need to do laundry."

"This duchess does. Lionel is quite actively proving a need for fresh linen."

She came closer and put the linens down on the bed. "Duke, you look tense. Did you strain getting up?"

Of course, it was a strain. It was terrible looking at her wearing another dress he admired, one that darted at the waist, above the hips and thighs and . . . not being able to know her.

He swiped at his mouth and pushed the big wheel of his chair forward. "I needed to be up. You haven't coddled me, Patience. Don't start now."

"Sorry."

Her face blanked of its smile.

He needed to soften his voice. It wasn't her fault. Did those topaz eyes hold at least a mild curiosity, if not a latent smolder, for her husband?

Easing his chair to within a foot of her, he posted. "I told you it was time for me to get up. I'm up. You need to listen more."

Her brow cocked. "Did you think marriage would change this?"

"There was always hope your hearing wouldn't remain selective."

"Why do you sound angry?"

Now wasn't the time for this discussion. When he could act upon his desires would be better. He made the wheeled contraption move to the door. "Is that Lionel? I think he's crying."

"He's not. Or he's just settling." She put her hand on Busick's shoulder, the warmth of her fingers searing through his shirt. "What is it?"

"You didn't sleep in our chambers last night."

"Lionel was up late. I must've fallen asleep. We brought the rocker downstairs. It's quite comfortable."

Spinning around, he glared at her. "Pity. I missed hearing your thoughts. You communicate more when you close your eyes. Very talkative in your sleep."

Her mouth dropped open. "What have I done? What rule have I broken? I'll fix it."

"I know you're frightened. Tell me why. Hamlin is secure. Your position is secure. Tell me what's going on in your head."

She looked down and crossed her arms. "You heard my ramblings. What do you think?"

"That you're still in love with Colin. That you miss him."

"He was my husband. Should I not have loved him?"

"Of course you should. He fathered Lionel. But you are still calling for him. You chased after a man who knew him. You're stuck in the past. Is this because I'm physically stuck, too?"

Clasping her bony elbows, she sat on the bed, the bed where he wanted to gather her up and make her his own.

"I don't want Colin, but he still haunts my head. I don't know how to make him stop."

He pushed back to her. "What can I do to make you secure? You have my name, my protection. You must know how I crave you. What else?"

She came near, knelt, and dropped her head into his lap. "I don't know. Lady Shrewsbury says Markham may strike up until my father, my late father's payment is settled."

Patience counted her fingers. "That's two more weeks. More time to go about tasks pretending I'm not looking for the fiend to come from the catacombs. Or that he has stolen Lionel, or has found a way to hurt you."

He lifted her face, fingering that wonderful cleft in her quivering chin. "I have troops patrolling. Gantry is outside. He's capable of protecting you."

Her wide eyes narrowed as she stood. "Do you think my fears are because you can't walk? Don't disparage me like this. You know me better than this."

"I think I know you, but you're the only one to ever deceive me twice. I need to know what you're thinking, and it can't come from your dreams."

She rose, towering above him like the queen she was. Chin lifted, she went into the adjacent room.

The noise of drawers opening, content shifting struck his ear.

When she returned, she placed a scrunched-up piece of parchment into his palm. "The last time I told a man what I thought, he walked into the Thames."

"I'm not Colin."

"I don't want you to be. I thank your Jove that you're not him. But we're not free, Busick. We're not. Waiting for Markham or Colin to appear will drive me to your rum. I don't know how to be around you and not be the cause of your suffering."

"It's not you—"

"Read it. Know my thoughts. They killed Colin."

Unfolding the paper, Busick saw a beautifully penned letter to his cousin. A few words stood out—*hate, can't forgive, tired, leaving.*

"I sent it to him when he left me again over the summer. I told him I was done being alone, that I wanted to go home. He should've laughed at that notion, knowing there was nothing in Demerara for me. My father's brothers—I can't call them uncles—they believe in enslavement. My sisters, they may all be enslaved."

"Patience, I'll find out what happened to them. I'll do that for you."

That look on her face—the angry and frowning purse of her lips when she thought no one saw, when she pounded loaves with her fists—made Busick feel worse.

"I don't want my words to kill you, Duke."

"Tell me your disappointments to my face. Let me know. No hiding, no disguises. Tell me, Patience. That's an order."

"What is it you want to hear? You want to know how I like to hear you breathing next to me? That I hate that you can't walk because it pains you so? Do you know I'm relieved that you're not traipsing to gaming hells with Markham and how I don't have to wait for him to come to Hamlin to tell me you're dead as he did Colin?"

"Markham was the one to tell you? Not the magistrate?"

"Halt!"

Men shouted from outside.

Busick clasped her hand and led her into the hall to view the front lawn. "Buck up. Maybe it's a note from Markham telling you he's given up."

He pushed his chair toward the stairs.

Patience came behind and put her hand on the seat as if she would assist.

Taking up her fingers, he kissed them. "I can manage."

"Must be a rule about not wanting my help."

Before he could answer her barb, he saw the rider coming up the driveway. The fellow wasn't in regimentals, but this could be a disguise to deliver a message straight from the battlefield. "Thank you, Patience, for never disguising yourself as a soldier. I still think of your hips in breeches."

"Why do you make me laugh when I'm angry?"

"It's good to know you don't feel apathetic toward me, Patience, and humor is the best way to deal with troubled hearts."

Busick swiped under his chin at the guards at the entry, the signal to let the fellow enter.

The guard went outside to greet the rider.

"You think this is a messenger from Wellington?" she asked. "Should I get you downstairs? I could call to some soldiers or Lord Gantry."

He pushed away from the railing. "I'll not be dragged down like I was carried off the field, even for Wellington."

Out of uniform, unable to stand to greet the rider—no. Busick pulled out his watch. "Lionel's story time. You get the message for me."

"What?"

"My duchess can handle this."

He left her there knowing she would indeed take care of things and went to Lionel.

The baby was up. He sort of smiled when Busick came close to the crib. He reached inside and drew the boy to his lap.

"My little soldier, are you ready to get your afternoon started?"

Lionel answered with that sucking noise he made with his puckered lips.

He held the boy at eye level. "We'll wait for your mother for that. I concede to your hate of pap milk. What would you like, crawling or a story?"

More whooping noises came from the baby.

"I guess that is a no. Want to hear about the Battle of Assaye? Want to know how old Repington, a lowly lieutenant general at the time, helped win the campaign? Wellington could count on me."

Lionel frowned, but with his little fingers he reached for Busick's drooping cravat.

Busick pulled him closer, snuggling the boy he loved. Then he hummed the shipwreck tune.

"I don't think my heart could create a better picture."

He lifted his gaze to the doorway.

Patience leaned against the molding. Her hand held a thick fold of papers.

She was a lovely sight, heaving at the threshold from running down and then up the stairs. That dress of dark gray flouncing at her trim ankles should have color. She needed to be free of mourning.

"My frustrations have cast you in shadows again. Wife, you deserve better. Your light needs to shine."

With Lionel secure in his arms, he moved to her. "Open it. I give you permission."

Rocking his little soldier, he waited to hear Wellington deny his request to return.

I needed to savor this picture of Busick and Lionel a little longer. I had a father to love my son, someone strong like my own papa, but the shadows under the duke's eyes, the flashes of anger in his voice foretold that nothing would last.

This letter would end it all, the peace of this brief marriage. "I don't want everything to go away by opening this letter."

Busick glared at me, his mouth tensing. "Go ahead, Patience, read it. News is never meant to wait."

Didn't he see the tears in my eyes, the bulge in my throat of my heart lodging there? I lifted the letter to him. "No."

"Fine. Then let's delay on opening it entirely. It's been two weeks since I've felt good enough to spend time with this boy, man-to-man. We've a bit of negotiating to do in private."

I shoved the parchment sealed in bloodred wax to him again.

He took it and put it by his side with my letter to Colin, covering them both with the madras plaid blanket I'd made for his chair. "It will keep."

"Duke, see what Wellington wants."

One arm holding Lionel, the other propelling his chair, he moved to the window.

"But you've been waiting for this. You want another day to pass not knowing if the war has need of you?"

He parted the creamy curtains. "Look at your fields, Lionel. It seems the men have let the snow get thick again. That won't do. You must take care of details. It is important."

I came behind them. "I could tell them to plow it."

"Why haven't you? Too much laundry?"

"I hadn't thought about it."

"You've been too busy fretting."

Had I said something to offend him? "You take the ramblings of a woman drowsy in sleep over one awake?"

"Awake and not talking versus you sleeping in chairs where I can't at least comfort you from your nightmare. These are difficult choices."

Was I back to walking on shells because I said something in my sleep? I folded my arms about my middle.

Fear left; rage swept in. "You're as infuriating to me in a chair as you are standing. Open the letter, let's face what it says together."

He rocked my yawning son in his arms. "An order, ma'am?"

I put all my effort into turning the chair so he'd see me. "Yes."

"If Wellington has granted my request to return to service or denied, it doesn't matter. Lionel's nap time takes precedence. It's something I can do, something I can control from this chair."

"Didn't you just tell me to face things just as we are? No disguises, no pretense?"

He grimaced, picked up the letter, and pushed it into my hands. "Then you open it, Duchess. Give me my orders straight. No softening. If Markham and Lady Bodonel know my inabilities, everyone does."

The scripting on the front didn't say Wellington or anything military. There was no franking from Spain.

My fingers fumbled on the wax.

The duke clasped my hand, his big palm covering the letter. "I asked you to go with me to the battlefield. You're my wife now, but you're not—"

"Yes."

"Yes, what?"

"Yes, I'll go with you. I'll march beside you. I'll follow you anywhere. You'd need to promise me that you'll be safe, never reckless."

"Reckless is your forte."

His smile returned for a moment, but my stomach spun. Hamlin had begun to feel like home, my only home now, and we'd have to leave it.

The duke released me. "Go ahead, soldier, read it."

My heart pounded. I broke the seal. "It's from my father's solicitors. Markham is questioning you as guardian and if you even have custody of Lionel. The solicitors are asking you to bring the baby to London."

The duke slumped in his chair. He hugged my yawning son. "It's not from Wellington." He slapped the side of the chair. "I've more time."

I should be glad for the duke, but my fragile heart shriveled. "See? Markham is still out there, still trying to gain custody of Lionel. He's not done."

"This is all wrangling. I'll have my solicitor tackle this."

Crumpling the paper, I backed away. "You put the baby to sleep. Guard him, so that evil man will have none of him."

"Patience, wait."

There was no staying or waiting. Fleeing was the only option. Saluting, I turned and ran.

I kept going until I was down the stairs and in the nook, hiding behind the useless marble gods. They weren't moving, so no one could see me be so weak.

For I was weak.

Wellington wanted Busick's mind.

Lionel, his arms and song.

But I wanted him—his mind, body, and soul—safe. Busick was my home, the place I felt secure.

We needed to leave England. Retreat now and win this war later.

Was I woman enough to tell the commander directly to retreat—not in a letter or in sleep talk, but aloud?

This Demeraran rabble would let my father's blood stir, my mother's bravery brew. I would tell Busick what I needed. All these feelings in my heart had to win.

CHAPTER 31

TRUST AND OBEY

Busick rolled the wheels of his chair back and forth in his bedchamber, moving from the window to the chest of drawers. He'd done this trek for the past two hours, watching the closed door leading to Patience.

He heard movement. Things being dragged but no door opened.

Lionel's cry was the excuse he needed.

He pressed on the door and entered.

Patience nursed Lionel sitting on a trunk. Items from her closet, like the fetching dress she'd worn for their wedding, were laid out on her bed.

"Packing, Patience?"

"Yes."

He pulled closer, close enough to see the crown of Lionel's head, his dark hair against her tawny skin. "You know, if you were going to leave me, you should have done it like the others, before the wedding."

"Yes."

"One-word answers. They are still annoying coming from your sweet lips."

"We should follow a battle strategy."

Half listening, still staring at her exposed bits of bosom, he clasped the chair arms. "What are you talking of, Patience?"

"Let's go to Wellington. Let's go now."

"Patience. That's not possible. One doesn't show up at the battlefield as if it were an invitation to a party or the theater."

"I've never been to a dinner party or the theater here in England. The ghost you are jealous of never took me."

"Maybe I want you to be dreaming of me. Maybe I see you tiptoeing about me and I want you to react, to express some sort of frustration at our plight. Fight with me like before, even if I can't chase you."

"You did chase. You r-rolled into here."

She wiped Lionel's mouth, and for a moment she was exposed, such a lovely round essence of motherhood, of womanhood, of a goddess.

"Excuse me, what were we talking about, Patience?"

She shook her head. "Lionel, are you full?"

The baby yawned smacking his gums.

Busick had studied the signs of contentment. He took the boy from her arms. When he was assured the napkin needed no refreshing, he placed Lionel in his lowered crib. "There, little one."

"Thank you," she said when he came back to her.

But he wasn't done being the helpmate she needed. He took her palm in his and drew her to his lap.

Her long legs curled about his good one as he powered the chair, moving those wheels in reverse. Back inside his bedchamber he cracked the door.

"Our boy will sleep a few hours, that should be long enough for me to make amends."

Her posture relaxed, as her head dipped to his shoulder. She smelled of soap and lavender and tears.

That last one wouldn't do; it would never do. "I'm sorry, Patience."

She held him tight, her arms draping his neck then his shoulders. "Why aren't you happy with me?"

"You should be adored and ravished. I haven't been able to make you secure. It has to be me in this chair."

"No. It's just you. You thinking I'd deceive you about being happy in your arms."

Her lips found his neck, and she curled into him, seductive and luscious in his arms.

"Patience, this contraption makes no difference to you?"

"None."

"Thanks, but you know my opinion of one-word answers. Talk to me. I'm not delicate. You can be disappointed or frustrated with how things are."

Her fingers gripped his collar tight. "You want me to own my feelings?"

"Yes."

"I'm frightened, more frightened than I've ever been."

"Because of Markham?"

"Because of Colin. I couldn't keep him happy. He wouldn't listen to me. And now you don't look happy. And you won't listen to me when I say I am."

"You're not good at this rake business. Or understanding the complexity of being happy that I married you and being frustrated that I'm not well enough to enjoy the fruits of this labor."

"If you are happy—"

"I am content for now. I want more of you. I want my name to be the only one on your tongue."

Busick lifted her chin, took her lips, and hoped to coax her to confess to the love he saw in her eyes. "I'm listening now, Patience."

She smoothed his shirt, her palm splaying down his shoulders. "To keep Colin from his moods, I couldn't be me. I don't want that with us. Take us to Wellington or some other place where Markham won't find us. Let me prove to you that I will pick up your sword and fight for you."

"No." He touched her cheek, swiped at a tear pooling at her chin. "You don't have to prove anything. I just need your voice, telling me what's inside."

Patience put his hand to her heart. "I believe in you. Let's go away. When it's safe, bring us home."

"Hamlin is our home?"

"Where you and Lionel are is home for me."

He put his arms about her, drawing her as close to his heart as possible. "Then why are you packing?"

"I needed to do something while I waited for you to come get me."

"An ambush then, that was your planning? So now you want to be a strategist?"

"Well, no one is a better teacher for me than you."

He nestled her long neck. "Your resident strategist knows how to make Hamlin safe. The answer is Colin's diary. Well, Markham and Colin's diary."

She squinted at him, and he smoothed away the wrinkles to her brow. "It's Colin's hand at the beginning, but the latter half is Markham's. Very close, very similar hand."

"Markham's?"

"Yes, he had been manipulating Colin, and now he's manipulating you. I have a plan to rid us of him. There are risks, but you won't have to do any disguises, only the thing you hate. We have to wait. We must have patience and wait him out."

"Then we are doomed, Busick."

"Nothing is doomed when we work as a team."

"Nothing?"

"Nothing, Patience. Now it's time for me to put you to bed."

"Busick, I had intended to sleep in the other room. I don't want to say something that hurts you."

"Well, intentions are fine and lonely, but I need you."

Her eyes brightened as she mouthed his words.

"Yes, the commander needs you, just as you are. Now put me to bed, I've dismissed my valet early. I will require help."

She climbed down from his lap and wedged herself under his arm.

He grunted and lifted as his perfect-size wife guided him to the mattress. The agony of the quick movement countered with the bliss of his head in her bosom, the arch of her back to him. He panted through the pain of lowering and laying atop her.

"It's obvious, my dear, that we need practice. This will be our new evening drill, something for our schedule."

"Weighty. You are weighty." She wiggled and tried to scoot free from her pinned position beneath Busick.

The true strategist had other ideas. A slow rotation put him and Patience side by side. After a thorough examination of this soldier for weapons and such, he released her to squirm to the pillows, and for his back to ease.

"Yes, each evening, we will work on this to improve our technique so that—"

Her arms went about him, and she kissed him. "You talk too much."

Patience had such a kissable mouth, kissable neck, kissable bosom, but she was wrong. He hadn't said enough. He'd tell her everything, all the hopes that filled his chest about her, his precious wife. Once he made Hamlin the safe home she needed, he'd tell her all.

CHAPTER 32

THE COMMANDER'S STRATEGY

I let my husband implement his plan and watched the life that Busick and his men had brought to Hamlin die.

Lights were dimmed.

Curtains pulled closed.

The friendly chatter in the halls—all evaporated like mist.

He'd dismissed most of his contingent force, leaving just two guards. The two with no homes to return to because the war had made them widowers. They stayed and exercised in the great hall, even pitching a tent to keep up with the routine Busick had created to aid in their recovery.

The scuffs on the tile didn't bother me. The purpose in their brilliant eyes was enough.

Jemina met me at the stairs. We walked up arm and arm. "The house is so different without all the light."

It was. This needed to be done soon. "The duke should restore his army at the first opportunity."

My friend nodded. "That will make the smile he puts on your face permanent."

Was I smiling? I was fretting wrong, my lips curving up instead of drooping. I clasped the rail, looked down at the inadequate marble gods. "Lord Gantry has gone to the city to complete the duke's ruse. This adds no comfort to me. Markham is wily, and if he indeed tries to return to Hamlin—"

"This will work. If Markham wants Lionel, he'll follow Gantry, but if he wants Jordan's diary, then he'll come here now that he thinks everyone is away to Town."

Jemina swept me up into a hug. "Go check on our fearless commander."

My friend floated up the stairs, her ash-gray skirts flapping as she marched up the stairs. She looked well in waisted gowns, too.

Standing outside the master's chambers, I wiped my perspiring hands. This wasn't walking on shells, this was worse. It needed to be over.

I went inside. "Duke, I think—"

Naked chest.

The man was a thing of beauty sitting bare but for his breeches in his wheeled chair. He tugged a bar tethered to ropes and weights and the old chandelier's pulleys. "Yes, my dear. What do you think? I want to hear."

He groaned and moved the bar back and forth, up and down. The rhythm was hypnotic. I felt it from across the room.

Busick stopped and turned in his chair. "Has something happened?"

Nothing new, just a craving to be in his arms, to lie against his expansive chest, one made for my fingers to smooth, with little tufts of hair that tickled my chin. The urge to hear the rumble of his laugh, the calm of his prayers for Lionel's health, for my safety and peace overwhelmed my reason. I wanted him.

"Patience?"

How do I say this? How do I tell him that the drills every night, the schedule or rituals of how we went to bed—

wrapped in his arms, my heart beside his—left me breath-less, so drawn to Busick.

"Come to me, Patience."

I ran to my duke, and he whipped me up in his arms, pulling me onto his lap. My bottom nestled on his leg, my thigh curled about his wooden stump and boot.

He snuggled my waist as my fingers skirted his scars, smoothed his skin.

There was no denying it. He was my beloved, and I was his.

I hoped I was.

"Patience, my plan will draw Markham out. Gantry's made a fuss of me being in Town. Inviting my mother to a dinner for her friends at the end of the week at my town house should get ears buzzing. Everyone will think I'm there with Lionel, not here with a goddess at my beck and call."

Such words while I was on his lap, but I loved it. For the first time in a long time, I was me, just me. This me was for him.

Those pretty eyes, clever and clear—I think he knew.

"You still talk in your sleep, but this time I heard my name."

My cheeks were on fire. "Sorry. I hate that I'm such a talker."

"On the contrary. I'm rather happy you're chatty. It helps me to know I'm doing things right, since you can't bake bread and get that smoky hearth signaling the family is here, not until this is over."

He planted a kiss at the base of my throat, then his lips skimmed the sensitive skin of my neck that my chignon often covered.

"See, I'd never know how that entices you, I think you whispered toes curl. I can't think of a more pleasurable in-terrogation to find secrets. No, I think I can."

I was wasting away, caught up in my fears, and he made fun. Trying to get up from the chair, I couldn't. His hands had shifted, tickling me, touching me, driving me mad. I'd slipped down that steep banister of the heart, but I'd flown. I loved Busick.

"Tell me. Wide awake, looking at me. What do you think of us?"

I wanted to confess and let him know I wanted his love, but I kissed him instead. My actions should confirm all he needed to know.

His mouth took mine, which mirrored my hunger, a matching sense to please and to show the lessons we'd learned, the things we'd practiced. I knew he liked my hands on his chest, never on his shoulder or thigh.

Surely, he knew I liked him holding me tight, so much so that I breathe Busick—a little sandalwood, a little sweet starch, and a tinge sassy rum.

"I feel strong, Patience. I think we need to discuss some of the legal clauses in our marriage."

What? Lady Shrewsbury's warning about reading paperwork stung the pit of my stomach.

A screeching, whining noise sounded below.

Busick put his hand to my lips.

Then we heard a curse. A loud, foul Markham-said expletive.

Running.

Loud booming commands.

Busick set me on my feet and pointed to his sword.

I grabbed the weapon and showed him my father's knife. It was a permanent fixture in my pocket.

"Keep it. You stay here with Lionel."

"But I should go with you."

"I married you to keep you protected, not to risk your safety. Now, that's an order. Stay put."

I wasn't in agreement, but I saluted.

"Oh. I intend to come back to finish this conversation. A man needs to let his wife know how much he loves her, but after he slays her dragon."

He tugged his shirt from the bedpost and slipped it on. Then, he took his sword and pushed his chair to the door.

His crutch remained by the bed table.

My son.

Lionel was in the other room. I blew open the compartment door, scooped him up, and put him in the basket. Then we went back into the master bedchamber.

At the side of our bed, I prayed like Busick to Jove, that my husband would be safe, that Markham wouldn't hurt us anymore.

I stared at the latch, forcing my mind to repeat what Busick said about loving me as I chastised my cowardly lips for not saying the same.

CHAPTER 33

THE DIARY TELLS ALL

Patience had said she loved Busick as she slept by his side last night. It was something she murmured between her well-wishes for Lionel and ingredients for a bread recipe.

Well, it sounded like bread.

Obviously, he was very high in importance to be ranked with her delightful baking. The woman was everything he needed, and she wanted Busick as he was, standing or not. Once he slayed this ugly dragon, nothing would stop them.

Their love was just beginning.

Curses and marching sounded below.

He looked over the balcony and saw the devil, old Markham, with flintlocks pointed at him. Busick rolled closer to the railing and clasped the newel post.

"Bring the skunk up here."

"Repington, have your goons unhand me."

"That is a colonel and a lieutenant. The only goon in Hamlin is you. You're trespassing."

Mrs. St. Maur came down from the third level halfway on those steep steps. "I heard noises."

"We have a burglar, ma'am. Go back to your quarters."

She curtsied and fled.

"You've rid the place of Mrs. Jordan and already have a new wench. You're so predictable."

"Well, I've always been popular. Unlike you, I don't have to drug my women for friendship."

Half up the stairs, Markham struggled but couldn't tug free. "What are you talking about?"

"The belladonna you used on Nanny Kelly and on Mrs. Jordan. My friend Gantry had a long discussion with the butler-gardener fellow in the village. Seems the night Mrs. Jordan was sent to Bedlam, her eyes were yellow. A strange color for lovely topaz eyes. Did you think you could seduce her before locking her into Bedlam?"

"I admit to nothing. Have these men release me. I came to get something I left."

Taking Colin's diary from under his seat cushion, Busick held it high. "You mean this book?" He flipped the pages. "What is in this thing that causes you to burglarize Hamlin? You know trespassers can be shot on the spot."

Busick made an exaggerated show of dangling the diary. "This is Colin's hand. It belongs to my ward. Bring the fool up here so I can show him why he'll be jailed for trespassing, all for naught."

Jerking and pulling at the soldiers, Markham stomped onto the second-floor landing.

Rolling backward so that the fiend would be led closer to the master's bedchamber, Busick pushed at the wheels of his chair. He needed Patience to hear the next part of his plan. This was for her freedom.

"You are an invalid. Lady Bodonel's blather was right."

"A little back strain. I've been a little busy with my cousin's widow."

"Disgusting. Colin would hate you for that, bedding his wife. The fool actually loved her. Was set to ruin what we worked for over a daft letter she wrote him. I know you are onto my scheme. You were at Piccadilly. You figured out the extortion plot from my diary."

The door to the master chamber was cracked open. *Stay put, my girl. This is almost over.*

"The book is Colin's." He held the diary up at a distance Markham couldn't grab. "See his handwriting?"

"Some of the notations are Colin's, but the rest is mine. It's my book."

"Well, my cousin's not here to say it's yours. My statement stands. You burglarized for nothing."

"You know very well I'm telling the truth. You know I taught Colin to write when he was a lad. You should've told me you were light in your funds. That daft mother has bled you dry. I know you and your partner LaCroy are trying to weasel your way into my scheme."

Yes, she was his partner, his life. Busick turned the wheels a little more. "Whatever do you mean?"

"You figured out Colin and I were extorting the gaming hell operator Sullivan. He's been cheating the club, charging patrons a fee for shaving a few guineas here or there off their debts. That diary is the record of over a year's worth of cheats summing to over thirty thousand pounds."

"Thirty thousand four hundred and twenty-six, to be exact."

Mrs. St. Maur's voice boomed. She must be like Patience, loathe to follow orders.

"Thank you, ma'am, but I ordered you to withdraw into your room."

Markham sneered. "Belladonna makes women compliant. You should try it."

"And suicidal. Men, too. We both know Colin didn't commit suicide. You killed him."

"What are you talking about? I loved him like a son."

"Colin wanted to end this gambling scheme. He wanted to be a better man for Mrs. Jordan and their babe to come. Her letter shook him, but it set him on a better path."

Markham shrugged, but the smirk on his face was proud, as if he relished his exploits being said aloud. "Repington, you don't know what you are talking about."

"Mrs. Jordan interrupted a meeting with you, Sullivan, and Colin. She heard your threats and those of Sullivan's but focused on Sullivan's. She believed that you loved Colin too much to be serious that you'd kill him if he quit your scheme. But you and I know the truth. Colin was your pawn, and you murdered him."

"He was compliant. Then she started to control him. That foreign voodoo did it."

Holding his sword out, Busick moved closer. "You knew that if she ever repeated your threats, everyone would suspect you of murder, particularly since you claimed Colin died in the Thames in December, when it was frozen over. The handwriting changes to yours in July. July is when her last letter is dated. July is when you killed him."

"All we worked for. He was going to toss it for her. You're here defending the woman from an invalid's chair. Did the witch get to you, too?"

"She did. She broke me wide open. I love her for it."

The door to the master chamber swung wide. Patience ran out waving her knife. "You repugnant fool. Colin trusted you. You must've forged that suicide note. You troll."

"What is she doing here? Do you like bedding a crazed wh—?"

The point of his blade sliced at Markham's throat. He'd not use disgraceful language about Busick's lady. "Yes, I do. Every minute of her rashness, her never following orders, her wonderful heart. Yes, she makes a very good wife."

Markham grasped at his neck and stepped backward. "You married the witch?"

Hearing her advance, Busick moved in front of Patience, lowered his sword, and blocked her advance.

"He killed Colin!"

Markham broke free of the distracted guards. He started to run but then stopped midstep. "I'm on my last nickel. I've nothing."

He turned back. "Yes, the tea worked well on him. He walked right into the Thames searching for you and your boat to Demerara. The belladonna-laced tea just made you run and scream. Foul woman, you can't even be drugged right."

Patience lunged again, Busick dropped his sword and caught her about the waist.

"Another slap. It's the least he deserves. Let me at him."

"He's not worth it, Patience."

"I did enjoy you suffering with that suicidal letter. You'd just had his baby. I thought it'd break you."

She swung over Busick's head, but he held her back. "Patience, he's going to swing on the gallows. We've heard his confession."

Lionel cried out.

"The mongrel's down here, not on the third level." Markham ran toward the master bedroom. "Maybe he should join his father, then you two can be free."

Dumping Patience to the floor, Busick caught Markham's coat and the two began to tussle.

Markham's erratic swings made the wheels move.

The heavy chair rolled backward, but Busick locked his arm about Markham's neck.

They fought, slugging at each other.

Both were dangerously close to the rail. A push the wrong way could send either of them through the stair posts and fall to the statues below.

The guards lifted guns, but no one would take a shot at this close range.

"Stop it, Markham! Let the duke alone." Patience came forward. She'd dropped her tiny knife and had picked up Busick's heavy sword and jabbed it against Markham's shoulder. "Back away, or I'll finish you now."

"Wench, you don't have the strength to kill, so step away. This is a man's fight."

Busick lunged backward, grasped her hand, and drove the sword forward, straight into Markham's chest.

"She may not, but together we do."

He gave Markham a final push.

The gasping man fell over the rail.

A gurgled scream released and then silence.

Busick spun Patience to him. He'd seen enough death. She shouldn't have to witness the fiend's crash onto the statues below.

But she turned again and witnessed Markham's body impaled on the sharp spear of the tallest Roman soldier.

"Maybe Agassou is not lifeless, Duke."

"Well, dear, those statues of Grandfather's have served a purpose." He put his hands to her face and drew her near. "The worst enemy to my family is no more. You're free. We're free."

He held on to Patience, and she latched her arms about his shoulders, immovable like a shield. She was a shield, a shelter to keep his heart safe. He loved her so. "Men, send for the magistrate and coroner. Then, we'll take care of the aftermath."

Looking over Patience's head, he saw Mrs. St. Maur sitting on the stairs. The poor woman had stayed. Surely, she'd seen Markham's fall, but the approving grimace on her face foretold that she'd known other tragedies.

"Ma'am, come down to my wife. Patience, go into the bedchamber with Lionel while I dispose of the trash. That's an order, ladies."

The women did as he requested. With arms entwined, they went inside.

Busick closed his eyes for a moment, thankful that Markham's threat to his family was over, but he wondered if Patience had been freed completely of the guilt gripping her heart.

In the large bedroom of Hamlin Hall, I settled my son. His appetite was as big as ever. Maybe more so. He was free, finally, truly free.

With him tucked in the bread basket, secure, dry, and warm, he eased off to sleep.

Jemina sat on the floor with her back to the footboard. She'd seen the fight, but she had no duke to comfort her.

I knelt beside her as I did when we were in rags at Bedlam.

She clasped my hand. "He deserved to die, Patience. Markham surely did. Some people die but don't deserve it."

Jemina's voice sounded low but held a sense of assurance. Then I realized that it wasn't the first time she'd seen someone die.

"My Colin was murdered in July. I didn't know. I thought he was mad because of my letter. Staying away because of it."

"Markham knew you bore a boy and thought he could get your father's payment without anyone asking questions. Good thing the duke became involved."

"A very good thing." I was so grateful this was over. I stood up and grasped Jemina's hand. "We are free."

Her eyes had that soft, distant look she had sometimes. "You're free. And I'm so happy for that. I will be free someday, too."

"You have me, the Widow's Grace, and I suspect the Duke of Repington to aid you."

The door opened, and inside came my duke.

His motion was slow in his wheeled chair, and I feared he'd injured his back again. "Everything has been handled in the hall. Mrs. St. Maur, I wish that you hadn't witnessed—"

"Your Grace, all is well. I'll return to my room."

I saw my knife, cleaned and shining in Busick's hand. Taking it, I placed it in Jemina's fingers. "Good night, my friend."

Jemina held my knife, nodded, then left the room.

Part of me wanted to give chase, but the look on the duke's countenance said, *No. Don't even think to move or breathe without my permission.*

I wasn't one to follow orders, but this time I'd make the exception.

"Are you much hurt, Busick?"

"If thinking you'd actually honor a request could cause pain, I am in agony."

"But words you knew I couldn't keep means nothing."

"You have a point. I'm a man of disappointed hopes."

I knelt at his side. "I'm not disappointed. How could I be when Colin's killer is no more, and you and Lionel are alive and safe?"

He tugged me onto his lap and held me. The strength in his arms was everything. His beating pulse next to mine told my heart I'd found home.

"Patience, I could not have borne you being hurt. How would Lionel stand to lose you? You know he hates pap milk," he said with a chuckle.

I swatted his arm. "I wasn't hurt, and I know I helped."

"It would be helpful if just once you listened."

"I have listened, but I hear first with the ears of my heart."

"Well, that's a good place to seek guidance. Your heart is honest, and it holds my happiness right behind that lace."

He put his hand to my jaw and lifted my lips to his.

I was moving. I thought I was, but I could be wrong. I couldn't tell anything when he kissed me like this, like I was air or coconut bread or water.

"Let's put Lionel in his crib."

He'd picked up the bread basket and set it in my hands.

The kissing began again, me to the duke, me to my Lionel.

Busick pushed us into the adjoining room, and I settled my snoring baby into his crib.

"I love you, Lionel," he said.

Placing his hand on my babe's forehead, he offered a blessing. I heard Colin's name in his whisper. Busick promised Lionel and me to keep us in safety and health.

Our boy's whistle snores sounded so sweet.

Then he turned to me. "I love you, too."

His voice was direct, like a command, weighty and forceful.

My heart obeyed. I loved him.

"You're nothing of what Markham said. You're good and trustworthy. You're beautiful. And mine."

We'd moved again. He'd crept right up to the edge of the bed.

"I am yours. Busick, I love you so very deeply. I trust you, and I always will honor you."

His lips on mine weren't searching, they were telling— telling me I was his and he was mine and the happiness and security I longed for, that I'd missed for so long was all mine.

And I'd never have to sacrifice me for peace.

Hands slipping to my hips, he lifted me onto the bed.

But that wasn't my place, not without him. I bounced up and stood beside him, right under his arm and helped him lift from the chair.

"My favorite crutch. I think I like you best, undressed for bed."

As we'd practiced, we lowered to the pillows in unison, not too fast, definitely not too slow. Then Busick took command, and I let him. Skin to skin, kiss to kiss, I was undone.

This mattress made for two held our love. We were one, the love between us burning brighter, growing slowly from embers to roaring flames.

I was consumed.

I was the woman Busick loved. I loved him, for he gave my life more beauty. This sharing of our spirits was pure, as pure as gold.

EPILOGUE

May 3, 1814
Hamlin Hall

The grand chandelier that Busick designed began its maiden ascent to its position above the hall. I watched the large wrought iron fixture with glimmering glass globes rise. A dance of sparkles surrounded me.

The duke, my dearest darling, sat off to the side with Lionel in his lap, pointing to the pulleys and chains. "See, my boy," he said, "that's how you brighten the hall."

The entry doors opened.

Gantry ran inside. He bowed to me and went to the duke.

Very carefully, Busick stood. The improvements he'd made to his reticulating stump with the catgut strings for tendons made his balance so much better. He could rise with Lionel safe and secure in his arms.

But the kitty, Athena, now stayed far away from him when the countess visited.

"Gantry, what is it?"

"Lady Bodonel is in a carriage following me. She's coming to visit."

"What?"

He ducked his head. "She'd seen Lady Gantry. I had to bribe her with something."

I left my stance under the light and came to Busick's dear friend. "Did you find her? Did you find your wife?"

"No, but I will. She didn't catch the boat to Demerara. She's still in London."

If his lordship was as determined as Busick, I knew he would find her.

My husband frowned and sat back in his wheeled chair. "What did you tell her for the information?"

"That you two were thinking of travel. She wants an invitation to come along."

Busick looked at me, and I nodded to him. The unspoken ask and reply transmitted between us. No one-word answers needed for him to know I'd entertain Lady Bodonel when she arrived to allow my duke to escape.

I took Lionel from Busick and smoothed my love's lapels that our boy had ruffled. The dove-gray tailcoat looked so handsome on him.

This man in uniform still made my head dizzy, but with the Peninsular War over, he didn't feel the need to wear his regimentals as often, just for special occasions like later, when I needed to see him coming from the drawing room under the light of the chandelier, or when he received wounded veterans for training.

Wellington sent his injured officers to Busick to get them back in the saddle as soon as possible. Other men he ordered to Hamlin to learn military tactics. Though Napoleon was in exile, my husband's old commander had a sense the man would rise again.

Busick clasped my hand. "You must truly love me, Patience."

"What kind of statement is that?"

He tapped his cheek, and I graciously planted a kiss to his sweet dimple. One to Lionel's, too.

"My duchess is so patient, Gantry, suffering my mother for tea. Soon, she'll be pretending her increased visits will be about Lionel and being a friend to him, but I don't know if she has the stomach to call herself a grandmother."

"Your gift of the marble gods to her house in Town touched her. I'm glad they are gone from here."

He laced my fingers with his. "Nothing to give you nightmares. Although, I do love hearing about myself in your dreams."

"Duke," Gantry said as he ducked his face into his palm. "I'm going to be in the drawing room with your brandy. Carry on with this loving stuff."

The poor man walked away sort of grinning, still sort of sad. I hoped he'd find Lady Gantry and that they could solve their differences and love as deeply as Busick and I.

My darling pulled me in his arms. He still wasn't comfortable using this improved version of Potts's limb for extended periods of time. It wasn't necessary, when he could spin me round and round better than any dancer.

Curled in his lap, I relaxed and settled Lionel between us.

"Hold on to our son. Let's examine the new chandelier before your guest arrives."

I lifted my eyes to the glimmering candles, but I glanced at Jemina sitting on the second-floor landing. Clutched in her hand, she had a piece of foolscap that Lady Shrewsbury brought this morning.

Jemina had been silent since breakfast, but I knew she'd tell me what this note said. She was my sister, my friend. I was determined to help her be restored.

For I was still a member of the Widow's Grace, and we never quit, not until we'd helped fivefold of our brethren find protection and favor.

Busick spun fast in the center of the hall.

I clung to him, but I listened for creaks and moans.

"We never determined if Markham had a hand in the destruction of the old chandelier or if those missing things or noises were his."

"Does it matter? Your father's payment gave us a new one. I rather like having something of your father here." He clasped my hand to his heart. "I've written to his estate to find out what happened to your sisters. I'm determined to recover them."

There was not a doubt in my mind that Busick would do what he said. He'd already given me enough of his heart to mend mine.

"Then turn us faster, my love. Another lap before Lady Bodonel makes it to Hamlin."

Lionel blew spittle from his mouth, sort of a *wwwheeee*.

"Once more, then Lionel and I will join Gantry for crawling practice in the drawing room."

"Crawling practice? He's six months, Busick."

"An excelled six months."

"What? Busick Stra—"

He smothered my complaint with one of his rakish kisses. It was his promise to make amends as only the duke knew how. Tea with his talkative mother wasn't a bad price to pay for the happiness Busick added to my life and Lionel's.

But I did intend to give my duke an earful when I slept tonight.

ACKNOWLEDGMENTS

Thank you to my Heavenly Father, everything I possess or accomplish is by Your grace.

To my beloved editor, the fabulous Esi Sogah, your belief in this series has meant the world to me. You make me better.

To my fabulous agent, Sarah Younger, I am grateful that you are my partner. Your guidance and support shine so bright, my days are rarely gloomy.

To those who inspire my pen: Beverly, Brenda, Sarah, Julia, Maya, Lenora, Sophia, Joanna, Grace, Kristan, Alyssa, Laurie Alice, Julie, Cathy, Katharine, Carrie, Christina, Georgette, Jane, Linda, Margie, Liz, Lasheera, Felicia, Alexis, and Jude—thank you.

To those who inspire my soul: Bishop Dale and Dr. Nina, Reverend Courtney, Piper, Denny, Eileen, Rhonda, and Holly—thank you.

And to my own HEA: Frank and Ellen.

Love you all so much.

Hey, Mama. We did this. Love you, always.

RECIPE

Patience's Coconut Bread

Busick and his men fell in love with Patience's coconut bread, and I thought you might want to know how to make it, too. In parentheses below are suggestions on how to lighten or make the bread a smidge healthier.

For the Bread
3 cups all-purpose flour, spooned into a measuring cup
    and leveled off with a knife to be exact
½ teaspoon baking soda
½ teaspoon salt
2 sticks unsalted butter (or softened 1 butter stick and
    ½ cup grape-seed oil)
2¼ cups granulated sugar
3 large eggs (or 2 eggs and 1 egg white)
1 cup (low-fat) buttermilk
½ cup toasted finely chopped coconut. To make, take
    shredded coconut and bake for 10 minutes at 300°F.
    Coconut toasts fast, so be aware and stir.
4 teaspoons fresh lemon juice
4 teaspoons coconut extract

For the Syrup
⅓ cup water
⅓ cup granulated sugar
4 teaspoons fresh lemon juice
2 teaspoons coconut extract

For the Glaze (Optional)
1 cup confectioners' sugar
4 teaspoons fresh lemon juice

2 teaspoons coconut extract
½ teaspoon toasted finely chopped coconut, packed
1 teaspoon unsalted butter, melted

Instructions

1. Set the oven rack to the middle and preheat to 325°F.

2. Spray two eight-by-four-inch loaf pans with nonstick cooking spray and dust with flour.

3. In a medium bowl, whisk or sift together the flour, baking soda, and salt. Then set aside.

4. In another bowl, cream the butter and sugar until light and fluffy, typically 3 to 4 minutes at medium speed. Scrape down the sides of the bowl. Beat in the whole eggs one at a time (and then the egg white if following the lighter recipe). Beat well after each addition.

5. Scrape down the sides of the bowl again.

6. In another bowl—yes, we are up to three bowls—combine the buttermilk, coconut, coconut extract, and lemon juice.

7. Turn the mixer to low speed. Beat in one-quarter of the flour mixture, then one-third of the buttermilk mixture.

8. Repeat. Beat in another quarter of the flour and another third of the milk mixture.

9. Repeat. Beat in another quarter of the flour and the remaining milk mixture.

10. Beat in the remaining flour mixture, then scrape down the sides of the bowl.

11. With a wooden spoon, give the batter a quick stir to make sure all the ingredients are well mixed.

12. Spoon the thick batter into the greased and floured loaf pans and smooth with a spatula. Bake for 50–55 minutes, or until a toothpick comes out clean. Start checking after 45 minutes.

13. Cool the loaves in the pan for 10 minutes on a rack.

14. Meanwhile, make the syrup. Combine the water and sugar in a saucepan and bring to a boil. Remove from the heat and stir in the lemon juice, coconut extract, and coconut.

15. Invert loaves onto a rack.

16. Slip a large piece of parchment paper under the rack to catch all the drips from the syrup.

17. Gradually brush the hot syrup over each loaf and the sides, letting it soak in. Take your time. Do not rush. Repeat several times.

18. Allow loaves to cool completely. Typically, about 1 hour is required.

19. When loaves are cool, transfer to serving platters.

20. To make the glaze: combine the confectioners' sugar, lemon juice, coconut, coconut extract, and melted butter in a medium bowl, mixing with a fork until smooth. Add more sugar or lemon juice as necessary to make a thick but pourable glaze. The glaze should have the consistency of thick honey. Spoon the glaze over the top of each loaf.

21. Cut a slice and eat.

AUTHOR'S NOTES

Dear Reader,

I hope you enjoyed Patience and Busick's love story and the antics of the Widow's Grace. This was a fun and heartfelt story to write about women taking control of their destinies and the men who love and support them, and how united they make their worlds better by partnering in grace and joy.

This tale covers many themes, showcasing a sliver of the diversity of the Regency, the treatment of the disabled, and the power structure afforded women. It is my hope that in Patience and Busick's journey, you find your own light and that it casts beauty about your footsteps. *Let your light shine in the darkness, for darkness cannot overcome it* (John 1:5).

Visit my website, VanessaRiley.com, to gain more insight. Make sure to sign up for my newsletter to be the first to know about upcoming books, events, contests, and more.

Mulattoes and Blackamoors During the Regency

The term *mulatto* was a social construct used to describe a person birthed from one parent who was Caucasian and the other of African, Spanish, Latin, Indian, or Caribbean descent. Mulattoes during the Regency period often had more access to social movement than other racial minorities, particularly if their families had means.

The term *Blackamoor* refers to racial minorities with darker complexions that included mulattoes, Africans, and West and East Indians living in England during the eighteenth and nineteenth centuries.

Mulattoes and Blackamoors numbered between ten thousand to twenty thousand in London and throughout England during the time of Jane Austen. Wealthy British with children born to native West Indies women brought them to London for schooling. Jane Austen, a contemporary writer of her times, in her novel *Sanditon* writes of Miss Lambe, a mulatto, the wealthiest woman. Her wealth made her desirable to the *ton*.

Mulatto and Blackamoor children were often told to pass to achieve elevated positions within society. Wealthy plantation owners with mixed-race children or wealthy mulattoes like Dorothea Thomas, from the colony of Demerara, often sent their children abroad for education and for them to marry in England.

Island and African Gods During the Regency

The mix of different people from differing parts of the world allowed for many beliefs to flourish in the Caribbean. Erzulie-Dantor is the goddess of women and sometimes referred to as the vengeful protector of women. Agassou is the guardian spirit. Erzulie-Ge-Rouge is the red-eyed goddess of revenge.

Potts's Artificial Limb

With England being in so many wars, the number of wounded veterans increased. Medical technology advanced to create artificial limbs. In 1816, James Potts crafted an artificial limb for the Marquess of Anglesey whose leg needed to be amputated as he fought alongside Wellington during the Battle of Waterloo (June 1815). The limb created was comfortable to wear and carved to be lifelike in appearance. By being made hollow, it was lighter than earlier models and possessed an articulating knee with ankle and toe joints to make walking easier and appear more natural. Catgut was added to simulate quiet tendons, so the clicking and clanging of his earlier models was no more. The new artificial leg was called the Anglesey leg.

Invalid Chair

Self-propelled chairs for disabled people date back to the seventeenth century. The most noted one is from 1655. Johann Hautsch made a three-wheeled chair that was powered by a rotary handle on the front wheel. The chairs were often armchairs with large wheels in the front and casters in the rear.

The Peninsular War

The Peninsular War, May 2, 1808–April 17, 1814, was a series of military campaigns between Napoleon's empire, Spain, Britain, Ireland, and Portugal for control of the Iberian Peninsula during the Napoleonic Wars. Napoleon was not fully contained until Waterloo in 1815.

The Battle of Badajoz

The Battle of Badajoz, March 16, 1812–April 6, 1812, was one of the costliest victories of the British, with their forces suffering more than four thousand soldiers killed. It is also where British soldiers lost control after the battle. The British soldiers abused, assaulted, and killed four thousand civilians of Badajoz, Spain, in the aftermath of the battle.

The Battle of Assaye

The Battle of Assaye, September 23, 1803, was a definitive, early victory in Arthur Wellesley, Duke of Wellington's career where the strategy was key to victory in the war against the Maratha empire.

Gaming Hells

Gaming hells were clubs for gambling. Some were filthy houses of disrepute. Others were high-end gentlemen's clubs. Games played were cribbage, hazard, and other dice and card games. The Piccadilly gaming hell was modeled after William Crockford's exclusive gaming hell, Fishmonger's Hall, with waiters, fine food, and wine to induce high-stakes, wealthy gamblers.

Duke of Wellington

Arthur Wellesley had a distinguished military career in service to the Crown. His advancements on the field led to the following increases in his military/titled rank:

Major General Wellesley—September 1802
Viscount Wellington—August 26, 1809
General, Viscount Wellington—July 31, 1811
Earl of Wellington—February 22, 1812
Marquess of Wellington—August 18, 1812
Duke of Wellington—May 3, 1814

Don't miss the rest of the
Rogues and Remarkable Women series
An Earl, the Girl, and a Toddler
A Duke, the Spy, an Artist, and a Lie

And be sure to check out Vanessa Riley's
new historical mystery series,
The Lady Worthing Mysteries
Murder in Westminster

Available now
wherever books are sold

Visit our website at
KensingtonBooks.com
to sign up for our newsletters, read
more from your favorite authors, see
books by series, view reading group
guides, and more!

BOOK CLUB
BETWEEN THE CHAPTERS

Become a Part of Our
Between the Chapters Book Club
Community and Join the Conversation

Betweenthechapters.net

Submit your book review for a chance to win exclusive
Between the Chapters swag you can't get anywhere else!
https://www.kensingtonbooks.com/pages/review/